THE OLDEST TRICK

THE OLDEST TRICK

Book 1 of the Saga of the Redeemed

AUSTON HABERSHAW

HARPER
VOYAGER
IMPULSE

An Imprint of HarperCollins Publishers

The Iron Ring copyright © 2015 by Auston Habershaw.

Iron and Blood copyright © 2015 by Auston Habershaw.

EPub Edition AUGUST 2015 ISBN: 9780062417220

Print Edition ISBN: 9780062417244

10 9 8 7 6 5 4 3 2

This novel is dedicated to my little brother, Preston, whose defiance, courage, and humor in the face of doom has inspired me to this day.
To all the little brothers out there: may they never, ever do what they are told. May they never, ever learn their place.

Part 1

THE IRON RING

"Morality is simply the attitude we adopt to those we personally dislike."

Oscar Wilde

PROLOGUE

The complete rout of an army in the field was never a pretty thing. When it broke, those thousands of men who once were an orderly, deadly machine of steel and flesh suddenly began to writhe and wither, like a slug dipped in salt. Friends trampled friends. Hallowed banners stamped with a dozen great victories were cast down in the mud. Cowards knocked heroes over the head and stole their boots. The ground became a gory, crimson slush.

The Mad Prince Banric Sahand did not tarry to watch his army disintegrate. Not yet forty, he had fought in more battles than most men twice his age, and he knew the signs of defeat when he saw them. He had been the commander of the most feared, disciplined, and deadly army in the West—the conqueror of kingdoms, the sacker of cities, the scourge of Galaspin, Saldor, and Eretheria. He had bent the whole of the

Trell Valley to his will; he had been on the verge of besieging the ancient city of Saldor itself. His enemies, bogged down in an endless war in Illin against the vast legions of the Kalsaari Empire, could do nothing but watch the victories pile about his feet and hear the tales of their defiant kinsmen's heads mounted on pikes. That, however, had been before the rout. Before Calassa.

Sahand could scarcely think about the place now without bellowing his rage, though there was no one but his exhausted horse to hear him. His mind was still reeling at how his enemies had managed to accomplish it. How he had been duped. Fooled. Made into a mockery for all the world to laugh at.

He pressed his heels into the horse's flanks. It was sweating, despite the chill of autumn and the harsh winds blowing down from the snow-capped Dragonspine to the east. The arrow shafts protruding from the horse's flanks gave it an uneven gait; he suspected it would die soon. It occurred to him that he had no idea whose horse this was. He didn't even know if it belonged to one of his men or one of the enemy. He supposed it scarcely mattered. Either way, he'd kill it under him and be glad of it.

Sahand's heart burned. Bile bit at the back of his throat. His eyes were wide and could scarcely focus on anything for long. He wanted to reach out and throttle someone—anyone—if doing so could just abate the mind-numbing anger that seemed to consume him from his toes to his ears. It would have been easier, *so* much easier, if the defeat had been someone else's fault—if he could not, even now, see how obvious the trap was in retrospect.

Calassa. City of Vineyards, heart of the Saldorian dominion, gatekeeper to the approaches of Saldor itself. A little walled city of crumbling battlements and pretty wooden houses; a road apple, a practice run for Sahand's siege crews. It was so obvious that he would attack there, Varner must have seen it coming for weeks. They were probably giving the fool parades at this very moment. The magi of the Arcanostrum were gifting him something grand and powerful and ancient; they were setting laurels upon his brow.

Sahand roared again as the horse stumbled. He leapt clear, rolling to his feet even as the beast hit the dirt. Its flanks shuddered with exhaustion; its tongue lolled out like a dog's. It didn't get up.

Sahand drew his broadsword, still bloodstained from battle, and muttered an angry and guttural incantation to draw the Fey energy into the blade. The steel shuddered and screeched with the influx of power and then glowed orange-white, as though just drawn from a furnace. He stomped beside the horse, sorcerous heat making its sweat steam, and looked in its wild, bloodshot eye. He raised the sword over his head and dropped it in one heavy stroke. The Fey energy was released in a titanic burst of fire and noise, ripping the horse apart into fist-sized chunks of charred flesh and boiling blood. Sahand looked at what was left of it—the saddle, now on fire, and some bits of bone—and roared again. He didn't feel any better. Overcome with heat, the sword began to melt in his hand; he threw it away.

It had been three days since the battle. He could still see the flames consuming the rooftops, hear the crackle of the painted facades as they withered beneath the heat. He smelled the smoke. He'd watched the city burn for thirty-six hours, congratulating himself on the quality of incendiaries he'd used, sending his compliments to the war engine crews, drinking *oggra* with his officers like it was the eve of his damned wedding. What an idiot he had been.

Then Varner sent Cadogan, that self-aggrandizing sell-sword with his team of cutthroats, swimming through Calassa's moat with ash on his face and a knife in his teeth to murder Sahand's officers in their sleep. Sahand had made Cadogan pay for it, of course, but by then half his best officers were dead.

That was when it all fell apart. Sahand, standing in his own tent just at dawn, his sword soaked with Finn Cadogan's blood, with the sound of silver trumpets carrying through the air. Not Sahand's trumpets, nor Varner's—it was Perwynnon, Falcon King of Eretheria, at the head of a host of glittering knights, charging at the flank of Sahand's army. The officers to prepare the defense? Dead, of course, and by Cadogan's hand. Sahand was only just in his armor as the Eretherians were turning his camp into cinders. Then Varner had charged from the city gates—on foot, as always, at the head of a hard-eyed host of war veterans, magi, and Defenders of the Balance. Every one of them was somehow untouched by fire, their eyes bright and their faces beaming as Varner's trap was sprung. The slaughter had been complete.

Now Sahand found himself fleeing alone across the empty grassy hills of the Galaspin hinterland without even a horse to his name. If there were a way, he would have murdered the whole world, right there and then, for refusing to be his.

He was able to walk another few miles, climbing steadily up into the thin air of the mountains, before he found himself too exhausted to continue. He hadn't eaten or drank since the night before the rout; he had sustained himself on a mixture of sorcery and raw, unfiltered anger, and he was now spent. The destruction of his former horse was the last he had in him.

Rolling on his back, Sahand looked up at the sunless, slate gray sky. He was near Freegate—a neutral party, a guild-run city of merchants and traders. He and Varner had sparred over it, each flirted with sacking it from time to time—there would be no friends there. They'd hand him over for the bounty, he was sure of it, the money-grubbing pigs. They wouldn't even have the courage to gut him themselves. He should have sacked them when he had the chance, just to hear them squeal as his men raped and pillaged their way across that wretched, tumbledown shanty town.

Sahand lay there, exhausted, indulging himself in revenge fantasies for what seemed like hours but may have only been seconds. A light snow began to fall, but he didn't feel cold. That meant he was probably freezing to death. Mumbling a few spells to heat his body, he found the magical energies gathering in his hands as easily as if he were dipping his hands in a warm bath. He had to be resting along a ley line— the natural streams of invisible power that pooled all five of the Great Energies together into one place. He'd studied them in school as a boy, of course—they assisted in navigation, shaped where cities had been built, and even how the land itself had formed, it was said. The one he laid on now probably ran from the mountains above Freegate, through Galaspin, Calassa, and all the way to the city of Saldor itself. He grunted to himself—all of his enemies, tied together by one unbroken stream of magical power.

That was all he could think about—his enemies. He could see Varner and his Defenders and Arcanostrum magi sitting in the old Calassa Keep, chuckling to themselves as they watched his camp through the veil of illusory flames. Sahand knew he should have been suspicious—he should have *known* a city wouldn't catch fire that easily, not with Varner in command. Not with magi like Lyrelle Reldamar pulling strings and working rituals. The illusion had been her idea, he just knew it—she'd sold him a pretty lie, and he'd swallowed it because he wanted to. Because he could already taste his victory and refused to conceive of anything else. It was the most basic of all cons; it was the oldest trick in the book.

He was an idiot, and the fact made him angrier than anything else.

For some reason, the face of Lyrelle Reldamar seemed to resolve itself above him. He saw her more clearly than any of his other enemies—her platinum hair piled high on her head and pinned in place with silver posts, her eyes the color of the sky, but colder and sharper. A woman of thirty, but already a master mage. He could almost see her leaning over him, her black robes fluttering in the mountain winds. She wore the pinched expression a mother would use on a muddy child. "You're finished, you know." Her voice was cool and calm, with a subtle firmness to it that reminded Sahand of ice beneath packed snow. "Even if you do survive to make it back to Dellor, you'll never have another chance at what you want again."

"Damned Kroth-spawned bitch!" He growled. He flailed his hands at the hallucination but touched nothing.

The image of Lyrelle wrinkled her nose at him. "Do you plan on dying here, then? Another bleached set of bones to adorn the wilderness. Another pile of teeth for some troll to make into a necklace. Fitting."

Sahand pulled himself into a sitting position. He shook his head. Lyrelle's image did not go away, but rather floated in front of him, just beyond reach. "You . . . you're really here?" He blinked a few times but nothing changed.

Lyrelle snorted. "Do you really think I would *walk*

out here to the middle of nowhere just to chat? Are you of the opinion that I intend to be strangled by those meat hooks of yours? No wonder you fell for the Calassa Shroud."

Hallucination or not, Sahand spat in her direction. It might have hit her face, were she solid. Instead, he realized he had just wasted what was possibly the very last of his spit. "I'll have my vengeance. I'll make every one of you pay—Varner, Perwynnon, you—even if it takes the rest of my life I'll—"

Lyrelle laughed the carefree laugh of a woman surrounded by friends in a sunny place. Sahand felt his face flush with what heat he had left inside him. He tried to stand but stumbled back to the ground. Lyrelle shook her head. "By the time you can raise another army and have another chance at conquest, you'll be too ancient to enjoy your rule and too feeble to keep it for long. That is, of course, assuming you don't die here on the side of a mountain or that the filthy hill-people you call your subjects don't lynch you the moment you get home." She smiled. "That is a lot of assumptions, don't you think?"

"Then what *is* this?" Sahand bellowed at her, hurling a rock through her translucent form. "You've come to gloat? You mean to kill me? Kroth take you! I'll have my fingers around your neck, so help me . . ."

Lyrelle ignored him. "Take this." On cue, a small, inert black sphere came into view. Moving about as fast as a trotting horse, the courier djinn wound its way up the hillside and stopped in front of Sahand, hovering a foot off the ground.

Reaching out, Sahand touched it. It vanished with a pop, and a wooden letter box dropped to the ground. He picked it up—it was solid, warm, *real*. "This is really happening." He muttered. He was too tired to wrestle with the implications, but something . . . a feeling, like a buzz at the back of his neck, woke him from his stupor just a little bit.

Lyrelle's voice rang in his ears as clear as church bells. "The war has changed the world, Banric. For the first time in millennia, sorcery was used on a large scale, and all those prudes in the Church and the Arcanostrum who'd been trying to keep the secrets of the High and Low Arts to themselves have been made to look like fools. Restrictions on magecraft are going to relax, warlocks and thaumaturges are going to multiply like rabbits, alchemists will be selling potions on every street corner in the West."

"What's that to me?"

Lyrelle smiled at him. "An opportunity."

Sahand frowned. "I don't believe you."

Lyrelle laughed. "Do you actually think what you *believe* matters, Banric? Understand this: *I* marshaled Varner and Perwynnon and Cadogan to fight you, *I* crushed your armies at Calassa, *I* have been the architect of the events that brought you here, now, because *I have use for you*. Your entire brutal, violent existence—your very life—is something that I have designed to suit my purpose, so whether or not you think I'm telling you the truth is completely inconsequential to the choice you must make at this very moment. Will you accept the offer before you or stay here alone and die the bitter, frustrated despot of a backwater nation? I await your answer."

Sahand scowled, the rage at his defeat again bubbling up inside of him to the point where he thought his eyes might catch afire. He opened his mouth to say something vile, but all he managed was, "Making a deal with me is treason, Lyrelle."

"It can't be treason, as the magi of the Arcanostrum recognize the authority of no king." Lyrelle looked out at the gray-green hills and valleys that surrounded them and took—or *appeared* to take—a deep breath of sharp mountain air. "That box is your link to what you never had before, Banric—secrets. You either take them, and everything that goes with them, or you don't. In either case, my time grows short."

Sahand opened the box. It was empty, but its interior surface was covered in sorcerous runes so carefully drawn it would have taken the efforts of a master like Lyrelle months to inscribe them. This was no mere trinket; this represented a kind of power Sahand had never had. A kind of power that had just been used to destroy him, and now was resting in his hands.

But at what cost? Nothing from the hand of Lyrelle Reldamar, that spider of spiders, could be trusted. Take the deal, and he'd be playing into her plans somehow—plans so far-reaching and so fathomless that he'd probably never know their full depths. The idea that he had been a pawn enraged him past all sense; were he not so close to death, his curses would have echoed from the mountainsides.

Then again . . .

Why offer him this directly? Lyrelle worked through proxies, never directly. She pulled the strings without the puppet's knowledge—that was her way. So why this now? He knew: it was an act of desperation. He, Banric Sahand, had done something she hadn't expected, forcing her hand. What was it he had done? It was obvious: he had lived.

This was an advantage he had never previously enjoyed, and he didn't intend to squander it, rage or not. "I accept."

"Welcome, Banric Sahand, to the Sorcerous League." The image of Lyrelle vanished with a barely audible pop, leaving Sahand alone on the mountainside, clutching the letterbox to his chest, wondering what kind of deal he'd just made, and what he might possibly owe to the people who fashioned artifacts like this box.

But something else occurred to him, too—something that made him happier than a starving, defeated, freezing ex-conquerer had any right to be: he was still alive, had been given access to sorcery he had never known before, and for the first time since Perwynnon's cavalry smashed through his picket lines and started burning his tents about him, he saw a way toward revenge. Though it might take him a hundred years, he'd have it, one way or another. His enemies would wade knee-deep in the blood of their children; he would ride the changing world all the way to that moment, and Reldamar would never see it coming. He could lie as well as the next person.

Lyrelle Reldamar wasn't the only one who knew the oldest trick in the book.

CHAPTER 1

THE BOY WITH THE GOOD CHIN

It was becoming obvious to Tyvian that bringing the boy had been a mistake. The thirteen-year-old wore his clothes—his very *expensive*, embroidered, Akrallian-made clothes—like they were sackcloth. Even as Tyvian was looking at him, the boy actually reached up and tugged on his fine lace collar *again*.

Tyvian wasted no time in cuffing him sharply behind his left ear, then pulled him close and hissed, "Now listen here, you miserable, gutter-born brat: if you so much as lay a single, grubby fingertip on that collar again, I will heave you headlong off the next bridge. Do you understand?"

The boy nodded, red-faced. "Yes, my lord. I'm sorry."

Tyvian cuffed him again. "No apologies! You are supposed to be an Akrallian attaché, a servant of *noble* bearing, not some groveling, half-witted scullery maid! What's more, *you don't speak bloody Akrallian!* Open your trap to say anything more than *oui* or *non* and we are finished!"

The boy held still and kept from flapping his lips. Tyvian sighed. To think that he might have had any number of simulacra conjured for himself in the form of an Akrallian attaché and never have had this difficulty. The thing would have obeyed his every command and looked the part perfectly, and there wouldn't have been any of this nonsense at all.

It might not have worked, though. Rameaux was probably a fool in many ways, but not in terms of magecraft—one whiff of the Ether used to make a simulacrum and the deal would be off. Pressed for time, he had to settle for the best-looking urchin he could find on the streets of Ayventry instead, and hope that the eight hour journey by spirit engine from there to Galaspin would be sufficient to train the whelp in the finer points of etiquette. With less than one hour to go, his doubts were almost complete.

From the head of the train the moans of the demons confined within the pistons of the engine intensified as they came to a steep hill. Peering out the window, Tyvian saw that they were now running parallel to the Freegate Road as it wound along the banks of the Trell. Past it, he could see the gently sloping farmland and sparsely wooded countryside of the Duchy of Galaspin glittering under a thin sheet of moonlit snow. He wondered if Zazlar was holding up his end of the bargain; shipping could be slow, especially in winter. Smuggling was usually even slower.

Turning back to the boy, Tyvian pointed to the closet of their stateroom. "Get my case and bring it to me . . . and for Hann's sake, stop *slouching*."

The boy frowned. "But I'm not—"

Tyvian threw up his hands. "*Why* are you speaking to me? Is that Akrallian coming out of your mouth? Well?"

"N-No . . ."

"No? Or do you mean *non*?"

The boy's face was alternating shades of red and white, but he said nothing.

Tyvian shook his head. "I swear, boy, you will be the death of both of us. Case, closet, *now*."

When it was brought to him, Tyvian laid the leather case on the small table in front of the train window and opened it. Lined in black velvet to hide the runes written in quicksilver that covered the interior, it had successfully allowed Tyvian to carry his equipment past the mirror-men at Ayventry Station without being detected. Any augury directed at the case saw nothing but a few bolts of cloth, a Book of Hann, and a pair of riding gloves. What it actually contained, however, was quite different.

The boy stood close by and watched as Tyvian reached into the case and slid a ring onto the middle finger of each hand. The one on the right was of mage-glass, and its translucent, crystalline design glittered in the warm light of the cabin. The left one was of gold and inlaid with a trio of pure blue sapphires. Into his pockets Tyvian placed a handful of marble-sized spheres and a short cylinder of ebony inlaid with silver about as long as his hand.

This last the boy recognized, and gasped. "That's a deathcaster! Does it work?"

"Unlike the common footpads and wretched, beer-sodden fools with which you are no doubt used to associating, I do not commonly carry enchanted items that do not function."

The boy had no answer. "It's just . . . they're expensive."

Tyvian rolled his eyes. "You are an uncommonly stupid boy, aren't you?"

The boy grumbled a bit under his breath, but no more.

"We will be in the city of Galaspin shortly. Remember: say nothing, do nothing until told, and pretend like you are the exact opposite of your actual self."

They left the stateroom and made their way through the rocking corridors of the spirit engine until they came to the dining car. It was late at night, and the two of them were alone as Tyvian slid into a leather-upholstered booth in the corner, his back to the wall. The boy, at his command, remained standing. The dining car, though in reality not much wider than the rest of the spirit engine, had been Astrally reconfigured to multiply its interior space so that it was comfortable and spacious enough to seat the train's entire complement of passengers—a sign of the luxury afforded those who could travel in this manner that was, no doubt, lost upon the boy. He merely blinked at the glittering feylamps set on each table and was, Tyvian concluded, calculating just how much each of those would be worth for sale on the black market.

"Do you ever wonder why you don't see those for sale on the street very often?" Tyvian asked.

The boy shot Tyvian a guarded look but held his tongue. After some consideration, he offered a slight nod.

"It's because the theft of sorcerous objects is a delicate art. You, like your average lowly criminal, would simply swipe a half dozen of those feylamps, stuff them in your coat, and then try to sell them to some back-alley, ink-thralled hustler for one-fifth their worth. Of course, what you wouldn't realize is that by touching those things and carrying them around, you'd be leaving a trail even the least competent Defender with a functioning mage-compass could follow. So, you'd be in the midst of spending your meager earnings when the mirror-men would find you and drag you away for the Illicit Sale of Magecraft."

The boy thought this over for a few moments, and then asked. "How'd you do it, then, so's you weren't nicked?"

Tyvian cuffed him. "There you are—talking again. To answer you, however, it's merely a matter of understanding . . ."

The boy sneezed, and Tyvian interrupted himself so that he could observe the boy's reaction to his allergic episode. Noticing Tyvian's eyes on him, he only sat up a bit straighter and did nothing else.

"Well?" Tyvian asked at last.

"Well what?"

"You just sneezed." Tyvian prompted.

"Oh!" The boy nodded, and raised the ruffled edge of his sleeve to wipe.

He didn't get it halfway before Tyvian, with a paroxysmal lunge, slapped his hand down. "Hann's boots! Don't they have *handkerchiefs* where you come from?"

"I'm sorry! How was I supposed to know?"

It took all of Tyvian's self-control not to scream. "You should know because that is all I have been talking about for *the last eight bloody hours*! Fool of a boy! I should have left you in the ditch where I found you!"

The boy's face was beet red, and his hands balled into fists. "I didn't—"

Tyvian threw up his hands. "Unbelievable! It's like trying to speak to a rock! Look at you—you are standing like someone smacked you with a pole, your fists are balled, your shoulders are hunched, and you can't stop speaking Trade for five bloody seconds. We're doomed, and all because I saw that marvelous profile of yours and thought, 'There you are, Tyvian, a fine young man with a good chin of whom you might be able to make something. Why, he's got the looks to be an Akrallian duke!' What a fool I was, to mistake looks for brains!"

"Stop yelling at me!" the boy snapped suddenly. His teeth were clenched and he stepped back from the table. "Ever since I took this stupid job, you've been riding me like a wooden horse on Feastday! I've had it! So I can't learn a whole lifetime of bloody stupid fancy-folk rules in a couple hours—so what? You're a bloody awful teacher, you know! I don't know what kind of job you got planned here or what, but I don't think it's half as dangerous as you say it is. I think you just like putting down folks so you'll feel all high and mighty, so I'm telling you now, mister, you cut it out, or I walk!"

Tyvian stared at the golden-haired street urchin, eyes suddenly alight. "Don't move!"

The boy blinked. "What?"

"You've got a name?"

"Artus."

"Artus, that's *it!* You've got it!"

"Got what?" Artus twisted slightly to look around.

"NO!" Tyvian caught his shoulders and moved them back into place. "Your posture! That's *it!* That's what I've been trying to get you to do all night! Just now, when you were carrying on about . . . whatever that was—I wasn't really listening—*then,* what were you thinking about just *then?*"

"How much of an arse you are?"

Tyvian snapped his fingers. "Perfect! Now, for the rest of the night, I want you to focus on how much of an arse I am and *say nothing*, understand?"

Artus nodded, skeptical. "Okay."

Tyvian smiled and straightened Artus's collar. "For the first time tonight I feel like we might pull this off. Now, stand just next to my right hand. We are arriving in the city."

As he said this, the mournful wail of demons being released back to their plane of origin shuddered through the night air. The engine slowed immediately, and through the windows of the dining car could be seen the weathered cobblestone streets and sharply peaked roofs of the Newbank district of Galaspin. It was an ancient city, like most capitals in the West, and its writhing streets and narrow alleys seemed to brood at the modern spectacle of the spirit engine as its brass wheels coasted along adamant tracks. It being a cold night, Tyvian saw no one in the streets and precious few lights in windows until they pulled up to the glittering edifice of the Galaspin Newbank Spiritberth and their nonstop journey from Ayventry came to a halt.

Tyvian slid the mageglass ring off his right hand and placed it on the table. He then placed the palm of his left hand on top of it and closed his eyes. The farsight augury enchanted upon the ring wasn't strong, but it was strong enough for him to see beyond the dining car and all along the length of the spirit engine as it was unloaded and loaded in preparation for its journey to Freegate. The images came to him as hazy and dreamlike at first, but the more he concentrated, the more detail there was.

He saw the conductor—a heavyset man with a broad white moustache in a dark blue coat with brass buttons. He was walking from the caboose toward the engine itself, swinging his feylamp to and fro as he whistled something formless and off-key. Tyvian moved past him—he was of no importance whatsoever. Next there were the engine warlocks—two of them—who bustled about the adamant pistons and mageglass chambers of their mystical vehicle, applying ritual unguents of warding to various gaskets and reinscribing incantatory runescripts along massive brass spirit-vessel that formed the heart of the magical conveyance's power. Soon, their ministrations (which, Tyvian noted, were carried out with a rather pedestrian and casual air) would lead to the reinfusion of Fey demons ("engine-fiends," to be precise) to force the hundred-ton vehicle along its way once more. Though the warlocks' lack of attention to their job raised some minor concern, Tyvian also moved past them—they were not what he was looking for.

Moving his perception past the parade of mail-bags and parcels being unloaded by a team of porters, Tyvian at last found his associate, Zazlar Hendrieux. The tall, thin Akrallian was barking orders to various thick-necked gentlemen who were wrestling several large boxes aboard one of the cargo cars. Observing his dress, Tyvian tsked under his breath, noting that his red breeches were at least four months out of style in the Akrallian court, and that his low-slung rapier was riding too loosely in the scabbard. If the man wanted them to come off as low-class penny-pinching provincial nobility, then he was doing a good job. Still, Zazlar had never been much for culture. It was enough to know that he was here, he didn't appear to be dipping ink, and he was holding up his end of the bargain. In fact, given the sheer number of crates being loaded aboard, the swarthy thief had outdone himself in acquiring the kind of goods Rameaux was likely to want.

Finally, Tyvian sought out Rameaux himself. Given that the platform at the berth was mostly occupied by servants and other laborers come to collect the goods and correspondence of their betters, he was easily found. Flanked by a pair of tall, broad-shouldered bodyguards in long green cloaks, Rameaux was a puffy toad of a man in clothing so exquisite his frame could not hope to justify them. His fingers seemed to be little but hooks for glittering jewels, and his ermine cape wrapped itself around his sloping shoulders like a beast clutching a suckling pig to its breast. He looked exactly as Zazlar had described—wealthy, proud, and foolish. If they could convince him they were legitimate nobility trying to liquidate their ancestral assets, they stood to make enough money to live comfortably for years.

The magic in the ring began to fade, and Tyvian lost the vision of Rameaux. He opened his eyes. Artus, he noted with satisfaction, hadn't moved from his place, but his fingers were fidgeting behind his back. Tyvian slapped them. "Be still! The moment is at hand."

The passengers taking the overnight engine to Freegate were few, but they did exist. As Tyvian and Artus waited in the dining car, isolated individuals, bundled against the cold winter night, shuffled past with their cases, packs, and trunks in tow. They looked to be merchants and couriers making the trip for business, not pleasure. Tyvian spotted a few distinctive brooches here and there denoting members of various guilds, but nothing that aroused much suspicion. That the Defenders might get wind of this deal was always possible, but Tyvian found it extremely unlikely. He and Zazlar had been careful.

Finally, Rameaux appeared in the car, flanked by his guards. The Akrallian looked left and right, eyeing the huddled shapes occupying tables in various corners with open suspicion. Tyvian resisted the urge to roll his eyes—the man couldn't have looked more like he was up to no good if he were prancing about with a bloody saber and a bag full of heads. Yawning, Tyvian brought his left hand to his mouth. The sapphires glittered in the gold ring on that hand, drawing the attention of one of Rameaux's guards. He nudged his master, and they came up to the table.

Meeting with Akrallian nobility was always difficult, especially when this particular noble—

Rameaux—was of questionable parentage and doubtful social standing. Zazlar had told Tyvian that the "Marquis" may have had a commoner for a great grandsire, a fact that had recently come to the attention of one of his political rivals. Such an impurity of the blood was unacceptable in the Griffon Court, and punishable by the stripping of titles and land. All of Marquis Rameaux's fabulous wealth would mean nothing in the face of this disgrace, and so he had scurried here—a thousand miles from his home country—to acquire certain artifacts that would establish his line as pure.

The thing that made this meeting difficult was how, exactly, the rules of etiquette applied to one such as Rameaux. If Tyvian were an Akrallian nobleman of good family but relative obscurity—which was to be his part for the evening—how would he greet a nobleman of comparatively higher status and wealth, who might not even be noble after all? Given the volatile nature of Akrallian pride—a facet of their cultural personalities that had gotten Tyvian into more duels than he cared to recall—the wrong response could likely result in Rameaux's guards drawing the blades they clearly had concealed underneath their cloaks and running both he and Artus through without even a *pardonnez-moi*.

Having considered this interaction for some time, Tyvian had concluded that the trick was to find a balance between stroking the Marquis's pride enough to keep him satisfied, but not so much that he himself would appear overly impressed. And then, of course, there was the ever-so-important formal Akrallian greeting.

When Rameaux came to stand across the table from him, Tyvian lifted himself off his seat just far enough to execute a truncated bow, and extended his left hand, palm upward, toward the seat opposite him. In flawless Akrallian he said, "I, Etienne DuGarre, Lord of the Blue Lake and guardian of its environs, salute you, the great Marquis Rameaux, Lord of Archanois, custodian of Pont de Mars, and the protector of its peoples, and offer you relaxation in my humble presence."

Rameaux blinked once, nodded, and sat down. He said nothing, but looked miserable. Tyvian immediately hated him; his response was nothing short of offensive. The very idea that Rameaux would greet a fellow noble that way was preposterous! Granted, Tyvian wasn't *really* an Akrallian nobleman, but Rameaux didn't know that. Were he not about to acquire half this man's fortune, he would have challenged him to a duel right there.

Well, Tyvian said to himself, *if he's going to be rude, so will I.* He smiled at the Akrallian, "Shall we speak Trade?"

Rameaux's accent was slight, which was evidence of a man used to doing business. "Yes. That would be wise."

Tyvian's eyes narrowed—he didn't like that answer either. "Forgive me if I seem impertinent Marquis, but you seem preoccupied. Are you perfectly well?"

"If I were, I would not be here at all. Forgive me if I am blunt, but I wish to handle this affair as quickly as possible." Rameaux drummed his fingers on the table and looked over his shoulder.

Tyvian's heartbeat quickened. *This man was not who he said he was.* No Akrallian marquis would be so forward. No Akrallian of noble bearing would drum his fingers like a nervous schoolgirl. No Akrallian would feel the need to check over his shoulder when flanked by two bodyguards. Tyvian needed a test, just to make sure. He thought about it for a moment and then said, "I took the liberty of ordering some *cherille*. Let us drink a toast to your success, and then carry on."

Rameaux looked at Tyvian, no doubt scanning him for some sign of deception. The smuggler kept his face impassive, but grinned inwardly; the impostor sensed a trap, and he was right. Tyvian's statement was, to those well-versed in Akrallian etiquette, a contradiction in terms. For the first part, it was unpardonably rude to presume to order refreshment for a person you had not yet met—a custom borne out of centuries of poisonings among the halls of the Griffon Court. However, at the same time, *cherille*—an ensorcelled wine that retarded the aging process—was fabulously expensive and a kingly gift, to be sure. Turning it *down* would be just as offensive, and, given their respective situations, the likelihood that Tyvian, masquerading as Lord Etienne DuGarre, might be poisoning him was extremely remote. The correct answer would be to drink, but only after a counteroffer of similar expense had been extended and accepted.

Several seconds of silence passed before Rameaux

replied. "You have honored me with your offer, but there is an ancient saying: business before pleasure. I beg you, let us conclude our mutual affair, and then share a drink to our health later."

Tyvian permitted himself a grin. "I humbly beg your pardon—of course you are right. How presumptuous of me to assume—"

Rameaux waved his hand—*interrupting* an apology—and said, "It is perfectly all right, cousin. You embarrass me with your humility."

"And you, me, with your magnanimity." Tyvian rose and motioned toward the exit to the dining car. "If you will deign to follow me, cousin, I will take you to the objects of your desire."

This man Rameaux was a Defender operating under a Shroud made up to look like a wealthy Akrallian noble. Looking back, Tyvian came up with a half-dozen signs he should have noticed from the platform—what kind of man goes to a secret meeting dripping in jewels, honestly? How had they gotten wind of this? It didn't matter—all that mattered now was cutting losses and getting away. As he walked to the door to the next car, he took his time, running backup plans through his head.

Once they were at the exit, they stood there a moment, staring at the closed door, until Tyvian finally looked at Artus and snapped. "Door, fool!"

Artus leapt as if bitten and quickly pulled the door open. As Tyvian passed, he whispered to the boy, "Don't look now, Artus, but we're nicked."

CHAPTER 2

ZAZLAR'S JOKE

Tyvian skipped a few paces ahead of Rameaux and his guards, dragging Artus by the elbow. Artus squirmed in his grip. "Nicked? What do you mean, nicked? Mirror-men?"

"*SHHHH!*" Tyvian hissed. "No questions. Go to the cargo car, find Zazlar Hendrieux. Tell him you're with me and that Rameaux is an impostor. He'll know what to do."

"But what about—" Artus began, but Tyvian planted a hand in the center of his back and shoved him on his way.

"Is there a problem?" Rameaux asked from behind.

Tyvian turned gracefully on his heel and smiled. "My attaché is poorly trained, cousin. I have sent him to prepare the items for your inspection."

Rameaux frowned. "I would like one of my guards to accompany him."

Tyvian's gasp was actually genuine—the *gall* of the man! "*Monsieur!* How *dare* you?"

Rameaux's face blanched. "I . . . I meant no offense . . ."

"I regret to inform you, then, that I *am* offended!" Tyvian stiffened his back and flared his nostrils, affecting his best impersonation of an angry fop. He even flapped his hands loosely at his sides. "Your crudity toward my person since our meeting has been most uncalled for!"

Rameaux exchanged a troubled look with his guards. "My lord DuGarre, if you would only listen—"

"*Non!* You listen to me, you insolent half-blooded toad! To preserve the honor of my fathers before me, I challenge you to a duel!"

The look on the false Marquis's face was priceless. Tyvian knew he would cherish it for years to come, though he hid his glee well behind a quivering facade of rage. He watched Rameaux and his two guards shift uncomfortably from foot to foot.

"But," Rameaux sputtered, "you do not have a sword!"

"Your guards do," Tyvian countered. "Let them

give up their blades—one to each of us—and I shall have satisfaction."

Again Tyvian's opponents stood flabbergasted. *Go on,* he thought, *go ahead and give me one of your weapons.*

Rameaux, eyes wide as his plot—whatever it had been—was rapidly unraveling, tried once more. "Really, if we could finish business first . . . could we see the items you promised and then—"

"Sir," Tyvian growled, "we do not go *anywhere* until my honor is satisfied."

Rameaux's face fell, and his guards looked worried. If Tyvian could read thoughts, he was certain Rameaux's mind was chaining together a number of colorful vulgarities. *That's right,* Tyvian told himself. *You can't arrest me if you don't see the goods, can you?*

The demons moaned in their piston prisons, and Artus stumbled as the spirit engine lurched forward. It picked up speed quickly, leaving Galaspin behind in the dark, and with it any chance of leaping off into the relative safety of the city's winding streets. Cursing Tyvian Reldamar for the hundredth time since meeting him, Artus pushed his way forward to the cargo cars.

Like the dining car, the cargo containers on this spirit engine were Astrally modified. Artus found the effect disconcerting; the magical alteration made it difficult to judge distances properly, and he constantly felt he might run into the wall or strike his head on the ceiling. Unlike the dining car, however, the extra space was the only amenity afforded the cargo section. It was a dark box with thin wooden slats forming a thin barrier between the sawdust-scented interior and the crisp, cold air of the Galaspin night. The wind and the cries of the engine-demons howled through the cracks in the wide-mouthed cargo doors on both sides of the compartment, and light was limited to a single feylamp swaying from a beam over the door. Large crates and heavy trunks stenciled in a variety of foreign languages were stacked in precise rows along the walls, throwing long shadows wherever the lamplight struck.

Artus reached up and took the lamp down. He took only a moment admiring its craftsmanship—a feylamp, they said, could burn for months without need for replenishment—and then turned his eyes to the dusty gloom. "Hello?"

There was no answer. He stood still, listening and scanning the shadows for movement. Then, from the other side of the car, he heard a low-pitched growl followed by a sudden thump, as though something heavy but soft had been thrown against a door. Moving slowly to keep his balance as the engine bucked and shuddered over the hilly landscape, Artus held the lamp in front of him as some kind of ward and called again. "Is anybody there?"

Silence for a moment, and then another growl, this one even lower pitched and more sinister than the first. It was deep and forceful, like a steel cart rumbling down a mine shaft. Whatever it was, Artus knew it wasn't human; no person could make a sound that menacing.

Wondering what sort of person this Zazlar might be, Artus willed his feet forward and slowly advanced on the noise. "Hello?"

A hand as strong as an iron claw seized him by the hair and yanked his head back. At the same moment, a knife was placed against his throat. Its edge burned in the cold air. "Name, whelp!" a man's voice snarled in his ear from behind.

"Artus!" the boy blurted, and added, "You Zazlar?"

Artus's hair received a twist and another yank. The knife bore down. "And why would you know such a dangerous name?"

"Reldamar sent me! He's brought me with him!"

The knife relaxed and Artus's hair was released. Stumbling forward, he turned to see a lean man dressed in a fine black cape. His face—long and unshaven—was impassive, but his icy eyes seemed to swallow Artus from head to foot. Slapping his dagger back into his belt, the man said. "I'm Zazlar Hendrieux. You weren't expected."

"Reldamar says we're nicked!" Artus said. "He said Rameaux's an impostor. He said you'd know what to do."

Zazlar laughed. "Is that so? Hmmmm . . ."

There was another crash, coupled with another inhuman roar that tapered into a howl. The sound made Artus cringe. "What is that?"

Zazlar smiled. "A little joke, is all."

"It don't sound very funny."

"Such a clever tongue in such a young head," Zazlar said. "Now, what's this about being nicked?"

Artus explained everything he knew, which was precious little. Indeed, the whole evening's affairs were an almost complete mystery to him, but as he talked, it all seemed to make some kind of sense to Zazlar, who nodded sagely at each pause in the story. When Artus had finished, Zazlar clapped his gloved hands together.

"Excellent! Tyvian was right to send you to me. Go and fetch him. Tell him once he's here, everything will be fine. I've got a plan."

Artus blinked. "Really? What is it? What's going on?"

Zazlar grinned. "And ruin the surprise? Now go— I've got preparations to make."

Artus looked around at the bleak interior of the cargo car, wondering what "preparations" needed making, but retreated. Zazlar vanished back into the shadows before Artus had replaced the feylamp and closed the door.

He couldn't put his finger on it, but there was something just a bit off about Zazlar Hendrieux.

Tyvian, meanwhile, had engaged Rameaux and his entourage in a staring contest of sorts. It was comprised, primarily, of Tyvian standing with his arms crossed and his chin elevated—the very definitional image of restrained outrage. Rameaux, sweat beading on his powdered forehead, stood flummoxed and likewise outraged, bejeweled fists balled at his waist. The two of them had stood in this way for the past three minutes straight, ever since they ran out of constructive things to yell at each other.

There was only so far either of them could push a bluff, and they both knew it. Tyvian knew Rameaux was a fake, but Rameaux wasn't *sure* that Tyvian knew yet. The only way for him to *be* sure was for Tyvian to break character, which, by choosing to react as he had, Tyvian had avoided. Rameaux knew he was in a pickle. He could simply order his guards to escort Tyvian to the cargo car, and then Tyvian—the contents of his pockets notwithstanding—would be powerless to resist. However, that would blow his own cover, and he assumed that Tyvian, being Tyvian, had certain useful items in his pockets that would make overt action risky.

For his part, Tyvian knew that *Rameaux* knew that his best bet was to get him to go to the cargo car under the assumption that he was still dealing with the Marquis Rameaux, and not whoever his true self happened to be. Unfortunately, because of Tyvian's (pretended) outrage, the only way for that to happen was for Rameaux to engage in swordplay with a man who, he was clearly aware, was one of the finest swordsmen in the West.

The end result was a lot of angry staring.

Rameaux heaved a sigh for the twentieth time. "Really, cousin, you are being ridiculous."

Tyvian raised his eyebrows. "I? Surely not—it is you who are being ridiculous. You are a coward and a braggart, and I demand—"

Artus entered the car, and Tyvian broke off midrant. The boy's face was flushed—Tyvian guessed it was nerves—but, to his credit, Artus did his best to assume the proper posture before bowing to the men in the room. He failed utterly, but that was beside the point.

"Well?" Tyvian asked, and when Artus hesitated, he nodded. "You may speak, but use Trade. Akrallian is too delicate a tongue for these brigands."

"Zaz . . . Master Hendrieux says all is ready, sir . . . m'lord."

"Tell him I am quite occupied. He will wait."

Artus's mouth flattened into a hard line. "I told him about the gentlemen, and he said he could . . . uhhh . . ."

Surprisingly, it was Rameaux who finished the boy's sentence. " . . . resolve this issue of honor, I'm sure. What say you, cousin? May we forestall our duel another hour? Surely that is customary."

Tyvian grunted. What was Hendrieux planning? Probably something like "stab them in the back when they came through the door." Not the most elegant solution, but Tyvian had to admire its simplicity. He still had the deathcaster in his pocket, which would easily account for one of them, probably two. Between that and Hendrieux's knife . . . Tyvian liked the odds. He nodded his assent. "Very well, though it pains me to do so, I will lead you to the objects, as agreed. Follow me."

As they made their way through the corridors of the spirit engine, Tyvian went over escape plans. Murdering the three men behind him, though regrettable, would be simple enough, but he couldn't guarantee their bodies would go undiscovered. He supposed he could always toss them out the door when they went over a bridge. Zazlar could assist him with the big ones, and there were plenty of tributaries to the Trell running through this countryside. After that, return to his cabin, act like nothing happened, and get Carlo in Freegate to store the goods for them when they got into the berth. A bloody plan with plenty that could go wrong, but a workable one nevertheless.

Then there was the boy. It was a pity, really. Had this all gone smoothly, he would have paid the brat to keep his mouth shut and that would probably be an end to it. Certainly the boy would have told somebody, but not immediately—not until the money he gave Artus ran out. Having him as witness to a triple murder, though, and with no money to buy him off with, was a different matter. The boy couldn't be permitted to talk; Zazlar would insist on killing him. Tyvian would try to talk him out of it, but he doubted Zaz would be reasonable. Zaz had poor nerves when things went wrong, and the only way he knew how to react was with brutality.

The additional trouble was that they couldn't kill the boy while still aboard the spirit engine—the conductor would likely remember him arriving with a companion and leaving alone, and when the other three didn't get off either, it would be an investigation that pointed directly at him. No, better to let Zazlar stick a dagger in the boy's ribs when they got off at Freegate. Tyvian would offer the boy a hot meal and a drink or something and they'd lead him out of sight. There were literally hundreds of places to drop dead bodies in Freegate, and the city watchmen never asked too many questions. It was too bad, though.

That settled, Tyvian's mind was clear when they came into the dimly lit cargo car that Artus had just left. The boy was to his right, the two guards were behind him, and Rameaux was behind them. Zazlar, though, was *not* where Tyvian had expected—which was to say, he wasn't hidden in some shadowy corner, knife at the ready. He was, instead, standing in the center of the car, feylamp in hand, cape thrown jauntily over one arm.

Zazlar bowed as they entered. "Welcome, my lords! How pleased I am that you could all make it!"

Tyvian, trying not to show his unease, stepped forward. "Gentlemen—by which I mean everyone present save the odious pig who has so gravely damaged my honor—allow me to present my cousin and associate, Zazlar Hendrieux."

Hendrieux grinned broadly. "Thank you, my lord DuGarre. If you three will just step into the car a bit—

yes, yes, don't be shy—I will arrange for the goods to be displayed."

Tyvian's eyes narrowed. Hendrieux clearly wasn't himself—he was very seldom so calm or collected in meetings like this. He was usually fidgeting with the pommel of his sword or scanning dark corners for an imagined ambush. He wasn't even speaking like Hendrieux; admittedly they had practiced covering up his merchant's accent, but Tyvian never remembered him doing so well as this. He must have been dipping ink before the meeting, but his eyes were unusually clear. Come to think of it, he had never seen Hendrieux's eyes so devoid of the rheumy clouds that marked an ink-thrall. Ordinarily this might have been a good sign, but not now. Too much was amiss this evening for Tyvian to discount anything as coincidence.

He felt the urge to put a hand on the deathcaster sitting in his pocket, but restrained himself. He wanted to save that as a surprise, and he knew the two bodyguards were watching his every move. He forced a smile at Zazlar. "Don't keep our guests waiting. Let's see the first case!"

Zazlar skipped over to a stack of trunks and, summoning some assistance from Artus, pulled the top one free and dragged it under the light of the feylamp. He waved his hands over the locks, muttering the keywords, and the lid sprung open. Tyvian looked inside, expecting an array of ornate talismans, decorative amulets, enchanted rings, and the like. Instead he saw a velvet tray in which was laid row upon row of finger-sized mageglass vials filled with a glowering, orange liquid.

Rameaux stepped forward to inspect them more closely, also surprised. "Gods, that's pure brymm."

Tyvian blinked. Brymm—pure, concentrated fey energy in a volatile liquid form—was the kind of stuff armies lobbed over walls to incinerate cities. What the *hell* was Zazlar up to?

Rameaux gingerly fished a vial out of the trunk and held it up to the light. "I wasn't expecting this, I must say."

Tyvian summoned up a scowl. "It is clearly the wrong trunk. Pardon me for a moment." He grabbed Zazlar by the arm and pulled him aside. "What in blazes are you doing?"

Zazlar grinned. "Trust me, Tyvian."

"Don't call me that. They're watching," Tyvian hissed, making sure his back was to the guards.

Zazlar looked back at the three men marveling over the volatile trunk and called, "If you lift up the tray, you'll find some additional items I think you'll find interesting, my lords!"

One guard did so, balancing the tray very carefully as he lifted. The two other men—and Artus—looked inside. Tyvian heard them gasp.

Tyvian opened his mouth to ask what was there, but Zazlar motioned for him to follow. "There's something I want you to see." They moved to the back of the cargo car, where an abnormally large crate was stashed in a corner. It was reinforced with iron studs, and its corners were shod in steel. As they drew closer, something inside of the crate moved, and a pair of copper eyes glittered through the slats in the flickering light. Tyvian stopped dead. "Is that what I think it is?"

Zazlar grinned in exactly the same way as before. "It's a joke."

Tyvian licked his lips. "On whom?"

Zazlar, still smiling like a wax sculpture, called out, "Back here, my lords!"

Tyvian seized him by the collar. "Zaz, why did you pack a bloody *gnoll* in a bloody crate?"

Zazlar said nothing, and Tyvian was forced to free him as the two guards, Rameaux, and a bewildered Artus found their way over. The guards were carrying the trunk, no doubt considering its cargo too dangerous to leave unattended. Rameaux had in his hand a weathered, leather-bound pamphlet. On its cover was a sigil that Tyvian couldn't place immediately until Rameaux held it up in front of him. "What is the meaning of this?"

Tyvian got a better look at the sigil on the cover and recognized it as a Kalsaari mark made by the Cult of the Devourer. His breath caught in his throat at the horrid implications. "Zazlar, what the hell are you up to?"

That same smile, that same answer. "Trust me, Tyvian."

Tyvian's heart sank. The mannequin smile of Zazlar told him everything he needed to know. "You're a simulacrum."

The revelation was punctuated by a thunderous growl from the crate behind him. Rameaux jumped at this, and then seemed to put two and two together as well. "This pamphlet is a forbidden work on the proscribed study of biomancy, which details the use of brymmic concoctions to alter wild beasts into demons of war. I can only presume you mean to sell me these things."

Tyvian backed up against the wall of the car, putting some distance between himself and the gnoll in the crate. "I note, Marquis, that your Akrallian accent has suddenly eluded you. It seems that none of us here are who we claim to be."

Rameaux scowled. "No indeed, Mr. Reldamar. Save Mr. Hendrieux, of course."

Tyvian smiled mirthlessly. "Whoever you are, sir, you are less than observant."

Rameaux cocked his head to the side. "I beg your pardon?"

Tyvian turned to Zazlar. "How do you feel, Zaz?"

"Quite well, thank you!"

Tyvian looked back at Rameaux and repeated, "How do you feel, Zaz?"

"Quite well, thank you!"

"Kroth!" Rameaux swore, and looked at his guards. "Somebody must have tipped him off. Inform Galaspin Tower that Hendrieux might still be in the city."

One guard produced a glowing blue sphere from his robes, the size of his hand—a sending stone—and moved off to a corner to operate it. If the mention of

Galaspin Tower weren't enough, Tyvian knew expensive objects like sending stones weren't common to bodyguards.

"You're a Defender, then." Tyvian remarked casually. "Pardon me, sir, but since you know who I am, might I ask you to return the courtesy?"

Rameaux grunted and waved his hand. The air shimmered, and the fat, toadish form of Rameaux evaporated into the tall, athletic build of a young woman in her mid-twenties clad in the silvered mageglass armor and white cape of a Defender of the Balance—a mirror-man, or woman, in this case. The glittering staff at her side indicated her rank as a Mage Defender, and, therefore, wielder of the High Arts. Tyvian saw her high cheekbones, glaring blue-gray eyes, and the golden braid thrown over her left shoulder, and recognized her as Myreon Alafarr. She and Tyvian had met before, and on similar terms.

"Look, Tyvian—it's your old friend!" The simulated Zazlar smiled and pointed.

"The real you set me up, Zaz," Tyvian growled. "I'll not forget it."

The simulacrum shrugged. "Sorry, chum. Had to be done."

One of the guards threw back his cloak, drew his sword, and advanced on Tyvian and the simulacrum. Alafarr tapped her staff on the ground once, and "Zazlar Hendrieux" vanished from existence with a sharp crack.. "It's over, Reldamar. Come along peaceably."

Tyvian's mind raced—had been racing—since the simulacrum revealed itself. Escape routes from a moving spirit engine were few, and from this particular corner were proving to be even fewer. He had his back against the wall, in both figurative and literal senses. There were two armed men and a mage-defender between him and any exits, and, if Alafarr's methods were consistent, there were likely some more undercover Defenders aboard as backup. Tyvian's assets were the deathcaster as well as the surprises stored in the crystal spheres in his pockets—and that was it. By themselves, they weren't enough. Not with Alafarr, with all her arcane power, looking right at him. The only other thing he could think of was the crate to his right containing an angry, growling gnoll. As far as Tyvian understood them, gnolls were bipedal dog-beasts that came from the distant wilderness of the Taqar. Given its current attitude, Tyvian doubted it would be likely to assist him. That was unless, by "assist" one actually meant "maul and devour."

Then again . . .

The guard was two paces away when Tyvian thrust his hand into his pocket for the deathcaster. Before he had even grasped it, however, Alafarr thrust her staff in Tyvian's direction and thundered the word, *"Azmor!"*

The spell slammed Tyvian against the wall and held him there. Keeping a keen eye on him, Alafarr said, "Search his pockets! He's likely armed."

Tyvian felt as though a one-ton wineskin were pressed against his chest, but he managed to turn his head enough to look Alafarr in the eye. "You're only surmising that *now*?"

The guard—the *Defender*, Tyvian corrected himself—sheathed his blade and rifled through Tyvian's clothing. Tyvian thought about requesting he take it easy on the lace fringe, but didn't think the brute was likely to listen. When he was through, Alafarr's underling had found the marble-sized crystals and that was all. He delivered them to Alafarr. "Just this stuff, Magus. Nothing else."

"That's not true!" Tyvian was aghast. How could the man have missed the deathcaster? He had put his grubby hand *right in* the pocket!

Alafarr and the Defender looked at him, blinking. "What do you mean?"

"I had a deathcaster in there! Your fool of a man missed it!"

Alafarr looked at her man, who shrugged and said. "You must be mistaken."

"I most certainly am *not* mistaken! I put it in my right pocket just before coming to meet you. I'm *certain*!"

Alafarr smirked. "Perhaps you lost it."

"*Lost it*? Do you have any idea how *difficult* it is to get one of those little beauties? It's not the kind of item you just casually toss around! What did it do, crawl out of my pocket and run away? I *demand* you search me again."

Alafarr and the Defender drew closer to him, making certain to maintain a bit of distance between them and the rattling, growling gnoll-crate. "May I remind you, Mr. Reldamar, that you are under arrest. You are in no position to demand *anything*."

Tyvian strained against the spell. "Well I *refuse* to let five months of scouring the black market of Tasis for an authentic deathcaster be lost to the winds because your fool of a man knocked it out of my pocket while he was pawing my waistcoat like some deputized ape!"

Alafarr rolled her eyes. "This is ridiculous."

Tyvian tried to move his head so he could see down. "Look on the floor—maybe it was jostled free when you hit me with the restraining spell."

"You know something, Reldamar," Alafarr sneered, and leaned close enough to Tyvian that he could smell her atrociously floral perfume. "I am really going to enjoy watching you turned to stone and placed in a penitentiary garden."

"Nobody move!" The voice was shrill and tremulous, but Tyvian recognized it at once—Artus.

The boy was standing with his feet spread apart and his hands wrapped around the sinister black form of a deathcaster. He was pointing it at Alafarr primarily, but the business end of the thing wavered between her and the other Defender. Alafarr put her hands up, but still had her staff. "Boy, don't do anything foolish, now. Put down the weapon."

"Shut up!" Artus snapped. "Drop the staff!"

"Boy—" Alafarr began.

"Now!"

Alafarr dropped it, and Tyvian was released from

the spell in the same instant. He immediately checked his own pockets, just to make sure, and then leveled an accusing finger at his savior. "You picked my pocket, you little bastard!"

As Tyvian took a step forward, Artus pointed the deathcaster at him, too. "Stay back!"

Tyvian stopped short, putting his hands up. "Artus? Maybe you don't understand how saving somebody works, but you're supposed to—"

Artus blinked. "I'm not saving *you*. I'm saving my own skin!"

"Ah, well—that makes much more sense. I apologize. There's one problem, though."

Artus was slowly backing up. "What's that?"

Tyvian pointed. "There's a Defender behind you."

Artus's expression was incredulous for the split second before the Defender behind him—having completed his message to Galaspin Tower—jumped on his back. Tyvian, Alafarr, and the first Defender all sprung into action. Alafarr crouched to retrieve her staff, while Tyvian threw a heel back into the groin of the first Defender, interrupting his attempts to draw his sword.

Spinning around, Tyvian caught Alafarr's staff by one end even as the mage was standing up with it. As Alafarr attempted to yank it free from his grasp, Tyvian went with the pull and drove the mage against the wall. A brief wrestling match ensued, with Tyvian trying to press the staff against the mage's throat. He was getting the better of it until Alafarr slammed a

mageglass-tipped boot into the smuggler's shin, causing Tyvian to drop to one knee. Grimacing with pain,
he rolled to one side before the back end of Alafarr's
staff could be brought into contact with his skull, but
this left him on his back, staring up at the recently
groin-kicked Defender, who had managed to draw his
sword after all. He looked quite angry.

Before Tyvian could be run through, however, the
tumbling brawl between Artus and the other Defender
over the deathcaster resulted in the magical device
being discharged. A wild, blazing bolt of green lightning cut an arc across the cargo car, splintering crates,
cutting support beams, and causing the Defender
standing over Tyvian to throw himself on top of the
smuggler to avoid being seared into halves.

The Defender had about thirty pounds and four
inches on Tyvian, and his bulk was sufficient to block
out all light and sound for a moment as Tyvian struggled to throw him off. In the midst of their grappling,
Tyvian's fingers came across the crystal spheres that
had just been taken from his pockets. He managed to
snag three of them in one hand before kicking the man
off him. Then Tyvian rolled to his feet . . .

. . . and found himself face-to-face with Alafarr and
the two Defenders, all with their weapons in hand.
Artus, Tyvian noted, was a bruised heap on the floor.
Tyvian raised his hands. "It's not too late to come along
quietly, is it?"

Alafarr's lip curled. "Tyvian Reldamar, I'll see you
in—"

The Mage Defender's words were suddenly drowned out by the spine-tingling bass of the gnoll's growl. They had all heard it consistently since arriving in the cargo car, but this time it was somewhat . . . closer. The sound was like a thundercloud looming overhead. All four of them froze, eyes wide.

The gnoll was out of its cage.

CHAPTER 3

WHAT TYVIAN DOES BEST

A six-and-one-half-foot mass of fur and teeth pounced on one Defender, tackling him to the ground like a cat upon a rag doll. The man didn't even have time to scream before the beast's jaws tore out his throat. All thought of arresting or being arrested vanished from the thoughts of the others present. Tyvian, who liked to think himself calm under pressure, felt a sick, nauseous terror at the prospect of being devoured by a wild beast who no doubt had been underfed for who knew how long in its prison.

Therefore, he found himself cheering on the

second Defender. Rapier in hand, he performed a textbook lunge at the beast, aiming to spit it through the heart. In a show of unnerving animal dexterity, however, the creature darted forward, ducking under the blade, and *grasped the man by the wrist*. Before Tyvian could fully rationalize his horror that the thing had opposable thumbs, the gnoll pulled the Defender off-balance, flipped him over its back, and charged at Alafarr, fangs bared. All its physical superiority, however, was no match for the power of a mage wielding the High Arts. Alafarr took a forceful step forward, thrust the tip of her staff at the beast, and spoke a word of power too nuanced for Tyvian to hear properly. A blue light burst from the staff, striking the gnoll in the chest, and propelled it across the cargo car and through the door opposite into the snowy night beyond.

Tyvian and Alafarr stood silently for a moment, looking at the black hole where the gnoll had gone, and regathered their calm. Tyvian regathered first, and remembered the three crystal spheres he had in his hand. "Alafarr," he said, tossing one of them, "catch!"

Alafarr blinked and caught it with her free hand. As soon as the sphere touched her, it popped like a soap bubble, and her mageglass armor—fashioned, as all mageglass, from Dweomeric sorcery given physical form—disappeared in a sudden puff of ozone. The mage swore and rubbed her hand on her breeches, as though hoping to dissipate any further effects. "Antispell!" she yelled to the other Defender. "He's got antispell!"

Tyvian was already moving. As the remaining Defender struggled to get up, Tyvian kicked the rapier out of his hand and scooped it up as he ran past. He looked back to see Alafarr sputtering in frustration as she tried to pull enough energy from the surrounding air to overcome the antispell. Chuckling, Tyvian ducked out of the cargo car.

Barricading the door behind him, he sprinted down the length of the spirit engine, making for his cabin to collect his belongings, and then to the end of the engine, where he hoped to leap off into the night. He barreled into the dining car and hit the floor just before the frame was splintered apart from a trio of explosive crossbow bolts; three Defenders, clad in their glittering armor, had set up a defensive position out of overturned furniture. Tyvian rolled underneath a nearby table while the men reloaded. "Dammit!" He yelled, noting the thick dust clinging to his shirt. "This floor is *disgusting*!"

An enchanted crossbow bolt splintered the table into kindling. Tyvian dove to another one, with two more bolts missing him by mere inches. He was running out of cover, and with Alafarr not far behind, he decided drastic measures were necessary. He took his second antispell sphere and chucked it against the wall of the car. He heard one of the Defender's snicker about him missing, but the laughter soon died on the man's lips when, suddenly, the whole dining car began to shrink. The antispell had undone the astral manipulations that gave the car its unusual size, and the result was a mass of tables, chairs, and carpeting being compressed toward the center of the room at high speed. As the Defenders stumbled to escape the crush of material, Tyvian nimbly slipped out the destroyed door he had just come through.

Now, back in the car he'd just left, he saw the barricade he had set against the cargo car entrance beginning to buckle. Knowing it was Alafarr and knowing that this time the Mage Defender would be ready for a projectile antispell, Tyvian shattered a window with the butt of his stolen rapier and climbed out.

Outside, the bitter winter air howled down the smooth sides of the spirit engine. Rapier tucked into his belt, Tyvian hauled himself onto the roof of the car and, back bent against the wind, made his way forward. If the Defenders had been waiting for him in the dining car, then they probably found his room, along with all of his possessions. As much as it pained him to abandon such fine quality items, he couldn't go back for them now. All that remained was to find a suitable way to escape the spirit engine without Alafarr tracking him. To his left there was a snow-blanketed forest, and to his right white-clad open pastures. Leaping off now would either leave him in the open or leave him broken in two upon the bole of some pine tree. There had to be a better way to escape and still leave Alafarr behind.

It hit him all at once. "The deathcaster!" He'd double back, grab the deathcaster, cut the cars behind him free, and leave Alafarr and her thugs trapped on an inert series of train cars in the middle of the Galaspin countryside. He was in the midst of congratulating himself when he heard his name shouted over the howl of the engine spirits.

Tyvian looked up to see the Defender whose rapier he had stolen. His green cloak flapped and jerked in the cold wind like it was being ravaged by a wild animal, and in his hand was the rapier of his friend—the one killed by the angry gnoll. The big man's face was screwed up into an immovable mask of anger, his dark eyes boring into Tyvian's chest.

"Hello, there." Tyvian drew the man's own sword and saluted. "I don't suppose I could bribe you?"

The Defender answered with an athletic lunge that aimed to put a blade through Tyvian's throat. The fellow's speed was good and his form admirable, but his movements were rather obvious—Tyvian parried the attack effortlessly. "Really now—you used that same attack on the gnoll and it didn't work then either."

The Defender grunted in reply and pressed his attack with four more thrusts, each of which Tyvian deflected with ease. While his opponent possessed competence with a blade, he clearly relied more on size and power than on skill. Against most opponents this would probably be enough, but Tyvian Reldamar was not most opponents. Every attack the man launched was preceded by a controlled roar, as though yelling would somehow guide his blade. The result, Tyvian concluded, was one of the more boring duels he'd ever had, the fact that he was fighting on the icy roof of a speeding spirit engine notwithstanding.

Tyvian parried a tenth attack; he had been pushed back almost to the end of the car. "You know," he called over the wind, "you really ought to watch yourself up here—it's very slippery!"

Frustrated and enraged, the Defender performed a flèche. This was an aggressive, lunging attack, but launched from the back foot rather than the forward, with a result halfway between leap and charge. It was a bold and risky maneuver, but if used in the proper circumstance, could be deadly.

This was not the proper circumstance.

During the duel, Tyvian had been cataloguing the Defender's attacks and concluded that his defenses had exhausted the man's repertoire of offensive maneuvers—all except the flèche, which every competent fencer knew. So Tyvian's opponent had allowed himself to be pushed back into a place where a flèche would appear wise; namely, backed up against the edge of the car. But the common retreat and parry defense for a flèche was not an option here. Tyvian knew this; the Defender knew this; any competent fencer would have known this. Tyvian, however, was more than merely competent—he fought dirty. When the Defender's rear foot left the ground to launch the flèche, Tyvian dove at the man's knees. As the sword pierced the empty space where Tyvian's torso had been, Tyvian's body knocked the man's legs out from under him. The Defender landed with a thunk on his sword arm and slid off the side of the car.

Tyvian rose, walked to the edge and peered over. The Defender was clinging to a window frame on the side of the car by one, white-knuckled hand. His feet dangled over the speeding tracks, his face set in panic. "Help . . ." he managed.

Tyvian chuckled and shook his head. "My dear fellow, just who do you think you're dealing with anyway?" He cut the man's fingers at the knuckles with one quick slash of his rapier and watched him tumble beneath the heavy wheels.

Tyvian swung himself inside the cargo car a minute later, whistling as he went. It was still dark, but the lone feylamp was still there, and it gave enough light for him to see his deathcaster lying on the floor next to the case full of brymm and the unconscious body of the boy, Artus.

He scooped up the priceless weapon-artifact and, casting a cursory glance over the other objects—a case of volatile alchemical ingredients and a worthless street urchin—turned to cut the remainder of the spirit engine loose.

"That's far enough, Reldamar!" Myreon Alafarr stood in the door, her staff glowing softly in the dark. Tyvian couldn't help but notice the lighting was rather flattering to her statuesque profile.

He grimaced. "Ah, Alafarr, I was just thinking about you. How exactly do you plan to explain your failure to your superiors this time?"

She snorted. "Still glib, I see. I've noticed, though, that you seem a bit more disheveled than usual. I'll take that as a compliment."

"Oh, but *I've* noticed that you seem to have run out of henchmen. You should take *that* as an insult."

Alafarr leveled her staff at Tyvian. "Give it up. You're no match for me, and you know it."

"You magi and your famous arrogance. If your so-called 'High Arts' counted for much, you would have caught me long ago." Tyvian took a step back toward the case full of brymm.

"You've got a plan, then."

Tyvian smiled. "One twitch from you and I'll blow the brymm."

"They're in mageglass containers—a deathcaster won't do anything to them." Alafarr snorted, but didn't move.

"Who said anything about using a deathcaster?" Tyvian said, and produced the last sphere of antispell in the palm of his hand. He held it over the case.

Alafarr frowned. "You haven't enough antispell in that little sphere to nullify the whole case. It would be only three or four vials, at most."

"Yes, but once freed, the combined brymm from those four vials will alter the magical ley of the case to a sufficient degree that the surrounding mageglass vials will destabilize, creating a chain reaction, and—"

"Yes, yes—I keep forgetting you've studied." Alafarr made a sour expression. "Such a waste."

"I beg your pardon?"

She sighed. "You could have been a great mage, Reldamar. With your intelligence and your connections, you could have earned your staff in Saldor and done a great deal of good."

"And been a civil servant to the sweaty, unwashed masses, you mean? You sound like my mother, Alafarr." Tyvian scowled.

"Your mother is a great woman."

"You *would* say that—she's not your mother."

Alafarr, oddly, looked offended. "I grow tired of this. You're a blight upon your family name and a scourge upon the earth, and I'm taking you with me this time. Put the antispell away—if you drop it, you'll kill us both, and you love yourself too much for suicide."

Tyvian grinned. "You don't know that. The nature of the Fey is chaotic, and brymm is just concentrated Fey energy. We don't know what it will do, precisely. It will destroy us both, yes, but maybe not immediately. Who knows—I might have time to escape while you, of course, would have to stay. You couldn't allow a whole spirit engine full of innocent people be blown to smithereens over little old me, now could you?"

"You're a monster, Reldamar." Alafarr stated coolly, hands tightening on her staff.

"No, Alafarr, I'm a gambler." Tyvian dropped the antispell and leapt clear.

The crystal broke on the lid of the case, and, for a split second, nothing happened. Then the whole case ceased to exist all at once and there was a rush of searing hot air as though belched from the open door of a furnace. Tyvian was thrown across the car and slammed, upside down, into the wall. While his head was still spinning, he observed that where the case had been was now the center of a fiendish display of fiery destruction. Tiny sprites of flame—complete with little legs and arms of pure fire—danced and twirled throughout the car, setting everything they touched instantly and completely alight. There were hundreds of these sprites and they moved with a gleeful and malicious intelligence. Tyvian knew he had only seconds to escape before he, too, would be little more than fuel for their consumption.

Black smoke stinging his eyes, he felt around for his deathcaster, but found instead a human hand. It was attached, he quickly realized, to the boy, Artus. Awakened by the explosion, the boy clung to Tyvian's arm and pulled himself closer, screaming, "Help! Help! What's happened! Oh gods!"

The boy was a panicky wreck, and Tyvian should have shaken him off, but he was unsteady on his feet from the explosion and the world was still spinning. "Help me up!" he screamed in Artus's ear, "Get to the door!"

Their one chance for escape—their *one* chance—was the open cargo door through which the gnoll had been propelled earlier. Holding on to Artus's shoulders, Tyvian pushed the two of them through the maelstrom of ever-growing fire. Somewhere in the chaos he heard Alafarr chanting incantations over the roar of the flames. Laughing despite himself, Tyvian wondered if the mage would be successful or not.

Then the door was before them. Tyvian pushed Artus as hard as he could, but the boy had, in a fit of panic, dug in his heels. He should have left him again, but Tyvian found himself screaming in his ear, "Jump!"

"But, no, it's—" Artus began.

Tyvian, his pants and shirt set alight already by twirling, dancing fiends, kicked Artus in the back of the knee and, as the boy buckled, heaved both Artus and himself through the open door.

He expected snow, he expected ground, he expected to hit something hard and roll; none of that happened. They fell through open air, and he abruptly realized what Artus had been trying to say. They had jumped off a bridge.

A brick wall of icy water hit Tyvian in the face.

CHAPTER 4

THE IRON RING

The smell of dead fish and the hiss of a woodstove woke Tyvian from his coma. He was looking up at the dusty rafters of a thatch-roof cottage, and his head was pounding. Sitting up gingerly, he saw that he had been laid on a straw pallet on a floor carpeted with beaver pelts, and covered by a thick blanket of itchy wool. He was wearing his underbreeches and nothing else. He spoke his first thought aloud. "If this is the afterlife, then I am sorely disappointed."

"I am impressed." A deep, weather-worn voice rumbled from behind him.

Tyvian craned his neck—a punishingly painful maneuver—to see a burly man with wild, graying black hair and a thick matted beard sitting on a stool that didn't seem quite capable of accommodating his weight. He was clad in heavy furs and had the hands of a laborer—thick, callused, and large. Tyvian sniffed the air tentatively—the man smelled faintly of mud and sweat. "You will forgive me if I do not return the sentiment. Where am I?"

The man chuckled. "Out of ten thousand men, only perhaps a score might have escaped the Defenders aboard that spirit engine. Of that score, I doubt that even one of them would have the presence of mind to be flippant after two days of unconsciousness. You are an incredible person, Tyvian Reldamar, despite yourself."

Tyvian's stomach tightened. He quickly scanned the room for a weapon, and spotted a long knife in a scabbard hanging by the rough wood door. When he looked back at the hairy man, he noted that the stranger's dark keen eyes had followed his every glance. He might be smelly, but the man sitting across from him was not a fool. "You know my name, but I don't believe I know yours."

"Eddereon."

"Pleased to make your acquaintance."

"You are a very good liar."

Tyvian scowled. "Thank you."

A teapot whistled, and Eddereon clapped his hands together and rose. "Ah! You must be thirsty, hungry. You haven't eaten for some time."

Tyvian watched him go to the stove and pour out two cups of tea, keeping his bulk interposed between Tyvian and the knife. Searching his memory, Tyvian tried to recall whether he'd heard the name Eddereon before. It was Northron, the lack of surname and his faint accent making that fact even more obvious. Tyvian had never crossed the Dragonspine into those cold, open lands; he never saw any reason why a person would feel the need. He couldn't have met this Eddereon there, then. The man had to be an expatriate, but Tyvian couldn't place him, precisely. His face looked vaguely familiar—those eyes especially. It was the face of someone he might have passed in a crowd or spied across a smoky tavern. That was all he had, though, and he didn't like it.

Eddereon held out a teacup. "It isn't poisoned, I promise."

"No thank you—I ate well on the engine."

Eddereon smiled, revealing an imperfect set of teeth. "No, you didn't." Tyvian's indignant expression prompted the big man to continue. "I spoke with the boy, Artus. He doesn't like you very much, you know."

The boy! Suddenly Tyvian's escape from the burning spirit engine came charging into harsh focus—the fire licking at his back, his pushing Artus from the train, the fall from the bridge. He glared at Eddereon. "I should have drowned."

"I saved you. You and the boy."

"From a freezing river at night? Why?" Tyvian spat.

Eddereon left the tea on the floor next to Tyvian

and sat back down, chuckling. "Interesting that you don't ask 'how.'"

"Answer the question, Eddereon."

Eddereon's face grew suddenly solemn, and strangely calm. "I saved the boy because he was an innocent, and undeserving of the fate you put upon him. I saved you, Tyvian Reldamar of Saldor—known smuggler, thief, and blackhearted killer—because I have seen in you the potential to be much, much more."

Tyvian rolled his eyes and lay back on the pallet. "I seem to be lectured as often as I am captured. I take it you work for the Defenders, or perhaps my mother? Is that how you know who I am?"

"No."

"You lie."

"I do not."

"Clever retort, but I am strangely unconvinced."

Eddereon sighed. "Have you asked yourself how it was that the Defenders got wind of your operation to defraud Marquis du Rameaux?"

Tyvian sat up again, eyes flashing. "*You* tipped Alafarr off?"

Eddereon nodded. "Not Alafarr, but her superior, Tarlyth, with whom I have dealt with in the past. I have been watching you for almost two years, ever since I heard of your exploits at the Blue Party in Eretheria. It took me that long to obtain enough information to set you up."

"I suppose you told Zazlar Hendrieux, too? Is he getting a cut of the reward money, then?"

"How Hendrieux received word, I do not know. He might have warned you, I suppose, but chose to betray you of his own accord."

Tyvian sprung from the floor and lunged at the knife. He drew it, but his legs, weak from inaction, caused him to stumble back to the ground. Still, he cocked his arm back, aiming to throw the knife through Eddereon's eye. Tyvian had the big man dead to rights, and Eddereon knew it, but he did not stir from his stool.

"Before I kill you," Tyvian sneered, "I want to thank you for saving my life. You seem a decent sort for a backstabbing, stinking vagabond."

Tyvian tried to throw, but a sudden, searing agony shot through his right hand like liquid fire running through his veins. His arm didn't—couldn't—move. He dropped the knife to cradle his pain-wracked hand to his chest. It was then that he saw the plain, dark iron band he wore on his ring finger. It was from there that the terrible pain erupted. Roaring, Tyvian attempted to pull it off, but he could not. The pain the ring was causing faded quickly, but no matter how he twisted, yanked, or scraped, the innocuous iron ring did not budge in the slightest—it was as though it was fused to the bone. "What the—" Tyvian gasped.

Eddereon stood up, his face again as solemn as a priest's. "It is the instrument of your salvation, Tyvian."

Tyvian picked up the knife in his left hand and dragged himself to his feet. "Get it off me."

Eddereon raised his hands. "It is beyond my power

to do so. Once put on, only the bearer may remove the Iron Ring."

Tyvian staggered at Eddereon, knife pointed at the man's throat. *"Get it off*, or I will kill you where you stand!"

"You have no call to kill me, Tyvian." Eddereon said calmly, hands at his sides. "I am unarmed. I have done you no harm. I am not your enemy."

Tyvian lunged at him, but fiery lances of pain from his right hand shot through his arm and across his shoulders, causing him to stumble, yelping in agony.

Eddereon stood over him. "You cannot kill me."

Tyvian dropped the knife as the burning pain continued. As soon as it left his hand, the pain quickly faded. "What . . . what enchantment have you put on me?"

"I am not the maker of the ring. I am only its bearer, and its keeper." Eddereon held up his right hand, and Tyvian immediately spotted a plain iron band identical to his own nestled there between wide pink bands of scarred flesh.

"Kroth, what madness do you peddle, man?"

The door swung open and Artus, clad in furs, came in with an armload of firewood. He saw the half-naked, panting Tyvian on the ground and looked at Eddereon. "Is everything all right?"

Eddereon smiled. "Yes, I am fine. Master Reldamar and I were having a chat."

Artus snorted. "So, what—he was insulting you and you gave him a smack?"

Tyvian scowled at him. "I should have left you to burn, brat."

"Hey," Artus snapped. "Next time you throw somebody out a spirit engine, maybe pick somewhere with ground, huh?"

"Artus, leave us." Eddereon said.

Artus's mouth popped open. "It's damned cold out, though! I'll freeze!"

Eddereon pointed at the door. "Out. It will not be long."

Grumbling, Artus left, shooting Tyvian one more rude look before going. When the door was closed, Eddereon held up his ringed hand again. "I, once, was very much like you, believe it or not. I was a brigand, a bandit. I and my men raided the caravans along the King's Highway that runs from Freegate to Benethor. I was elusive as the wind, mighty as the lion, and brutal as winter. All men knew my name and feared me."

"Let me guess," Tyvian snorted. "Then some cheeky, moralistic git stuffed a magic ring on your finger and it trained you to jump through ethical hoops, too?"

Eddereon nodded. "My reaction was much the same to my Initiator. I tried to kill him several times; I sought to cut the ring from my hand, with little success. I cursed it and cursed all who saw it put there. The ring is not as restrictive as I thought, however. It does not tell you what to think. It does not seek to make you a sheep. You will find it can be resisted sometimes, and there are those who endure its effects for decades, continuing in their old lives, if with markedly less pleasure."

"If it isn't meant to control me, then what, pray tell, is its purpose?"

"You are no sheep, Tyvian Reldamar. You are a wolf, just as I am. It is not our destiny to settle down on a farm or weave baskets in a humble shop. We are too volatile and too restless for that. We need adventure, challenges that tax the body, mind, and soul. Before the ring, we found that life as villains. The ring will guide you to that same life," Eddereon smiled broadly, "but this time as something far more noble."

Tyvian glared at Eddereon for several moments, working up the proper reaction. Were his mouth not so dry, he might have spit in the burly stranger's face. He took a sip of tea, but it was bitter and too hot to help in that regard. Besides, he thought perhaps that spitting on Eddereon might be misinterpreted; Tyvian was willing to bet Eddereon washed his face with his tongue.

Instead, he rose. "Where are my clothes?"

"Quite destroyed by the fire and the river, I'm afraid. You may wear the leathers and furs I acquired for you over there." Eddereon pointed to the corner of the cottage, where Tyvian saw a pile of material he had hitherto thought some kind of trash heap.

He marched over to the clothes, scowling, and pulled on a pair of leather breeches and a fur vest. He felt like a wild animal—no, an *impoverished* wild animal. He turned back to Eddereon, lip curled. "I am going to Freegate. Once there, I intend to find a talismonger or thaumaturge whose art exceeds that of your masters, whomever they are. Then, I will have him *excise* this odious item from my hand, after which I will track you down and take great pleasure in putting a rapier through your heart."

Eddereon stood and handed Tyvian a waterskin, the knife, and a small pack. "Food and hearthcider for the journey. The knife for protection. I fear that you will find the ring hard to remove, however. It will only release you when you have become Redeemed."

Tyvian took the items with a scowl. "I am through talking with you now."

Eddereon nodded. "I will never be far away, should you need me."

Tyvian pulled on a great fur cloak, slapped a hat made from a river otter on his head, and left the cottage. He made certain to slam the door.

Artus, who had been sitting with his back to the cottage, stood up. "Oh, it's you. Is Eddereon still in there?"

Tyvian gestured at the door. "You better hurry. He may run out of simplistic ethical aphorisms any moment."

Tyvian turned his back and walked away on unsteady legs as Artus went inside. The cottage was situated a mere fifty yards from the banks of a narrow river—a tributary of the Trell, no doubt—and he could see the bridge from which he had fallen two days earlier stretching over it. The engine track cut across the snowy landscape ahead of him, a barren black strip of lifeless ground in a field of white. He traced the track east with his eyes, toward the imposing gray and white peaks of the Dragonspine, knowing that the Freegate road would run in the same direction, though it might be as far as a mile from the track itself. He considered his route. It was cold, and the heavy leather and fur boots were poorly sized for his thin feet. Between this and his exhaustion, Tyvian felt like he was dragging wooden blocks behind his legs.

He heard the door to the cottage slam open behind him. There was the crunch of footsteps in snow and he turned around to find Artus planted in front of him. "Hey! Hey, what did you tell him?"

Tyvian rolled his eyes. "Let's see—I called him a backstabbing, stinking vagabond and a cheeky, moralistic git. What is it to you?"

"He's gone, is what! He just up and gone! He left a note!" Artus held up a scrap of paper. Tyvian could see the crudity of the handwriting from where he stood.

"I presume that you can't read, then."

Artus shook his head. "Can you?"

Tyvian scowled and snatched the note from the boy's hand. He glanced it over, and after parsing Eddereon's blocky script, saw that it read:

Artus,

Remember this: it was not I who saved you from the spirit engine, it was Tyvian Reldamar. No matter his faults, which are many, he is a man destined *for greatness who is possessed of a noble soul. He is embittered, though, and angry, and will need help along the way. You offered to serve me in return for saving your life; I ask you to transfer that debt to Master Reldamar. He doesn't have many friends, Artus. Be his friend, despite his sharp tongue, and neither he nor you will regret it.*

Saints bless and keep you well,

Eddereon

"Well?" Artus asked.

Tyvian cleared his throat. "'Dear Artus, please bugger off and leave Tyvian Reldamar alone. Your hairy friend, Eddereon. P.S. Learn to read, for Kroth's sake, so as not to annoy your betters.'"

Artus frowned. "It don't say that!"

Tyvian threw the note over his shoulder and began to follow the riverbank downstream and away from the spirit engine tracks and the road.

The boy fished the note out of the snow and trotted after him. "Well, what *does* it say? Tell me!"

"No."

"Why not, dammit?"

Tyvian spun around. "Allow me to be clear, boy. Our relationship is *over*. You and I have nothing more to say to one another." He pointed down the river. "When we follow this river to the Trell, you are going to turn downstream and go to Galaspin. You'll like the gutters and alleys there, I'm certain. I, meanwhile, will go upstream, to Freegate, where there is a comfortable bed and some decent clothing. Thus will end the tale of Tyvian Reldamar and Artus the street urchin."

Artus snorted. "Fine, but you owe me ten marks."

"Ha! Whatever for?"

"The job—what else? I fooled that guy for you, didn't I?"

Tyvian hissed out a laugh. "You did nothing of the kind. The man wasn't Akrallian nobility; 'he' wasn't even a man. *She* was a glorified constable and she certainly wasn't tricked."

"That don't matter! I went with you, didn't I? I did everything you said, right? You owe me my money!"

"First of all, it is 'doesn't matter,' not 'don't.' Second, in case you hadn't noticed, Artus, I no longer *have* any money! That crazy hermit you are so fond of somehow managed to lose my change purse."

Artus scowled. "That ain't fair."

"By your age, I would think an indigent orphan would come to expect unfairness."

"I'm no orphan." Artus said. His voice dropped an octave and he stopped walking. Tyvian turned to see the boy's hand on his knife. "I've got a family, and I won't have you say nothing bad about them."

Tyvian pursed his lips and stood calmly. "Or you'll what?"

"I'll have your blood, is what."

"Don't be ridiculous."

"Try me."

Tyvian rolled his eyes. On other days he might have kept walking—he didn't feel up to a knife fight and was guessing the ring might have some adverse effect on the contest as well. Even now it was throbbing on his finger, as though threatening him. Then again, he was in a vile mood, and thought perhaps teaching the brat some humility might do him so good. He leaned forward and sneered at him. "That's just the kind of stupid bravado I would expect some toothless, ugly peasant wench to teach her boy."

Artus roared and charged, seeking to draw his knife as he ran. Tyvian stepped into the charge, simultaneously seizing the boy's knife hand by the wrist and bringing his knee into his groin. Artus doubled over from the strike, and Tyvian pulled the boy's knife arm out to the side. He forced the blade out of the lad's hand with a twist, and as Artus struggled to free his arm, Tyvian kicked him in the back of the knee.

Artus collapsed, face-first, into the snow, with Tyvian on top of him. The boy struggled, but Tyvian had one knee in the small of his back, one on his free arm, and a fistful of his hair in his hand. Tyvian drew his own knife and placed the flat of the blade along the side of Artus's cheek. The ring burned and pulsed in warning, but nothing more. Tyvian grit his teeth against this minor pain and hissed in the boy' ear, "I could kill you here, and nobody would ever know or care. Draw a blade on me again, and I just might do so."

Tyvian pushed Artus's face into the snow and stood up. He walked away, assuming the boy would stay down, but Artus was not so easily cowed. He scrambled for his knife and charged again. Tyvian hadn't been expecting this and was less prepared to deflect the attack. For a boy of thirteen, Artus knew his way around a knife, and his first two slashes came dangerously close to relieving Tyvian of his nose. He ducked and retreated before the boy's assault and waited for the opening. In every rage-filled attack, no matter how fast or skilled, there was always an opening; the more passionate and emotional the enemy, the bigger the opening became. Tyvian was certain that a young teenage boy defending his family honor would leave a fatal one.

When it came, it came in the form of a lunge that left Artus overextended. Before he could recover, Tyvian yanked on his arm, pulling the boy even more off-balance. Tyvian's own blade rushed unerringly toward Artus's unprotected heart, and he saw the sudden look of terror in the boy's face as he knew his death approached . . .

. . . but the blade didn't strike. A bright, horrible blossom of pain that ran from his hand all the way to his eyes caused Tyvian to cry aloud and collapse to the ground. The world was bathed in bright orange spots, and his right hand curled as though afflicted with a severe palsy. Tyvian cradled it and rolled onto his back, waiting for the horrible, icy-hot pain to subside. He tried to roll away from Artus, but neither of his agony-locked arms would obey.

When at last his eyes cleared, Tyvian saw Artus standing over him, a look of wonder on his face. "What happened? Are you all right?"

Tyvian managed to uncurl his ring hand—aside from a faint ache that filled his arm, there was no physical sign of the pain the ring had inflicted upon him. When he spoke, he was short of breath. "Nothing. It's nothing."

Artus looked at him skeptically. "It's that ring, isn't it?"

"Weren't you trying to kill me a moment ago?"

Artus ignored him. "I saw Eddereon put it on you, after we was pulled out. It glowed in the dark, real bright, too—like the sun. You probably want if off, huh?"

Tyvian looked up at the boy. If episodes like this kept happening all the way to Freegate, he was probably going to need a little help. Then, of course, there was the fact that he would need somebody to carry supplies, somebody to fetch things, somebody to keep watch at night . . . "I'll pay you ten marks if you help me get to Freegate."

Artus looked around at the snow-covered fields of Galaspin. The only thing in view besides the stream and the bridge was the tumble-down remnants of a ruined watchtower. "Why should I?"

"Because it's ten marks, that's why."

Artus snorted a harsh laugh. "True enough. Well, I ain't got nothing better to do. But lay off the insults, huh?"

He reached down and helped Tyvian up.

CHAPTER 5

IN PURSUIT

The warm spiced wine coated Myreon Alafarr's raw throat, but did little to calm her. She sat perched on the edge of the sturdy oak chair in the private library of the Thostering War Academy and found herself glancing at the ancient spirit clock every half minute. With her free hand, she tugged at the charred ruin of her braid. Cutting it off would have only taken a moment, but she didn't feel like she had even that much time.

Master Defender Ultan Tarlyth took a long drink from his goblet and set it down on the table. In his youth he had been a mountain of a man and a wrestler of some renown, and even now, in his old age, his wide shoulders filled the high-backed chair. His lantern-jawed face, though, looked on the young Mage Defender with kindness. "Saldor has opted not to continue pursuit."

Myreon leapt to her feet, nearly spilling her wine. "Reldamar's alive—I know it! With any luck, he's injured and stuck somewhere. I need fifty men, some horses, another seekwand—"

Tarlyth held up a broad long-fingered hand spotted with age. "Galaspin Tower's complement is only seventy-five, and half of those are already engaged in other activities."

"Switch them off, then! This is Tyvian Reldamar we're talking about!" Myreon barked, and then, remembering who she was talking to, added, "Master, he's almost in our grasp!"

"I know you are frustrated, Myreon—I would be, too, if I had spent three of my five years bearing the staff chasing one man. You have to put things in perspective, however. Even presuming he is alive, Tyvian Reldamar is still only one wicked man in an ocean of wicked men. The fisherman who chases the whale to the exclusion of all others is the fisherman who goes hungry."

Myreon frowned and swirled the wine in her goblet. "With all due respect, Master Defender, Reldamar is not a fish. Two nights ago he killed two of my men, injured three others, released a wild gnoll into the Galaspin countryside, and was responsible for the destruction of an entire spirit engine—and that was among the more minor of his offenses. I caught him peddling biomancy, sir—*biomancy*. What if Sahand of Dellor were to get his mitts on that?"

Tarlyth nodded and put a hand to his chin. "Yes, the biomancy bit *is* troubling. It is also, however, an unusual choice for Reldamar, is it not?"

Myreon sighed and nodded. "It is—he usually restricts himself to artifacts and basic magecraft. This is the first time we have him dealing in the High Arts, or with Kalsaari arcane texts."

"What does that indicate to you?"

"I haven't worked up the proper augury to tell me—"

"No, no," Tarlyth warned, waggling a finger at her, "not with sorcery. What does that indicate to your reason—your *mind*."

Myreon blinked. "What do you mean?"

Tarlyth sighed and sat back, taking up his goblet. "Do you know why Tyvian Reldamar consistently eludes us—note that I say 'us' and not just 'you,' Myreon—you are not the only Mage Defender whom Reldamar has thwarted. Well, do you know?"

"I . . . I can only conclude that he is uncommonly lucky."

"No, he is uncommonly smart. He knows that we rely on the High Arts—on our auguries and sorceries—to find and catch him. What he has realized and that so many of us have not is that the High Arts and, indeed, even the Low Arts of magic, are just *tools*. Powerful tools, certainly, but tools nevertheless, and tools are only as good as the men wielding them. Too many of our order—especially since the end of the Delloran and Illini Wars—have come to rely too heavily on their arts to perform their duties. They have forgotten that, before the wars, when more conservative elements controlled the Arcanostrum, Defenders were taught to be investigators first and magi second."

"Of course, sir." Myreon nodded, restraining the urge to throw her goblet at the wall and scream. Reldamar was still at large and here she was, being *lectured*?

Tarlyth laughed. "You are young—I don't expect you to agree with me. Not yet, in any case. Let me ask you this, though, to see if I can't prove my point: what does a seekwand do?"

Myreon shrugged. "It is an enchanted device of about twelve inches, usually made of bone, that can read the Etheric ley of an area to see if someone has passed. If you have something that belongs to a person, you can isolate their trail and track them with the Law of Possession. Coupled with some simple auguries, you can usually track anybody over any distance with very little error."

Tarlyth nodded. "Good, but what are its limitations?"

"Like any Etheric device, it functions poorly in areas where Lumenal energy is dominant—cornfields, dense woodlands, fields of wildflowers in direct sunlight, that sort of thing. It's also rather breakable, and it requires a good bit of time to narrow down on the proper trail if the quarry is moving along a heavily trafficked route, and the Law of Possession only works for a short time. Still, it is perfectly accurate. I've found smugglers in—"

"I am well aware of its benefits, Myreon," Tarlyth interrupted, "but consider this: to most of our quarry and, indeed, to most people, the function of a seekwand is mysterious and frightening. They think that they cannot hide, and fail to realize just what protection a sunny field of daisies might afford them. They hide in the dark and away from prying eyes, which is just where the seekwand works best. The problem with this is that Reldamar, and those like him, *are not most men.* He is perfectly aware of how a seekwand works—his great uncle, Hann rest him, invented the damned thing—and so you can bet a pretty penny that right now Tyvian Reldamar is in a crowded garden party, standing in the sun, with a stick of burning incense in his pocket. Gods, I bet he's only buying things in sevens, too, just to make sure. Your precious seekwand won't find him in a hundred years."

Myreon scowled and threw up her hands. "Well, then what would you have me do? Get a team of trained dogs from somewhere and try to chase him down like a wild boar?"

"Mind your tone, Magus!" Tarlyth warned, and then sighed. "In fact, that's what we *used* to do, but we don't keep dogs anymore, more's the pity. No, what I'd have you do, Myreon, is find yourself a tracker—a *real* tracker, who finds people with his eyes and his nose and his tongue. You need a man who can glance at a dirt road and tell you how many people have passed in the last hour, how much they weighed, and whether they were carrying a pack or not. *That's* the kind of man who will find and catch Tyvian Reldamar."

Myreon bowed her head for a moment and sipped her wine. "Do we have such a man in Galaspin Tower?"

Tarlyth shook his head. "No. A couple good tails, some fine rumormongers, three or four men who can spot counterfeits from twenty paces, and a wagonload of strong sword arms—no trackers worth a damn. If you wish to continue pursuit of Tyvian Reldamar, you are going to have to hire a bounty hunter, and do so 'off the record,' or so to speak."

"Really, sir, if I could just have twenty men, then I could—"

Tarlyth held up his hand, and stated firmly, "You have exhausted more resources on Reldamar than the Lord Defender in Saldor thinks he is worth. I agree with him. As wicked and dangerous as Reldamar is, he is but one smuggler among hundreds operating in the Trell River Valley alone, and so the official pursuit of Reldamar ends here for the time being. That said, I cannot abide the thought of abandoning his trail entirely, which is why I've come all this way from Galaspin to speak to you in person. You will hire a bounty hunter to track him down, and direct him to bring Reldamar in by any means you find prudent. You will be afforded no Defenders to assist you and will be operating as a Magus

Errant; Reldamar is now yours and yours alone to deal with, and you report directly to me. Is that clear?"

"It is, Master." Myreon nodded. She wasn't sure whether to be thankful or not. Certainly, the opportunity to pursue Reldamar was exciting, but Magus Errant was somewhat . . . worrying. No backup, no support, no reserves to call in. Was she good enough to do this herself? Was it even wise?

Tarlyth smiled and stood. "Come with me."

The snow on the parade ground of the Thostering War Academy had been mostly trampled into a soupy mixture of mud and slush by the thousand boots of five hundred cadets, marching in rigid formations at the barking command of the March Master and his officers. Ordinarily, the slog across the wide yard to the gatehouse on the other side would have been a soggy one, but both Tarlyth and Myreon made certain to abjure cold and moisture from their boots as they walked, keeping their feet dry as good kindling.

Some cadets saluted as they went past, but Myreon didn't acknowledge them. She kept her eyes fixed on Tarlyth's broad back, and tried to forget the faces of the men she had led against Reldamar just a few days before. Carlis, with the big laugh and strong hands, had been crushed under the spirit engine—dead. Markon and Baness, who had worked with her since she earned her staff, had both been permanently crippled from the crushing wounds they received in the collapse of the dining car. Then there was Evard—sweet, funny Evard, with his kindly smile—he was slain by a gnoll and consumed by a sorcerous fire. The only thing his family would get back were ashes and a gruesome story. As it stood, she had barely survived herself; the burns on her arms and shoulders and hands had been mostly healed by the War College's alchemist, but every move of her body felt like she was tearing her skin apart like parchment.

And all of it was Tyvian Reldamar's fault.

Myreon found herself at the center of the courtyard, where a grand, ten-foot statue of Finn Cadogan—the Academy's most famous graduate and the so-called "Patron Saint of Sell-Swords"—stood just inside the main gate, overseeing the campus. The sculpture depicted the improbably handsome visage of the career soldier whose heroic sacrifice had, in large part, saved Galaspin from the ravages of Mad Prince Sahand twenty-seven years earlier at the Battle of Calassa, where the Dellorans were finally defeated. Cadogan's magic sword, Banner, was raised high, and he stood upon the broken shields and weapons of his defeated foes, his breastplate carved with the image of men-at-arms standing side by side.

Myreon looked up at one of the four great heroes of the age. Cadogan had led a daring midnight raid on Sahand's camp to assassinate Delloran officers, putting the Mad Prince's army in disarray when the Falcon King Perwynnon's reinforcements arrived at dawn. None of the Iron Men returned—it was said Cadogan died at the hands of Sahand himself.

She knew that Master Defender Tarlyth as well as some of the older Sergeant Defenders in Galaspin Tower had served alongside Cadogan's "Iron Men" in Illin. When they spoke of him, it was only to say he was a soldier of integrity and steadfast courage. "I know what you're thinking," Tarlyth said, grinning up at the statue. "That it was all a myth. That we old men have cooked up stories about Cadogan and Varner and Marik the Holy and Perwynnon and the rest."

Myreon sighed but didn't say anything. Cadogan had been a mercenary; he was paid to fight for the Alliance. Any of the men inside Thostering Academy could be the enemy or friend of Myreon's goals, based only off the contents of her purse. The whole of Galaspin was awash in such men—mercenaries infested the place like weevils. Just because the ones who could pay sent their sons to Thostering to learn how to pretend to be gentlemen didn't make it so. They were no more to be trusted than Reldamar was.

Tarlyth kicked the wet snow off the base of the statue and read the epigram.

> Captain Finn Cadogan
> Soldier, Hero, Favored Son
> "If Men of Honor Hold Together,
> No Evil May Pass."

The Master Defender sighed. "The man I am going to introduce you to is a man of honor. You may not like him and he may not like you, but he is the best at what he does. I trust him, and so should you."

Myreon nodded. "I defer to your wisdom, Master."

Tarlyth smiled and put a hand on her shoulder. The pressure there made Myreon's burns scream with pain, but she held it in and only tightened her grip on her magestaff. "Good," Tarlyth pointed through the gate behind them, "because here he comes now."

Myreon looked and saw a grim-faced Illini guiding a black mare through the village market that pressed up against the borders of the War Academy. He had eyes like coals and a mane of matted raven hair that reached his shoulder blades. Myreon cocked her head to one side. "Wait, is that . . ."

Tarlyth nodded. "Yes, that is Hacklar Jaevis. I am paying him two thousand marks to assist you."

Hacklar Jaevis dressed in muddy leathers studded with rusty iron disks, and knee-high boots inlaid with tarnished silver. He had a thick, black beard that was clasped at its bottom with a ringlet of bone etched with a Hannite cross. He wore a thick black fur cape, underneath which, Myreon could tell, were hidden a variety of weapons, both magical and mundane. He was known to be humorless, gruff, and unpleasant. When he dismounted, she noted that he smelled very much like a wet dog.

But everybody said he was the best.

Jaevis did not bother introducing himself. He pointed a grubby finger at Myreon's chest and muttered, "Pretty Mage Defender does not come to Hacklar Jaevis to catch famous Reldamar *first*. She comes to Hacklar Jaevis *last*. You will listen to what I say, or you will go away and hire fool. Choose now."

Myreon held her breath and held out her hand. Jaevis didn't shake it; he spit in it. She looked back at Master Tarlyth, mouth agape.

The Master Defender only smiled. "He likes you!"

CHAPTER 6

MAN VERSUS BEAST

" . . . Five, six, seven. Stop." Tyvian put an arm out to stop Artus in his tracks.

The boy groaned. "How is this helping us, again?"

Tyvian scowled. "I'm sorry if my attempts to keep us from capture are bothering you. Perhaps you'd like to run and hide in some dark alley somewhere?"

They were standing in the center of a muddy road that paralleled the wide, blue-black expanse of the Trell River. Around them there was nothing else but the snow-dusted fields of Galaspin, empty, windy, and cold. Artus gestured at the open countryside. "How is *this* better than hiding? We're the only damned people on the road, and it's broad daylight!"

"Are you ready to go another seven paces now? You're slowing us down, and there's a river-inn ahead about a mile, if I'm not mistaken. I don't know about you, but I am quite hungry."

Artus threw up his hands. "What is with the seven-paces-and-then-stop thing? I thought we was in a rush!"

Tyvian began to count out another seven paces as he muttered, "*Were* in a rush. You thought we *were* in a bloody rush."

Artus stuffed his hands under his armpits to keep them warm and stomped after the smuggler. When Tyvian got to seven paces, though, Artus took an eighth and stuck his tongue out.

"Are you an idiot?" Tyvian snapped.

"I told you no more insults!"

"It wasn't an insult, it was a question."

Artus snorted. "Why are we walking seven paces at a time, Reldamar? We've been doing it for *hours* and it's driving me nutty!"

Tyvian rubbed his hands together and blew into them. "Tell me something, Artus. For exactly how long have *you* evaded capture by the Defenders of the Balance?"

Artus blinked. "I never had no cause till I met *you*!"

Tyvian rolled his eyes and nodded. "Yes, yes—a fact that you, no doubt, will harp upon for the days to come. However, allow me to point out that I have evaded their capture for almost eight years now. Now, what does that tell you?"

"That you're a slippery bastard."

"A rather cruder turn of phrase than I, myself, might have used, but accurate enough. Suffice to say that *I* know what I'm doing and *you* do not, so when I tell you to walk seven paces at a time and stop, *you should bloody well do it!*" Tyvian yelled.

Artus groaned. "Fine, fine—whatever. Can we just get to that river-thing faster?"

Tyvian looked at the sky. "At last! Now, with me—one, two, three . . ."

The Trell River ran south and west from its headwaters near the city of Freegate, gaining strength from the many tributaries running out of the Dragonspine, until it became a broad and powerful waterway that ran all the way to Saldor and the Sea of Syrin. Back before the Delloran Wars, it had been a fortified border, with watchtowers and garrisons of the duke's petty barons patrolling regularly. Sahand's invasion had, of course, put an end to literal fire and brymmstone and as many rows of impaled heads as he could manage. After the war the lack of fortified keeps was found convenient by the guild-lords who ruled much of Galaspin, and nothing much had been rebuilt while tariffs had been kept low. Accordingly, the river was a busy trade highway year-round, so long as it didn't freeze, and trading posts and settlements were common along its banks.

The Wandering Fountain was one such settlement. It was a "river-inn," which meant it was a barge or series of barges converted into a floating boardinghouse that provided shelter, supplies, and food for travelers along the banks or the river. Their advantages, as Tyvian understood it, were chiefly legal. No Galaspiner petty barons or guild-lords held legal authority over the waters of the Trell—a by-product of the great Treaty of Aldentree, which ended the Guilder Wars that tore the country apart over a century ago—and therefore any building that existed upon it was free from harassment and taxation from any authority on shore. Furthermore, if a local ruler made himself too troublesome, a river-inn could easily be floated downstream or to the opposite bank, thereby changing which local lord they would deal with.

The most beneficial thing about river-inns, as far as Tyvian was concerned, was the fact that nobody save a Defender of the Balance would have the authority to arrest him while he stayed on one. That didn't mean somebody couldn't try, of course, but any discouragement at all was helpful, given his current predicament.

Long before they came around the bend in the river that obscured the Wandering Fountain from sight, Tyvian and Artus smelled it—wood smoke and stewed meat—and it was intoxicating to the famished and cold pair. When the establishment came into view, however, Tyvian was immediately reminded of the drawbacks of such places. It comprised probably three massive barges upon which had been built three stories of rickety wooden construction that not only looked drafty but also not entirely safe. Each floor was ringed by a veranda painted with a haphazard coat of whitewash that somehow managed to make the place look even older than it probably was. From the center of the river-inn rose a single rusty tin smokestack that belched out the pleasant aromas that had enticed the two of them closer; Tyvian noted that this smokestack was poorly secured and wobbled in the wind. Like the rest of the place, it looked like a massive firetrap, and he wondered how it had managed not to burn down already.

"Looks great!" Artus said, trotting down the road toward its entryway. Rolling his eyes, Tyvian followed.

The Fountain's common room—or "galley," as the quaint riverfolk called it—was belowdecks in the first barge. As Tyvian and Artus entered, they found themselves drowned in a sea of smoke and raucous conversation. The warmth of the low-ceilinged chamber made Tyvian's numb cheeks start to tingle, but he could identify few other positive attributes to the place besides the heat. Taking a table somewhere in the middle of the room, he sat gingerly on the edge of a dirty chair and scanned the local patrons. Artus threw himself unceremoniously across from the smuggler and hunched over the table as only a teenage boy could. He frowned at Tyvian. "What's the matter?"

Tyvian motioned to his fur-and-leather-themed

attire. "I have discovered, to my dismay, that I am appropriately dressed for this venue."

Artus sniggered. "Serves you right."

Tyvian disregarded the goad. "How much money do you have?"

Artus blinked. "Nothing."

Tyvian grimaced. "Not *anything*?"

"Look, you're the one always saying I'm a worthless street urchin. What'd you expect?"

Tyvian pursed his lips. "I *expected* you to have picked a few pockets on our way in."

Artus's mouth fell open. "Steal! Here?"

Tyvian leaned forward. "Please *lower* your voice."

Artus leaned to meet him, glancing over his shoulder twice as he did so. "I can't steal from these folks."

"I notice that you had no qualms about picking *my* pocket."

"Yeah, but I don't like you."

Tyvian rolled his eyes. "Am I to believe that you only rob people you dislike? Gods, no wonder you were living in a gutter."

Artus opened his mouth to protest, but Tyvian cut him off. "Never mind. I thought we might utilize your one apparent talent to purchase ourselves a hot meal."

Artus held up his pack. "We still got the dry rations Eddereon gave us. We could heat them on the cookstove over there."

Tyvian stood up. "Warm crackers do not constitute the kind of sustenance my stomach has come to expect from me. Since you are so unwilling to accommodate us, I see I will have to do everything myself. Don't go anywhere."

Tyvian left Artus at the table without waiting for an answer and passed among the crowds of sweaty rivermen and fur-clad wagoners that filled the Fountain. Picking pockets from half-drunk laborers was child's play. The trouble was, they hardly had anything worth stealing. After a few minutes all Tyvian had was a handful of copper peers, a few buttons, and a set of dice that looked like they had been shaved by the least subtle cheater in the history of gambling— the thug must have tried doing the job with an axe. During this time, he was forced to press bodies with men who had never bathed, women who had never brushed their teeth, and the odd filthy, belching child. This, of course, would have been bad enough, but the sharp bites of pain Tyvian received from the ring every time he snagged another coin only made the experience that much more unpleasant.

He decided that his life had reached a new low point. This was it. The bottom of the barrel—picking pockets in the bilge of a Galaspiner river-inn. Gods.

When Tyvian returned to the table, he found Artus with his feet up and a steaming bowl of black stew in front of him. Tyvian threw the coppers on the table. "Where the hell did you get that?"

Artus grinned broadly as he slurped from a wooden spoon. "The serving lady come by, and she says I looked so nice she gave me a bowl of stew for free!"

Tyvian considered his throbbing right hand. "You are a son of a bitch."

"Hello there!" A matronly woman with large red cheeks draped an arm around Tyvian's shoulders. "You must be this young man's father, then?"

Tyvian smiled at her. "Madam, I would hardly consider myself old enough."

The woman smiled and blushed. "Madam, am I?" She looked at Artus. "Sweet talker, your da is, eh? What'll it be, love?"

"I'm afraid you haven't told me the menu."

The woman laughed. "Menu, now? By Hann, you're the toast! We've got stew or a roast."

Tyvian eyed the greasy liquid Artus was slurping down with skepticism. "What is in the stew?"

The woman gave him a blank look. "In it? It's *stew.*"

Tyvian produced a restrained grin and slid a copper across the table. "I'll have the roast." He added five coppers to the pile. "And a cup of your best hearthcider."

The woman winked. "Back before you know it!"

As she left, Tyvian grumbled, "Roast what, is the question."

Artus was staring at him. "How did you do that?"

"Do what?"

"You had her eating out of your hand!"

Tyvian pointed to the stew. "Of the two of us, you are the only one who has free food."

"No! I mean . . . I mean, well, she *liked* you." Artus blushed.

Tyvian rolled his eyes. "We are not having this conversation."

"I bet you're a hit with the ladies. Knew a guy who always said they liked jerks."

"No!" Tyvian slapped the table. "I am *not* discussing this with you. How old are you anyway?"

Artus puffed out his chest. "Almost fourteen!"

"I would wager you know as much about women as you need to know at this moment, Artus. The remainder you ought to learn like every other man—through painful trial and error."

Artus frowned. "C'mon! Just a trick or two, is all! Please?"

Tyvian took a deep breath. "How about we talk about something more immediately useful, such as how to get to Freegate without being caught."

Artus nodded. "Okay—yeah! How come you know they're after us? Maybe they think we drowned."

"Alafarr is nothing if not thorough. She's after me for certain. The question is only how much of a head start we have. We can only keep up the seven-step for so long before it becomes a disadvantage."

"Are you gonna tell me what that does?"

Tyvian grimaced. The thought of educating Artus seemed a rather tedious enterprise, especially given how ineffectually the boy had absorbed the exhaustive etiquette lessons he gave him on the spirit engine to Galaspin. Still, he reasoned that giving the boy the basics could only work to his own advantage, as the likelihood he would make a stupid mistake would be bound to go down. He sighed. "Very well, then. Taking seven steps at a time in broad daylight is an adequate way to enhance the luminal ley of any given area."

Artus blinked. "What?"

Tyvian tried again. "The ley errs slightly toward Lumenal energy when taking steps in sevens, because the Lumen has an affinity with that number."

"What's the Lumen?"

"Gods, boy, how much schooling have you had anyway?"

Artus snorted. "I can't read, remember?"

Tyvian rubbed his forehead and sighed. "Of course—how foolish of me to expect so much. Fine then, let's put it this way: the world—the very stuff of existence itself—is comprised of five energies. They are the Lumen and the Ether, the Dweomer and the Fey, and lastly the Astral, which binds them all together. These energies manifest in different quantities in different places—in a bright place there is more of the Lumen, for instance, or in a cold one there is more of the Dweomer, and so on and so forth. How these energies are distributed is called the 'ley' of a place."

Artus slurped his soup. "Could you use smaller words?"

Tyvian closed his eyes and tried to restrain his urge to scream. He wasn't sure if this conversation could get any more painful than if the ring were actively torturing him. "Look, all that really matters is that each of those five 'govern,' or at least *affect*, everything you can think of. All of this energy tends to flow and change with the seasons, the time, and so on, but congregate in great metaphysical pathways, called ley lines, which is largely how ships navigate at sea and have played an important role in where cites have been founded and, probably, how the geography of the world itself has been formed. Understand?"

Artus licked his lips, trying to take in both what Tyvian said and the ring of greasy broth that had formed around his mouth. "So what's this got to do with walking seven steps and such?"

Tyvian threw up his hands. "It affects the ley by . . . look, it just *does*, Artus. It's *maaagic*." Tyvian twiddled his fingers like he was casting a spell.

Artus brightened. "So it's white magic."

Tyvian groaned. "The terms 'black' and 'white' magic imply some kind of moral governor over the energy itself, which is erroneous. The Ether is no more evil than the Lumen is good. I need only point out the instances in which deceiving someone with the Ether actually does them a favor, whereas telling them the truth with the Lumen would destroy them. Morality has nothing to do with sorcery whatsoever, no matter what you learned in church."

"'Ere you are, love." The serving woman returned, grinning, and plopped a chipped mug and a wooden plate in front of Tyvian. The "roast" was a dark, greasy hunk of unidentifiable meat coupled with some mushy potatoes in a black gravy. The woman took a pair of coppers for her trouble and melted back into the crowd.

Tyvian was transfixed by the meat. "It seems I

should have had the stew. She didn't even leave any flatware."

Artus shrugged. "Just use your hands."

Tyvian curled his lips at the suggestion and pushed the plate away. "I am going to kill Hendrieux *slowly* for this."

"What? Everybody uses their hands."

Tyvian snorted. "Your definition of 'everybody' seems to leave out the intelligent, cultured, clean, and polite."

Artus leaned back and crossed his arms. "You're an ass."

Tyvian put up three fingers, one at a time. "An ass who saved you from a burning spirit engine, who refrained from killing you when you came at him with a knife, and who is paying you ten gold marks when you get to Freegate, so *shut the hell up.*"

They both fell quiet and Tyvian took the respite from Artus to examine the iron ring affixed to his finger for the hundredth time. There were no sigils or runes inscribed along its surface, no visible marks of enchantment, not even any jewels or studs around which to focus magical energy. It was a featureless iron band—as fascinating a talismanic work as it was enraging. The material, if it were iron, would indicate an association with the Dweomer, though without a mage-compass he couldn't tell for certain. Dweomeric energy would make sense, though, if its purpose was to make him adhere to certain rules of behavior. How it was able to know *which* rules he would be constrained to obey, though, was something he couldn't figure out. Conventionally they would have to be inscribed upon the ring itself, but Tyvian could see nothing. Even presuming the writing was along the *inside* of band, there was hardly enough surface area to accommodate much Dweomeric lettering. He supposed somebody could have used Astral enchantments to artificially expand the area on the inside of the ring, but that was an enchantment of such complexity Tyvian felt it hard to believe a single ring could contain such power, especially when coupled with the behavior-triggered effects and the enchantment to keep it on his hand.

"Does it hurt?" Artus asked, watching Tyvian's hand.

"Not just now. Insulting you isn't on its list of things I shouldn't do, apparently."

Artus licked his lips. "If it hadn't stopped you, you woulda killed me, right?"

Tyvian didn't smile when he answered. "Yes, Artus. I would have."

He looked Artus in the eye. The boy was trying to look nonchalant, but his face was too tight and too controlled. He was afraid. "I ought notta attacked you. Sorry."

Tyvian nodded. "Apology accepted."

"You gonna apologize to me?"

"I can't imagine for what."

Artus's eyes flashed and his face flushed. He opened his mouth, probably, Tyvian assumed, to call him an ass again, but he didn't get it out.

At that moment there was a commotion up on deck. Tyvian stood to see what was happening, and through the smoky gloom he spotted a pair of men supporting a pale woman between them. She had been half dragged, half carried in from outside, where the sun had just set, and was panting as though she had been sprinting. "Monster!" she gasped. "Monster coming!"

It was then that Tyvian could hear the screams of injured men coming from somewhere above. Around him the locals began hasty speculations. Nurlings? Trolls? It was the wrong season, some insisted, while others called for the tavernkeeper to bring weapons.

In moments the tavernkeeper was distributing cudgels and quarterstaffs he had taken from the back room, and half-drunk men were charging into the night to drive off the invader, whatever it was. Tyvian watched the excitement with a dispassionate eye, hoping the mob would keep any inhuman beasts from assaulting his person, but also incredulous that any such group of toothless yokels could ever constitute a competent fighting force.

"Should we go help?" Artus asked.

Tyvian snorted. "Don't be ridiculous. This has nothing to do with us."

No sooner had Tyvian spoken those words than a distressingly familiar gnoll appeared in the doorframe . . .

. . . and it was looking straight at him.

The galley was still as the patrons gaped at the gnoll's muscular bulk. Snow blown in from outside played about its feet and glazed its golden-furred shoulders; its copper eyes glittered in the guttering lamplight. About its waist was fashioned a crude lanyard from which hung an assortment of dead rabbits, but it was otherwise unclothed and unarmed. Unarmed, that was, if one didn't count the white fangs it no doubt concealed inside its snout.

It leveled a thick, hairy paw at Tyvian and pointed. For the second time, the smuggler's insides twisted at the thought of the beast possessing such humanlike hands. Everybody in the tavern followed the beast's gesture, and found Tyvian and Artus on their feet, faces pale.

"It wants them travelers!" The tavernkeeper yelled.

What happened next, Tyvian had to admit, was a credit to Galaspiner hospitality. Two men advanced on the gnoll, stools in hand, aiming to brain the creature before it went another step. Tyvian, who had seen the beast in action before, knew what was going to happen. The gnoll dropped a shoulder and rammed one man to the floor while blocking the other man's blow with the precise sweep of a massive forearm. It then followed up this block with a punch to the guts that folded the man in half and dropped him, weeping for air.

Threatening travelers might have encouraged a pair of men to attack, but the casual pummeling of two of their own was enough to raise the whole place against the intruder. Angry drunks with bottles, bar stools, clubs, knives, and even fists descended on the beast, their courage bolstered by their liberal intake of beer in the hours before.

The battle did not go well for the forces of humanity.

The gnoll, possessing an agility that belied its massive size, felled men as easily as one might whack the heads off daisies. Its broad, sloping shoulders absorbed blows that might have killed lesser beings with little apparent distress, and its counterattacks never failed to remove a man from the melee permanently. It didn't use its teeth, but then it didn't need to—the creature possessed a skill in hand-to-hand combat that no pack of drunken country Galaspiners could ever match. If they came at it with weapons, it took their weapons away. If they threw things, it dodged. If they jumped on its back, they found themselves hurtling through the air.

Artus snatched up a half-empty beer mug and moved to join the defense, but Tyvian caught his arm. "Artus, back door, now!"

"But it'll kill them!"

Tyvian winced as the ring bit down on his hand like an iron vice. He hissed through clenched teeth, "Better them than us."

A man with a bloody face flew at the two of them, causing Tyvian to dive to the floor. The unfortunate victim smashed chin-first into their table, knocking it over and spilling stew, roast, and hearthcider in every direction. When his limp body at last came to rest in a sprawling heap, Tyvian could see that the man wasn't likely to get up anytime soon, and even then probably not without some medical attention. Tyvian scowled at him. "Idiot. Trying to fistfight a gnoll, indeed."

"YAAAAAAA!!!!" Tyvian heard Artus yell, and looked up to see the boy charging into the fray, which had moved away from the door and was halfway across the room toward Tyvian. In between its devastating attacks, he noted that the gnoll was still casting significant glances in his direction.

Tyvian grimaced and, hoping Artus's sacrifice would give him a good head start, beat a hasty retreat.

He had barely made it up the back stairs to the deck of the river-inn and slammed the door behind him when he was doubled over by a white-hot flash of searing pain. He fell to a crouch and beat his hand against the planks. "Stop . . . it . . . stop . . . it . . . you . . . son of a bitch!"

The pain did not stop, but Tyvian managed to stand anyway and ran, blindly, along the slick, snow-dusted decks of the Wandering Fountain. With every step, he felt as if more of his hand began to blister and burn away, but he ran anyway. His mind raged, *I will not be controlled. I will NOT be controlled!*

He tripped on a rope and rolled down a flight of stairs, hand and arm clutched to his chest, his breathing ragged. Barely aware of where he was, he screamed down at his hand. "KROTH'S TEETH! What do you want me to do? You want me to go back there and die? What would that accomplish?"

Face a mask of determination, Tyvian rolled to his knees and shuffled back up the stairs and onto the deck. His vision was blurred with tears as the ring seemed to brand his very bones with its infernal heat, the pain throbbing from his fingertips to his shoulders. He dared not look down, convinced that all that remained of his right hand was bones and ash.

Ahead, dimly, he thought he saw a stable. Yes! A horse! If he could just climb atop one and spur it on, it would take him away. With any luck, the gnoll would be too injured from the fight to follow. Determination revitalized, he staggered to his feet and across the deck, vision tunneling so that all he could see was the door to the stable in front of him. The ring blazed on, punishing him, but with each step, Tyvian felt the pain fade. He was beating it! He laughed, thinking of that prig, Eddereon. "Your ring's no match for me! I knew it! I knew it!"

He reached the door, the pain almost all gone. He pulled it open, stepped inside . . .

. . . and found himself in the back hall of the galley again.

"What? Kroth!" Tyvian whipped the door back open and looked out. There, in the growing moonlight, he could see his footsteps silhouetted clearly in the snow. They staggered from side to side along the river-inn's decks, but ultimately went in a circle.

He glared down at the ring. His hand was completely unharmed. "You sneaky bastard."

There was a thunderous crash from the galley, and

Tyvian heard Artus yell in pain. The ring pinched him.

Tyvian, scowling, shook his head. "Well, since I have no choice . . ."

Artus was the only human left in the room who wasn't unconscious or too injured to move. His mouth was bleeding and his left eye was swollen shut, but he wasn't down yet. His knife lay on the floor halfway between him and the hulking mass of fur and teeth that was the gnoll. The two of them circled around it, but neither advanced.

What little Artus knew about fighting he had learned as a child with his older brothers and then, later, as a matter of survival in the alleys and slums of Ayventry. In both cases the winners were usually the bigger and meaner parties, unless the little guy used a cheap shot. In the case of the gnoll versus himself, Artus had little doubt who was the bigger and meaner fighter. It only remained to be seen if he, Artus, could get in that cheap shot. Trouble with cheap shots, though, was that if they didn't win the fight immediately, you'd better be able to run away real fast.

Somehow Artus doubted he would outrun the gnoll.

Tyvian, it seemed, was long gone. Artus wanted to say he didn't care, but he couldn't, quite. The smuggler was an ass, true, but he was educated, refined, quick-witted, wealthy, dangerous . . . in short, he was pretty much the most interesting person Artus knew and the only one who seemed the least bit interested in talking to him. He had hoped—

"*Ooof!*" The gnoll's front paws hit Artus in the chest. He found himself on his back on the floor, the mighty beast on top of him. Artus lay, open-mouthed—the creature must have covered the five paces between them in one leap.

"Get off of him!" Artus craned his neck and saw Tyvian standing there, knife drawn. "He's not the one you want."

The gnoll turned its copper eyes from the vanquished Artus to look at Tyvian. Then it spoke. "Put away your knife." Its voice was surprisingly soft and smooth, but with a heavy cadence that indicated it was used to being obeyed.

Tyvian blinked, but that was all the indication of surprise he gave. "If you were in my position, would that seem like a wise idea?"

The gnoll pondered this, then said, "This is not your pup."

"You mean Artus? Hann, no! Why does everyone keep saying that? Surely there isn't much of a resemblance." Artus could see Tyvian's weight shift to the balls of his feet. He might have been speaking casually, but the smuggler was ready for a fight at any moment.

The gnoll got off Artus's chest and picked him up by the collar. "Take him." Artus was unceremoniously tossed across the room.

Tyvian didn't look at him, but asked, "Are you all right?"

Artus spat blood. "No."

The gnoll pointed at Tyvian. "You will help me."

"Why would I do that?"

Around them, various patrons of the Wandering Fountain began to return to their senses, moaning and coughing. The gnoll's triangular ears swiveled to record this. It spoke in a thunderous semigrowl. "All of you will *leave* now! This is my place!"

Tyvian smiled and nodded. "We'd be delighted to."

The gnoll glared at him. "Not you. You will come with me."

"Not a chance."

The tavernkeeper crawled out from under a table, his left leg bent at an unnatural angle. "Help! Help! Beast!"

The gnoll trotted over, grabbed the man by the front of his shirt, and heaved him through the exit like a sack. It then looked back to Tyvian. "Then I go with you."

Tyvian scowled. "Why on earth would I let you do that?"

The gnoll looked around at the patrons stumbling to their feet, their eyes bleached with stark terror. "*I SAID LEAVE!*" It roared. Within a few seconds the room was empty.

"They'll go get help, you know," Tyvian said. "There are more people in the inn than just those here."

The beast snorted. "Not anymore. I threw them all in the water before I came down."

Tyvian smiled again. "Ah, naturally. Well, they will come back, and next time they'll have weapons. I can't really think of a particularly good reason to associate myself with you in that case, can you?"

The gnoll fixed Tyvian with its predatory glare again. "You need help to kill the man who tricked you and got you caught by the wizards. I am strong and fast and better than this pup." It gestured at Artus, who was only now managing to stand up. "I can track stupid humans across miles and miles, and if you won't let me go with you, I will eat your face."

Tyvian, for the first time Artus had met him, seemed at a loss for words. Then he cleared his throat and said, "For a monster, you are remarkably convincing."

The gnoll held up the tavernkeeper's apron and jingled it. "I also have lots of money."

Artus and Tyvian exchanged glances. Artus asked, "How far is it to Freegate, again?"

Tyvian looked back at the gnoll. "Right, then— you're in. Off we go."

After looting the empty river-inn of supplies, a tent, and some other essentials, the strange trio of smuggler, boy, and gnoll slipped through the dark of the winter night until they found an empty barn in which to take shelter. The gnoll wanted to continue on, but

Tyvian managed to convince it (he had no idea how) that to rest a few hours would be wiser.

Artus found a lamp somewhere and lit it with a flint. Tyvian would have preferred an actual fire, but the risk of discovery was too great. Besides, the hearthcider he had drank in the Wandering Fountain was actually working—he didn't feel cold at all, despite crouching on the hay-strewn floor of a uninsulated and empty barn on a winter night.

The gnoll's unnerving gaze was fixed on Tyvian. "How long do we wait?"

"I told you—an hour or two. Then we put some distance between us and here until morning."

"Then what?" Artus asked.

Tyvian gestured to the gnoll. "Then our new companion gives us the money he's acquired and we purchase passage on a riverboat heading north."

Artus nodded, his eyes—well, *eye*; one of them was swollen shut and purple—darting constantly to where the gnoll was crouching as he tried to subtly move a few paces farther away from it. The boy had been ill-at-ease ever since it apparently dawned on him just how dangerous it was traveling with a savage monster. To his credit, he hadn't said anything aloud on the subject. Tyvian only hoped that the human facial expressions indicating anxiety and terror that were so prominently displayed on the boy's face weren't as readily understandable to gnolls as they were to other people.

"Where are you going?" the gnoll barked, paying Artus no heed.

Tyvian sighed. "Gods, do the two of you ever run out of questions?"

The gnoll slapped the ground. "You tell me!"

"Freegate! Satisfied now?" Tyvian snarled. He wondered how long it would take him to get rid of the beast now that it was in his company. Unlike Artus, its uses were limited to the money it had in its stolen apron and its obvious physical prowess. In every other way it was a liability, even provided it *didn't* eat them both in the middle of the night. He silently cursed the ring . . . again.

The gnoll curled itself up on the ground in a very canine posture. "I will sleep now. Don't you run away! I will know!"

Tyvian mustered up a smile. "We wouldn't dream of abandoning you, sir."

The gnoll's ears shot up. "I am a *lady*!"

Tyvian blinked. "Oh . . . I beg your pardon, ma'am."

"You call me Hool," it said, and then closed its eyes. A few minutes later, with the two humans watching it in silence, its breathing became rhythmic and its ears laid back against its broad skull.

Tyvian broke the silence with a soft whisper. "It's asleep."

Artus, visibly trembling, examined the beast's sleeping form. He then hissed at Tyvian, "What do we do now? You don't really aim to stay with this thing, right?"

Tyvian shrugged, smirking. "You didn't object in the tavern."

"That was 'cause it was gonna kill us! I thought we would get outside and make a break for it. Maybe call for help."

Tyvian rolled his eyes. "Yes, because those locals so recently pummeled by the very same wild gnoll would have done such an *admirable* job of containing it and we could *easily* outpace a creature that can, evidently, track like a hound and run like a mountain cat."

Artus gestured to the sleeping gnoll. "It's sleeping! Why don't we just call them now?"

"Or better yet," Tyvian said, drawing his knife and offering it, hilt first, to Artus. "Why don't *you* do her in?"

Artus looked at the knife and looked at the sleeping gnoll. "You do it."

"Come now, Artus. Is this the same lad who charged into the fray with his fellow patrons at the Wandering Fountain? Take the knife, cut out the middleman, as they say, and slice her throat."

Artus shook his head. "I don't want to."

"Don't want to because she might wake up, or don't want to because you don't think it's right?"

"Both. I don't know." Artus sighed.

Tyvian nodded. "Exactly as I thought, boy. Never taken a life in your whole time in the world, Hann bless you. I, meanwhile, have this." He held up his right hand, where the iron ring glowered blackly in the lamplight. "And I would wager its perverted sense of self-righteousness would prevent me from slaying yonder sleeping beast, no matter how much my prac-

ticed hands might want to. So, barring your spontaneous generation of a spine or my freedom from this iron
anchor, nobody is going to do anything to our new
friend, Hool."

"But we can't *travel* with it! No town will ever let
us in. We'll never be able to stay at an inn or ride on a
riverboat or anything!"

Tyvian frowned—that *was* a sticking point, but
there was little point in echoing the boy's sentiment.
"No matter. Besides, if that river-inn is any indicator of
the kind of lodgings one can expect along the Trell, I
doubt we are missing very much."

Artus looked back at the sleeping gnoll. The apron
with the money was securely buried beneath her body,
with only its tassels visible. "I wonder how much silver
she's got in there."

"The equivalent of at least two marks, two crowns,
and eight peers, and probably a bit more," Tyvian remarked absently, rising and walking to the barn door.

Artus's mouth fell open. "You're making that up."

"I most certainly am not," Tyvian shot back, peering through the cracks in the door into the darkness
beyond.

"How'd you know?"

Tyvian shot him a withering look. "I *counted*, you
ninny. What do you think I was keeping an eye on that
whole time you were asking me stupid questions?"

Artus gasped. "You were gonna rob the place all the
time!"

Tyvian nodded. "Did you really think it was my

original intent to *walk* all the way to Freegate? Between the money the tavernkeeper had in that apron and the safe he clearly kept under the bar, I estimated we could buy a pair of ponies or some such the next town up as well as book passage on a riverboat as far as Headfort. We wouldn't travel in style, but at least we'd travel fast. Plus, animals exude a consistent Lumenal trace, which would assist us in evading Alafarr."

Artus slapped his knee. "Saints, you're sharp!"

Tyvian returned and sat down, his face impassive. "Thank you very much for noticing. Such praise from you is a priceless gem that I shall cherish forever."

"Well, you don't have to be a jerk about it."

"Forgive me, Artus, if I am in a bad mood lately. You see, a longtime business associate of mine recently betrayed me, I have a magical torture device affixed to my hand, and I am wearing furs and sleeping on a barn floor with a chattering juvenile delinquent and a bloody *gnoll*."

Artus's lips pulled into a tight line. "Sorry."

Tyvian pulled off his fur hat and fashioned for himself a makeshift pillow. "That's perfectly all right. Only one of my six problems has anything to do with you, after all. Get some sleep. We'll leave in an hour."

Artus nodded and lay down, uncertain of how insulted he was supposed to be, but decided to let it go. Tyvian just liked insulting people, he guessed. The more he took it personal, the longer his trip to Freegate would be.

His face still hurt from his fight earlier, though his

mouth had stopped bleeding. He tossed and turned, trying to find a comfortable position on the hard floor. Though hardly the first barn he had ever slept in, he didn't feel tired, and his thoughts were racing. He thought again of the letter Eddereon had written him and what it might really say. He thought of his home across the mountains, in the broad farmlands of the North, and what his mother was doing right then. Most of all, though, he thought of the gnoll lying not four paces from him. He thought of her long white fangs and her predator's eyes; he thought of her standing over him in the night and tearing out his throat with a bestial howl.

His eyes popped open. There, twinkling in the semidarkness, one of Hool's eyes was half open and looking at him. Artus gasped and sat up straight, but the eye snapped closed as soon as he did so.

Artus knew then, beyond any doubt, that the gnoll had been awake the whole time.

CHAPTER 7

ON THE ROAD

Myreon Alafarr sat uncomfortably in the saddle of a borrowed horse, her magestaff across her knees, and mused on the truth to Jaevis's reputation as the bounty hunter crouched over some muddy, snow-filled tracks in the center of the narrow road that ran along a tributary to the Trell River. What he saw in them, Myreon had no idea, but it was apparently very interesting, as he had been examining the tracks in earnest for a full minute. After another half minute or so, Myreon cleared her throat. "Mr. Jaevis, would you care to share what it is you are looking at?"

Jaevis looked at Myreon over his shoulder. There was something about the man's thick eyebrows and dark eyes that put his face into a perpetual glare. "Two peoples. One man, very fit, not so tall. One boy, maybe fifteen, go with him. They were here day before yesterday. They walk strangely—in sevens."

"That sounds like Reldamar and his accomplice to me. He's using the seven-step to foil seekwands. Fortunately it will slow him down. Come, let's—"

Jaevis held up a thick, dirty hand. "That is not all, Lady Magus. There are other tracks."

Myreon sighed. "This is a *road*, Mr. Jaevis. I'm certain there are other tracks."

"These are not people tracks. These use four feet, like wolf or big cat, but are not wolf or big cat. Front paws are hands. Weigh maybe three hundred pound, moving quick."

Myreon frowned. "You're certain?"

Jaevis glared at the Mage Defender. "Of course."

"There was a gnoll on the spirit engine when I confronted Reldamar last. It escaped during the fighting, but I had presumed it dead."

Jaevis looked back at the road and examined something. "It favors left side a little—probably bruises there. Not enough to slow it."

"Why would a gnoll follow Reldamar?" Myreon asked aloud.

Jaevis shrugged. "You are wizard. Use augury."

"An augury to determine another being's *intentions* is something quite beyond my capabilities, Mr. Jaevis, and, even if it weren't, it would take too much time. We are after Reldamar, not the gnoll. If it interferes, I will simply make certain to destroy it this time. Can we be going, now?"

Jaevis did not respond. He mounted his own horse, Kuvyos, and spurred her into a canter. Myreon shook her head and followed.

Catching Reldamar didn't seem terribly likely. The smuggler had at least a two-day head start on them and, as Tarlyth had predicted, was counteracting most of the conventional auguries Myreon knew for catching criminals. Even by creating a possessive link to the smuggler with a small stockpile of his items retrieved from the spirit engine, the best information she had acquired were things she knew already—Reldamar was heading north, and Reldamar was not alone.

The light mix of rain and snow that plagued the days since they left Thostering had finally cleared, giving way to a bright but cold sun that reflected off the isolated patches of snow spotting the Galaspin countryside. As if that hadn't put enough of a damper on her relationship with Jaevis, even when the weather cleared they did not speak. Not only was Jaevis's Trade imperfect, Myreon couldn't think of a topic of mutual interest they might discuss. The tracker didn't seem inclined to make friends, in any case.

Myreon was fairly certain Jaevis didn't like magi and probably had a low opinion of women, though she had no real proof to back that up and was never good at the empathic auguries that would tell her for certain, as channeling the Fey had never been her strong suit. She did note, however, the Hannite cross Jaevis wore around his neck and the Hannite talisman affixed to his beard—almost certainly a life ward—and concluded that such accessories were probably sufficient to indicate his piety and, by extension, his opinion of the High Arts, if not the fairer sex.

The Church had become more and more critical of the Arcanostrum of Saldor since the death of Keeper Astrian X shortly after the conclusion of the Illini Wars. With the conservative Astrian dead, a more progressive member of the Archmage Council was able to achieve the Fifth Mark—the former Archmage Del'Katar of the Blue College, now known as Polimeux II, Keeper of the Balance. Polimeux had wasted no time repealing what he considered "antiquated policies" regarding the distribution of ensorcelled goods and the development of alchemical or thaumaturgical technologies. This was followed by the invention and distribution of things like spirit engines, sending stones, hearthstones, feylamps, and the rest of it. As far as Myreon could tell, the West had benefited enormously from these changes—the economies of the Allied Nations had exploded; the war-ravaged infrastructures of Illin, Rhond, Saldor, and Galaspin had been restored in record time; and the people prospered.

The Church, however, didn't seem to appreciate all of this. Such "irresponsible" use of the art was a sin, they said. It would lead to the destruction of the world, they insisted, and every slight magical mishap or natural disaster was said to be evidence of "Kroth the Devourer stirring in his bonds." Myreon personally believed the Church was just bitter that their priests and healers were receiving fewer donations now that materials like illbane powder and bloodpatch elixirs were more readily available to the average person. She imagined that the sale of luck-charms and various divinatory almanacs also had a deleterious effect on their blessings and holy ceremonies. Why kowtow to a bunch of didactic holy-men when you could see if your child was born under a fortunate star with a couple silver crowns to a local talismancer?

In any case, as much as she might like to discuss these topics, Myreon doubted Jaevis would appreciateit. Illinis were known to be a superstitious and pious lot and were famously intolerant of those who didn't agree with them. There was no sense in sticking one's finger in a pot one knew was boiling, and so she kept silent until they came upon the angry mob along the banks of the Trell River.

Like most mobs, they lacked subtlety. A group of about ten men armed with spears, scythes, and hatchets came clambering out of a copse of trees near a bend in the river. They were bundled in heavy woolen fleeces and crude beaver-pelt caps, and their faces were scoured raw with cold and exhaustion. Their eyes, however, were still blazing with equal parts fear and anger. When the mob caught sight of Myreon and

Jaevis, they ran toward them, waving their arms and shouting "Hold" and "Danger."

Myreon looked over at Jaevis to find the bounty hunter had a small crossbow already loaded and resting across his knees. "Mr. Jaevis, I trust you will use discretion with that device?"

Jaevis didn't look at her, but grunted in what Myreon assumed to be assent.

"Hold!" The apparent leader of the mob was a middle-aged man with a thick beard and wide, flat cheeks. He had a wood-splitting axe that he was waving in the air like a banner. "Come no further if you value your life! Go back!"

Myreon raised her magestaff so it could be easily seen and pulled back her hood. "I am Myreon Alafarr, Mage Defender of the Balance, in pursuit of a criminal fugitive. This is an associate of mine, Mr. Jaevis."

The sight of the magestaff took something of the bravado out of the group. The leader paled slightly and let his woodsplitter drop to the ground. "Begging your pardon, Magus. Been trouble hereabouts, and we've been keepin' travelers away." The man looked about at his companions and, perhaps for the first time, realized how a pack of armed men jumping out of the bushes might be misinterpreted. "For their safety, you know. Obviously. We ain't no bandits or nothing. Honest."

Myreon nodded, face impassive. "I surmised as much, sir—bandits are usually a bit quieter when approaching their prey. What has happened?"

"Well, night before last there was a row at the

Fountain—river-inn, maybe two miles up. Monster of some type crashed in there. Fought the whole place, it did, and put ten men on their backs in a healer's bed, threw a half dozen into the river and half froze 'em, plus a couple more got bruised up so bad they don't know what's comin' or goin'. There was some talk from witnesses and such that seen the fight that the beast was in league with some strangers, but I don't know more past that. We been out ever since trying to hunt the thing down—we know it slept in a barn nearby anyway."

Myreon gave the mob a good hard look—they were farmers, woodsmen, fishermen, and craftsmen, by the looks of them. That gnoll, she suspected, would tear them apart if they actually caught up to it. "Why not report this to your local baron? Surely his men-at-arms would be better equipped for this sort of thing."

The men shrugged. "He's gone off to winter up in Freegate, the slug—all the fancy folk go up there before the heavy snows set in. His keep has got just a few fellows about, and they're helping with another group upriver."

Myreon rolled her eyes—typical Galaspiner politics. People claimed the nobility were more responsible since the war, but they hadn't changed. The average Galaspin peasant was expected to fend for himself, and they usually did, or pooled their money to hire mercenaries. Putting that issue aside, Myreon focused on what was most interesting in the mob leader's tale,

"How many travelers do you get passing through at this time of year?"

The leader of the mob conferred with his compatriots for a moment before producing the answer. "I dunno. Two or three barges head up- or downriver a week. Them's mostly folks we see regular, you know? They ain't from around here but they ain't strangers neither, right?"

"What about on foot? How many then?"

The leader of the mob blinked. "On foot in the winter? None—who'd walk to Thostering at this time of year?"

"Hey!" one of the other members of the mob shouted from in the back. "Weren't those two strangers on foot that night? I swear I heard that!"

Myreon grinned. "Thank you, sir—that was what I wanted to hear. If you don't mind, my associate and I are going to the Fountain to investigate."

The mob leader knuckled his forehead. "Yes ma'am. You think we should keep looking for the monster, then? Is there danger?"

Myreon weighed her options for a moment and decided to remain positive. "Keep up the good work, gentlemen—you are a credit to your community!" With that, she and Jaevis spurred their horses past the group and rode off.

The Wandering Fountain was a disaster area, as the mob had explained. The broken furniture had all been removed from the galley, but there were still signs that a large melee had happened. The wall boards were cracked, support beams were scratched and nicked by errant weapons, and the bar itself had a monumental fissure running from one end to the other.

The tavernkeeper's wife met them at the door, and upon seeing the magestaff in Myreon's hand, ushered them in without delay. In the galley, Jaevis spit on the floor, rubbed the saliva around in the dust, and then tasted it.

Myreon made a face and muttered to herself, "I hope that is worth the taste."

"Pardon, m'lady?" the wife asked.

"Nothing, madam, and the title is 'Magus,' please."

She threw up her hands as though surrendering. "We don't have naught to do with fancy folks 'round these parts, no ways! That was why the stranger caught me eye. He was a fancy one, sure enough. Saldorian like yourself, I shouldn't wonder. Anyway it was all strange to hear ol' Abe tell it. He's sore hurt, m'lady . . . uh, Magus. Face all swole up like a toad's!"

Myreon narrowly avoided hitting her temple on a low beam as she paced around the scene. She held out her hand and channeled enough Ether to conjure a glamour of Reldamar. It sparkled and rotated in midair before the wife's wide eyes. "I am looking for this man. Have you seen him?"

The tavernkeeper's wife put a hand to her heart. "Hann guide me, but that's the man! He had a boy with him, too, maybe thirteen years. After their beast done thumped all the men and threw our guests overboard, they nabbed the till!"

Myreon blinked. "What, they *robbed* you?"

"Then run off," the woman confirmed.

"Ran off *together*?"

The man's wife nodded, tugging at Myreon's sleeve. "Have you ever heard the like, m'lady? Men in league with monsters like that? It is some kind of unholiness at work, I know it!"

"Well?" Myreon looked at Jaevis, who was standing in the center of the common room, arms crossed.

"There was fight. Can't tell more—too many peoples walking through here, sweeping up, mopping, washing . . ."

"Well, then," Myreon said, raising her staff, "Allow me."

Closing her eyes, she chanted the proper incantation for a psychometric augury, turning slowly at the center of the room. She felt the astral energy that bound the place together humming in resonance with her spell, and soon flashes of light were skipping behind her eyelids. Focusing her power a bit more, Myreon refined the flashes to actual images. She saw the floor being laid by a shipwright twenty-four years gone. She saw an endless cavalcade of boots and shoes treading over the top of it. She saw men warming their feet before the stove, and saw decades' worth of food and drink being eaten, spilled, and enjoyed. She rushed past these, trying to limit her visions to the most recent ones. It took some time, but then they were there—a pair of broad furry feet, like paws—moving with practiced precision around the room. From the stove she could see the gnoll mercilessly pummeling the tavern's defenders, and reminded herself not to let the beast get anywhere near her in the future. Finally, the end of it came into clear focus, and Myreon paid close attention.

The gnoll was there, and it was *speaking* in a deep, velvet smooth voice. *You come with me.*

Reldamar's voice was firm. *Not a chance.*

Then the tavernkeeper's yelp. *Help! Help! Beast!*

Myreon saw the gnoll heave the man out the door. *Then I go with you.*

As the rest of their negotiations unfolded, Myreon found herself aghast and in awe of what she was witnessing. Was this for real? How could it be possible for Reldamar to make some kind of pact with a wild animal?

Then came the clincher. The gnoll was speaking, *You need help to kill the man who tricked you and got you caught by the wizards. I am strong and fast and better than this pup. I can track stupid humans across miles and miles, and if you won't let me go with you, I will eat your face.*

Then Reldamar nodded. *For a monster, you are remarkably convincing.*

That was it. That was all Myreon needed to see. She opened her eyes to find Jaevis glaring at her, arms still crossed. "What do you know?" he asked.

"It's settled," Myreon said, hurrying out of the tavern. "Reldamar's making for Freegate. We need to catch him before he reaches it. Oh, and apparently he's working with a gnoll."

The winter wind seared Tyvian's cheeks raw as the Freegate Road wound about the broad base of a rocky hill. Behind it, he knew there would be another hill, and another, and another after that. They were climbing up the sides of the Trell River Valley, and the foothills of the mighty Dragonspine were making travel difficult. The sun was setting, and they would have to camp soon.

Tyvian looked behind him to see Artus hiking up the road with a smile on his face, the large frame pack with their supplies clanking quietly on his shoulders. The weight of the thing, which was not inconsiderable, seemed to bother the boy about as much as would a simple blanket-roll. Tyvian found that frustrating, but reminded himself that such spite was beneath him.

"The mountains are pretty, ain't they?" Artus remarked, peering past the crest of the hill where, along the horizon, the snowcapped peaks of the Dragonspine glowed in the light of the setting sun.

Tyvian scowled, deciding to reevaluate his position vis-à-vis spite. "Yes, quite fetching."

Artus took a deep breath, savoring the crisp air. "I mean, look at the way they glow—all warm and bright."

"'Warm' strikes me as a very inappropriate adjective. It's getting dark. We'd best set up camp."

Artus looked around at the bald crown of the hill. "What, here?"

"No, in the stable over there." Tyvian pointed.

Artus looked. "I don't see nothing."

"That's because I was being bloody sarcastic! Just set up the damned tent, will you?" Tyvian snarled. "Where's that gnoll, anyway?"

"Here!" Hool loped to the top of the hill, a few fresh rabbits affixed to her belt. She threw the meat at Tyvian's feet and looked at Artus, who was taking off his pack. "What is he doing?"

"Setting up camp."

Hool snorted. "Not here. This is a stupid place to make camp."

Artus nodded. "That's what I wanted to say."

"Could that be because it is outside in the middle of the bloody winter?" Tyvian motioned to the cold, austere countryside around them. "Because I wholeheartedly agree, but since we are traveling in the company of a bloodthirsty monster, we can't exactly stop at the next roadside inn and ask for a room, can we? Remember what happened at the last place?"

Artus rubbed his head reflexively. "They threw pots at us."

"Right!" Tyvian nodded. "So, unless we can convince Madam Hool here to go away, I don't see why we can't just pitch our damned tent anywhere we damned well please."

Hool stood up. "This is the top of a hill. There is lots of wind and no firewood. You will get cold and will have to eat the food I caught for you without cooking."

Tyvian began a pithy reply but quickly noted that what the gnoll said made a good deal of sense. "Fine. Where would you suggest?"

Hool pointed to the next hill. "The back of that one has small bushes for burning and is hidden from the wind. Let's go there now."

Tyvian doffed his cap and bowed. "Lead on, wise gnoll." He then looked at Artus and his half-unpacked tent. "Looks like we're moving. Pick all that up."

It had been three days since they left the Wandering Fountain in the company of the gnoll, and Tyvian found that her presence had complicated things even more profoundly than he originally thought. For one thing, purchasing ponies was completely impossible. Not only was approaching civilized people difficult, given the gnoll's predilection for being nearby, but the barest whiff of her scent was enough to drive horses to the point of hysteria. Since both he and Artus were in her company for the better part of the day, this meant that they, themselves, reeked of gnoll enough to cause one horse trader in a small village twenty miles back to banish them from the sight of his corrals for rest of their natural lives. This, coupled with the fact that staying at inns had become likewise difficult and that Hool steadfastly *refused* to travel on the river, meant they were reduced to hiking and sleeping outside for the remainder of their journey, doubling their travel time, and making it more uncomfortable besides.

They had left the banks of the river and moved slightly north to pick up the Freegate Road—the best and only highway that lead directly to the city. It was also the slowest and least comfortable of all possible methods of travel.

On the bright side, Hool was an exceptional huntress and had kept them all well fed on rabbit and grouse, the latter of which Tyvian had no idea how she caught with her bare hands. She acted as a scout, too, giving a report to him of the layout of the local land every day when she returned from hunting. Though their lack of transportation made it almost certain the Defenders would catch up with them, Tyvian felt oddly secure in the knowledge that Hool would let him know they were coming long before they arrived.

The gnoll's reason for accompanying them, or more specifically, accompanying Tyvian himself, was still a mystery. Hool was oddly concerned with his whereabouts, and with the exception of her hunting expeditions, wouldn't let the smuggler out of her sight. She hadn't yet revealed the reason for this, though Tyvian surmised that if it was sufficiently important to necessitate her assaulting an entire tavern's worth of people, it was a lot more than simple curiosity or fascination. Tyvian hadn't asked. This was partly because he didn't think she would tell him—she was waiting for the right moment, he was certain—but he mostly hadn't asked because he didn't care.

At the gnoll-recommended campsite, Artus set up their tent with his usual skill as Tyvian hacked up some of the dry, scraggly bushes that grew in the area with a hatchet they had purchased with some of Hool's stolen money. The gnoll, meanwhile, skinned and gutted the rabbits on a broad, flat rock. The place Hool had chosen was a small basin on the leeward side of a large hill. Tyvian was forced to admit that it was a far better choice than his rather arbitrary choice, as this spot was removed from the road by a few hundred yards, hidden from sight on three sides by large stones jutting out of the side of the hill, and warmer by some ten degrees.

Since they had run out of hearthcider, warmth had become a major consideration for Artus and himself. All they had to protect them against the wind and cold were the furs on their backs, the itchy woolen blanket rolls, and the thick canvas of the tent walls. Against the biting chill of a winter night in the foothills of the Dragonspine, it was all poor protection. Hool, meanwhile, seemed unaffected. Her shaggy coat was evidently more than enough insulation to deal with the local conditions, a fact that was of great relief to both Artus and Tyvian, since the prospect of sharing a tent with the beast would have been too much to bear.

Tyvian gathered the brush together at the center of the gulley and produced a hearthstone. Striking it sharply against a rock, he tossed it quickly into the pile of brush and watched as the magic in the simple, rust-red rock ignited the fire. Hool was watching him with her unwavering gaze as she skinned the game with the practiced ease of one who had been stripping small animals of their flesh for most of her life. "Are you a wizard, Reldamar?"

Tyvian shook his head. "Certainly not."

"Do you know about wizards?"

"Yes, I do."

"Tell me about them." Hool had a note of finality in her tone that was unmistakable.

The hair on the back of Tyvian's neck stood on end. He spoke carefully. "What do you want to know?"

"Do they die?"

Tyvian licked his lips. "Well . . . yes. They're just human beings, after all. Are you looking to kill some wizards, Hool?"

"Yes."

Tyvian managed a chuckle. "That's what I like about you, Hool. You are delightfully straightforward. Any wizards in particular?"

Her eyes gleamed like metal disks in the firelight. "Yes."

Tyvian nodded, disliking the direction the conversation was going. "Well, then I pity the poor chaps. I most certainly would not like to be your enemy."

"You say we are going to this Freegate-place. What is it?"

Artus hammered the last stake into the earth and clapped his hands. "Yeah! What are we doing when we get there?"

Tyvian scowled at him. "Just to make things perfectly clear—once we get to Freegate, *we* are not doing anything. I am paying *you* ten marks from my personal holdings there, and then *we* are going our separate ways."

Artus frowned and sat in front of the fire. "Oh right—sure."

Tyvian nodded. "As for 'what is Freegate,' it is a city. It is, perhaps, one of the most wonderful cities in the whole world. Indeed, I often wonder why I ever leave."

Artus shook his head. "I dunno. I was there once, and I didn't think it was all that great."

Tyvian nodded. "That's because you passed through as a moneyless wretch, Artus. Freegate is no place for the peasantry."

The boy looked at his own tattered fur clothing. "Good thing we're going there in style, then."

"Are there wizards in Freegate?" Hool asked.

"That depends—are you planning to go on a wizard-killing rampage when we get there?"

"No."

"Then yes, there are lots of wizards."

Hool placed a skinned rabbit on a stick and handed it to Artus to suspend over the fire. "Don't drop it in or it will burn."

Artus frowned. "Saints, Hool, I *know*, okay? You tell me that every time."

"That is 'cause you hold your stick too loose. You are going to drop it in." Hool handed another stick to Tyvian. "Reldamar does it better than you."

Artus scowled and grumbled under his breath, staring into the fire.

"Don't look at the fire. You will ruin your eyes for

night-seeing," Hool scolded again. "Then when the wizards come for us you won't be ready."

Tyvian perked up at that. "Any sign of them?"

Hool nodded. "There are horses behind us. They were many miles away, upwind from us. One of the riders is the one who tried to catch you."

Tyvian smiled. "Good to know Alafarr hasn't given up. I was a bit worried about her, to be honest."

"Why do they chase you?" Hool asked.

Tyvian shrugged. "Because I'm a bad person. I deal in the illicit sale and trade of enchanted and alchemical items, which is a serious crime, you know."

"You're also a jerk." Artus muttered.

Tyvian nodded. "Ah, yes—thank you, Artus." He turned to Hool and said, "I am also 'a jerk,' though exactly how that differs from being a 'bad person,' I can't say."

Artus glared at him across the fire. "Jerk."

Tyvian raised an eyebrow at the boy. "Well, *your* mood has certainly soured. Why don't you look at the pretty mountains some more?"

Artus didn't say anything and kept looking into the fire as the sunlight vanished behind the crest of the hill. The smell of roasted rabbit filled the air, and Hool passed around a waterskin. She then went about checking Artus's pack and reloading anything that had shifted over the course of the day's walking. She even checked its leather straps for any wear or tear. Not until she had finished her inspection did she sit down to roast her own rabbit.

Tyvian watched the gnoll quietly through the firelight, trying again to figure out how it was she had come to be here. Wherever Hendrieux had gotten her, she couldn't have come cheaply—catching gnolls was a daunting enough prospect as it was, Tyvian imagined, but shipping them alive across half a continent couldn't be substantially easier. It would have cost a fortune, and he knew Hendrieux was not in a position to spend that kind of money on what amounted to an elaborate trap. Hendrieux could have planted a dozen equally incriminating things in the cargo in question without needing to go that extra mile for a full-grown gnoll in a box. Granted, the biomantic text Alafarr mentioned had dealt specifically with altering wild beasts, and gnolls fit that description admirably, but it still didn't make sense that Hendrieux would choose *that* specific crime. Unless . . .

"You aren't the only gnoll," Tyvian whispered to himself.

Hool's ears swiveled in his direction. "What do you mean?"

Tyvian blinked. "Oh . . . your hearing is quite keen, isn't it? It was nothing, really—just thinking aloud."

Hool's ears went back, a gesture Tyvian had come to associate with annoyance. "No. You tell me what you meant."

Tyvian put up his hands. "I only meant that you are probably not the only gnoll Hendrieux has. Actually, let me amend that, you aren't the only gnoll that whoever is *paying* Hendrieux has in his, her, or their possession."

Hool was across the campsite with her fists gripping handfuls of Tyvian's jacket in the blink of an eye. She shook the smuggler like a rag doll. *"YOU TELL ME WHERE THEY ARE RIGHT NOW!"*

"Saint's eyes!" Artus jumped at the sudden attack; he immediately dropped his rabbit in the campfire.

Tyvian wriggled in the gnoll's iron grip, his own hands prying at her furry fingers to no noticeable effect. "Kroth, beast! Unhand me! Let go, I say!"

Hool shook Tyvian so hard he thought his head was going to pop off his neck. *"YOU TELL ME NOW OR YOU DIE!"*

Artus snatched up the mallet he had used to hammer in the tent stakes and hit the gnoll on the back as hard as he could. Hool dropped Tyvian immediately and backhanded the boy across the face hard enough that he spun around and fell flat on his face.

Tyvian was on his feet immediately, knife drawn and backing away from Hool. "Calm down! I don't know where they are, all right? I didn't take them!"

Hool's aggression quieted somewhat, the ridge of hair running along her spine slowly lowering to its normal height. "Who did?"

"I know a man who knows who took them. His name is Hendrieux."

"The fake-man on the screaming snake-thing."

Tyvian nodded. "The spirit engine, yes—that's the

thing. The *real* Hendrieux double-crossed me, you see, and he knows where the other gnolls are, understand?"

Hool pointed at him. "You will take me to this Hen-droo."

Tyvian nodded, grinning. "Nothing would give me more pleasure, Hool. Now, are we done assaulting each other for the evening?"

Artus was slowly getting to his feet. "I'm all right. Thanks for asking."

Hool retreated back to her place on the other side of the campfire.

Tyvian, knife still drawn, crouched back down to get nearer the warmth of the flames. "Gods, Hool! I'm not one in favor of slavery, mind you, but I must say your reaction to the bondage of your fellow creatures is a bit . . . extreme. Do you know them, by any chance?"

Hool's face grew suddenly still. "I know them."

"Friends of yours?" Tyvian asked.

"They are my puppies." Hool's copper gaze focused on Tyvian's face. "Hen-droo has my *children*."

Tyvian suddenly felt his guts clench in terror. "I . . . I see."

Hool said nothing, her gaze still fixed on Tyvian. The smuggler read a lot of things in that gaze, for the gnoll's eyes were deeper and larger than any human's. One thing, though, stood above the rest—there was nothing on this earth that Tyvian Reldamar could do to Zazlar Hendrieux that could ever hope to equal the terrible wrath of a mother gnoll. If she caught him, his death would not be quick.

Then, as suddenly as it had arrived, the feeling of terror faded. Tyvian found himself smiling more broadly than he had for days. "Let's to bed, shall we?"

That night, Artus dreamed of home. It was springtime, and Ma had the shutters open to let in the fresh air. Outside, he heard the rhythmic chop of his second-eldest brother, Marik, splitting wood. The back room of their four room cottage was quiet, save for the humming of the insects.

Days like these Artus would spend helping Ma and his sisters with the chores while Conrad, Marik, Balter, and Handen would be plowing the fields. Artus ran outside to the yard, looking for Marik. He wanted to see his favorite brother again, more than anything. He ran across the soft grass, trying to round the corner of the cottage to where Marik had always stood, his broad shoulders bare to the sun, axe in hand. Or it could have been Conrad, or Balter, or even Handen—whichever brother who would tell him what year it was. Conrad, the eldest, was the first to be drafted—he had died in Roon, under Sir Markus Gravel. Then Marik, whom they had never heard from again. Then Balter and Handen went together, and came back cripples in the same wagon. The villagers said the boys up at Jondas Crossing had a curse on their heads. Ma said the curse was that the army-clerics knew where they lived.

Artus couldn't round the cottage. He was lost somehow, in a sea of waist-high wheat, rolling over the gentle hills in golden waves. Suddenly he could see the cottage and the barn in the distance, the smoke from the fire snaking out of the chimney in a thin gray line against an azure sky.

"MA!" he yelled. There was no echo.

He ran toward the cottage, but he got no closer. His feet churned up the soil, the wheat slapped against his bare knees but he felt nothing. He stopped and screamed again. "MA!"

"You can't go back, kid." The voice was felt more than heard. There was something amiss, like it wasn't quite there. Still, Artus knew it was Marik.

Marik stood in the sun, stripped to the waist, sweat glistening off the thick hair on his chest and arms. His beard was short and his eyes were smiling, like always. Marik was ten when Artus was born, the day after Da got called up to the army. Da had told Marik that the baby was his responsibility while he was gone, while Conrad was to care for their three sisters. Marik had held true to that promise, even when Da never came back. Where Balter and Handen were always teasing and fighting with him, Marik was his protector. Marik told him what was what.

"Marik!" Artus said. "You're back!"

Marik shook his head. "You can't go back, kid. She don't want you."

"It's suppertime. You'd better put on a shirt." Artus tried to look back at the cottage, but he couldn't find it.

"She don't want you, understand? Stay away."

"I can't! Who'll chop the wood? Who'll see to Maya and Kestra and Tori?"

Marik only put his callused hand on Artus's shoulder and shook him . . . and shook him . . . and shook him . . .

Artus's eyes popped open to see Tyvian shaking him. "Will you wake up already? Gods, you sleep like the dead." The smuggler whispered.

Artus sat up. "What is it? Is someth—"

Tyvian slapped a hand across his mouth. "Shhhhh!".

This time, Artus whispered. "What?"

The cool gray light of dawn illuminated the walls of the tent with enough light that Artus could see Tyvian's eyebrows pinched together in thought. "Hool's gone."

"Where'd she go?"

The smuggler shook his head. "More important is *why hasn't she returned*? This time of morning she's already back from her predawn hunt. Something prevented her from coming back."

It dawned on Artus suddenly, and he gasped. "Mirror-men! You think they've found us?"

Tyvian nodded, grimacing. Clutching his right hand to his breast, he handed Artus a fur cloak. "We need to split up. Here—take this and run west, I'll head east. They can—" Tyvian gasped and wrung his hand in the air. "They can only catch one of us."

Artus frowned, his eyes on the iron ring that was clearly torturing the smuggler. "What's wrong?"

Tyvian, teeth clenched, threw the fur cloak on Artus's back. "We haven't time! Just go, will you? Run!"

Artus found himself shoved through the tent flap and into the breathtaking chill of the morning air. The charred remnants of their campfire were coated in a sparkling layer of frost, and a crisp breeze made him shiver and clutch the cloak more tightly around him, noticing that it was a bit large on him. It was Tyvian's.

Before Artus had much time to ponder why the smuggler would give away his own cloak, he heard the sound of hoofbeats at a gallop closing in. Cursing, Artus ran to take shelter behind the tall rocks that circled the camp, getting out of sight just as two mounted figures—one woman in gray robes with a magestaff across her knees, the other a man in black and worn leathers—appeared on the crest of a nearby hill. The woman had a slender wand in her free hand, its tip a swirling pool of pure shadow. From his hiding place, Artus could see her focusing upon this strange darkness, and watched as she altered the course of her mount in accordance with some perceived change in its the shape or demeanor. He had never seen one of these before, but he knew them by reputation clearly enough—it was a seekwand.

She was the Mage Defender—Artus remembered her name was Alafarr—and her dour, bearded associate who rode into their camp. While Alafarr puzzled at some strange indication by the wand, the man dismounted, making for the tent. Artus held his breath—Tyvian was still inside!

"Jaevis!" Alafarr snapped, pointing her wand directly toward where Artus was hiding. "Reldamar's not in the tent. He's up there."

Jaevis's head snapped in Artus's direction and he drew a short sword with a wickedly curved blade from underneath his worn black cape. He advanced on the rocks quickly, but carefully, his black eyes missing nothing. As he did, Artus realized Tyvian's plan and why he had stuffed him in his clothing. Patting down the cloak's crude pockets, he found Tyvian's knife, as well as a pair of worn-out socks that weren't his. "That son of a bitch . . ."

Tyvian popped out of the tent silently, clad in *his* cloak. Jaevis and Alafarr didn't see him, as both were fixated upon Artus's hiding spot. As Tyvian grabbed the bridle of Jaevis's horse, a hot flash of anger caused Artus to stand up and point. "You damned *liar!*"

Both Alafarr and Jaevis spun around in time to see Tyvian swing up into the saddle of the bounty hunter's sturdy mare. Alafarr dropped the wand and moved to raise her magestaff, but Tyvian quickly snatched the staff out of the Defender's lap and jabbed his heels into the mare's sides. It sprung into a gallop as the smuggler raced out of the campsite, laughing as he went. "Thanks for the staff, Alafarr!"

The Mage Defender, face red, turned her horse and spurred it in pursuit. Artus watched in fascination as the two rode recklessly down the steep slope of the hill, certain one or the other's horse would stumble and fall. Both mounts, however, proved to be sure-footed and they hit the floor of the small valley below with riders intact.

Jaevis, meanwhile, sprinted to where Artus stood and, looking down on his fleeing mount, put his fingers to his lips and produced an ear-splitting whistle. *"Kuvyos! Rixte!"*

The mare Tyvian rode stopped suddenly, digging its hooves into the frozen ground and rearing back, pitching him from the saddle and throwing him flat on his back. Alàfarr pulled up short, and, extending her hand, summoned her staff to it with a single word. Leveling it at the prone Tyvian, she shouted. "Stand down, Reldamar!"

Abruptly realizing what was happening, Artus tore his eyes away from Tyvian's arrest to flee for himself. The bounty hunter Jaevis, however, blocked his path. The dour Illini thrust his fat curved blade at the boy's chest, but stopped short of impaling him. "You stay," he stated.

Artus put up his hands. "Okay . . . you got it."

They were nicked. Again.

CHAPTER 8

THE OL' SWITCHEROO

"I'm surprised, Reldamar. That was the kind of trick I expect out of sneak-thieves and thugs, not you." Myreon Alafarr was unaccustomed to gloating and so she wasn't doing it right. Tyvian was relatively certain that enduring such subrate mockery was worse than the genuine article. At least in the latter case one could appreciate the artistry of the insult. Alafarr was like a child painting with mud and bringing it to the art gallery for approval.

Tyvian and Artus were bound hand and foot and sitting on the bottom of a soggy river barge as it was solemnly poled downstream by a gray-haired Galaspiner with one eye. Tyvian had always thought depth perception would be important in the riverboat trade, but evidently he was wrong. Either that or this trip down the Trell River was doomed to a cold, wet end. In any case, his mood was hardly improved by their method of transportation.

The bounty hunter named Jaevis had a compact Kalsaari-make crossbow across his knees and he was watching the riverbank exclusively, confident that Tyvian and Artus constituted less of a threat than any potential attack from the shore, which lay some thirty or forty yards off. Tyvian had heard of Hacklar Jaevis and was singularly unimpressed with the man's appearance—he was dirty and unkempt to the point where the shaggy Hool was manicured by comparison—but he was forced to admit the man knew his business. It had been eight hours and he hadn't yet been able to loosen the knots around his wrists one bit, which was no mean feat, especially without enchantment of some sort. Most bounty hunters were good trackers and fighters, but only the best of the best could tie knots like that.

"What? Nothing pithy to say?" Alafarr chuckled. The Mage Defender was riding a barrel of beer side-saddle directly across from Tyvian. Her cheeks were red from the icy gusts of wind coming across the water, which only made her smile look all the more cheery.

Tyvian ignored the Defender, looking instead at

Artus. "I thought I told you to run, not reveal my position."

Artus, who had been quiet since his capture, scowled. "You set me up, Reldamar! You hung me out to dry! They was chasing me, and you were gonna leave me!"

Alafarr laughed. "Oooo . . . he's mad at you, Reldamar."

Tyvian sighed. "Yes, Artus is quite unused to the comings and goings of criminal enterprise. He, apparently, was raised with some perverted sense of fair play. His mother's fault, I shouldn't wonder."

"Why you son of a . . . I'll kill you!" Artus struggled against his bonds, squirming like an angry snake as he tried to head-butt, bite, and ram into the smuggler. Jaevis grabbed a handful of the boy's shirt and pulled him off.

Alafarr shook her head. "Reduced to baiting fourteen-year-olds, are we?"

Tyvian shrugged. "Say, Alafarr, how is it that Jaevis here comes to be working with you? I thought Defenders did all their manhunting in-house, so to speak."

Alafarr shot Jaevis a glance, but the bounty hunter was still peering at the riverbank and wasn't paying attention. She glared at Tyvian. "Don't worry yourself about it, Reldamar. You should just wonder what kind of statue a Saldorian court is going to make you into and for how long."

Tyvian nodded—it was a good question. "I hope a

fountainhead. You know—something pretty, but not too gaudy."

"I'll see to it they make you a birdbath, so animals will shit on your head for years on end," Alafarr snarled.

"What are you talking about?" Artus asked. "What do you mean 'birdbath'?"

"Saldor is a civilized country, Artus," Tyvian said, "We don't whip or maim or clap criminals in irons. The guilty are made to contribute to society in the form of stone statuary by way of a semipermanent Dweomeric alteration ritual. For us, that means we will be transformed into stone benches or flagstones or something and left as an attractive piece of public artwork in some penitentiary garden for however long as we are sentenced to 'serve,' all the while being left alone with our thoughts."

Artus turned white. "How . . . how long?"

"For being an accomplice to Tyvian Reldamar," Alafarr stated, "you are looking at a minimum five years, barring any association or collusion with the several murders he's committed."

Tyvian nodded. "More than enough time for you to either go completely insane or become a perfect citizen thereafter. I must warn you, though, that the 'insane' bit is far more common."

Artus's mouth opened and closed for a few moments. "But . . . but . . . I'm only a kid! You can't do that to me! I don't want anything to do with this guy!"

he sputtered, pointing at Reldamar. "He didn't tell me what we was doing! I didn't kill nobody! He was just going to pay me ten marks—only *ten*!"

Alafarr nodded. "I understand, boy—you'll have an opportunity to plead your case. If you serve as a witness against Reldamar, it could go well for you."

Artus was still pale as a sheet. "Oh, oh thank you, Magus! I'm sorry—I really am."

Tyvian smiled quietly and caught them boy's gaze. "And now tell me, Artus, who is hanging whom out to dry?"

Alafarr grinned. "Looks like he's catching on to the 'comings and goings of criminal enterprise' after all, isn't he?"

Tyvian looked out at the river. It was dark and wide, and though it was too warm for large chunks of ice to form in its waters, he knew it was cold enough to kill a man before he got to shore. The scenery on the bank consisted of isolated stands of bare trees and firs, as well as an occasional mill, ruined old watchtower, or ferryman's boathouse. Judging by their speed, he estimated they would be in Galaspin in less than two days, and every hour put Freegate farther and farther away. He wanted to swear, to jump up and down in rage, but there was little point. His only plan for escape involved some of the equipment he had left aboard the spirit engine and some spontaneous mishap that would delay their progress southward. Neither of them, he knew, were likely to happen.

It was just at that moment that there was a whistle

of air and the boatman cried out just before pitching overboard.

Alafarr stood so suddenly she almost fell overboard herself. "Kroth's teeth! What the hell . . ."

"Silence!" Jaevis suddenly barked, leaping to his feet with much more grace than the Defender had, crossbow at his shoulder. "Get down!"

Alafarr crouched, muttering an abjuration under her breath that Tyvian couldn't quite follow, save that it was channeling the Lumen. Over this, Tyvian could hear a rhythmic whirring coming from the riverbank. Rolling himself over to get a good look in that direction, both he and Jaevis searched for the source of the noise, whatever it was.

The whirring grew higher and higher in pitch until, suddenly, a monstrous golden-furred head and torso appeared over the riverbank and released a long strap. Jaevis threw himself to the deck, but the sling-stone wasn't targeted at him. White sparks flashed a foot from Alafarr's head as the projectile smashed against her magical guard. Even unharmed, the shock of it was enough to make her fall backward.

Tyvian grinned. So *that* was how Hool was catching those birds . . .

Jaevis lined up his crossbow for a shot, but Hool had already vanished from sight, and the whirring started again. The bounty hunter swore in Illini.

Meanwhile, the horses, who had only recently accepted the presence of the gnoll-reeking Tyvian and Artus, began to panic at the nearness of the real thing.

Their nostrils flared and they yanked at their bridles, which were looped around a rail at the center of the barge. Alafarr stood up, putting a hand on the reins of her own horse and yelling, "Jaevis! Control your horse!"

"Silence!" Jaevis roared over the scream of his own steed and Alafarr's yelling. "I can no hear sling!"

Another sling-stone caught Jaevis in the hand, sending his crossbow skittering onto the deck and under the horses' hooves. The bounty hunter swore and fell to his knees in an attempt to recover it.

Tyvian saw his window of opportunity. Throwing himself on his back at Alafarr's feet, he kicked the Defender in the stomach with both legs. The force was enough for Alafarr to stumble backward and fall overboard, though she managed to catch the rope-railing that ran along the gunwales before vanishing completely into the river.

Tyvian stood up just as Jaevis got his crossbow back. The bounty hunter lost no time in pointing it directly at him and firing, but a sudden buck of a horse fouled his aim and the bolt slammed into the floor of the barge with a loud crack.

Hool let loose again with the sling, but this time Jaevis dove clear and the projectile put a bloody hole in the rump of Kuvyos, who screamed in pain and tore loose from her bonds. Jaevis flailed for the animal's reins, yelling, "*Kuvyos, eirhus!*"

Tyvian dropped to the floor by Artus, whose eyes were wide with a mix of terror and fascination. "Artus! Pull the quarrel—cut me loose!"

Artus scooted next to the smuggler. "No, you cut *me* loose!"

Tyvian glanced over his shoulder at Jaevis, who was still struggling with his horse. From the corner of his eye he could see a red-faced Myreon Alafarr slowly climbing back aboard. "There is no time to argue!"

"So don't! Cut *me* loose!"

"Dammit, child! Between the two of us, who do you think has a better chance of outfighting an angry bounty hunter?" Tyvian snapped.

Artus scowled, and then turned around to work the quarrel free with his bound hands. It came loose with a popping noise, and it was accompanied by the *blub-blub* of river water that began to seep through the hole in the bottom of the barge. It was a slow leak, so Tyvian was unconcerned—they would either both be dead or free long before the barge actually sank.

Alafarr was halfway into the boat, lips blue and chattering from the water. "Reldamar, you son of a bi—"

Tyvian kicked her in the face, putting her back over the side, but both of the mage's hands still clenched the rope railing.

Tyvian's own hands were cut free and he sprung up just as Jaevis had subdued Kuvyos. The bounty hunter glared at the smuggler with his coal-black eyes and drew a slender throwing knife. His arm cocked back to throw and, for the second time, a sling-stone struck him, this time in the side. It caused Jaevis to buckle over in pain, and bought Tyvian another several seconds. "I'm going to have to buy that gnoll dinner some-time," he muttered to himself, taking the quarrel from Artus and sawing his ankle-bonds loose enough to shake them off.

"What about me?" Artus asked as Tyvian rifled through Alafarr's saddlebags.

Tyvian pointed at the Mage Defender, who was, again, trying to climb in the boat. "Keep kicking her over the side!"

"But she's a *lady*!"

"DO IT!"

Jaevis, keeping low, moved to the other side of the barge, where he would be shielded from sling-stones by the two horses. He drew a pair of short curved blades and stalked toward Tyvian. In another second or two, Tyvian knew he'd be in easy lunging distance, and then, well, then his throat was as good as cut.

He upended the saddlebags, sending scrolls, a variety of potions, a change purse, and a heap of odds and ends skittering across the wet deck. Scanning the pile, he noticed several of his own items—the very ones he had left on the spirit engine. One, in particular, caught his eye; it was a simple hand-sized leather-wrapped cylinder, shaped to fit in his palm perfectly and capped with a crystal sphere of excellent clarity. It was called a "trigger"—a small enchanted object that conjured something out of mageglass.

Tyvian snatched it up and leapt back just as Jae-vis's first cuts passed through where his face had been. Smoothly dropping into en garde position, Tyvian extended his right hand with the crystal end of the handle pointing at Jaevis. The bounty hunter looked at him suspiciously. "What is that?" he grunted.

Tyvian grinned. "My sword." He then spoke, in perfect Akrallian, *"Bonne chance!"*

A rapier of pure, translucent mageglass formed around Tyvian's hand, complete with cross guard, basket-hilt, and crystalline pommel. True to its name, it had always brought him luck. Tyvian executed a brief salute and faced Jaevis across three paces of deck.

His back to the water, Tyvian elected to advance, thrusting at the bounty hunter with some exploratory attacks. Rather than parry, Jaevis retreated, his twinned blades weaving a sinuous dance in front of him. Tyvian had heard of the style—Salasi, it was called. It specialized in feinting attacks and soft defensive moves, but that was about all he knew. Rather than risk trouble, Tyvian decided to use Maldraith to counter, despite the style's rather boring focus on technical footwork and a balanced offense.

Jaevis circled left, placing each foot carefully among the coiled lines and discarded equipment strewn across the barge's deck. Tyvian pivoted to match, knowing that the bounty hunter was trying to get under the rapier's longer reach with his shorter blades. Tyvian kept up the pressure, thrusting and slashing in quick, controlled bursts, but didn't lunge or advance. At the moment it was *he* at the center of the barge and Jaevis who was circling along the outer edge, and he had no interest in giving up that advantage. His simple attacks, though, found no target behind Jaevis's defense. Tyvian knew he would either have to execute a much more forceful attack or expect their duel to last until the barge sank to the bottom.

He flashed a quick cut at Jaevis's face, but the bounty hunter ducked the attack and countered with a flurry of fast slashes that forced Tyvian to retreat two paces, sparks flying from Chance's blade as he parried. "My, my, my," Tyvian scolded, "you'll dull those little cleavers fighting like that against mageglass."

Jaevis whirled in for another barrage, but this time Tyvian sidestepped, parrying each blow again. "No, no! You've got it all wrong, Hacklar—you're really not very good at this, are you?"

Jaevis's black eyes bored into Tyvian. "Silence."

Tyvian smiled. *Vulnerable to taunts, are we? Well, now . . .* "Orders?" he chuckled. "You must be confusing me with your horse."

This barb earned Tyvian a lunge from the bounty hunter, who brought both his blades upward in an arc that would have surely gutted the smuggler from groin to breast if he hadn't retreated in the nick of time. Tyvian didn't have to look down to know the attack had been close enough to cut open the front of his fur vest. There was no doubt about it—Jaevis was *good*. Too good to keep dueling with, certainly. With more room and more time, well, Tyvian was fairly confident Jaevis's temper would prove too much of a disadvantage. Stuck on a sinking barge on a freezing river wasn't the ideal circumstance.

Jaevis attacked again, driving Tyvian back with a flurry of slashes and short thrusts. Tyvian found himself in ankle-deep water so cold he gasped—he had been driven to the end of the barge, which was sinking. Jaevis stood between him and escape, and the Trell boxed him in on the other three sides. The bounty hunter, his blades spread wide, nodded solemnly to Tyvian. "I kill you now."

Tyvian looked at Jaevis, arms out to the sides, and knew the attack that was to come. Jaevis would trap Chance with both weapons and run under Tyvian's guard. In close, the bounty hunter's shorter weapons would make short work of him, and Tyvian had no knife and nowhere to retreat in order to save himself. In terms of fencing, the only technical trick that might save him would be a double disengage from both blades, evading their attempts to bind Chance. One disengage against a talented opponent was hard enough to manage, but two against Jaevis would be impossible. Tyvian could keep his blade free from one of them, but not both, and any way he looked at it the end result was him getting gutted and tossed into the river.

So, Tyvian did the only thing he could think of: just as Jaevis began his charge, Tyvian threw Chance into the bounty hunter's exposed stomach with a flick of his wrist. While an ordinary rapier thrown with such little force would have simply bounced off the leather jerkin Jaevis wore, mageglass was different. Unyielding, nearly weightless, and razor sharp, Tyvian's flick was all it took to cut through the bounty hunter's crude armor like simple linen. Chance didn't sink deeply into Jaevis, but enough to cause him to stop short in shock and pain.

Tyvian took a half step forward and kicked Chance in the pommel, driving it hilt-deep through Jaevis and pushing the blade out his back. The bounty hunter, face frozen in a mask of agony, fell to his knees, dropping his weapons. Tyvian grabbed a fistful of the Illini's tangled hair and threw him onto the sinking bow of the barge. Jaevis tried to get up, but Tyvian put a foot on his neck and ripped Chance from his belly. The bounty hunter's eyes rolled back in his head.

Noting the religious talismans on Jaevis's person, Tyvian hissed, "Give my regards to Hann," and kicked him overboard.

Jaevis tumbled into the frozen water and sank beneath the currents of the Trell.

"Reldamar!" Artus shouted.

Tyvian spun to see Artus in a halfhearted wrestling match between his still-bound self and a mostly frozen Myreon Alafarr. Chance in hand, Tyvian approached the pair, ready to run Alafarr through and have done with it. As the thought occurred to him, though, the iron ring gave his finger such a wrenching squeeze that he had to drop his sword. "Dammit!" he swore, clutching his wrist.

Alafarr had a hand on Artus's face and was halfway in the barge, her now-blue lips drawn into a grimace of determination. Artus bit her in the fingers, but they were clearly too numb to feel it. With his mouth full of the Defender's digits, Artus yelled a muffled, "Hurry up!"

Tyvian frowned at the ring, which pulsed quietly on his hand in warning, and then sighed. "Very well, have it your way."

Grabbing Alafarr by the hood of her sodden robes, Tyvian heaved the Mage Defender into the barge. Recovering Chance, he placed it at Alafarr's throat. "Congratulations."

Alafarr's teeth chattered as she spoke, and she wrapped her arms around her shoulders in a pathetic attempt to get warm. "F-F-For wh-what?"

Tyvian smiled. "In a fit of uncharacteristic mercy, I have decided to take you prisoner. This is your lucky day." He looked at Artus, who was trying to manipulate one of Jaevis's short blades to cut his bonds. "Artus, stop wasting time and get those silly ropes off. You need to pole us to shore before we sink."

Alafarr, like all good Defenders, had a pair of casterlocks in with her things. Designed as a way to both restrain wizards and to keep them from casting spells, they were a number of compartments in a single iron cylinder, arranged to immobilize every finger on both hands. The result was that a person in casterlocks looked an awful lot like they had their hands stuffed into a kind of cast-iron muff. Not being a wizard himself, Tyvian had never worn a pair, but he understood them to be quite uncomfortable. The look on Alafarr's face after he had clamped them over her hands was enough to confirm that rumor.

Beyond the casterlocks, Alafarr and Jaevis's saddlebags contained a variety of other useful goods. Besides some hearthcider, some more hearthstones, and a variety of Tyvian's things, there was a sizable amount of silver, the seekwand, and a copy of *Marcom's Abridged Compendium of Dweomeric Sorcery*. The amount of money these items could fetch at market would more than finance their expenses to Freegate, and the silver was enough to make one innkeeper look the other way when they brought a gnoll into his riverside establishment.

They were in a large room on the first floor of said inn, complete with its own fireplace and an array of comfortable if crudely upholstered furniture. Tyvian sighed and put his feet up before the fire. He had done away with his dirty leathers in exchange for various articles of his clothing Alafarr had been dragging around. They included a fine shirt of lamb's wool, heavy green breeches, and a pair of suede, knee-high riding boots. When coupled with the beaver-pelt cloak he had purchased from a wandering merchant, he looked almost respectable. "If these are the rewards for capturing Defenders, I will make a point to do so more often."

Artus was in the process of devouring a loaf of bread, and spoke with his mouth full to Alafarr. "Why'd you have his stuff?"

The Mage Defender was staring at the fire, casterlocked hands hanging between her knees. Her teeth still chattered as she spoke. "None of your business."

"Now Alafarr, no reason to be morose," Tyvian scolded. "The reason, Artus, is that personal items are how a seekwand works. You attune the wand to the item that belonged to the person in question, and then it leads you to that person, or alternately, you attune it to the owner and it leads you to their things. The only thing I'm surprised at is the sheer amount of my things Alafarr had with her. Really, Myreon, I appreciate your delivering them, but I can't imagine doing so was strictly practical."

Alafarr sighed deeply. "The Law of Possession was against me. I needed more things to maintain the link, given your head start. It was already so weak by the time we found you that the wand could barely tell you apart from the other things you owned."

Artus blinked. "Law of Possession?"

"It is one of the basic sorcerous axioms upon which a great many auguries are founded, Artus," Tyvian said, leaning back in the chair. "Essentially, the act of ownership imparts a small amount of yourself into the item you own. The trouble is that it isn't permanent. If I own a hat, for instance, and I give it to you, it will still be 'mine' for a while, but eventually it will lose all trace of me and be replaced by you. Since my things were in Alafarr's possession for a number of days, they were beginning to take on her signature, weakening the seekwand's bond. I just didn't realize taking more of one's things delayed that process. It makes sense,

I suppose, but I hadn't considered it." He shrugged. "Worked out well for me, at any rate."

From the shadowy back corner of the room, Hool rumbled from where she had curled up on the floor. "No more magic talk!"

Alafarr shot the gnoll a withering glare. "Your taste in company is eroding, Reldamar. You always associated with scum, but at least it was human scum."

Hool's lip curled up, revealing a row of inch-long teeth.

"You are hardly one to criticize another's company, Myreon. The late Hacklar Jaevis's hygiene was in no way superior to Hool's, here. Furthermore, the man had the personality of a tree stump and would have only been interesting company if, like a tree stump, he were to have birds nesting on his person."

Alafarr looked at Tyvian's grinning face with a somber frown, and then looked back at the fire again. "What are you going to do with me?"

Artus stuffed the last of the crust down his throat and sat up straighter. "Yeah! What do we do when the other Defenders come looking for her?"

Tyvian cocked an eyebrow. "Other Defenders?" He nodded to Alafarr. "Should you tell him, or shall I?"

Alafarr shook her head. "I don't know what you're talking about."

Smiling, Tyvian leaned forward. "Let me jog your memory, then—there *are* no other Defenders."

Hool's ears stood up. "You cannot know that. They could be setting a trap."

Alafarr said nothing, but only kept looking at the fire.

Tyvian kept at her. "Oh no—I know there are no others coming, because I know you, Alafarr, and I know the Defenders. You've been chasing me for some years now, and I've never known you to willingly traipse about the countryside with naught but a dirty Illini bounty hunter. When you raided my safe house in Akral, you had twenty men. When you attempted to abduct me in Ihyn, you had half the city watch with you. On the spirit engine from Galaspin you brought at least five plus yourself. No, if you were out here with just Jaevis, that tells me you've been cut off. You're Magus Errant."

Alafarr's eyes darted to Tyvian and then went back to the fire. "I'll be missed. They'll send somebody."

Grinning, Tyvian shook his head slowly from side to side. "No, they won't. They don't *know* you are missing, you see. Magi Errant, as you know, are quite autonomous. They aren't required to report back more than once a fortnight—even longer if they don't have a sending stone, like you don't. Now, let's see—we captured you yesterday morning, so if my estimates of how long you've been after us are correct, we have at least five days before anyone will notice your absence."

Alafarr's face sank into a scowl. "By then we'll be in Freegate."

Tyvian nodded. "And beyond your order's jurisdiction."

"Unless we pay the proper bribes."

"Bribes? My dear Myreon, who is going to pay that kind of money for little old me? Saldor has already sunk wagonloads of marks into your little operations. The fact that you were reduced to hiring Jaevis is proof that they've given up any kind of concentrated efforts to apprehend me—they can't afford it anymore."

Alafarr managed a fake-looking smile. "Are you an accountant now?"

"Far be it from me to say I'm not worth it. I happen to think I am a very dangerous man who needs capturing. I must admit, though, that while I might be Lord of Sorcerous Smugglers, I'm not very high on the list of general priorities for the Defenders or the Arcanostrum of Saldor, given the political climate. The Mad Prince Sahand still rules Dellor in the north, the Kalsaari Empire is growing more threatening along the Illini and Rhondian borders, and then there's the League—"

"The League doesn't exist!" Alafarr snapped.

"Yes it *does*, and don't change the subject," Tyvian snapped back. "My point is that you, Myreon Alafarr, are the last Defender on my case. There will be no reinforcements, because neither I *nor* you rate them. Maybe next year they'll wiggle out a little piece of the budget to look for you, but not until then."

Artus raised his hand. Both Alafarr and Tyvian stared at him until, finally, the smuggler said, "Yes, Artus?"

"Okay, so what do we do with Alafarr *until* then?"

"I say we kill her," Hool said.

Tyvian felt the ring pulse with heat at this statement and he jumped in his chair. "Dammit, no! We can't kill her."

Hool's ears went back. "Why?"

"Well . . . we can't have her body found. It will raise suspicions."

Hool nodded. "I will eat her."

This caused Alafarr to sit up straight. "I . . . I beg your pardon?"

Tyvian blinked. "I appreciate the offer, Hool, but you don't have to eat her."

"Good," Hool stated, but did not elaborate.

Tyvian didn't pry. "Let's focus on getting to Freegate first, then we can decide what to do with Alafarr there."

Artus raised his hand again. "The innkeeper says there's a barge heading north on the river tomorrow. We could buy passage and make it to Freegate in four days."

"No!" Hool snapped. "I will not go on the water."

Tyvian rolled his eyes. "Of all the silly . . . Hool, you *have* to go on the water."

"No."

"Yes."

Hool's ears pressed flat against her skull. "No."

Tyvian grimaced. "Hool?"

"What?"

"You want me to help find your pups?"

"Yes."

"Then you'll get on the bloody barge!" Tyvian pounded the armrest of his chair.

Hool considered this for a moment and then nodded. "I will go on the water, but I will not get wet." She then turned herself around in a circle and buried her head into her fur.

Tyvian sighed and turned back to the fire. He found Alafarr looking at him. "How did you ever manage pick up a pet gnoll?" she asked him.

"First, she is no one's pet, and second, I'm just lucky, I guess." Tyvian stood up and spoke to Artus. "I'm to bed—you keep watch on our prisoner. If she does anything funny, tell Hool to eat her."

Tyvian retired to the large bed at the center of the room and was quickly asleep. His steady breathing was drowned out by the rumbling drone of Hool's snoring and the crackle of the fire. Artus came to sit in the chair Tyvian had occupied and nodded politely to the morose Defender.

"Sorry about this," he said.

Alafarr blinked at the boy, surprised by the genuineness of the sentiment. "Thank you. You must understand, though, that when I escape—"

Artus held up his hand. "I wouldn't try it."

Alafarr managed a half smile. "I assure you—I am quite well-trained."

Artus cast a careful glance over his shoulder and then leaned in to whisper in the Defender's ear. "Look, I shouldn't be telling you, but I just want to let you know that Hool over there ain't really sleeping. She looks it, but she ain't. You so much as stand to use the pot without asking and she'll have you skinned and spitted 'fore you can say 'Saint's praise.'"

Alafarr peered toward the hulking mass of fur and muscle slumbering in the corner. "Thank you for the warning."

Artus nodded. "I'm not such a bad sort. A guy's gotta make a living, though, you know?"

"Reldamar isn't the best way to do that."

The boy nodded at this. "Yeah, well, I dunno. He's a jerk sometimes, but I get the feeling I could learn a thing or two watching him. You could, too."

Alafarr scowled. "I do not learn from criminals."

"Might be why they keep escaping, then, ain't it?" Artus smirked.

Alafarr noted the style of insult. "You *have* been learning."

The boy beamed at that, and produced a length of rough rope from a satchel on the floor. "Shut it now, if you please. I gotta tie you to this chair and give you a gag. Again, no hard feelings?"

CHAPTER 9

IN THE FREE CITY

The Independent City-State of Freegate lay like a loose field of mismatched wreckage bunched against one side of a stone bowl. Half of the city lay at the bottom of a steep valley, surrounded on all sides by the imposing gray cliffs of the Dragonspine and the ancient, empty ramparts the long-dead Warlock Kings had carved into those cliffs. The other half had been built almost vertically up one side of the valley in a precarious series of terraced buildings, staircase avenues, and winding ramps. A low and permanent cloud of soot and dust hovered over the irregular steeples, minarets, towers, and artifactory stacks of the lower districts, while the Cliff District—as the vertical portion of Freegate was known—mired its way through the poisonous layer of fumes until, at its heights, it peeked over the clouds and glimpsed blue sky and snowcapped mountains.

The Freegate Road and the spirit-engine tracks to Galaspin both speared the irregular mass of Freegate's lower half in the same place, terminating at the western edge of the city proper, in the midst of a sea of ramshackle tents, huts, pavilions, and other temporary dwellings that formed the Western Outskirts. The red-tiled roof of the Freegate Spiritberth marked the start of the city's Grand Avenue, which cut a swath between numerous guild-owned and operated boroughs—the Woodcarver's District, the Mason's District, Cobbler Hill, Tailor Town, and so on—until reaching the vast, mile-wide expanse of the Beggar's Market at the heart of the city. There, housed beneath a huge dome of green copper, the Municipal Trading House squatted like an obese spider at the center of an overloaded web, the seat of Freegate's Lord Mayor and Municipal Council.

The Beggar's Market and its attendant Trading House was only the largest of innumerable other markets and bazaars that filled Freegate, however. A city wedged between the Alliance to the southwest, the Principality of Dellor to the north, and the Twin Kingdoms to the northeast, commerce was the focus and purpose for its existence. As Tyvian led Artus, Hool, and a hooded and gagged Alafarr through the throngs of merchants, peddlers, and pickpockets that filled the Grand Avenue, he referred to the larger markets. "The Cloth Market is to our left, up Barricade Avenue, while the Perfumer's Market and the Glitter Market are to our right, past the Holy District and Brewer Town, respectively. We are headed to a side street off the Stair Market, which is in the heart of the Cliff District."

Artus tugged a reluctant Alafarr past a pair of peddlers hawking discount luck talismans, his eyes scanning the crowd nervously. "I don't know about this—what if somebody asks why we've got a woman tied up and hooded? What do we say?"

Tyvian smiled. "We just say we're going to Corpse Alley to see the Phantom Guild."

Artus's eyes grew even larger. "What's that?"

"The local thieving guild. They run a lucrative trade in kidnapped persons, particularly women." Tyvian caught the baleful eye of Hool and added, "Not that I know from personal experience, of course. Hendrieux is a member there and spoke about it at exhaustive length."

Hool snorted loudly at this, which caused a number of passersby to back up even farther than the two-yard bubble the crowd was naturally maintaining around her person. The gnoll had her ears back and her hackles up ever since they reached the city limits, but hadn't spoken except to repeat the words "I don't like this place" and "Everybody here smells bad" at regular intervals. She did so again at Tyvian's mention of the Phantom Guild, but this time added the adverb "really" to each sentiment.

Tyvian shrugged. "The wells here are privately owned, so clean water and bathing are at a premium. The average Freegater spends most of their water budget to be able to drink and live. Being clean is not a priority."

"That's stupid," Hool concluded.

Artus frowned. "Hey, you don't smell like a bunch of flowers yourself, you know."

One of Hool's ears swiveled toward Artus. "Not the bathing part. The part where these stupid people pay for water. Nobody *owns* water."

Tyvian led the party off of Grand Avenue when it reached the Beggar's Market and steered them onto Main Street, which headed southeast toward the cliffs. Main Street was considerably narrower and all uphill, but that didn't mean there were fewer people there. Without Hool to break the press of the crowd in front of them, it was likely they would have been forced back into Beggar's like so many leaves caught in a stream.

"Why are there so many people here?" Artus asked, guiding Myreon over a drunk passed out in the gutter. "I didn't think Freegate was this big."

"It isn't. Two out of three people in Freegate are visitors. Why there are so many visitors here *now* is somewhat odd, I admit. Probably a lot of holdovers from the Hearth Festival, or perhaps Trell's Pass has been snowed in on the Northron side early this year and most people are just waiting for a thaw. In any case, get used to it." Smiling at his own narration, Tyvian casually picked an apple from a passing cart without the carter's knowledge, but then yelped suddenly and dropped it in order to cradle his spasming hand. "Dammit all!"

Artus politely ignored the episode, but Hool did not. "What is wrong with your hand?"

Tyvian heaved a heavy breath and worked his fingers. "Nothing."

"You are a liar."

"Mind your business, gnoll," Tyvian snarled.

Hool went back to scaring locals out of their way and conversation stopped. Tyvian navigated his three charges up through the winding alleys and steep avenues of Freegate without comment, ignoring the ceaseless, oceanic roar of the crowds, to be left with his own thoughts.

The journey from where they captured Alafarr to Freegate had taken four days, just as predicted. The barge crew had been hesitant to take a gnoll and a gagged prisoner aboard, but Tyvian paid extra and, to her credit, Hool caused no trouble. That she was uncomfortable on a boat was clear—she insisted on sitting at its exact center and could not be persuaded to move. Tyvian also noted that she only looked at the deck or straight up at the sky and wouldn't entertain conversations regarding the depth, breadth, or temperature of the river. Still, he had seen many humans act less rationally toward their fears than the gnoll, and he supposed he owed her some degree of tolerance, as she had saved him from the Defenders twice now. He had left her in peace.

Artus, however, was another matter. Tyvian knew the boy was becoming attached to him for reasons that were not entirely clear. Granted, he was well aware of the impressive figure he cut and knew how his clever wit and resourcefulness might encourage a certain amount of awe in a young teenage boy, but he had made a *point* to antagonize and insult Artus at every convenient opportunity. He knew these insults had their effects on the lad—after he used Artus as a decoy in an attempt to confuse Alafarr's seekwand, the boy had been irate. The trouble was, the very next morning Artus had *apologized* for being angry. He'd said, "I understand what you were doing, and it was a pretty smart plan and all, so I guess I'm sorry I was cross." Tyvian had informed him that he *ought* to be sorry, and that he was a pretty dull lad in situations pertaining to life-and-death. Artus had looked annoyed at this but didn't comment.

At any other point in his life, Tyvian might have secretly abandoned the boy while he slept without a second thought. Hool's presence, though, complicated that considerably. Somehow, the gnoll had gotten it into her head that the three of them were some kind of transitory family unit, with her as mother, Artus as child, and Tyvian himself as father. He was relatively certain that the beast would become quite upset if he had introduced the "abandon Artus" plan and, due to Hool's unusually acute senses and incredible tracking ability, Tyvian seriously doubted he could escape without her permission.

Then, of course, there was the infernal ring. Tyvian had come to understand that it, much like Hool, attached some level of significance to Artus. He imagined this was somehow integral to the sorcery Eddereon had used to attach it to his body. This would explain the note Eddereon had written for the boy, as well as the device's rather extreme reaction to his attempts to kill Artus during their brief knife-fight, as well as during his attempt to abandon Artus to the tender mercies of Hool in the Wandering Fountain, *and* to his efforts to disguise Artus as himself four days ago, though that instance had been less intense. Nevertheless, because of the ring, Tyvian was uncertain he was going to be rid of Artus easily.

To be fair, Artus had been useful during the trip, as Tyvian had hoped he would be. The boy had the resilient constitution of a young person who spent a great deal of time working with his hands, was gullible enough to be easily manipulated, and was savvy enough to be trusted with basic tasks without failing utterly. He could pick a pocket, pitch a tent, and watch a prisoner—all tasks Tyvian would have been hard-pressed to do on his own without assistance from Hool, which seemed unwise. Still, the boy was young, irritating, and in no way his responsibility. If Eddereon had hoped to give the young vagabond a father figure in the form of Tyvian Reldamar, he had sorely misinterpreted the smuggler's temperament. He had every intention of paying the lad his ten marks and setting him on the streets of Freegate with his conscience clear. After all, *he* had learned to stop relying on adults for guidance long before *his* fourteenth birthday, and Artus would be fine on his own, no matter what an imperious gnoll or a self-righteous ring thought.

The Stair Market was aptly named. Running for nearly a mile from bottom to top, it was a hundred-yard-wide terraced market of granite stairs that ran for nearly the entire length of the Cliff District, beginning in the haze of the city's pollution layer and reaching all the way up to the crest, where the elite of the city maintained impressive homes along the shores of Dain's Lake—an ancient and artificial reservoir that rested in a basin atop the southern edge of the valley. Thanks to the lake being at such a high elevation, a narrow stream fed by its waters cascaded from broad stair to broad stair at a rapid rate down the center of the Stair Market and ended in a large fountain at its base. As the water was drawn from the lake, it was said to be safe to drink. This was, of course, discounting the fact that most local merchants used it as a dumping ground for the waste they did not wish to carry off, permitting the stream's rapid speed to carry the offending material off to the bottom. This practice meant drinking the water was risky at best, particularly at lower altitudes, and also explained why the fountain at the base was known as the "Chamber Pot."

By the time Tyvian and his companions reached the Stair Market, the crowds had abated somewhat.

It was late afternoon and the sky was gray with rain clouds. Those peddlers and pushcart merchants who had elected to brave the rain were erecting colorful oil-cloth awnings over their carts or had drawn out umbrellas, ready to be opened. Uncharacteristically, they did not call out to Tyvian and company as they passed, though whether it was due to the gnoll glowering at them or the hooded, casterlocked woman they had in tow was unclear. In any event, Tyvian appreciated the relative quiet.

Artus, who had to guide Alafarr up every stair, was taking up the rear of the group when he called to Tyvian, "Watchmen, Reldamar!"

Tyvian saw them then—a squadron of four city watchmen clad in iron-studded leathers and bearing arm-length cudgels, standing in a circle on the front steps of a gambling house. One of them was watching them casually as the other three were engaged in conversation. Tyvian smiled and nodded to him. He nodded politely back and returned his attention to his compatriots.

Tyvian looked at Artus. "They aren't interested in us."

"Not even . . ." Artus jerked a thumb at their prisoner.

"The enforcement of laws in Freegate is spectacularly lax, Artus. Those men have probably been bribed to beat some unfortunate fellow somebody suspects of cheating at dice, and have evidently been paid well enough to completely disregard a gnoll and a blindfolded wizard being led through the city streets. Even if they were interested, for the cost of a mark per man we would be given a rather lackadaisical warning to 'behave' and they'd go their way."

Artus shook his head at this, a mix of disbelief and amazement on his face. "Wow."

Tyvian smiled and shrugged. "That's why I love this city. Come, now—we're almost there."

"Where are we going?"

"To visit a warlock and thaumaturge of my acquaintance."

"What's a tham . . . thouma . . ." Hool's snout struggled with the word.

"Thaumaturge—thaumaturgy is one of the Low Arts, related to alchemy but more abstract. Thaumaturges distill essences and traffic in materials for sorcerous rituals and such. Boring people, but rather useful contacts to have." Tyvian said, steering them toward the edge of the market.

Hortense's shop had the same cheery green awning and brightly painted sign as the last time Tyvian had been here. The sign depicted a stereotypical wizard's cap with stars and moons and such, which was generally enough information for the primarily illiterate population of Freegate to identify his general specialty. In truth, Hortense was a master of his craft. Nobody Tyvian knew of was a better hand at sussing out the details of odd and rare magecraft.

As they got closer, however, he noted some key differences in the shop's appearance. The broken lock, for instance, as well as the slightly ajar door, the bare shelves, and the thick layer of dust covering the floor, counter, and almost everything else. As he peered inside, Artus looked in over his shoulder. "Is he out of town?"

Tyvian pointed at the forced lock. "Why would he break into his own shop?" He knew the place was likely empty, but decided to be thorough. "Hello?"

Something fell over and broke within the shop, and a scruffy, bearded face popped up over the shop's bare counter. The man had far too many sores on his face to be Hortense, and his fingers were stained purple—a squatter and an ink-thrall. "Eh? Watchawant?"

"Ew!" Artus said, "Is that *him*?"

Tyvian glared at the boy. "Don't be an idiot." He looked at the squatter. "You, idiot, how long have you been staying here?"

The man's unfocused eyes dilated at this, but produced no satisfactory answer. "You got any chicken?"

Tyvian threw a copper at the man. "What happened here?"

The sound of a coin hitting the floorboards cleared some of the squatter's mental haze. "Kidnapped, most like. Phantoms' been paying good gold for magic folk. You know any, you should go down there. Knew a guy that mugged him an alchemist, and he got—"

Tyvian slammed the door and turned away. "Dammit. How could Hortense let himself be carried off in the middle of the night? He had wards and paid his bribes . . ." Something occurred to him, so he opened the door again. "Did they kidnap his daughter, too?"

The squatter was facedown on the counter, fast asleep and muttering to himself, his finger stuffed in an ink pot.

Tyvian walked over and recovered his copper, then left and slammed the door again.

His companions were looking at him, Artus expectant and Hool mildly curious. "C'mon. To our next stop."

Tyvian led them out of the Stair Market and down a narrow alley that twisted and turned to squeeze between buildings in the process of sliding off their foundations. Here the light was blocked by teetering chimneys and sharply angled walls, and the cobblestones listed so sharply to one side that there were points where they needed to walk with a hand against a wall. Finally, just past the alley's most claustrophobic section, it opened into a circular courtyard of blue and white tiles, and at its center stood a bubbling fountain. A sign standing just before the fountain, written in a neat hand, read: Drinks for Patrons Only; All Others One Piece of Silver. A clay cup had been helpfully placed next to the sign.

Past the fountain, on the opposite side of the courtyard, Tyvian saw was a small, blue door with a silver knocker and a knob of crystal. "Wait out here," he said. "I'll be back shortly."

"Good." Hool dropped her things and dunked her head in the fountain.

"Don't you have to pay?" Artus asked, examining the cup.

"Don't be stupid," the gnoll replied.

"For once," Tyvian said, "I agree with Hool."

He opened the door and went inside.

Carlo diCarlo was a Verisi political expatriate, thanks to the public humiliation he had inflicted upon the Baron of Veris fifteen years earlier. Tyvian, at that time only a handful of years older than Artus, had been there to witness the event and still could not recall a time he had laughed so hard at so powerful a person. It was because of Carlo that current Verisi law required all royal garments to be flame resistant and all pigeon owners to be licensed by the state.

Carlo's "office" was a low, domelike room that required Tyvian to duck to enter. It reeked of tooka smoke and was thickly carpeted with a mixture of furs, silks, and gaudy embroidered pillows. Carlo himself sat cross-legged on the largest of these pillows, a smoking pipe on one knee and balancing a simple blasting wand on his other. It had been over two years since Tyvian had seen him, and he noted that the short, wiry Carlo had been replaced with one no taller but considerably fatter, and festooned with a waxed handlebar moustache, to boot. He was wearing an ornate silk robe of Kalsaari style and a crystal eyepiece pinched between the cheekbone and brow of his left eye. He smiled as

Tyvian entered the light, as though just noticing him. Tyvian knew perfectly well the old pirate had seen him coming from the moment he entered the alley that led to his home.

Carlo's smile revealed a pair of gold teeth. "Tyvian Reldamar, my friend! Why ever are you not dead?"

Tyvian pulled up a cushion and sat down. "Is that the word on the street?"

"Just so. Have you come to kill me?"

"Have you given me cause?"

Carlo considered this and then laughed, smiling even more broadly. "Yes, I think I have."

"Please explain," Tyvian said calmly. It was impossible to read whether Carlo was kidding or not—the man's face had no connection whatever to his thoughts, a fact that had frustrated as many interrogators as it had gamblers. Tyvian had spent years studying how Carlo did it, but despite his own considerable skill at masking his expression, he had to concede that Carlo was the master.

"I will, but first—tea!" Carlo clapped his hands, and a barely clad woman with golden hair sauntered into the room with a silver tray and two cups. Tyvian found himself thinking she looked just a *little* bit like Alafarr before shaking himself back to his senses.

He held up his hand. "No thank you."

Carlo laughed again, but this time so violently that he shook his eyepiece loose from its fitting. Tyvian only got a glimpse of the gaping socket behind it before Carlo's lightning-quick fingers replaced the item. "Tyvian, my good friend, I am not going to poison you! You are dead, remember?"

Tyvian snorted. "Not for long. Somebody must have recognized me in the city today. Word will get out. The Phantom Guild will sell the information for pennies to any interested parties."

"Ho, ho! In the Freegate of two months ago, perhaps, but not today. There is too much other business for the rumormongers to bother with you, Tyvian."

Tyvian cocked his head to the side. "What's happened?"

Carlo took his cup of tea and waved the woman with the pot back toward the smuggler. "Drink some tea—there is much to tell, and you are thirsty. Do not worry, Tyvian Reldamar, Carlo diCarlo is still your friend."

CHAPTER 10

A CONVERSATION WITH CARLO

If one were to call Carlo diCarlo a banker, they would simultaneously insult both Carlo and bankers everywhere. Still, the tasks banks undertook were not altogether different than what Carlo offered to his select group of patrons. Both he and banks kept things safe for those who employed them, and both "invested" the assets in their care for the purpose of profit. But there the similarity ended. Banks, according to the one-eyed Verisi, were engaged in an institutionalized con that involved making money off of people who thought they were being done a favor, when all they were *really* gaining was the assurance that the bank would not steal from them—something any decent business wouldn't do anyway. Carlo, on the other hand, asked that you pay your money up front, and the services he provided you in return were commensurate with the scale of that remuneration. The "profits," as it were, served to benefit both Carlo *and* you.

An additional and important difference between Carlo and a bank was the kind of things Carlo kept. He would not keep money for anybody—any coin that passed into his nimble hands was henceforward *his*, no matter what the former owner thought about it. No, Carlo diCarlo kept safe two things: *items* and, more importantly, *information*.

In the first case, it worked something like this: if a person owned a home in Freegate but was leaving town for a while, he would ask Carlo to care for that house in his absence. Carlo would ensure that the house remained free of squatters, unvandalized, and unburgled until such time as the owner returned. However, during that time, Carlo would use the home as he saw fit—he might rent it out to visitors, use it to host parties, or exploit it in a variety of much less savory and semilegal ways. Then, upon the owner's return, Carlo would give the owner a percentage of the profits he made from his use of the house—a sum that could range from a few coppers to a king's ransom, depending on how profitable the house had been for Carlo.

Information worked in much the same way. If a person had a secret they thought might be worth something, they could go to Carlo. Upon accepting knowledge of the secret—which, in itself, was payment up front—Carlo would go out into the seething river of rumors and illicit information that ran through Freegate and see how the information could be used to his advantage. In most cases it became a matter of selling the secret to somebody else, in others it led to other secrets that, themselves, were more profitable than the original, and in some others it could lead to blackmail, conspiracy, or other potentially advantageous criminal behaviors based around secrets. In any event, the person who supplied Carlo with the secret was entitled to a portion of the profits, be they monetary or informational in nature.

Carlo's peculiar business was quite lucrative and his reputation was impeccable, once you accepted that if you left a good coat in his care you would never see the loose change in the pockets again. Furthermore, thanks to the nature of his business, Carlo had his fingers in more pies and his head in more plots and schemes in Freegate than anybody Tyvian knew of. He was a very useful man to know and an even better person to be able to call friend.

So, while Tyvian sat across from Carlo diCarlo on a cushion in the Verisi's smoky office, he took comfort in the fact that whatever he was about to be told, it was going to be both useful and at least more than half true.

Carlo took a sip of tea. "I take it you will be recovering the things left in my care."

Tyvian nodded. "The keys to my flat and a strong-box. I hope they were useful to you."

"Very much so."

"How much do you owe me?"

Carlo produced an abacus and did some quick calculations. "One hundred thirty-five marks, sixteen crowns, and five peers."

Tyvian nodded. "Keep the silver and the coppers—you do good work."

Carlo peered up at Tyvian and smirked. "Your generosity is overwhelming. My stomach thanks you for the singular meal with which you have provided it."

"Given its proportions, I should advise your stomach, for its own good, to consider the meal in question its last for some time." Tyvian permitted himself a small smile. "Have the money delivered to my flat; send it by djinn. Now, you haven't yet told me what has happened—does it by any chance have anything to do with the unseasonable crowds clogging the streets?"

"It does." Carlo nodded, waving to his scantily clad assistant to leave them. "There is a Kalsaari Hanim in town. She's throwing money around like she's allergic to it. Every enterprising boob in the Trell Valley is here trying to nab a piece."

Tyvian frowned, "And every spy in the West is here trying to get a look at her. What the hell is she doing here, though?"

Carlo smiled then, a twinkle in his real eye that Tyvian usually associated with a god-awful amount of trouble. "Exiled, they say."

Tyvian blinked, but wished he could take back the gesture. Carlo was watching his face like a cat watches a bird. "By whom? The Emperor? Her family? The . . ." He lowered his voice to a whisper. ". . . *Nine*?"

"*They*"—Carlo said the word with a kind of sinister weight—"aren't the kind to exile people. If you cross them, you simply vanish. Besides, if you ask me, it is all an act—those queenies are always up to more than it looks like, and this is no different. She isn't here to be spied on, she's here to do the spying."

Tyvian let the information sink in for a minute or two. The Kalsaari Empire rested half a continent away, across thousands of miles of deserts, mountains, and one sea. The primary aggressor in the Illini Wars twenty-seven years ago, it took the combined might of four Western nations to fight them to a standstill. Since the Treaty of Al Maharik, the two sides had barely spoken. Everyone expected the Kalsaaris to invade again, but they hadn't. Trade had resumed eventually, but it was very slow and few Western merchants were permitted to travel beyond the city of Tasis at the edge of the Empire's vast realm, so very little was known of what occurred or what was occurring within their borders. The West, of course, returned the favor, so one could assume the Kalsaaris knew as little about the modern West as the West knew about Kalsaar. That one of their nobility—and from an Imperial House, too—would have taken up residence here, in Freegate, was something of a revolutionary occurrence.

On a personal level, Tyvian had interacted with his

fair share of Kalsaaris in his line of work. Besides the valuable silks, spices, and clockwork that constituted most of the legal trade between the two regions, magical goods were of paramount interest to both sides. The war had proven, of course, that Western magi were far more innovative, talented, and knowledgeable than their Kalsaari counterparts when it came to the High Arts, but the Kalsaaris knew a surprising number of strange and terrifying tricks of the arcane. Kalsaari magecraft was as valuable and rare as it was illegal, including the proscribed arts of both biomancy and necromancy, and their talents with the Low Arts of alchemy, talismancy, and thaumaturgy were clearly superior to those practiced in the West. Considering that he had recently been framed for trafficking in biomancy *and* had even more recently fallen victim to a rather advanced case of talismancy, Tyvian thought the presence of a Kalsaari princess in Freegate was more than a coincidence.

At length, he snorted. "She's probably just here slumming on her father's dime."

Carlo shrugged, "Who knows? The Lord Mayor, of course, is up in arms about the whole situation, and nobody listens to him anyway, especially when the gold keeps flowing from the Hanim's purse. All I know is that my usual contacts have been trying to get some information on this for weeks and have come up with precious little."

Tyvian snorted. "Well, it's none of my concern, in any case. I have unfinished business."

"Hendrieux," Carlo said calmly. It was not a question.

"Have you seen him?" Tyvian asked, trying to keep his voice calm. The thought of Hendrieux's betrayal was enough to boil his stomach.

Carlo grimaced. "Tyvian, Tyvian—you know my policy. I never get involved in vendettas."

"Just tell me if he's in the city."

"Should he come to me and ask me about you, should I return the favor?" Carlo countered, draining his teacup in one quick gulp.

Tyvian licked his lips; conversations with Carlo were usually rife with subtext, and the underlying inferences that could be drawn from that last statement were tantalizing. "He won't come. He thinks I'm dead."

Carlo leaned back on his cushion and closed his one good eye. "Hendrieux is in Freegate."

"That was all I needed to know."

Carlo opened his eye a crack. "That information wasn't free, you know."

Tyvian nodded. "Of course. How much?"

Carlo pointed through the wall behind Tyvian. "Tell me who that tall, willowy beauty in the caster-locks is."

Tyvian sighed. "A Mage Defender of the Balance."

"Which one? A name, please." Carlo yawned. "Tell me more about Hendrieux and I'll consider it." Carlo was hinting at something; Tyvian knew he knew much more than he could let on, but Carlo's evasiveness seemed to suggest that he wasn't comfortable letting him *know* that he knew. That either meant Carlo was involved in something extremely dangerous, or that Carlo was actively plotting against him. Those two options, of course, were not mutually exclusive.

"Oh," Carlo chuckled, "haggling, are we? Forget it—I don't care so much as that."

"Really?" Tyvian said, eyebrows rising, "I have a captive Defender of the Balance—a blonde, at that—and you don't care what her name is? Unlikely."

Carlo pointed at the door. "That's the way out, Tyvian."

Tyvian stood and turned to leave. "You know, you never *did* tell me what you've done to make me want to kill you."

"I was joking." Carlo said, and then shooed Tyvian away like a fly.

Tyvian put his hand on the doorknob and stopped suddenly. *That was it.* He looked over his shoulder. "Allow me to guess—you've been doing a lot more business with Hendrieux lately, haven't you? He's been buying a lot of information."

Carlo shook his head. "Not true."

Tyvian turned back and sat down. He grinned broadly. "Yes he has—why else would you be worried about him asking for me? Hendrieux would have no reason to come to you about me, as I said, so that means he's coming in here all the time for reasons completely unrelated to me, doesn't it?"

Carlo glared at Tyvian but said nothing. To eavesdroppers—and Carlo *always* assumed he had eavesdroppers—it would seem Tyvian were prying information out of the old Verisi. In the private language that Tyvian and Carlo had built up over the years, however, it was tantamount to a thundering yes.

Still, Tyvian knew he had to play it all up. Talking with Carlo was always half real, half elaborate mummer's farce. "Does it have anything to do with the fact that the Phantom Guild is buying practitioners of the Low Arts off any lowlife with a club and a sack?"

Carlo snorted. "As though Freegate has any shortage of lowlifes, clubs, and sacks. The kidnapping trade is what it always is."

Tyvian kept his gaze level—that last meant Carlo wasn't sure himself. Fair enough. "Information, Carlo. Give it to me."

"Why should I? You know my policies—why jeopardize them for a dead man?"

"I'm *not* dead." *I'm in danger, am I?*

Carlo didn't blink as he spoke. "If you start fooling with Hendrieux, you will be soon enough."

"Hendrieux's a sleazy cutthroat and a thug. He doesn't worry me." Tyvian, though, felt a tiny knot of worry nestling itself into his innards. Carlo was being far too direct now; it might be that he actually *was* worried about him.

"It's not Hendrieux you need to . . ." Carlo sighed. "*Kroth's teeth*, boy—I'm not telling you anything else. You'll endanger my reputation."

That meant Carlo was too close to the trouble,

whatever it was, and couldn't even hint at more without some kind of external coercion on his own part. Fortunately, he had just the thing. He jerked a thumb through the door behind him. "You see that gnoll out there? She's after Hendrieux, too. She can track a man over miles of snow-covered country, so she can probably find out if Zazlar's been here—his stink is probably on the curtains or the pillows. Suppose I were to mention to her that you've *seen* Hendrieux and that you might know what Hendrieux has done with what she's after?"

Carlo's crystal eye was fixed on the door, or, rather, the gnoll beyond it. "What is she after, then? Money?"

"Not money, Carlo. Her *children.*"

For the first time in Tyvian's memory, the color drained from Carlo diCarlo's mustachioed face. He swallowed a lump in his throat, which Tyvian granted was a wonderful effect. "This . . . this is extortion."

"How clever of you to identify it."

"You . . . you don't understand, Tyvian." Carlo spoke hurriedly and softly; Tyvian honestly couldn't tell if the man was actually terrified or not. "You haven't seen what gnolls can do. They attack settlements in Veris sometimes—they skin people like rabbits, make them into *capes.*"

"I think she'd get a whole greatcoat out of you, Carlo."

Carlo jumped as though bitten, causing his crystal eye to fall loose. "Ah! She's looking this way!"

"Tell me where Hendrieux is."

Carlo favored the smuggler with a bitter look. "After all I've done for you, this is the thanks I get?"

Tyvian repressed a grin—it had been years since he and his old mentor played this little game, but they had fallen right back into their familiar roles. "Don't bore me with sentimental tripe. *Where is he?*"

Relenting, Carlo sighed. "He's staying in the Blocks, or thereabouts, but keeps moving around. That's all I know."

Tyvian stood up. "Thank you very much, Carlo."

Carlo frowned. "You are a son of a bitch."

"Ah, I see you've met my mother." Tyvian skipped over the cushion to the door. "By the way, just for old times' sake, the Defender's name is Myreon Alafarr."

As the smuggler darted out the door, Carlo called after him, "I *should* have poisoned the bloody tea!"

Outside, Tyvian found Hool squatting in front of Carlo's door, her ears rigid and upright. "What did the man inside say?" she asked.

"That he should have poisoned me. Why do you ask?" Tyvian winked at her, but the gesture was clearly lost on the gnoll.

"Is he your enemy?"

"More like a grouchy uncle. I wouldn't worry—he won't stay angry for long."

Artus had taken off Alafarr's hood and gag and was

letting her drink from the fountain. Tyvian, seeing this, pushed past Hool. "What the hell are you doing?"

Artus's voice squeaked. "She was gonna pass out! We haven't given her a drink since this morning!"

Tyvian cuffed Artus upside the head. "What part of 'never take off her gag' don't you understand?"

Artus's face turned red. "She's still got the caster-thingies on. Plus Hool was watching her."

"And suppose she knows verbal invocations, eh? What happens when she speaks Sumptain's Word of Baffling and runs off?"

Alafarr frowned. Her voice was rough and dry. "Nobody can make that spell work. The only person I know of who has mastered it is . . . your mother. Oh."

Tyvian pointed at the mage. "Stop talking. Hool, put her gag back on."

"You do it," Hool countered, arms crossed.

Tyvian rolled his eyes. "Unbelievable."

Alafarr didn't struggle as the gag and hood were replaced. Artus watched sullenly as Tyvian turned the mage around and pushed her toward the alley that would lead back to the Stair Market. "Where are we going now?" Artus asked, finally, as they kept climbing the Cliff District.

Tyvian sighed. "I am going home. You are going to be paid, and then you are going to get lost."

"But—"

The smuggler held up a hand. "That's enough, boy."

"What about Hool?" Artus asked quietly, eyes downcast.

"The gnoll is welcome to go wherever she pleases. I will help her find Hendrieux, but not until tomorrow. None of this, by the way, has anything to do with you."

"Okay," Artus said, kicking some minuscule mote of debris across the cobblestones. He didn't look up at Tyvian until they had reached his flat.

Tyvian maintained a penthouse apartment at an exclusive address along Top Street. The lower floors of the five-story building were partitioned into deluxe suites that were rented seasonally by noble families from Eretheria and Akral. He could tell by the locked blue shutters and dark front hall that none of the tenants were currently occupying the place, which was ideal, as he had no desire to parade the dirty Artus, monstrous Hool, or captured Alafarr in front of the tender eyes of the naive nobility. Plus, he himself was not dressed to his usual standard.

On the steps of the building Tyvian saw a small black cube that seemed to suck in the ambient light—a messenger djinn, he thought, no doubt sent by Carlo. Messenger djinn were sorcerous entities of pure Dweomeric energy that were used by courier services wealthy enough to employ conjurers. One simply had to insert an addressed letter into the baffling darkness of the floating cubes and they would speed off directly to the addressee. You didn't even need to know the party's location—the person's first and last name would be enough, assuming they weren't working under an alias. While not as adaptable as human couriers and not as fast as sending stones or wraiths, they were reliable, trustworthy, could carry hundreds of pounds, and were virtually impossible to stop or waylay. Here on Top Street, one could easily spot a half dozen of the strange little black cubes cruising around at any given time.

Tyvian announced himself to the entity and it vanished with a pop, leaving in its place a small chest. He popped it open and examined the pile of gold that gleamed from within.

Artus's eyes grew wide. "Wow . . . that's a lot of money!"

Tyvian palmed through the coins, taking an approximate count. "No, it isn't. It is an adequate amount of money."

Artus looked up and down the street, but it was largely empty. "Shouldn't you open that inside?"

"Yes, but that would necessitate taking the two of you inside with me, which isn't going to happen." Tyvian counted out ten marks and slid them into a pouch. "Here you are—ten marks, as agreed." He slapped the money into Artus's hand.

Artus looked at it, and Tyvian watched him screw up his courage. "Look, I was thinking, what if—"

"We were to work together on a more regular basis?" Tyvian said, cutting him off. "Absolutely not. You are a boy, Artus. You are naive, unskilled, annoying, and possessed of a confounding and contradictory moral compass. You and I have no future together."

Tyvian watched Artus's face crumple. "Oh . . . okay."

The ring gave Tyvian a slight jolt, but he ignored it

in order to lift the chest and set it just inside the front door. He turned back to see Hool standing in front of him, her ears back. "You are throwing him away? Why?"

Tyvian took a heavy breath. "I realize this may be difficult for your gnollish mind to grasp, but Artus and I are in no way related. I owe him nothing, and he owes me nothing."

"That's a lie!" Hool barked. "He helps you all the time. You are mean to him, and he still helps you. That means you are a pack. You can't just give him stupid gold and make him go away."

"I can and I will." Tyvian maneuvered Alafarr inside the door and then tried to make himself look taller by stepping up on his front stairs and throwing out his chest to the imposing gnoll.

Hool displayed her teeth and ground out a slight growl that made Tyvian's insides vibrate.

Artus put a hand on Hool's arm. "No, he's right, Hool. He just owed me the money. It's okay."

Hool's ears swiveled forward as she looked at Artus. Then she stepped back from Tyvian, who guessed the discussion regarding Artus wasn't over, only in recess.

"I will wait for you to come out in the morning," Hool said to him. "Then you will tell me where to find the human who has my puppies."

Tyvian nodded at the gnoll, assuming this meant the creature would be curled up on his front doorstep all night long, and secretly hoped she didn't eat any of his neighbors. "Good-bye for now, then."

The smuggler was about to shut the door, but Artus called out to him. "Hey! Thanks . . ."

"For what, exactly?"

"Thanks for saving me from the spirit engine," Artus said quietly, looking at his feet. "You didn't have to do that."

The ring burned like a circle of scalding steam on his finger. Tyvian grimaced, bit his lip, and decided to say one more thing. "Go home, Artus—use that money to go home. If you really do have a family somewhere and they are worthy of the pride you take in them, then that is where you belong."

Artus looked up, and Tyvian noticed his brown eyes were watery with tears. "Yeah," he managed, "yeah, okay."

Tyvian, his mouth set into a firm line, closed the door in the boy's face.

CHAPTER 11

BLASTS FROM CERTAIN PASTS

Exhausted did not adequately describe how Myreon felt. She felt wrung-out, stretched thin, hollow. Reldamar had not laid a single violent finger on her since her capture, but he hadn't exactly been lavish with niceties like water, food, and rest. Were it not for the boy, Artus, and his constant worry over her well-being, she would be worse off, for certain. As it was, she could scarcely climb the stairs to the villain's flat without her knees wobbling.

She did not let them wobble, though. She would not let Reldamar see her as weak.

The hood came off. She was standing in the front hall of a lavishly appointed flat—Akrallian provincial in style, elaborate crown moldings and sunny yellow wallpaper; a vaulted ceiling with a mageglass chandelier. She might have made a sarcastic remark—she wanted to—but her tongue felt thick in her mouth and she was so tired she needed all of her attention to remain upright.

Reldamar had his back to her. She saw his shoulders sag as the door closed behind them both—shut by a serving specter, no doubt. Most of the wealthy homes in Freegate had them to perform most menial tasks. They were very expensive to conjure and bind to a home, but they took up no space and were unfailingly loyal—two qualities in high demand in cramped and corruption-filled Freegate.

Reldamar let out a long, slow breath. "Put her in the guest room." he said.

An invisible presence seized Myreon under each armpit and forcefully steered her through a living room and into a dark bedroom, all of them as richly decorated as the front hall. The force wasn't overwhelmingly strong—she might have struggled with it, if she had the energy—but for now she let herself be piloted into the room and locked inside. There was no feylamp, but instead an old-fashioned oil lantern set upon an end-table. Her hands still entombed in her casterlocks, she had no way to light it; the only illumination came from the single barred window through which filtered the dirty, smog-filtered lamplight of the Freegate streets.

There was a pitcher of water, too, but without any means to pour herself a drink, Myreon was forced to lap at the surface like a dog. Anger at her imprisonment flared, but she kept it bottled up—no outburst of rage was going to get her out of this.

She knew she was on Top Street somewhere, a short walk from the Stair Market. The flat was on the fifth story of the building—the penthouse. The lack of fey-lamp or illumite indicated that the room was warded with Astral sigils, which would keep all the energies—except the Astral—from being usable while inside. So, enchanted objects wouldn't work here. This meant the specters couldn't enter unless the wards were down, and *that* meant the wards would only go down when the door opened.

It wasn't much, but it was something to go on. She sat on the bed. Across from her, mounted on the wall, was a painting of a stately country villa, all ivy-covered stone and carved flarewood, with a narrow tower rising from its heart to pierce a summer sunset. Myreon knew the place.

Glamourvine. The family estate of Lyrelle Reldamar. The sight of the place again sent Myreon's memory reeling.

She had only been a few years old when her mother and most of her family was murdered by bandits out of Galaspin. She spent most of her life raised by her

father, Drython Alafarr, who worked as a longshore-
man and riverboat hand, barely making ends meet.
Each night, she would stare into her father's eyes as her
told her stories, and imagine what her mother looked
like when she had danced.

When Myreon was sixteen and old enough to enter
the Arcanostrum, Drython spent every penny he had
ever saved to bring her to Saldor and support her appli-
cation. When she had been accepted, her father danced
with her in their leaky room tucked under the eaves
of a crosstown inn. She entered the Arcanostrum the
next day.

Her father was murdered a week later. The innkeeper had done it—a dispute over the bill, they said

Myreon remembered standing before his grave,
unable to believe he was dead. His life—so full of
love and joy and honesty—was utterly wiped away.
There was not an acre of land, not a stitch of fabric,
not a scrap of paper that bore his name. As the tears
came, she knew that nobody noticed he was gone
except her.

She was wrong.

Myreon received a summons to attend Lyrelle Reldamar, Archmage and Chair of the Black College, at
Glamourvine the very next day. Terrified and uncomfortable in her worn-down shoes and patched robes,
she went. She stood in a hall of crystal and ancient
stone, surrounded by a kind of opulence her imagina-
tion had never dared theorize as real, and waited for
the most powerful woman in the West to come speak

with her. What would she want? What could she possibly need with her?

When the Archmage appeared, Myreon's anxiety bloomed into full-on terror. Lyrelle was a legend and she had the bearing of one—tall, graceful, her hair falling about her shoulders like molten gold, her midnight gown swallowing the light from the gothic windows. She did not walk—she glided. Myreon remembered mumbling awkwardly and falling to one knee.

Lyrelle Reldamar stood over her and, ever so gently, placed a hand on Myreon's cheek. Myreon looked up to see the Archmage of the Ether smiling down on her. Her voice was warm and firm, like that of someone who doesn't accept excuses. "I am very sorry to hear about your father."

Tears came then. Myreon remembered her face tightening, trying to stop them, and cursing her failure to do so. Lyrelle pulled her into a motherly embrace and held her there, in that ancient hall beneath the hoary old gaze of long-dead Reldamars, until at last Myreon had collected herself.

"I'm sorry," she had said, wiping her hot cheeks. "I'm so sorry, Magus. I'm ready to do what you wish of me."

Lyrelle smiled again and shook her head. "I called you here for this, Myreon—for this moment. I wanted you to know that you were not alone."

Myreon hadn't understood then—indeed, she wasn't certain she understood now—but that moment marked the start of four years of her working as the

Archmage's famulus as she progressed through her initiate studies at the Arcanostrum. They were some of the happiest years of her life. They marked the first time in her life where she could guess what it would have been like to have a mother. Were it not for Lyrelle Reldamar and Glamourvine, Myreon almost certainly would have dropped out of the Arcanostrum before achieving her first mark and entering the apprenticeship.

"And then," Myreon sighed to herself, "I wouldn't have ended up here, the prisoner of her ungrateful, criminal son. The irony."

Fate truly was a cruel prankster.

Somewhere in the flat, beyond the locked door of her room, Myreon heard Tyvian cursing. The sun-kissed memories of Glamourvine faded entirely, overwhelmed by an empty stomach, an exhausted body, and fingers so numb and cramped that she worried whether they would ever cast another spell.

Lyrelle had rarely spoken to her of her youngest son, but Myreon had often heard of Tyvian. Before he was a smuggler and a criminal, he had been a duelist and womanizer, well-known in Saldorian circles as a blight upon the family name and a short-tempered bravo. Myreon had always thought it sad that Tyvian could do such a thing to his family.

When he ran away to become a pirate—or so the rumors claimed—Myreon could see the pain it caused Lyrelle. The great sorceress had seemed . . . off-balance, brittle somehow. Myreon imagined that it was as though Tyvian, with that one act of self-important rebellion, had shown Lyrelle just how powerless she was over the people she loved. She knew that feeling herself—she had felt it when her father died. It was a gut-wrenching pain, made all the worse by knowing there was nothing you could do to make it stop.

By then Myreon had been apprenticed in the Gray Tower, seeking to earn her staff and become a Mage Defender. At that moment, she had promised herself she would bring Tyvian back home—for Lyrelle, to give her closure. It was a promise she still intended to keep.

For now, though, she needed rest. Myreon lay down on the plush featherbed, wondering whether she would be able to sleep, knowing that Tyvian Reldamar was only yards away.

She was asleep before her head hit the pillow.

A life ward is a troubling thing. Long provided by the Hannite Church to those dubbed "Champions of the Faith," they were talismans with powerful Lumenal enchantments bound specifically to the wearer's soul. They allowed the wearer to cheat death, but the cost was high. They did not save your bones from being broken. They did not put the blood back in your body, or replace lost limbs, or banish the poison or pestilence from your flesh. They only let you outlive the moment of your death, and then only for long enough for the bearer to, presumably, get the medical attention necessary to ensure their continued survival thereafter.

Legend stated that the earliest missionaries of the Hannite faith were granted life wards to impress the savage tribes of what eventually became Eddon and Akral. No doubt it would have been fairly impressive to hack off that annoying priest's head, only to have the head still admonishing you for your unrighteousness. Impressive enough, possibly, to get you to swear fealty to the God of Men.

Hacklar Jaevis had been granted a life ward when he was a boy, receiving it from the blessed hands of Prince Landar the Holy himself shortly before he disappeared. Jaevis had earned it for killing three Kalsaari soldiers—unrighteous and heretical invaders at the time. The bounty hunter had worn the life ward ever since, and had never needed to expend its power. Never, that was, until he was run through and pitched into a freezing river by Tyvian Reldamar.

Now Jaevis lay on his face along the riverbank, a small fire flaring weakly beside him—it was all his numb white fingers could manage. He had imbibed the bloodpatch elixir from his belt to stop the bleeding from his wound, but nothing but the fire could stop the deathly cold from freezing his muscles and bones into a solid lump of numbing paralysis. The fire would be enough, though. It had to be enough. The life ward was practically gone, the Hannite cross talisman now corroded into near nothingness.

Soon he would be expected to remain alive all on his own.

He would live. He swore it to himself. Even if he were never warm again, he would not die here. He, Hacklar Jaevis, would stay alive for one purpose and one purpose alone:

Vendetta.

CHAPTER 12

ESTEEMED COLLEAGUES

The plain wooden letterbox on Banric Sahand's desk was so nondescript that a visitor to his voluminous field pavilion might have noticed it anyway, given that everything else in the tent was unforgettable.

An educated person would quickly note that the contents of his bookshelf ran in two varieties—military strategy and proscribed magical texts—and that the vast majority of the books had long been thought lost or been banned throughout the West. A businessman or merchant would have noted the ostentatious quality of the Kalsaari rug that covered the ground, or the expense and rarity of the iron-and-mageglass chair that loomed behind his massive, hand-carved desk. A soldier would note the rune-inscribed broadsword on the rack by the fire not only for the weapon's quality, but also because it was clearly kept sharp, oiled, and in regular use, as were all of the various weapons and armor supported by racks and stands and attended to by invisible specters bound to Sahand's will. An uneducated person, meanwhile, would have likely been distracted by the imposing person of Sahand himself—his heavy fur cloak; his polished, silver-toed boots; the dark, iron circlet resting on his rugged brow; the goblet he drank from, made from an arahk's skull.

All of these things were amazing, terrifying, and incredible to varying degrees, and then, as some kind of strange, mundane joke, there was the plain wooden letterbox, sitting alone in a corner of the desk of a man who had once sought to conquer the West.

Of course, few ever noticed it, or anything else at all about the room. They were usually too busy lying on their faces before the Mad Prince, groveling for their lives, to take in the finer points of His Highness's personal living quarters.

On this particular afternoon the groveler was Hortense, a thaumaturge and warlock from Ayventry by way of Freegate. He was perhaps forty, with a teenage daughter, highly recommended as a man of skill, principle, and genteel bearing. Sahand's right-hand man, the towering Gallo, pressed a heavy boot into the small of the man's back, pushing his face toward the ground; watching this, Sahand noted yet again how quickly one's "bearing" slipped when faced with imminent death. Hortense was weeping tears, drool, and snot on Sahand's expensive carpet. "Pl-*Please*, Your Highness, permit . . . just . . . just permit me one more chance . . . I—I—I *know* we're close . . ."

Sahand sighed and looked out the open tent flap, where the snow was falling in heavy sheets along the upper slopes of the Dragonspine. "Hortense, what did I tell you last fall?"

Hortense tried to look up, his eyes blinded by tears, but Gallo pressed his face back down. "Oh! You said . . . that . . . that I had one year to get the machines to work."

"And how long ago was that?" Sahand asked calmly.

"Fourteen months . . . but . . ."

"Silence." Sahand nodded to Gallo, who pressed harder on the warlock's back. "Now, I am not certain how they read contracts in Ayventry, Hortense, but if it is anything like in the rest of Eretheria, twelve months equals a year. That means you are two months behind schedule, which means *I* am two months behind schedule. This strikes me as unfair, Hortense. Doesn't that seem unfair?"

"V-Very unfair, milord . . ."

"I agree, it *is* very unfair. It seems that you are in a breach of contract, even *after* I so graciously granted you an extension to complete your work and even went to so great a length as to kidnap *numerous* thaumaturges, alchemists, and warlocks to assist you, and procured literally *scores* of wild beasts from *all over the world* to make your work possible. Are you aware of how much such activities cost me?"

Hortense's voice was mangled by his cheek being pressed into the carpet. "A great deal, milord."

"Do you hear yourself, Hortense?" Sahand asked, standing up. "Are you aware of just how cavalierly you just uttered the phrase 'great deal'?"

Hortense's breath heaved in heavy sobs. "I . . . I didn't . . . I don't . . ."

Sahand crouched besides the prone warlock. "Of course you don't, Hortense—this, I believe, is the problem we are having in our professional relationship." He grasped the man by his hair and jerked his head back until he could see his eyes. "You simply do not appreciate my problems. My goals, my aspirations, my operations, my *finances* are abstractions to you, aren't they?"

Hortense didn't answer save to produce a nasal whine through his running nose.

"I have a solution to this problem—a way to bind your self-motivation more closely with my own interests. Now, of course, you are too valuable to punish physically—an injured, ill, or starving man does not work well. However, I have found men with *families* in jeopardy show a great will to succeed in their tasks."

Hortense's bloodshot eyes widened and his face crumpled into an even less flattering expression. "Oh . . . oh please, Hann, no! Anything! Anything but . . ."

Sahand permitted himself a tight grimace. "For every day you do not meet the goals I set for you, on that night I grant my officers access to your daughter. It is my understanding that they are not gentle lovers."

Sahand rose and nodded to Gallo, who released the sobbing warlock. Hortense simply sat in the center of the pavilion, tears streaming down his face, his palms upward in his lap. "It's . . . it's *impossible!* It cannot be done! I . . . I . . . *can't!*"

"Well, then, Hortense," Sahand said, sitting behind his desk, "congratulations—you will soon be a grand-father."

Gallo seized Hortense by the scalp and dragged him from the pavilion like a dead tuna. The tent flap closed behind him, leaving Sahand alone. He glowered at the dark stains on the rug where the warlock had been. Ten years! He had spent the past ten years of his life painstakingly preparing for this winter, and now to think he might fail *just* when success was closest. He wanted to flay the skin of that inept fop of a warlock himself. He wanted to make the entire city of Freegate wade in rivers of blood. He wanted to call down all the powers of the world to crack the fortresses of Galaspin open and feast on the flesh of the fools inside like a bird cracking open a snail. He clenched his fists and teeth until he heard the leather in his gauntlets cracking and his teeth grinding with the stress.

He stood up and released his rage into the Shatter-ing. The heat and raw power of the Fey roared through his blood and blasted forth into one of his bookshelves with a spectacular boom, reducing the shelf and the books to flinders and torn pages. The Mad Prince watched the paper flitter around the tent for a moment before taking a deep breath and sitting down. Then he heard something drop into the letterbox.

On the inside of the lid of the plain wooden container, the spiderweb of intricate Astral runes linked the interior of the box with a spatial rift through which secure messages could be sent. Even the mighty Arcanostrum of Saldor did not possess such devices. The Sorcerous League, however, possessed many secrets the magi of Saldor did not.

The letter inside had a red seal, marking it as important and specifically addressed to him—the whole League would not be privy to its contents. Waving his hand to seal the tent from intrusion, Sahand broke the seal with the proper word of power and flipped open the letter.

6th Ahzmonth, 26th Year of Polimeux II

> *Esteemed Colleague of Dellor,*
>   *You are summoned to attend a meeting this midnight to discuss and report on the progress of your activities and, additionally, to be made aware of an additional complication and opportunity that is emergent in Freegate.*
>   *Curse the Name of Keeper,*
>   *The Office of the Chairman*

Sahand frowned. The vague wording wasn't unusual for a letter from the Chairman—it was the highest priority of the League to maintain its secrecy, and so any official correspondence would lack detail in case the message were intercepted. The League assumed, of course, it was aware of his actions in Freegate—they had afforded him material support in a variety of ways—but what they would consider a "complication and opportunity" was very much a mystery. Especially since they had no idea what his real plan was, else they never would have agreed to support him in the first place. Whatever the reason, the meeting would have to be attended. As usual, the timing was very poor.

Sahand summoned Gallo back into his tent. Gallo was a man of similar stature to his lord, but far less social grace. Even in this cold, he wore dull and dented plate and mail with a wolf's-head helm that only partially hid his horrendously flame-scarred face. His breath was a choking rasp that gurgled and wheezed constantly, as though the man were constantly drowning in his own saliva. His face was a ruin of burn scars, with only a ragged hole for a mouth and two, dark fish-dead eyes. Of all Sahand's underlings, he knew he could rely on Gallo. He was that rarest of creatures—a man without ambition or compassion. Whatever fire had melted off the warrior's face had also taken with it whatever made him human. It was, ultimately, only Sahand's skill with life wards that kept the man alive.

"I am not to be disturbed for the remainder of the evening for any reason, on pain of death," Sahand ordered. He found threatening death to be the most reliable way to keep his idiot underlings away from him for any lengthy period of time, and he knew Gallo would follow through without hesitation. Referring to the spirit clock in his tent, he saw that he had only seven hours before midnight—just barely enough time for the ritual to be completed. Again he wondered what could be going on for the meeting to be called on such short notice.

Gallo's voice was a hollow rasp. "Is that all?"

"No. Keep Hortense working, and inform the city that we will need to get the idiot more help. You are dismissed."

Gallo executed a stiff bow and went out.

"Time to address the sheep," Sahand grumbled to himself. He sealed the pavilion, threw the letter in the fire, and got to work.

The nonplace called simply the "Black Hall" seemed to be fashioned from shadows made somehow real, as though condensed and distilled from a midwinter's night. A thirteen-sided hall with thirteen doors and thirteen terraces of the strange black shadow-stuff, sinking down to a platform at the center of which rested a broad well of oily black liquid, its surface smooth and still as lacquered ebony. This was the Well of Secrets.

The terraces were full of black-robed figures that wore faces not their own: Shrouds. The young looked old, the thin looked fat, the women appeared as men and vice versa; among the many secrets of the Sorcerous League, the identity of its membership was among the most jealously kept.

Sahand was the only member to openly flaunt this custom, and this he did to make clear to them that he was above their petty needs for security. He was Banric Sahand, Prince of Dellor, Scourge of the West. His power had made the nations of the West tremble; while others in the League might fear the wrath of the Arcanostrum and its Defenders, he feared nothing. Let them see his face, he thought; let them know who it was they dealt with.

When Sahand arrived in the Black Hall, he saw that the officers had already arrived and were in conference around the edge of the Well of Secrets. As usual, their appearance varied widely, as all of them had worked new Shrouds to make them look young or old, tall or short, ugly or handsome, according to their whim. They could only be identified through the distinctive scepters they bore, which signified their office. Besides himself and the officers, Sahand noted that the two wizards who were assisting him in this last phase of his plan—one disguised as a young red-haired man and another as a wizened old woman with a cane—stood on the level just above the officers and the Well and on opposite sides, as though drawing too close to one another would automatically compromise their identity somehow. They were each speaking with the Chairman, whispering to him from either side, their voices obscured beneath the din of the other members as well as by the sound-deadening air of the Black Hall itself.

Sahand strode through the crowds of black-robed sorcerers. They hushed and parted around him as he made a beeline for the Chairman and planted himself on the first level, directly over the "leader" of the League. By the time he reached his place, the Black Hall was silent.

The Chairman's blue eyes—he always had blue eyes, regardless of his form—narrowed at him. The face he had chosen for this meeting was broad and plain—the face of a laborer or porter—and Sahand thought it made him look stupid. "You are the last to come."

"What of it?" Sahand barked back. "This meeting deals with me and my activities. It begins when I choose to arrive."

The League muttered at this, whispering to each other and exchanging significant looks. There were many in the League who saw the Chairman as some kind of important or respected office and coveted it, as well as the other officer positions, but Sahand thought these individuals did not appreciate the symbolic architecture of the Black Hall. It was the first and only organization Sahand had encountered where the leadership occupied a level *lower* than the common members, literally looked down upon. They were servants of the League, nothing more—facilitators of an organization far greater and more powerful than they. If they hadn't been such fools, he might have pitied them. As it was, he found them and the airs they put on a contemptible, if unavoidable, aspect of his membership.

The Chairman raised his scepter and spoke in a voice that boomed throughout the chamber. "This meeting will come to order." The request was unnecessary—everyone already had their attention trained on the officers. Nevertheless, the Chairman gazed across the Shrouded faces staring at him, just to make sure. Finally, he said, "Our Esteemed Colleague from Dellor is recognized by the League and has the floor." The Chairman gestured toward the hulking figure of Sahand with his scepter. "You may report upon your progress, sir."

Sahand let his gaze flicker to the Well of Secrets. Its waters were still and dark for now, but should a lie be spoken in its presence, the waters would react—a lie detector, in essence. The Secretary stood at the Well's edge, gazing into the waters, waiting for the well to consume the lie with a flicker of light. If she was quick enough, she could often divine the nature of the lie and what it concealed before the pool of pure Etheric energy swallowed it with darkness again. The League thought its system foolproof, and meetings in the Black Hall were considered to be the most reliable source of League information.

How wrong they were.

Sahand addressed the assembly. "It may yet be possible that all of us will live forever."

A pause as everyone watched the Well: it remained

dark. Applause from the League rippled around the hall.

"Your work on Rhadnost's Elixir goes well, then?" The red-haired young man asked, folding his big hands behind his back.

Sahand regarded the man coolly. He—an Esteemed Colleague from Galaspin—had proven instrumental in keeping Sahand's operations in Daer Trondor secret. Sahand guessed he had a wide variety of connections with the Duke of Galaspin's spy network, or something similar. The man was not to be taken lightly. "My work in tapping the power sink of Daer Trondor is nearing completion. Success is close at hand."

Again the Well remained dark. The red-haired man, however, looked unconvinced. "I know we would like specifics, Your Gra . . . pardon me—*Esteemed Colleague*."

Sahand shrugged. "I am not an academic and am very busy doing things *apart from* toiling to unlock long-lost sorcerous arts. When this project of mine bears fruit, you will be among the first to know."

The red-haired man opened his mouth to speak, but the Chairman cut him off with a wave of his scepter. "Rhadnost's Elixir represents the greatest achievement of the ancient Warlock Kings—eternal life for those skilled enough to achieve it, as is only fitting for those of us who wield the High Arts. Though we are also disappointed that our Esteemed Colleague from Dellor has been working without consultation from the League at large, we should be thankful that he has devoted his vast resources and indomitable will to completing it. Though it will herald a great victory for him, it will be as great a victory for all of us."

Scattered applause across the assembly. Even the red-haired man favored Sahand with a few claps, but only a few. Sahand grunted to himself—some of them were growing suspicious. He had means to circumvent such problems, though. "I am a man who keeps his promises," he said. "You all know my reputation."

More applause, this time healthier. Sahand grinned at them. *Tell them what they want to hear, and they eat it up—how well old Lyrelle taught me that one. . .*

The Chairman brought the League to order. "We proceed to another matter directly pertaining to our Esteemed Colleague from Dellor's activities in the Freegate area." He nodded to the old woman— Sahand's other supporter. "We recognize Our Esteemed Colleague from Kalsaar."

The woman appeared ancient beyond reckoning, her white gloved hands clutching a gnarled walking stick. She tottered down to the center of the room besides the Well. "As you all know, I and my Esteemed Colleague from Galaspin," she motioned to the red-haired man, "have become involved in supporting the efforts of our Esteemed Colleague from Dellor for some time now. There is a new development entering into our operations in Freegate that may require our attention. His name is Tyvian Reldamar."

There was a wave of ruffled cloaks and shifting feet among the assembly. Sahand, though, didn't move, his gaze fixed on the old woman's wizened face. "I heard that Reldamar was dead."

The old woman shrugged. "An exaggeration. I have it from a very reliable source that he is alive and well and back in town."

The red-haired young man's voice was calm. "Why would this be a problem? Reldamar is no enemy of ours, and though he might know of our existence, he has no way of finding us."

The old woman looked at the Chairman, "By your leave, darling?" When the Chairman nodded, she turned to Sahand and the other man. "Tyvian Reldamar has brought a Defender of the Balance to Freegate . . ."

An outburst of dismay and anxiety from the League deafened all conversation for several seconds. A variety of suggested curses and plagues were shouted, as well as admonitions of caution hollered at the top of the lungs. Several members walked out of the hall then and there.

"So what?" Sahand said once the Chairman had restored order. "Reldamar is no friend of the Arcanostrum—he probably has the fool in casterlocks and plans to sell him to the highest bidder."

The old woman tapped her cane on the floor. "I hadn't finished, my duck. Had everyone listened a second longer before butting in, you all would also have learned that Reldamar has been given the Iron Ring."

The League, officers included, did all but gasp at

this, and the red-haired young man reflexively reached up to stroke a beard that he didn't currently have. Sahand looked at them and rolled his eyes. "You are referring, I take it, to that trinket occasionally affixed to scoundrels that tortures them into being nice to people? *This* is your 'complication and opportunity'?"

The old woman grimaced at him. "The Iron Ring is an artifact of profound power. The magecraft used to construct it is—"

"Of academic interest and little overall importance to myself, my holdings, or my aims," Sahand finished for her.

"We forget, occasionally, just how concerned Our Esteemed Colleague from Dellor is with the practical." The Chairman smiled. "Perhaps if Our Esteemed Colleague from Kalsaar could explain more clearly the practical applications of Reldamar's appearance and the possible interest we may have in his ring."

The old woman curtsied with the help of her walking stick. "Thank you, Mr. Chairman. Now, the reason why we are interested in the Iron Ring is because it operates in a fashion that is beyond our current understanding of talismancy. Clearly the power it is able to exercise upon its 'host,' if you will, far exceeds that which could conventionally be held inside an item as small as a ring. If we could understand how this works, we could greatly improve the standing of the League. Now . . ." The old woman looked at Sahand with a bemused smirk. " . . . before you fidget yourself right out of that impressive cape, my duck, let me explain why *you* should be interested in Mr. Reldamar and his new ring. It seems that one Zazlar Hendrieux recently staged an ambush for his former partner, Mr. Reldamar, aboard a spirit engine bound for Freegate a bit more than a week ago. It was this ambush that placed the ring on his finger and put the Mage Defender in his custody."

Sahand stiffened. He could connect the dots as well as anyone. "You expect this will lead back to me."

The Chairman nodded gently, along with the rest of the officers. "Ordinarily we wouldn't be able to ascertain such intelligence for one of our members, but given your . . . reticence . . . to maintain your anonymity among us, we could not help but notice a certain confluence of events that might lead to some interference with your activities. Reldamar has a score to settle with one of your underlings, a ring that forces him to behave nobly, and an operative of the Defenders by his side. He is dangerous to you."

"No," Sahand corrected, "He is dangerous to Hendrieux. He won't touch me—I'll see to it."

The old woman chuckled softly. "We wouldn't dream of it, my duck. I propose you let *us* handle Reldamar. We wouldn't want to distract you from your very important work. We merely thought it would be important to keep you in the loop. Your success in your endeavor is a success for the League as a whole."

Sahand tried not to let his lip curl. "Yes. Of course. I'll leave you to it, then. As you point out, I have very important work to attend to."

The Chairman bowed ceremoniously. "Our Esteemed Colleague from Dellor is excused, of course."

Snorting at the audacity of the Chairman "excusing" him to leave, Sahand spun on his heel and marched out of the Black Hall, the crowd parting for him again, just as though they weren't there.

The space outside the hall was ill-defined—a nebulous darkness without clear dimension. A few strides into the blackness and a fixed idea of where one wanted to be would bring the departing sorcerer exactly to that place. In this instance, Sahand had his own tent in mind, and a hundred other tasks lined up that needed his attention. It was no surprise, then, that he didn't see the young woman until she grabbed his arm.

At the touch, Sahand pivoted on instinct, pulling his assailant so that she was facing him. His free hand seized her by the neck and yanked her head down across his body and into his knee in one savage motion. The woman fell on the floor, blood spurting from a cut lip.

To her credit, she collected herself quickly, wiping her mouth on her black robe. "I beg your pardon, Your Grace."

Sahand squinted at her. She was Shrouded, of course—no telling who she was by sight. The Shroud, though, was familiar to him. She had been a vocal supporter of his in the League early on. He made no move to help her up. "What do you want?"

The woman rolled slowly to all fours, but had some trouble rising from there. An old woman, then.

She was lucky he hadn't landed that knee solidly—he might have broken her neck. As it stood, he reflected, a broken neck might be in her future anyway. "I . . . I had a question about the Daer Trondor power sink."

Sahand felt his face stiffen, and knew that was a mistake. The old woman watched him with young eyes. "What about it?"

Slowly, the Shrouded old woman got herself into a squat and, grunting like a birthing sow, drew herself to her full height. Her breath came in labored gasps. "If you can release the power there, how do you intend to control it? That ancient old sink has been pooling all five energies without being tapped for . . . gods . . . for centuries at least, if not millennia. If you can tap it, it will be like breaking a dam . . ."

Sahand frowned. "Such power is required to produce the Elixir. I've explained this before."

"Yes . . . but it's just . . ." The woman opened her mouth, then closed it. "Yes. I suppose you're right. I was only . . . I was hoping I could help."

Sahand watched her eyes and how they blinked. This was not a woman who was seeking to help. This was a woman who was afraid. Deathly afraid.

He appropriated a smile, but it was not a natural expression for him. The woman backed away a pace. "Your help, madam, is not required."

She curtsied—it was the flawless curtsey of a noblewoman, probably Eretherian. "As Your Grace commands."

Sahand nodded and backed into the shadows.

Soon, the darkness fell and the woman vanished from view.

He was back in his tent in moments, the darkness and stillness of that half-place still clinging to his garments as he stood before a roaring fire he had left burning in a brazier for just this reason.

"Gallo?" he called, and the massive warrior appeared, his ruined face betraying not the least curiosity of where his lord had been. "Tighten security, just in case. Tyvian Reldamar is alive and he may come after Hendrieux. If that happens, I want our operations here secure."

"Telling Hendrieux?" Gallo rasped.

Sahand frowned. "No. Their feud has nothing to do with me, and I want it to stay that way. Understood?"

Gallo bowed.

"One more thing," Sahand added. "We're going to need to visit that necromancer, Arkald." He reached down and wiped some of the old woman's blood off his knee and held it up in the firelight. "I have somebody I need to find."

Gallo bowed again, this time more deeply. "I will prepare an expedition immediately."

"No," Sahand shook his head. "I will go alone. This shouldn't take long."

CHAPTER 13

HOME AT LAST

Tyvian laid back in the saffron-scented bathwater, a glass of white Dorthian '22 cradled loosely in his left hand, as the rain beat a steady rhythm upon the skylights overhead. He tried to relax but he couldn't bring himself to close his eyes.

The ring finger on his right hand—the *ring's* finger—ached slightly, as though he had jammed it against a wall or some such, though he knew very well he had done no such thing. He tried to block the pain out but it was no good. The blasted thing wouldn't let him unwind.

He had hoped to recover himself inside his sumptuously appointed domicile. His servant specters—invisible Dweomeric constructs that maintained his house—had prepared his bath exactly to his specifications and were, even now, roasting pheasants he had preserved in his stasis box a year ago. The scent of rosemary and braised game bird wafted through the rooms of the flat, blending with the pleasant smell of the bath to create a perfectly luxurious environment . . . and that Kroth-spawned *ring* was ruining everything.

He knew the ring was trying to encourage a feeling of guilt in him for casting off Artus. He had to applaud the cleverness of its attempt—no sharp, searing pain, but just this dull, constant ache. Had he felt guilt with any regularity, Tyvian thought he might have been able to confirm beyond doubt that the sensation caused by the ring was a close amalgam of the feeling created by the emotion itself. As it stood, the ring only made him angry and frustrated. He had nearly been killed, had spent almost two weeks in the muddy, frozen wilderness, and now that he was *finally* somewhere civilized, he wasn't permitted the relaxation he so richly deserved.

He wanted to ask the ring what it was hoping to accomplish with this "guilt" charade, but didn't. He had slipped into speaking with the thing before and immediately recognized how insane it made him appear. The ring was *not* intelligent, it was merely sophisticated. No enchantment, no matter how advanced, was capable of truly simulating human intelligence.

Tyvian took a sip of wine, then placed his glass on a levitating silver tray beside him and, for the fifth time since getting in the bath, attempted to wriggle the ring off of his oiled and soapy finger. Pull as he might, and no matter how much he scraped or scratched at the flesh around his finger, the ring didn't budge. It didn't even rotate. He recalled the scar tissue built up around Eddereon's ring finger, and shuddered as he considered the implications.

"You drive men mad, don't you?" He said to the little iron-black circlet, and then grimaced. *Don't talk to it! It isn't bloody alive, stupid!*

"Bring my clothes," Tyvian announced to the specters. They carried off the wine and returned with the outfit he had selected for the evening—a fine silk shirt of gleaming white with a flaring collar, a long maroon coat with green embroidery along the sleeves depicting cliff serpents in flight, matching breeches, a broad black belt inlaid with silver studs, and supple suede boots. This, along with a variety of jeweled rings—a sapphire to compliment his eyes, a sliver flower to play off the belt and draw attention away from the iron ring—and he was ready.

"Set the table for dinner. Bring the prisoner from the secure room." He took a deep breath. Dinner with Myreon Alafarr was certainly going to be interesting.

Myreon woke up thanks to the painful aches of an empty stomach. She lay quietly in the dark, wondering what kind of people Reldamar usually kept in so comfortable a cell. She came to the conclusion that it was probably for actual guests. Though it was really a cell, few but actual trained magi would have been able to recognize it as such, and Myreon thought it appropriate to Reldamar's personality that he wouldn't trust even those he invited into his own home.

Every cell, however, had its weakness, and Myreon hadn't earned her mage's staff from the Arcanostrum for nothing. The only thing stopping her were those infernal casterlocks. With them in place, there was almost no sorcery of note she could work. After trying a few forms of purely verbal magic and failing utterly, she settled upon wiggling as much feeling back into her fingertips as she could until sleep, again, tugged at her eyelids. As she drifted off, the same thing kept running through her head—a lesson taught to her by none other than Lyrelle Reldamar shortly before Myreon had earned her first mark: *Your fate lies in your fingers.*

Two hours later Myreon was awakened again by the specters and dragged by the elbows to the dining room. Dinner was served, it seemed.

At the other end of a fabulously ornate table made entirely of mageglass, Tyvian Reldamar sat in a high-backed chair of white birch. Another, similar chair sat at the opposite end of the table. Everything was set for dinner, and the smell of the food instantly set Myreon's mouth watering. The specters pulled out the empty chair for her, and she sat down.

Reldamar grinned at the mage. "My goodness, Myreon—you look awful."

Myreon had long grown tired of verbal jousting with the smuggler over her days of captivity, so she only nodded. "Am I supposed to eat like a dog?" She held up her casterlocks. "Or are you just going to torture me by making me watch."

Reldamar clutched his heart in feigned pain. "Gods, what kind of monster do you think I am? There are *two whole* pheasants there, my dear. Do you really think I would eat *all* of them?"

Reldamar produced a key from his coat pocket and supplied it to one of the specters, which dutifully unlocked the steel cylinder that had been affixed to the Defender's hands for days. When the cylinder had been removed, Myreon could see that her hands were a mixture of pale white and raw, bleeding red. Gingerly she closed each of them into a fist and extended them again, clenching her teeth against the incredible pain caused by old cramps and muscular atrophy.

"Please eat your fill, Magus." Reldamar said, and Myreon's plate was supplied with a full half pheasant, some vegetables, and her glass was filled with white wine.

Myreon knew that stuffing her face would engender jibes from the smuggler, but she didn't care. She dove into her food, eschewing silverware both thanks to her hunger and the fact that her hands were too weak to clutch a fork and knife with any amount of dexterity. She made a point to play this angle up—she wanted Reldamar to think her hands weaker than they were. It was the only possible way she would get out of this.

To her surprise, Reldamar remained silent, his sharp blue eyes following her every move. After she had downed her second glass of wine in a few swift gulps, the smuggler took a bite of his own food. "If I had been told I would be dining with Myreon Alafarr in my own home at the end of this month, I would have been overcome with incredulity. Yet, here we are." He held up his glass. "To vanquished foes."

Myreon only glared at him for a moment and then returned to her meal. There were a half-dozen invocations she could think of that would blast Reldamar through the wall or sear his flesh from his bones, but none of them were going to be cast with her hands in the state they were in. They would take days to recover, and Reldamar knew it as well as she. The smuggler wouldn't have released her hands otherwise.

She looked out of the floor-length windows that lined the side of the dining room. They overlooked the remainder of Freegate, which lay far beneath Reldamar's Top Street penthouse. The city was black and obscured by a misty layer of smoke and fog, with only the tallest steeples and towers piercing its gloom. It was raining steadily, the lights of a few streetlamps flickering in the dark. Myreon cleared her throat. "Why haven't you killed me yet?"

Reldamar finished chewing a dainty portion of meat before answering. "I have use for you."

"You're lying."

"Since when have you been any good at telling when I'm lying? By my count, you have believed at least seven lies I have told you during the course of our . . . let us call it our 'professional relationship.'"

"I can only count five." Myreon frowned.

"Thank you, Magus, for proving my point." Reldamar held up his glass in salute.

"You're changing the subject. You haven't killed me and there is no reason for it. Every moment you keep me alive jeopardizes you. If I escaped, if I managed to get a message to someone, if anything went wrong, I could tell the Defenders where you are, where you live, whom you associate with in Freegate—"

"Now, Myreon," Reldamar interrupted, wagging a finger at her, "what makes you think you will escape?"

"Not my point. My point is that you are not stupid enough to take the risk."

"Perhaps the point is that I am not a murderer," Reldamar snapped. "Have you considered that?"

Myreon felt a cold hatred bubble up from her stomach. "Amos Claret, Venn Wasmeer, Sylva Arteen, Evard Hamson, Carlis Dogger, Hacklar Jaevis." She spat the names like poison darts.

Reldamar's face was stony. For a moment the only sound was the rain beating on the windows. "I suppose those are all people in your service I've killed."

"You *suppose* correctly."

"They were trying to kill me, you know. That makes a difference."

"They were trying to *apprehend* you. *That* makes a difference."

It was Reldamar's turn to look out the window. "What, then? Do you want an apology? 'I'm sorry Magus Alafarr that I didn't go meekly in shackles to be made into a statue'?" The smuggler snorted, "Fat chance."

Myreon said nothing. The faces of those five men and one woman came swimming up out of the depths of her memory. She recalled conversations she had with them, remembered the sounds of their voices. They had been good people, every one. Even Jaevis had been noble, in his way.

Reldamar swirled his wine around his glass. "Well, *Jaevis* was trying to kill me. He even said so."

"Doesn't change anything," Myreon said. "It also doesn't answer my initial question."

Reldamar shrugged. "I thought I'd already answered it. It isn't my fault you won't accept the explanation."

Myreon frowned. "Am I supposed to believe you've somehow acquired a sense of mercy?"

"No . . . no, of course not," Reldamar answered hastily, and Myreon noticed he withdrew his right hand to beneath the table.

She wondered if the smuggler had a weapon hidden there, but discarded the notion as foolish. Reldamar *might* have poisoned the wine, but there was no way he was going to put a knife in her heart or discharge a deathcaster in his own dining room. She recalled then the plain iron ring she had noticed on Reldamar's right hand during their journey. It had looked incongruous on the vain smuggler's fingers, but she wrote it off as part of Reldamar's "common folk" disguise. He wore it with as much apparent distaste as the rest of his crude clothing at the time—constantly scowling at it and scratching the skin around it, as though it burned to just wear it. She'd assumed it had been thrown away as soon as they entered Reldamar's home. But what if . . .

"May I see your right hand?" Myreon asked.

Reldamar's face was an unreadable mask. "Why?"

"Why not?"

"It seems a strange request." Reldamar shrugged.

"Please, I insist."

"You aren't in the position to 'insist' upon anything, Myreon."

"You are trying awfully hard to not show me your right hand, *Tyvian*."

Reldamar pursed his lips together, probably considering another retort, but then sighed. With visible reluctance, he held up his right hand. There, on his ring finger and partially obscured by an ostentatious silver ring, was the gray-black band of plain iron.

In spite of herself, Myreon smiled. "You can't take that ring off, can you?"

"It is a size too small. I plan on having it cut off to-morrow."

Myreon nodded—the explanation was plausible. "How did you come by it?"

Tyvian shrugged. "Stole it from a farmhouse. The same place I found the furs and such for me and the boy. I really don't understand your interest in it."

"You never mentioned how you made it out of the river alive that night. Surely the fall should have knocked you unconscious, and the water was cold enough to kill."

"We were assisted by a local fisherman."

"Who was fishing in the middle of the night and dove in to save two strangers?"

Reldamar glared at Myreon. "Galaspiner hospitality is greatly underrated, I have found."

Myreon smiled. "That ring isn't the wrong size—it's *meant* not to come off. It's enchanted, and with Lumenal energy no less. *That* was why my seekwand didn't spot you in the tent that morning. You were in an obscuring ley, so it defaulted to the boy—the next closest thing to you."

Reldamar clapped his hands slowly, a sardonic expression on his face. "Congratulations. You've earned dessert."

"What does it do?"

"That is none of your—"

"Let me guess!" Myreon blurted. "You can't kill me, *because it won't let you.*"

Reldamar rolled his eyes. "Don't be ridiculous. It let me kill Jaevis."

"Self-defense, as you yourself pointed out. But when I was on the floor of the barge, half frozen to death, it wouldn't let you. That's why you made that face before pulling me back into the barge. I remember you even *looked* at the ring!" Myreon was halfway out of her chair.

Reldamar had a bitter, deflated expression on his face—it was one to savor, so she basked in it while waiting for the smuggler to respond.

"Very good, Myreon—you get high marks for deductive reasoning. It doesn't matter, though. Within the week I intend to secure the services of a Kalsaari Artificer, who will cut this thing off my hand with great dispatch."

Myreon couldn't help but laugh. "An Artificer? Ha! Those recluses only work with Kalsaari nobility, and reluctantly at that. Even if you could find one around here, what possible reason would they have to help you? You have nothing to offer them in return."

Reldamar raised an eyebrow. "I don't?"

The realization hit Myreon suddenly, and her jaw dropped. The Kalsaaris would pay almost anything to get their hands on a staff-bearing mage, and particularly a Mage Defender. They would pick her brain apart like a spirit clock if it meant unlocking one of the Arcanostrum's secrets. In her work in Illin, Myreon had seen what became of magi who were taken by the Kalsaaris—they were like vegetables, their minds scooped out like porridge by Kalsaari sorcery. "You . . . you *wouldn't*."

It was Reldamar's turn to laugh. "I *told* you I had a use for you."

Myreon recovered herself and fixed the smuggler with a baleful glare. She worked her stiff, raw fingers back and forth beneath the table. *My fate lies in my fingers. My fate lies in my fingers. . .*

CHAPTER 14

LOOSE LIPS

Artus was drunk, and he was yelling. "Tyvian Reldamar is a son of a bitch!"

Two bearded men in the dingy bar looked up from their game of t'suul. "Keep it down, boy!" one of them snapped. Artus returned the men's glares until they turned back to their tiles.

Artus had no real idea what part of Freegate he was in—it was five blocks *below* Tyvian's Top Street address, somewhere off the aptly named Low Street in the midst of the Free City's smog layer. It was not a good neighborhood, certainly, but it did look like a cheap one. The bar he was in had no name he could recall—just a sign shaped like an ale-tankard. No one had welcomed him when he entered, and he waited almost an hour before the barkeep—a one-eyed, rail-thin Ihynishman—asked if he wanted ale or food or both. Artus insisted on ale and ale alone. He was on his third tankard. It was tasteless and watered down, but it did its job.

This was not the first time he had been drunk. On his tenth birthday, during Marik's going-away party, Balter and Handen had dared him to drink a cup of whiskey. He'd downed it all at once, just to spite them and show them he wasn't afraid. They had to have one, too, then—Balter was fourteen and Handen was fifteen, and none of them were supposed to drink. Ma had found them stripped and wrestling in the barn. They were all too dizzy to stand up. He remembered laughing a lot then. Even Ma, in the midst her yelling, couldn't keep in a chuckle.

This kind of drunk was a very different experience. This was the kind of drunk Artus had seen a lot of in the year since he'd left home—the kind he saw in the alleys and run-down bars of Ayventry, Galaspin, and now Freegate. Men who sat hunched over their bottles, staring into the distance, gulping down liquor with faces fixed with a rictus grin. "I am happy," the grin said. "No really, I am happy. Honest."

Artus found himself assuring those around him of a similar thing. He was celebrating, he said. He was celebrating a big job. A lot of money.

He was celebrating being abandoned.

"Kroth take him, anyway." Artus spat on the table. "Tyvian Reldamar is a son of a bitch." He drank sloppily from his tankard.

At home, a boy of not-quite-fourteen in a tavern drinking through his sorrows would have garnered some attention. Here, nobody cared so long as he kept it down. The bearded men were involved in their t'suul game, laying silver down on their tiles with greasy fingers. The barkeep fondled the barmaid openly by the till. Three others sat in a circle around an uneven table in the back, empty vials of ink discarded by their feet, their faces slack and eyes dilated as the alchemical drug ravaged their senses. These three were dressed in rags, their bodies gaunt and spotted with sores. They hadn't moved since Artus had entered. "Hey!" he yelled at them. "Are any of you dead?"

The t'suul players glared at him again. "Shut up, boy!"

"Kroth take you, too!" Artus retorted. The men didn't flinch at the profanity and returned to their game.

"So," he muttered, "alone again. Always alone for Artus. S'like poetry." Artus snorted at this, and forced a laugh. "I'm clever. Clever . . . er than he thought anyway."

He should be used to it, he knew. His father had gone away and died. Conrad had gone away and died. Marik had gone away and died. Balter and Handen had gone away. Ma had sent him over the mountains. Reldamar didn't need him anymore. It was all the same. Everybody had their reasons, but it was all the same. He was the kid, the runt, the youngest, the boy who didn't know anything. Why keep him around? What's the point?

Artus fished Eddereon's letter out of his jacket and squinted at the blocky script there, as though staring harder might make sense of the letters. Eddereon had pulled him from the freezing river, had fed and clothed him, had treated him with respect and kindness. Artus knew immediately he was a man to be admired and followed—a lot like Conrad or Marik. Artus felt drawn to him; he felt like Eddereon knew exactly what he was going through, where he had been. He had sworn to serve Eddereon, to be his servant or page or whatever the great man had thought necessary, and then Eddereon had just vanished into thin air and left this letter. He couldn't even read, but he knew what it said.

"Dear kid," Artus said, affecting a deep voice in imitation of Eddereon. He moved his eyes from side to side, like folks who read did. "I think you're a good kid, but I got things to do. Adult stuff that's too important for a . . . for a kid. 'Bye! Regards, Eddereon."

One of the t'suul players slammed a fist on the table, rattling the tiles. "Dammit, boy! I'm *trying* to *concentrate!*"

Artus stuck out his tongue.

The man stood, drawing a dagger from a belt sheath. "Kroth! I'll cut that tongue off, you miserable brat!"

Artus started to wonder where his own blade was when he was grabbed by the collar by the bartender. "Hey!" The barkeep thrust a bony finger at the angry t'suul player. "No blood in the bar! You want to cut the whelp, do it in the gutter."

"You can't thrown me ow . . . out," Artus slurred as the bartender, showing remarkable strength for a man of such slight stature, dragged him to the door and then kicked him into the street. Artus tripped and wound up on the cobblestones, his head spinning. He shouted in what he thought was the general direction of the bar, "I'm a payment custo . . . custo-momer. You can't do this t'me, dammit."

The door to the bar slammed closed. The t'suul player never appeared—apparently the game continued to require his utmost attention. After a minute or two Artus tried to stand up, but the world spun a bit too much and he laid back down on the cobbles. Night had fallen. Intermittent feylamps flickered from lampposts here and there, but for every working one there were three that had been vandalized or simply stolen. The yellow-orange flames of those that remained reacted with the smoky air to create great circular nimbuses of gloomy light that made the unkempt buildings along the street look gaunt and skeletal, their windows as dark as empty eye sockets. It was damp and cold, and no one was out.

Artus weighed sleeping there against the odds of being trampled by a horse. He didn't remember seeing too many horses in Freegate on the way in—

the vertical nature of the place made it awkward for horsemen—but that didn't mean there weren't any horsemen at all. He decided on a compromise. "Hey!" He shouted upward. "Nobody trample me, 'kay? I'm sleepin' here!"

Somewhere, from a dark distant window, someone yelled, "Shut up!"

Artus found this hilarious, and laughed to himself for a while. He rolled onto all fours and began to see about standing up without assistance when, out of the corner of his eye, he saw a group of eight legs stop in front of him. Two sets of legs wore heavy leather boots, while a third was barefoot. The fourth was wearing soft, thigh-high riding boots with silver lacing, unkempt but expensive. The owner of these boots was the first to speak. His voice was sharp and softly accented; Artus had heard it somewhere before. "Now what have we here, Ketch?"

"Drunk boy, sir," one of the heavy-booted men said.

Artus rolled himself into a sitting position. He looked up at a pair of broad-shouldered, hard-faced thugs wearing black cloaks, steel helmets, and chain mail. A frail, shivering man in a dressing gown with a sack over his head was in the process of being frogmarched between the two thugs. The fourth man, the one who had first spoken, was wearing a thick woolen cape fastened by a silver chain at his throat, had a rapier and a dagger at his hip, and had the same blade-thin physique, tousled black hair, and narrow, unshaven features that Artus remembered from their first meeting. "Hey," he snorted. "You're Zazlar Hendrieux."

"I'm sorry, lad, but have we met?" Hendrieux smiled, but only with his mouth. He looked like a predator showing its teeth.

Artus frowned. Now why wouldn't he remember? The details were a little fuzzy in his head then, but something inside told him to play dumb. "Oh . . . sorry. Must be wrong, then."

Hendrieux sniffed the air over Artus's head. "Oh dear me. What's a young lad like you doing drinking alone in a place like this anyway?" He nodded toward the bar.

"Sir?" Ketch grunted, nodding his head toward the shivering man held between him and the other thug.

Hendrieux held up a finger. "Just a moment, Ketch."

"He's just some orphan," the other one said, and added, "So what?"

"He's just some orphan who *knows me*. Doesn't that strike you as odd?" Hendrieux sneered at his companions.

"I'm *not* an orphan!" Artus stood up on a pair of wobbling legs. "I've got a family and *lots* of important friends!"

Hendrieux snickered at that. "Really? Such as?"

"Well . . ." Artus cast about for a moment—who would Hendrieux think of as important? Of course! "Tyvian Reldamar is my friend!"

Hendrieux laughed louder; his companions joined

in. "Tyvian Reldamar didn't associate with dirty street orphans even when he was *alive*. Nice try, though."

Artus snorted. "Reldamar isn't dead."

"I'm surprised you haven't heard." Hendrieux chuckled. "Killed by Defenders on the Galaspin spirit engine. Terrible disaster, from what I understand. Shame really—had nothing but respect for the chap."

The words came rushing out of Artus's mouth before he could stop them. "No, he escaped and now he's in Freegate and he's going to kill you for double-crossing him, you son of a bitch."

The mirth and the color drained from Hendrieux's face at the same time. "You shouldn't throw around wild stories like that, boy. Reldamar's *dead*."

"Alive. And he's come here. And he's got a mirror-man . . . err, woman . . . prisoner. And he's killed Hacklar Jaevis. And he's—"

Hendrieux seized Artus by the collar and pushed him back on the ground "Well . . ." he hissed. "Haven't *you* been helpful." He turned to the two thugs. "Ketch, this boy is a problem. Kill him."

"What, 'ere?" Ketch looked up and down the street.

Hendrieux grasped the arm of the shivering man, who by this point was shaking both from cold and, probably, from terror. "In the alley if you prefer. Make it quick and meet up with us later."

"Yessir."

Artus tried to scramble to his feet, but he slipped and fell flat on his back again. Hendrieux grinned over him. "Very nice meeting you."

Ketch grabbed Artus by the feet and dragged him behind the bar as easily as if Artus had been in a wheelbarrow. Artus tried to draw his knife but couldn't remember where it was. He began to call for help, but Ketch kicked him in the stomach and his cry was replaced with a wheezing "Ooooooo."

Artus wriggled and rolled, but the big man easily pinned him in place with a knee and held a long, thin knife up to the lamplight. "'Ere now, bobbin'. Don't wiggle so much, eh?"

Those would be the last words the man ever uttered.

Hool leapt upon his back from a rooftop, crushing him to the ground underneath her substantial weight. Even as Ketch was screaming in surprise, her powerful arms had wrapped around his head and yanked back. His spine broke with a visceral *pop*; the sound made Artus snap back to almost total sobriety.

Hool dragged Artus to his feet. "You smell like drunks."

Artus couldn't take his eyes off the burly Ketch, folded in half like a picnic chair. "Sweet Hann's mercy, Hool . . . you . . . you just . . ."

"Why was this man going to kill you?" Hool asked, sniffing Ketch's body as she rifled through his pockets.

Artus struggled to find the words. "How did you find me?"

"I followed you, stupid. I was going to leave you alone, but you aren't so smart."

"Yeah, I know." Artus nodded, gradually realizing

what his chat with Hendrieux had done. Reldamar—he'd told Hendrieux about Reldamar. "Oh gods, Hool! Hendrieux!"

Hool dropped Ketch's limp body. "Where?"

Artus looked around, the world spinning. "I . . . I don't know. They went somewhere."

Hool put her nose to the ground, took a few exploratory sniffs, and shot out of the alley like a racehorse. Trying to keep himself steady, Artus followed after her, slipping and flopping down the gloomy street. He heard her roar from another alley and got to the mouth of the place in time to see Hool seize the other thug by the nose-guard of his helmet and throw him face-first into a stone wall.

The helmet took most of the blow, but it bought Hool the time necessary to snatch a dagger from the thug's belt. By the time the man had spun back around and drawn his sword, Hool pounced yet again, nimbly knocking aside his blade and knocking him flat on his back. The knife was at his throat, and Hool was growling loud enough to make the cobblestones rattle.

The big man's formerly gruff voice was cracking like a boy of Artus's age. "Great Hann save me! Oh gods, *don't!*"

Hool's teeth seemed to glow in the dim light. "*WHERE ARE THEY!*"

The thug was paralyzed in the gnoll's gaze. "I dunno! I dunno! We only go by the door!"

Hool's eyes blazed. She stood slowly, hoisting the

man up against the wall until his feet dangled a full six inches off the ground. *"TELL ME NOW!"*

"I don't know! I *swear* I don't know!"

Hool shook him so hard his head looked likely to snap off. *"YOU WILL TELL ME NOW OR I TEAR OFF YOUR HEAD!"*

"Let him go, Hool!" Artus ran to the gnoll's side and pushed her, but she didn't budge.

Hool glared at him. "You will shut *up!* I am busy now."

"What happened to Hendrieux?" Artus asked. The alley was a dead end, save for a single door. That door stood open, but beyond it was simply a brick wall—a door to nowhere.

Hool slammed the thug against the wall. Artus heard bones crack. "Filthy magic! Filthy *cheater* magic! Tell me how it works!"

"I don't know!" the man squealed. "They don't tell us!"

Hool's voice was made ragged by the rumble of her growls. "If you know nothing, I will kill you now."

"Ple—" The man didn't finish his last sentence before Hool's jaws snapped closed around his neck, crushing it with a spurt of blood. She threw the body on the ground like a pile of rags, where it twitched for a few seconds before falling still.

Artus threw up in the gutter. When he finished, Hool was sitting on her haunches, looking at him with her glowing copper eyes. "You should not drink poison," she announced. Blood stained the fur around her lips.

"What happened?" Artus asked, his stomach still tumbling.

"Hendroo and an old man went through that magic door. He left this stupid man to fight me, but he was too slow and I killed him." She looked at the body and then back at Artus. "You were here for that part."

Making certain not to look at the dead thug, Artus went over to inspect the door. He was no wizard and knew virtually nothing about sorcery, but part of his still ale-soaked brain hoped maybe there was some sign of magic writing or some such to show how the door worked. There was none. It was just an old door— probably a former side or back door to some building. When the building had been renovated or rebuilt, the masons had likely bricked up the door from within, but never bothered removing it entirely. Beyond its architectural oddity, nothing else seemed unusual about it. "I wonder what happened," Artus mused aloud.

Hool shrugged. "It is late. Let's find a barn to sleep in. Tyvian Reldamar will solve this wizard-puzzle in the morning."

Artus pointed to the dead body. "We can't just leave *him* here!"

Hool cocked her head to one side. "I am not hungry."

Artus shuddered. "I can't believe you would *eat* him."

The gnoll prodded the body with her foot. "He is too big to eat myself. Enough meat for three days."

"You're disgusting." Artus folded his arms over his queasy belly and left the alley.

Hool followed him a moment or two later. "Do you want a sword?" she asked.

Artus shook his head. "First you kill them, then you rob them?"

Hool blinked slowly. "Dead people don't *need* swords." She spoke as though speaking to a child.

"I know that."

"You are stubborn and dumb," Hool said finally, tossing the dead man's sword back in the alley.

Artus sighed. "Hey . . . thanks."

Hool fixed him with her hard copper eyes and nodded slowly. "We are a pack, no matter what Reldamar says. He is stubborn and dumb, too."

A cold rain began to fall, quickly soaking Artus to the bone, so he was shivering as they wandered the streets at night. The water beaded on Hool's thick fur, but she didn't flinch from it as she loped along at the boy's side. She seemed comfortable and happier than she had been since Artus had known her. That, along with the image of her breaking that Delloran's back in the street, playing over and over in his mind, made him shiver even more.

Arkald the Strange, Necromancer of Talthmoor, ran for his life. Behind him, his mossy old tower burned with a supernatural flame. Within, all his books, all his ritual ingredients, all his creations—his entire career—

died a final death that not even he could reverse. Part of him wanted to go back, to throw himself in the fire, to die with his work. It would have been more fitting that way. Arkald, though, had never been a brave man.

The ground was a mixture of mud and slush, the provenance of a week's worth of sleet and rain. Arkald's sandals could scarcely find purchase. He kept falling, slipping, tumbling down hillsides in the dark of the night. His breath came in ragged gasps; he was so cold he could scarcely breathe. Fear was the only thing to keep him going. It seemed as though a blazing spike of terror was nestled in the center of his back somewhere, radiating out to all his limbs and pushing them to frantic activity. *Sweet Hann, he had to get away!*

Arkald knew who was coming for him. He didn't know how he had been found, but he knew who had done the finding. He wished to every god he knew that he was wrong, but he just wasn't that lucky.

He chanced a glance behind him. He'd made it perhaps a quarter mile from his tower, and there, in the blazing phosphorous-white light, he saw the silhouette of a man built like a rampart—tall, broad, and blunt. There was a glint of silver at his shoulders and on his brow—armor and a simple iron circlet. The sight filled the necromancer's gut with a new wave of terror.

Arkald felt the sorcerous energies that made up the world shudder just before the ground exploded beneath his feet. The heat and force of the blast was absorbed by the wards he had placed on his cloak, but no sorcerous ward would defend him from being tossed ten feet in the air and landing with a crunch against a rock. Arkald screamed into the night sky; his hip was broken. He rolled in the mud, trying to draw the Lumen into a spell that might knit his bones back together, if only temporarily. The ley did not favor him, though. The Lumen was found in places of light and life and happiness; the muddy winter hillside in the middle of the night was a place of darkness, death, and terror.

Channeling the Ether, the Lumen's opposite, was significantly easier, and so Arkald was able to cast a deathbolt at his pursuer despite his frozen fingers and pain-wracked body. The arc of green lightning that erupted from his fingers, though, was casually batted aside by the broad man in the iron circlet. Arkald tried again and again, each time pouring more of his fear and hatred into the spell to enhance it, but each time the man countered it with wards and dispels of his own. Arkald's attacks didn't even force him to break stride.

As though mocking his weakness, the man channeled the Fey—the energy of heat and chaos—to cause a ring of fire to leap up around the prone, shivering body of the necromancer. There would be no escape now. Despite cold creating a favorable ley, Arkald was too weak to channel a countering energy, the Dweomer. A miscast or mistake in the spell could be catastrophic—it could freeze him dead or kill his ability to feel. Instead, Arkald curled up into as much of a shivering ball as his screaming hip would allow and waited for the man in the circlet—the Mad Prince, Banric Sahand—to arrive.

Sahand calmly stepped through the ring of fire, the flames parting for his armored bulk like waves against the prow of a battleship. He towered over the wretched form of Arkald, his dagger eyes practically digging furrows in the necromancer's pale cheeks. "Well well, Arkald, it's been a long time." Sahand's voice was heavy and rough, like a shirt of mail dropped on a stone floor.

Arkald couldn't meet the Mad Prince's gaze. When he spoke, his voice was barely a whisper. "How could you know? I was so careful . . . so careful . . ."

Sahand crouched, his mail jingling softly. "I have been working on this project for over ten years, Arkald. I've had you and the rest of the League eating out of my hand all this time, and you thought I'd grown complacent, is that it? That I would forget about my nosy little friend, Arkald, and all his very useful talents?"

Arkald felt tears welling in his eyes. He'd expected rage from the Mad Prince, he'd expected a quick and violent end. He found himself, instead, facing the cold, passionless glare of a man who did things not from impulse, but from somewhere deeper, darker, and infinitely more terrible. "Puh-Please don't kill me. I didn't tell anyone. I swear it!"

Sahand slapped him in the face. It stung but it didn't hurt. "Stop that. Is this the necromancer who terrorized the village of Alwood into paying him tribute? Isn't this the man who summoned the spirits of Varner's dead scouts to come and spy on me? Surely such a man isn't going to weep in the mud like a child? Surely you don't intend to *grovel*."

Arkald was weeping now. He couldn't stop—the pain, the cold, the terror were too much for him. "My tower! My work! You've destroyed me, Sahand! You've already destroyed me!"

Sahand flipped Arkald onto his back so that he could stare into his eyes. "Arkald, I would think a necromancer, of all people, would have a more optimistic appraisal of their own ability to rise from the ashes, as it were. Besides, let's be honest—the Defenders would have found your little tower eventually anyway. Being a sorcerous criminal doesn't mix well with a fixed address; we don't all have private armies to defend us, now do we?"

"But I don't even know what you're really doing!" Arkald said, clutching at Sahand's loglike forearms. "What could I tell anyone? That you're not working on Rhadnost's Elixir? No one would even believe me! Tapping the Daer Trondor sink is an impossible task— it's like trying to move a glacier with your hands! Why would you put in all the effort if *not* for the Elixir? What else could you possibly be doing? If I told, I'd look like a fool!"

Sahand nodded. "Very good try, Arkald—people don't tend to believe you, do they? Arkald the Strange, the fellow who animates dead squirrels and communes with restless spirits so he has someone to talk to—who would believe him? Why, killing you would be a pointless act, as you are so despised."

Arkald grinned and nodded vigorously. "Yes! Yes, just so, Your Grace! No one in the League listens to me! I'm a nobody! A fool!"

Sahand leaned in close to Arkald so that the necromancer could feel hot breath on his icy cheeks. Arkald could now see through the cracks in Sahand's calm, calculating facade. Behind it there was nothing but rage—pure, hateful, white-hot rage. "If I wanted you dead, Arkald, I would have killed you already."

Arkald's breath caught in his throat. Dare he hope? "But my tower, my work . . ."

"A waste of your time, Arkald, and a liability to your continued existence—Defenders, remember? No, Arkald, I've just done you a favor."

Arkald's whole body quivered. He could scarcely breathe.

"You work for me, now. I'll build you a whole new tower in Dellor where you can juggle corpses to your heart's content." The Mad Prince smiled like a panther. "I'll even supply the bodies."

Arkald was trembling now, so forcefully he could scarcely speak. He still wanted to run, to flee into the dark and the cold and never come back. "What's the . . . the catch?"

Sahand reached into a sleeve and produced a scrap of fabric stained with blood. "I have somebody I need you to find. Somebody too curious for their own good."

"A League member? I can't do that. I'll be censured!"

Sahand pushed Arkald back into the mud and then

slammed the heel of his boot into Arkald's broken hip. The world went white with pain for an instant. The necromancer realized he was shrieking before he actually heard himself. Sahand laughed down at him, as powerful and inviolate as a god. "Arkald, what makes you think you have any choice?"

CHAPTER 15

LONG NIGHT

Tyvian didn't sleep. He lay in his heated bed, between
silk sheets, down-stuffed comforters to his chin,
feather pillows all around, and *didn't sleep one wink*.
The very idea that he should have slept *better* in a
smelly tent on the hard ground was enraging. He lay
on his back, staring up at the darkness of his room,
his arms crossed, and stubbornly waited for fatigue to
take him. It would not.

It was all the ring's fault, of course. It continued to
throb quietly throughout the night, and Tyvian cursed
it yet again for ruining the triumph that was to be his

first night home. He had planned it out in his head along the road. With every miserable indignity he suffered in the snow-dusted wilderness between Galaspin and Freegate, he had forestalled his rage by plotting this very evening. He was to arrive home, bathe, dress well, eat pheasant, gloat over Alafarr, and then sleep like a babe in his comfortable bed, his every need and want fulfilled. Then, in the morning, he saw himself kicking in the door of whatever rat's nest Hendrieux had inhabited, feeding him to the gnoll, and whistling all the way to lunch at Callaix's on Angler Street. He even knew the table he would sit at.

Now it was all ruined. He *hadn't* enjoyed his bath. Gloating over Alafarr had been almost a complete failure. He couldn't sleep! In the morning, that meant glassy eyes with dark rings under them and a groggy feeling that would persist all day unless he drank astronomical quantities of karfan, which would then stain his teeth. *That* meant, Tyvian thought, when he stood over Hendrieux's bloodied body and smiled, the last thing the wretched Akrallian thug would remember would be how badly his teeth looked in comparison to the white shirt and coat he intended to wear.

"Dammit all!" he swore aloud, and assaulted a pillow with his fists. It did not satisfy him.

Rolling out of bed, Tyvian pulled on a silk robe and ordered a specter to bring a feylamp. With the light floating just behind his left shoulder, he padded through his darkened flat toward the kitchen. The rain continued its steady assault upon the skylights and long windows outside, filling the halls with the steady sound of water pattering on glass. He remembered then that he had intended to replace the glass with mageglass from the earnings the deal with the "Marquis du Rameaux" would have brought, since they muffled sound better and were unbreakable. He had even lined up a conjurer who could do the work. Of course, once Hendrieux had betrayed him and the "Marquis" turned out to be Alafarr, all possibility of acquiring mageglass windows vanished. Tyvian knew he would be forced to endure the sound of rain or the noise of the city for the foreseeable future. He cursed again.

In the medicine chest in Tyvian's kitchen was a ten-hour sleeping draught of which he had only used two hours. He had purchased it from an alchemist recommended to him by Carlo diCarlo and knew it worked very well, as did a pair of customs officials in Eretheria who together had accounted for those two missing hours. He had only to find it, take it back to his room, down it in one gulp, and he'd be sleeping like the dead until mid-morning. He would have sent a specter to retrieve the draught, but he had forbidden his servants from accessing the medicine chest, ever since the little busybodies had reorganized the whole thing by weight and he had nearly died trying to find a simple blood-patch elixir.

In the kitchen the marble tiles were frigid under Tyvian's bare feet, and he shivered as a cold, wet draft blew up his robe. Frowning at the temperature, he manipulated the rune lock and opened the medicine chest. Finding the sleeping draught where it belonged—under S—he stuffed it into his robe's pocket.

Another cold breeze blew past his ankles. Where was the draft coming from? It wasn't like his specters to leave a window open in a rainstorm, nor was it likely they would forget to close the chimney flue after cooking. There was, however, a third possibility. He took a step forward, found the floor slick with frigid water and saw, at the extent of the lamplight, a specter-driven towel wiping up the mess. That settled it.

Snatching a cleaver from the kitchen table, Tyvian threw the hood over the feylamp, blocking out the light. Feeling with his toes, he tracked the trail of rain-water back to a broken window in his study, whose shutters a third specter had already closed to keep out any additional rain. Moving silently, Tyvian eased them open and peered out into the dim night. There, affixed on a ledge a foot beneath his windowsill, was an iron grappling hook.

Somebody had invaded his home.

The question of who and why they were here was of immediate importance. Whoever had come in had been here for a matter of minutes, and the flat, though large, was not so large that the invader or invaders would be denied their objective for long. Thieves would be looking for valuables, and they wouldn't have had to go any farther than the study for those—solid gold candlesticks, a spirit clock, and one hidden desk drawer that had a bag full of fifty gold marks—yet nothing was disturbed. If not thieves, that left two options: rescuers for Alafarr or assassins for him.

Tyvian hedged his bets on the more likely of the two and stole back toward his own bedroom. The lack of light was no hindrance, since he had personally laid out every square inch of his abode according to his own specifications. Nothing would be out of place since the specters, who never slept, would never allow it. He glided silently and quickly through the pitch-blackness of the night and didn't trip on a thing.

The invaders were not so lucky. Tyvian heard a clatter that he knew was the end-table just inside his bedroom door being knocked over. He grimaced at his own good luck—*had* he been asleep in bed, that noise would have woken him, but too late for him to do anything about it.

Coming up to his door, Tyvian lay flat against the wall just outside. Inside, he heard a man curse. "Kroth! 'E's not 'ere."

"Shhhh!" a second man hissed.

"What?" the first man muttered, "If he ain't here, then it ain't a problem."

"This bed's been slept in."

Tyvian placed the accents—Delloran, or very rural Galaspiner. Hired thugs, he guessed, but exactly who hired them wasn't immediately clear—he had several guesses, though. Not that it mattered at the moment.

"Let's 'ave a light, eh?" the first man said, and shortly thereafter the soft blue glow of an illumite shard emanated from within Tyvian's room.

This was the moment Tyvian had been waiting for. He stepped into the door frame, cleaver cocked back. Inside, he saw two men—one squat and broad-shouldered and the other somewhat taller, but equally as heavyset. The squat one held a well-oiled broadsword while the tall one cradled a loaded crossbow. Tyvian aimed for the larger target and threw the cleaver at the tall man's chest. It spun through the air and ought to have cloven straight through the assassin's breast bone, but instead Tyvian heard the sharp clink of chain mail being tested and saw the cleaver bounce off. The tall man clutched his chest. "Ow!"

"It's 'im!" the squat man roared, and charged. Tyvian ducked back as the tip of the broadsword sliced through where his head had been and embedded itself in the door frame with a meaty *thok*.

As the assassin struggled to free his weapon, Tyvian quickly stepped inside his guard and thrust a thumb into the man's eye as far as it would go. The man cried out in pain and released his sword to cover his face. "Oy! Kroth!"

The tall man had recovered from the shock of being struck and brought his crossbow to his shoulder. Tyvian slammed the door as he fired, serving the double purpose of trapping the broadsword and blocking the quarrel, which punched a full three inches through the other side of the door, stopping only a hairsbreadth from Tyvian's throat. Activating the lock, Tyvian smirked. "Pure oak—worth every penny."

At that moment the door shuddered as the men

inside attempted to get out. Backing away, Tyvian estimated he'd bought himself two minutes, maybe more if they were now unarmed. The appearance of an axe-head through the door's heart revised that estimate to something more akin to thirty seconds. Running through his contingency plans for this situation, he found few that didn't result in him fleeing his home in his robe during a rainstorm, meaning they were entirely unacceptable. However, with his sword in the room *with* the killers, he was left with only an array of kitchen knives to defend himself against two heavily armed and armored men.

"Get our guest out here!" Tyvian yelled to his specters as he ran back toward the kitchen. He snatched up a small double-edged dirk in a sheath and stuffed it in his pocket, where his hand brushed across the sleeping draught.

With a violent crash, Tyvian's pure oak doors were reduced to splinters and the two assassins emerged, roaring. "Oy, Reldamar!" one bellowed. "Come out and die like a man!"

Tyvian snorted at the notion. Apparently, to them, "men" were supposed to die like idiots. He remained hidden and heard them thumping around the flat, yelling for him, but they didn't yet come to the kitchen. They were sticking together, which was smart, and searching systematically, which was also smart. These men were well trained—not thugs, not assassins, but soldiers. Delloran soldiers came in two varieties: mercenaries who once worked for the Mad Prince Banric

Sahand or mercenaries who *currently* worked for the Mad Prince Banric Sahand. Troubling . . .

Finally, Tyvian heard the sound he had been waiting for. Myreon Alafarr was half asleep and sputtering as she was dragged into the living room. "Here now, what nonsense is this? Unhand me, you wretched constructs!"

Both mercenaries immediately homed in on Myreon's protests. "You!" one yelled. "Where's Reldamar! Where is 'e, ye whore?"

The ring gave Tyvian a sharp jolt as he heard the two Dellorans strike Myreon to the ground. Clenching his teeth, he hissed, "I'm on my way . . . all part of the plan, you wretched thing."

Tyvian stole quickly to the living room. The squat one, sword in hand, was kicking a prone Myreon Alafarr next to Tyvian's hand-carved Verisi sofa, while the tall one scanned the surrounding gloom with his crossbow reloaded and recocked. Choosing his moment carefully, the smuggler leapt out of the shadows and threw the dirk, embedding it in the stock of the tall one's crossbow, just in front of the string.

The tall mercenary looked down and smiled. "Missed."

"I did nothing of the kind." Tyvian advanced as the mercenary pointed the crossbow at his chest.

When the tall Delloran pulled the trigger, the string intercepted the blade of the dirk, which cut it as it fired. The result was a crossbow bolt that flew only halfheartedly across the room at a speed and awkward angle that Tyvian found easy to catch. Already close to the stunned mercenary, Tyvian flèched, the bolt held in his hand like a short rapier, and pierced the mercenary's throat just below his chin. Eyes wide in shock, the tall man fell backward, blood bubbling through his lips.

Tyvian whirled to face the squat one, who had stopped kicking Myreon as soon as the smuggler appeared. He held his broadsword blade down—a defensive stance. The barrel-chested Delloran chuckled at Tyvian as he retreated. "Yer pretty smart, eh? Captain told us yer fulla tricks."

He slashed at Tyvian, who retreated and winced as the mercenary's blade cut through a crystal candelabra. "I really wish you would focus on *killing* me and not damaging my property."

"Told us you was funny, too." The Delloran chuckled and dropped a downward cut designed to spit him in two. Tyvian darted to one side, narrowly avoiding the blow. The squat man displayed a set of mostly decayed teeth in a wicked leer. "What? No other knives? No fancy tricks? Ye can't run for always, mate."

Tyvian retreated before the armored mercenary, letting him gloat and leading him into the dining room. He scrambled over the top of the table, placing it between him and the Delloran. "Perhaps we can talk about this?" Tyvian asked, pulling out a chair and gesturing toward it.

"Sure, come on over 'ere and we'll 'ave a chat, you an me." The Delloran laughed, clearly pleased with himself. He circled toward Tyvian around the table, and Tyvian circled away.

"I meant in a more civilized fashion. Would you like something to drink?" Picking up on Tyvian's cues, the specters rushed in a pair of crystal glasses and a pitcher of chilled wine from the kitchen.

"Yeah—yer blood," the mercenary spat. He and Tyvian had now completed a one-hundred-eighty degree circuit of the table, with the Delloran standing right in front of the chair Tyvian had pulled out.

Tyvian smiled. "Won't you sit down?"

The specters pressed the chair against the back of the mercenary's knees, and the man stumbled back into it. He was pushed up against the table, his sword trapped underneath. Tyvian scrambled atop the table, the sleeping draught in his hand. Popping out the stopper, he stuffed it in the mercenary's mouth mid-bellow and upended it. The squat Delloran ejected the small vial with his tongue, choking on the oily black liquid and trying to spit it out, but it was too late. Tyvian knew even if he had spit out six of the eight hours' worth of sleeping draught, there was still a full two that had slipped down his throat.

The mercenary's eyelids drooped shut and, in the middle of a curse, the man's head fell on the table. He snored like a bear.

Tyvian sighed. "Well, there goes any hope of getting my *own* beauty sleep."

He wrestled the heavyset Delloran out of his chair and pried the broadsword out of his hand. Laying the soldier on his back, Tyvian held the tip of the heavy blade over his neck. The ring shot spiderwebs of agony through his hand and up his arm, and he retracted the sword as though stung. "Oh, very well, very well. I'll just have to kill him when he wakes up, though, you bloody stupid trinket."

When Tyvian returned to the living room, he noted to his dismay that the fine, hand-woven rug he had chosen for the center of the floor before the fireplace was stained maroon with the blood of the other Delloran. He scowled at this and was mentally calculating how much this particular home invasion would cost him when he heard a choked groan and remembered Myreon, who was still curled up in the fetal position before the couch. "I say, Myreon, are you all right?"

Myreon pulled herself slowly to all fours and looked up just to glare at Tyvian.

The ring pricked Tyvian, but he ignored it. If the goddamned thing wanted somebody to help up his old nemesis, it could bloody well grow its own arms and legs. "Sorry about the beating, but I needed a diversion and you were the most convenient one available."

Myreon pulled herself onto the couch and lay back gingerly. "The other one's dead?"

"Sleeping, actually." Tyvian held up the ring, "I'm still afflicted with bouts of 'mercy,' you see."

"Do I get a roommate, then?"

"Don't tempt me."

The Defender looked down at the dead man in the center of the living room, eyeing a silver device on his crossbow. "These men were Delloran soldiers, and not expatriates either. They're wearing Delloran wool, and this fellow's crossbow has the imprint of a Delloran weaponsmith. Why would Sahand want to kill you?"

Tyvian nodded, confirming what Myreon had noticed. The broadsword, also, bore the mark of a Delloran bladesmith, and Dellor wasn't much for exporting weapons. "I've been asking myself the same question. I've never even been to Dellor. To be honest, his attention is quite flattering."

Myreon raised an eyebrow. " 'Flattering' is not the right word. I'd pick *terrifying*."

Tyvian smirked. "Funny, I never would have picked you for a coward."

The Mage Defender only rolled her eyes. "That was simply juvenile."

Tyvian shrugged. "My apologies—it has been a long night and my wit is suffering. I shall endeavor to insult you more effectively in the future.

"In any event, Myreon, this is an interesting development. The only person who would have a concrete reason to try and kill me in my own home would be Hendrieux, and he certainly lacks access to a pair of Sahand's soldiers."

Myreon stood up, still slightly hunched. "I've been assaulted enough for one night."

"Sleep well. Oh, and Myreon?"

"What?"

"You wouldn't be attempting to escape from in there, would you?"

Myreon held very still, which was enough for Tyvian to know the answer. After a moment, the Mage Defender sighed. "What else would you expect? I may be caught, but I'm not dead."

"Good to know. Good luck with it." Tyvian nodded and grinned to his prisoner as she limped back to her room/cell.

After Tyvian heard the door close and the specters lock Myreon in, he took the briefest moment to admire her tenacity—there could be little doubt the Defender was quite a woman. If she weren't such a . . . well, such a *Defender*, he might have considered . . .

No. He banished the thought from his mind—it was completely idle, unproductive, and the result of a man who hadn't had the company of a woman in almost a month. There was work to do.

Tyvian went back to the dining room and stripped the slumbering mercenary bare. He then clapped his hands to summon the specters. "This is a side of beef I want packaged and wrapped for shipment immediately. I will summon a courier djinn for pickup in one hour—have this meet it downstairs."

The specters set about their work, and Tyvian went to his study, lighting the lamps as he went. He was never going to sleep tonight, so he might as well be productive. By telling Myreon that Hendrieux was the only man who had a concrete reason to kill him, he had stirred loose a rather odd possibility. He long suspected that Hendrieux hadn't acted alone when setting him up for the fall—Carlo had intimated as much during their meeting—and Sahand, it seemed, was the perfect backer. Sahand *would* have access to pure brymm, he *could* arrange for a gnoll to be boxed up on a spirit engine, and he definitely *did* possess a variety of proscribed sorcerous texts that covered biomancy and even more reprehensible topics. It would also explain Carlo's discomfort with the whole situation—the Mad Prince was not to be crossed. The *why* of all this was still a mystery, but if his hunch was correct, there were several things he could do about it right then and there.

Taking up an autoquill, Tyvian spread out a piece of paper and wrote a letter, taking care to use his best handwriting. When he was finished, he put it in an envelope, put his seal on the wax, and addressed it to Prince Banric Sahand by name, but left the location blank. It might take a bit longer, but courier djinni could of course always deliver things by name alone, for an extra price. They would also move a good bit slower, which helped him a great deal.

He got dressed, belted on Chance, and fetched Myreon's seekwand and the mageglass ring with the farsight augury he had used back on the spirit engine. If he guessed right, he was going to see the look on Banric Sahand's face when His Highness got a certain late night package. He had no doubt the expression would be priceless.

Myreon hadn't been sleeping when she was used as a distraction against the Delloran mercenaries; she had been trying to improvise a sorcerous ritual. Her fingers had now swollen to twice their normal size, and every tiny motion was agony, but still she tried. There wasn't much magic she could channel—the wards on the room made sure of that—but there was one energy the wards couldn't stop: the Astral. Known as the "universal energy," the Astral was the glue that held all the other energies in check. It was inert, having no opposite energy and no influence over the ley of a particular area, and governed such weighty concepts as space, time, and fate itself. No ward could do much to slow it down, even other Astral wards, and it was an instrumental factor in most counterspells against such wards. It was also the primary energy used to send a wraith—a method of long-range communication that involved sending an image of herself to a distant location to deliver a message.

The drawback of the Astral was, of course, that it was notoriously intractable and reticent to be channeled or drawn from the surrounding world. With her magestaff in hand and in top condition, Myreon counted herself as a very talented manipulator of Astral energy. In her current condition, it was like trying to suck tree sap out of a sugartree with only her lips. She had gathered enough of the energy into a single candlestick to create a makeshift *sha*, but drawing the *veta* was extremely slow going. Since she had been interrupted and beaten, she'd had to start over. Now she was almost done . . . again. She only hoped her shaking, weakened fingers hadn't made any errors in the sigils she had marked on the floor in enchanted wax.

Though she tried to keep her doubts out of her mind, the fact that Reldamar basically *told* her that he knew the mage was trying to escape was driving her crazy. Why would he do that? Why not stop her? Why not put her back in those infernal casterlocks? Myreon knew—she just *knew*—that this had something to do with some elaborate plot the smuggler had concocted for his own purposes. Myreon admitted she couldn't imagine what such a plot could be, but she still felt as though every step closer she got to sending a wraith to signal for rescue was a step closer to fulfilling Reldamar's plans.

Forget it, she scolded herself. *He's just playing mind games with you. This is the right thing to do. This is your only chance. Don't make a mistake.*

Sorcerous rituals of every description—and, indeed, all spells—needed three elements to work: the *veta*, the sorcerer, and the focus. The *veta* was the physical framework meant to elicit the proper energies from the surrounding world. In the case of a simple spell, the sorcerer's posture, gestures, and even emotional state served this purpose, but in a ritual, the framework was drawn with an enchanted wax implement known as a *sha*—or a weakly enchanted candlestick, as was the case now. If mistakes were made in the drawing of the *veta*, the energies would be misdrawn, and the spell would either fizzle harmlessly or be miscast with a wide variety of unexpected results, depending on the energy involved. Miscast an Etheric spell and you could rot from the inside out or fall into deep despair; miscast while channeling the Lumen, and people had been known to grow additional fingers or drop into fits of uncontrollable giggling that went on for months. Miscasts, it was said, gave wizards worldwide a healthy sense of humility. One did not channel the energies of creation itself without risk.

Mistakes when performing any sorcerous ritual—where the energies drawn were typically larger than those simply channeled through the body—were even more dangerous things, but the Astral had been known to cause some very peculiar effects when miscast. Some wizards had been frozen in time and space for weeks, months, or even years on end. Some had aged, while others had grown younger. Some had been flung miles away in an instant, while others were cursed with terrible luck for the rest of their lives. When fiddling with the energy of space and time, all manner of things could go wrong. This, also, Myreon tried to keep out of her mind. *You can do this,* she told herself. *You've done this ritual dozens of times.*

In a simple spell, the other two elements—the sorcerer and the focus—were one and the same. The sorcerer enacted the spell with a word of power—or series of words, depending on the complexity—and the focus was the thing through which the *veta* channeled its power. This could be quite tiring and even painful for the sorcerer, and quite a lot of instruction in the Arcanostrum was devoted to ways to reduce sorcerous fatigue. In the case of a ritual, the energies drawn were often too powerful or intense for the human body to realistically manage, and therefore they would use something external for a focus. In the case of the Astral, objects made of sedimentary rock were best. For Myreon's makeshift ritual, the best she could manage was a pebble that had been lodged in the tread of her boot. It looked very small at the center of her thickly drawn, barely legible *veta*. She concluded she would be lucky if she could channel enough energy to even risk a miscast. More likely nothing would happen whatsoever.

It took her hours, but finally, with her semimagical candlestick worn almost to the nub and the first rays of dawn breaking over the horizon, she was ready to enact the ritual and send her wraith. She couldn't send it far—only to that river-inn along the Trell where Reldamar's gnoll had assaulted all the patrons. Assuming the spell worked, she only hoped the people who witnessed her knew what she was and what to do . . . and that somebody would be awake, at dawn, in the galley of a river-inn. Myreon sighed; it was the long shot of long shots.

Fingers trembling with fatigue, body aching in every pore, she chanted the activation words under her breath, just below a whisper, and gradually increased volume to something just below a speaking voice. She tried to keep her mind balanced, calm—the Astral reacted well to even-tempered people . . . usually. Her tongue and lips carefully slid across the complicated syllables of the activation words with practiced ease, but the *veta* remained dark and the pebble didn't shudder. She was about to give up when, with a sudden flash, the wax *veta* sizzled like bacon in a pan and the tiny pebble grew dark as onyx and seemed to fade in and out of existence for a moment. The ritual was working.

She knew it wouldn't work for long, so Myreon lost no time in delivering her message. "People of the Wandering Fountain," she said aloud. "Do not be alarmed. I am Mage Defender Myreon Alafarr of Galaspin Tower, and I require assistance." If anyone was seeing her, she had no idea—no one there was capable of sending a wraith back to her, she was certain. She had to hope they would listen, though. She was due for some luck.

"Please inform Galaspin Tower that I am a prisoner of Tyvian Reldamar in Freegate. He is holding me in a penthouse flat on Top Street, two or three blocks from the Stair Market." Myreon imagined the patrons of the bar sitting around, looking at each other with wide eyes, as her ghostly form chattered on about such outlandish things as Freegate and Tyvian Reldamar and Mage Defenders. She hoped whoever was there wasn't so hung over they discounted this as a hallucination.

The spell was fading, so Myreon sped up her message. "There's a reward for this news being passed to Master Tarlyth of Galaspin Tower. Your service to the Arcanostrum will be appreciated. Please hurry—I am in grave danger!"

Myreon felt the spell fade, and with it, a profound

sense of weariness overcame her. *Please, Hann. Let someone have seen the message.*

With the last vestiges of her energy, she pushed the bed over where the ritual had been performed and threw herself under the quilts. She had to hand it to Reldamar—at least the bed was comfortable. She slept like the dead.

CHAPTER 16

STALKING HENDRIEUX

The Blocks was a neighborhood in Freegate that lay at
the very base of the Cliff District, just above the more
industrious trade-oriented quarters on the valley floor
and just below the fashionable, wealthy, and comfortable areas above the smog layer. It was a place that had
no real purpose beyond housing the teeming masses of
human detritus that drifted through the Free City, and
was widely considered to be the most god-forsaken
place in town, full of run-down brothels, diseased ten-
ements, and dank ink-dens. It was a tangled warren
of trash-strewn streets, rickety catwalks, flimsy stair-

cases, and narrow alleys built more to accommodate rats than people.

Hool crouched in the shadows of one such crooked alley, her nose testing the cold morning air. What Tyvian Reldamar had told her early that morning was not a lie—Hendrieux was close. His smell was dirty and foul, like rotting garbage, and he was excited, perhaps afraid. Her nose and ears told her that he was within the filthy building that jutted into the street not twenty yards away, even though there was no sign that the place was occupied. It had a sign with a picture of some kind of snake coming out of a pool of water. Hool didn't like snakes, didn't like water, and thought the sign was ugly.

She closed her eyes and tried to remember the scents of Api and little Brana, her two missing pups. She imagined the open plains of the Taqar, alive with spring wildflowers, and the blue sky that went on forever. She remembered the feeling of bounding through the tall grass after an antelope, the smell of a brush fire on a dry summer evening, the warmth of her cubs, nestled against her as they slept beneath a million stars. Api would count them—she was a good counter—and Brana would ask Hool stupid questions. Where does the moon go? Why do we sleep? What is metal made from? Hool purred to herself, took a deep breath . . .

. . . and choked on the poisonous fumes filling the air of the foul, dark, human city—the city where her pups were held, somewhere. The city she would tear apart until she found them.

If Hendrieux had been alone, she would have already gone into the run-down building, found him, and broken his bones until he told her where Api and Brana were. Hendrieux was not alone, though—Tyvian had told the truth about that, too. He had with him six men. These men wore armor and carried weapons, like the ones from last night. Unlike those men, though, these men were wary. Hool could tell by how still the ugly building was that they were waiting for something to happen. That meant she could not strike, not yet. She would have to wait.

In their meeting that morning, Tyvian had told her that she should simply follow Hendrieux to his hiding place, but Hool didn't like that plan. It was too slow, too uncertain, and she couldn't be sure that her enemy wouldn't just disappear again, like he had last night. Tyvian had said that was impossible; he had told her things like that were too expensive. Hool didn't believe him, though—how would *he* know how much money Hendrieux had?

She decided instead to see if Hendrieux would *talk* about where he was hiding. Humans were always talking about things they did or were doing or wanted to do. It was like they all wanted the world to care about them for some reason. Hool reflected that this was probably a result of poor upbringing.

Being quiet in the city was much easier than being quiet in the country. There was so much noise in the city, Hool barely needed to look where she stepped as she crawled out of her alley and slunk across the street to the side of the ugly, smelly house. Even though it was morning, there were very few people around. Many of them, Hool knew, were sleeping in their dirty beds as their bodies worked off a whole night of drinking poison and doing wicked things. Many others smelled like fear; its oily scent seemed to stick to every building and house in this tumble-down district.

Hool wedged herself between a barrel of rainwater and a pile of rotting firewood below one of the boarded-up windows of the house and swiveled her ears to their best listening angle. Hendrieux and his six men were inside, but so was another group of men. These men smelled like the human poison called "beer" as well as something filthy and magical and not altogether different than Hendrieux. She could tell there were four or five of them, plus a few others farther away that smelled like they were dying.

"I'm not pleased, Tupa. I was expecting more from you." Hendrieux's voice was clear as day through the flimsy boards on the windows. Hool had to restrain her urge to burst through them and tear his throat out. As it was, she curled her lips back and felt her hackles rise.

The man who was probably Tupa belched noisily. His voice sounded like he had stones stuffed in his cheeks. "So now you comes for me, eh? Every alchemist, talismonger, and thaumaturge in town has themselves holed-up in their shops like they is under siege. Thought maybe, seein' as how I keep you wrist-deep in the stuff, you'd might be makin' an exception. Guess you've finally got to the point where you're scrapin' the bottom, eh?"

"Don't make this bloody, Tupa Fat-Hands. You can drug up cheap alley-muscle all you want, but they'll never be a match for my boys here, and you know it."

"You come one step closer, and me back-alley muscle is gonna show you what they thinks of your Delloran stooges. You touch me, and it's a poison needle in the ear. I disappear, and the Phantom Guild will put the spot on you, they will. You'll have knives in every alley, poison in every drink, and don't think it won't happen! I've got connections, so don't come back 'round here, or I'll feather ye one between the— *Aaaghghhh!*"

Hool cocked her head. She was pretty sure Hendrieux had thrown a knife, and it had stuck in Tupa's hand. She listened as the black market alchemist screamed and moaned, and then there was more fighting. Swords were drawn and men shouted curses at one another. Hool knew who was going to win long before it happened, though; men who smelled of beer and foulness didn't kill men who smelled of boiled leather and oiled metal. The metallic tang of blood filled the air, which made Hool hungry. She made a mental note to catch and eat a rat later—the rats around here were as big as beavers.

"Here," Hendrieux barked, "get Tupa and stuff him in that chest—watch out for poison needles. You, get some of the wretches to do the heavy lifting."

Tupa's voice cracked as he bawled, "No! No! You can't! I don't— *Mmgghhhmmmpffff!*"

There was a thump and somebody locking something. Hendrieux barked some more orders and then said. "Let's go, and stay wary—that gnoll could be out there somewhere."

The door to the building opened and two men in long cloaks and carrying crossbows stepped out. They scanned the street carefully from side to side for a moment, and Hool was very still. They did not see her, and nodded to those inside. Four others came out, but these were not soldiers. They were skinny and smelled of sweat and deathly sickness, wearing only rags, a big chest slung between them that they labored to carry— Hool's gnoll ears could hear Tupa sobbing and calling for help from inside. These men looked cold and in pain, and Hool wondered what was wrong with them. Finally, the four other guards came out with Hendrieux, who was wearing a suit of mail that hung off his sloping shoulders like an ill-fitting second skin.

The procession set out down the street, and Hool watched them go without being noticed by the wary eyes of the armored men. Waiting until they had rounded the corner, she picked up the trail, following them easily while staying out of their line of sight. Even still, she kept to the shadows, using the murk and grime of the Blocks to her advantage as she stalked her prey.

The buildings around Hool did not improve much

in quality, but they did improve in cleanliness. Instead of smoke and ash, she smelled liquor and sweat, as well as a fair amount of blood. Here the road ran close to a muddy ditch about ten yards across, through which moved a rapidly flowing flume of brown water. Along its banks were a series of mills, each one larger and more impressive than the last, their great wheels grumbling and clattering as they turned, filling the air with a mechanical riot of noise. It was here, in the awful racket and stink, that Hool lost the trail.

Laying her ears back against her skull, she doubled back and checked to make sure she hadn't missed a turn, then searched the area in gradually widening circles to pick up the scent again. She got it, and quickly, but it was different. She tracked it to an alley with another old door at its end. Ripping it open, she found it led to a dusty, empty storeroom with nothing but piles of empty crates and no other exits.

She snorted. "Magic."

Hool checked the sky and guessed it was midmorning. She turned and left the alley, then, making her way toward the center of the city—it was time for Reldamar to make himself useful.

Imar's was a restaurant of the highest quality but not of the highest breeding. It was the premiere meeting place for the wealthiest businessmen, guild members, and merchants in Freegate, and Tyvian found its thick carpeting and ostentatious hardwood furniture the most crass and obvious display of tasteless wealth in the city. The potted plants were too large, the chandeliers too ornate, and the waiters strutted around in cartoonish imitation of their actual, nobility-bound counterparts. The food, though, was excellent, and this, coupled with the opportunity it gave Tyvian to turn his nose up at the middle class, made it one of his favorite spots.

"It is a bit early for lunch, Tyvian." Carlo diCarlo said quietly. Sitting across the table from the smuggler, he gazed over Tyvian's shoulder at a table full of Saldorian tailors splurging on expensive wine and roast duck.

Tyvian sipped his tea, admiring its delicate flavor while simultaneously sneering at the ridiculous pattern of the cup. "I had an early morning, Carlo. Not everybody sleeps until noon, you know."

"You are lucky I came, with the way you treated me yesterday."

"The invitation involved food and a business proposition. Why wouldn't you show up?"

Carlo snorted and reviewed his menu. "I am getting the lobster, just to spite you. What are you getting?"

Tyvian held up two fingers. "Firstly, I wouldn't tell you what I was getting even if I knew, since I know for a fact that one of the cooks here owes you a favor. Secondly, I haven't the slightest idea what I'm getting, since I don't know what they are serving today."

Carlo pointed at Tyvian's menu, as yet untouched and unopened. "You could find out."

Tyvian sneered at the menu. "The very idea that they expect me to *read* what food they have available is precisely why they will never attract anyone of higher social station than those tailors over there. I mean, why even *have* a servant if you are going to do all the work anyway?"

Carlo rolled his one real eye. "So speaks the man who showed up at my door yesterday in dirty furs with a gnoll by his side."

"Tragedies of circumstance, Carlo, that's all. Tragedies that will be set right soon enough, by the way." Tyvian smiled and sipped his tea.

Carlo put his eye back on the menu and spoke casually. "I heard you had some excitement last night."

"Your rumormongers are talented, I'll give you that."

Carlo nodded. "So now you know who you're dealing with."

"Hendrieux."

The Verisi pirate slammed his menu down. "No! Sahand!"

Several tables full of various blacksmiths and fur traders looked over in their direction. Tyvian, remembering his breeding, didn't return their gaze. Instead, he remarked coolly to Carlo, "You are not yourself, my friend."

Carlo regained his composure rapidly. He removed his crystal eye and buffed it with a napkin. Tyvian watched, catching the simple cues; the secrets passed through innuendo. "Times have been stressful, and you are making everything worse." *What you're doing is going to hurt Hendrieux*.

Tyvian laughed softly. "Now Carlo, how can that be? I've only been in town for twenty-four hours. Surely I couldn't have—"

Carlo popped his eyepiece back in to complete a stern glare. "Stop playing coy with me, Tyvian. You know as well as I do that you are shaking things up. For Hann's sake, boy, you've done that your whole life. This time is different, though. This time it isn't a game."

"Who said I'm playing, Carlo? That skinny ink-thrall Hendrieux betrayed me, and I'm settling accounts. It's business, not games."

"You can't settle accounts without getting in Sahand's way, and that's the kind of trouble you *don't* want, Tyvian. I tried to tell you this yesterday, but you had to go threatening me with that bloodthirsty monster . . ." Carlo shuddered. "You might be able to handle Hendrieux—he's a fool, as you say—but Sahand is out of your class, Tyvian. He's both brutal *and* intelligent, and don't let anyone convince you otherwise."

Here, the implication was clear enough. Tyvian smiled broadly. "He's in town, or near enough, you know."

Carlo choked on his glass of water. "How . . . how in blazes do you . . . wh-where did you see—"

Tyvian laid a finger beside his nose. "Tut tut, Carlo—a secret of *that* magnitude will cost you *quite a lot.*"

The waiter arrived, and Carlo ordered the lobster, as threatened. Tyvian, after demanding a recitation of the menu, whispered his order in the waiter's ear and sent him on his way. Carlo shook his head. "I'm not going to poison you, Tyvian."

"Yesterday's conversation would indicate the contrary," Tyvian countered.

Carlo folded his arms. "Fine. What is your proposition?"

"I want you to set me up a meeting with the Kalsaari Hanim."

"Hilarious. What do you really want?"

"A meeting with the aforementioned Kalsaari Hanim."

Carlo cleared his throat. "You are aware that I do not get along well with the Kalsaari nobility. I spent a good few years under Mudboots Varner and Finn Cadogan in Rhond, cutting Kalsaari throats."

Tyvian rolled his eyes. "Don't play the whole 'patriotic Westerner' card with me, Carlo. You were a mercenary—you were paid."

"Ten percent under market rate, mind you. I don't truck with queenies."

"I can make it worth your while."

"No, you can't. Even that little tidbit regarding the location of Sahand in the city isn't worth my directly entangling myself with those vipers."

"Carlo, if you do this for me, I will split the result with you, fifty-fifty."

Carlo sat very still for a moment. "Seventy-thirty."

"Not on your life."

The Verisi's eyes narrowed. "What does this have to do with Hendrieux?"

"Do you really think I am so one-dimensional, Carlo?"

"Answer the question. I want to see you lie."

Tyvian grinned. "It has nothing directly to do with Hendrieux. Can you do it?"

"How much are we talking, here?"

"You remember my house guest? The one my gnoll was babysitting yesterday?"

Carlo sat up straighter and grinned. "Yes. Yes I do."

"How much do you suppose the Kalsaaris would pay for her?"

Carlo folded his hands on his paunch and added figures in his head while Tyvian watched closely. "At least five thousand marks. Probably in gems and other goods that could be bartered for more. Gods, Tyvian, that's not bad!"

Tyvian nodded. He already knew the price. It was a terrible tragedy that neither he nor Carlo would ever see a copper of it. Even the ring burned with disappointment on Tyvian's finger. He knew it was disappointed by his misleading Carlo, not with the loss of money, but Tyvian decided to believe otherwise. For once, he and the ring were upset in concert. What the ring didn't quite seem to appreciate, though, was that

Carlo should undoubtedly be aware of the deception. Tyvian was counting on it, actually.

Carlo was still plotting and arranging in his head. "The Hanim is throwing a party tomorrow night. I think I know a few favors I can call up, perhaps get us an invitation."

"And a personal audience."

Carlo chuckled. "Impossible."

"*Possible* if you rise before noon."

"Why should I?"

"Your share of five thousand marks."

Carlo sighed. "Make it sixty-forty and you have a deal."

"Fifty-five, forty-five."

"An insult."

"You are a greedy, Verisi pig," Tyvian said, and added, "*That* is an insult."

"Fifty-five, forty-five," Carlo countered, "and you give me that tidbit about Sahand, or you stand at the back of the crowd just like everybody else, no matter what names you call me."

Tyvian delayed his response just long enough to make Carlo think he was mulling it over, and then answered. "Very well."

Carlo let a gold-plated grin escape him. "Excellent. Now, let's hear it."

Tyvian leaned forward, careful to cover his mouth to prevent lip-reading. "Sahand isn't *in* the city. He's camped up in the mountains, among the old ruins of Daer Trondor, with a fairly sizable armed party."

Carlo's real eye went wide, but he only nodded. "Interesting. Didn't think there was anything left of much use up there."

"What do you know about what he's up to?"

Carlo frowned. "You haven't the assets to purchase that information from me even if I knew, Tyvian, and it's for the best, believe me. Whatever it is, it's important enough for him to kill anybody who gets in his way, understood?"

"Why Carlo, you almost sound concerned for my well-being. How touching."

Carlo rolled his good eye. "Spare me, you grinning jackanapes."

They waited in silence for a few minutes. Tyvian had nothing to say and Carlo was likely too busy plotting away to notice the lack of conversation. The monolithic spirit clock of gilded brass that stood against the opposite wall of the dining room told Tyvian it was nearly half-past twelve. He was exhausted and wanted very much to take a nap, but knew doing any such thing was unwise until he had a safer place in which to do it. After last night, he had set Hendrieux back on his heels, that was certain, but that Akrallian skunk would regroup soon enough. As soon as he could, he would send more assassins, and this time they wouldn't be as subtle. Tyvian conjured up images of hired invokers pitching balled lightning and firestorms through his window, or perhaps a pack of heavily armored thugs, sorcerously abjured with enough guards and wards that they were basically invulnerable to attack, kicking through his door and bludgeoning him to death. Neither were pleasant thoughts and, with the ring restricting his behavior, his recourses to avoid such tactics were limited.

Tyvian was keenly aware that the metaphorical waters he now sailed were getting ever more treacherous. To achieve his aims—revenge on Hendrieux and the removal of the ring—he would have to navigate his way between several powers much larger than himself. On the one hand was Sahand, whom Tyvian knew enough about to have a healthy respect for his capacity for destruction and vengeance, and on the other were the Kalsaaris, who could not be trusted—Carlo was very much right about that. The problem was, to kill Hendrieux would require him to anger Sahand, and to remove the ring would require him to trust Kalsaaris. It wouldn't work, obviously. Sahand would make a target of him; the Kalsaaris would betray him. Of course, if he did nothing, the ring would remain on his finger and Hendrieux would eventually find a way to destroy him out of self-preservation. His points of leverage, though, Tyvian thought, might just work all of this out in his favor. A good offense, as old Mudboots Varner was wont to say, was the best defense.

His musings were interrupted by the food arriving and a man screaming somewhere near the entrance of Imar's. The scream was of a timbre Tyvian quickly identified, so while patrons and waitstaff fled from the door in barely constrained panic and Carlo quickly activated a variety of defensive guards placed upon his many rings, Tyvian smeared some mint jelly on his lamb chop and cut off a delicate bite. He had it on his fork and was about to eat it when Hool stomped up to his table.

Her fur was covered in black soot and grime, and she smelled very much like an open sewer. "Hendrieux used magic again," the gnoll announced.

Tyvian ate the bit of lamb. It melted in his mouth, perfectly spiced and tender. "He and his entire entourage vanished?"

"Yes. It was another magic door," Hool confirmed, and then looked at Carlo, who had his back pressed to the wall, his face a mask of terrified concentration. "Who are you?"

"Forgive me—where are my manners?" Tyvian said. "Carlo diCarlo, allow me to present to you Hool, the gnoll I've talked about. Hool, this is Carlo diCarlo."

"You have a stupid name," Hool announced, and then crouched on the floor.

Tyvian snapped his fingers at one of the cowering serving staff. "We need another chair over here."

A quiet argument erupted among the servants until, at last, Tyvian's own waiter was thrust forward. He slowly made his way to Tyvian's elbow, his face pale and his hands trembling. "Sir . . . your guest is not . . . *dressed* appropriately."

Tyvian took another bite of lamb, chewing and swallowing completely before answering. "I see. Now, what is it that you consider 'appropriate' dress?"

Disinterested in the exchange between Tyvian and

the servant, Hool picked up one of Carlo's lobsters and sniffed it. "Is this a fish?"

Carlo shook his head. "No . . . lobster."

Hool tore the head off of the lobster in one massive bite. After giving it a few savage chews, she swallowed and nodded slowly. "Lobster is good."

"Appropriate dress—" the waiter began.

"Is it anything like you are dressed, sir?" Tyvian interjected.

"Well . . . yes sir, I suppose so."

"So you would have my friend wear an ill-tailored jacket, breeches that are too tight around the thighs, a lace collar that clearly needs laundering, and a shirt that was obviously purchased off a bargain cart in Tailor Town? No sir, I think not." Tyvian pulled out two gold marks and slapped them on the table. "Get a basin, as well as some soap, and allow her the opportunity to wash up, and I think you'll find that she is more 'appropriately' dressed for her station than anyone else here."

The servant's ears turned red, but no other expression registered. "The owner will call the Watch, sir."

Tyvian nodded. "I suppose Imar would, but if you would be so good as to inform him that I have already paid the Watch two hundred marks *not* to show up, he may change his tune. Furthermore, allow me to demonstrate something for you. Hool?"

Hool's mouth was stuffed with lobster, so her only answer was her ears swiveling in Tyvian's direction.

"Could you please lift Mr. diCarlo over your head?"

Hool blinked at him, shrugged, and then grabbed Carlo by the belt and swung him over her shoulder like a bag of dirty laundry while the Verisi pirate howled incoherently. The server, upon seeing this, bobbed his head and vanished with a "Yessir."

Hool put Carlo down and swallowed her lobster. Carlo was panting. "Reldamar, this indignity is . . . is—"

Tyvian put up his hand. "Please, Carlo—you were the one who taught me just what too much dignity could get you. You are a back-alley fixer, not the Prince of Illin, and Hool didn't mean you any harm."

Hool pointed at Carlo's glass of white wine. "Is that wine?"

Carlo sighed and waved his hand at it. "Go ahead, it's yours."

Hool snorted. "I hate wine. I want water."

Carlo scowled and looked at Tyvian, who was eating with gusto. "You are attracting a lot of attention, you know. This will only cause trouble for me."

"Nonsense, Carlo!" Tyvian smiled. "This will only tell everyone that I'm one of your clients and that the gnoll who killed two of Sahand's men last night is as well. The only way that would actually cause any trouble would be if *you* were working with *Sahand*. Now, you aren't doing that, are you?"

Carlo shook his head. "Of course not! Why would a prince need me?"

Tyvian smirked and shrugged. "I don't know, Carlo. Why would he need Hendrieux?"

Carlo diCarlo scowled. "You are an incredible nuisance, Tyvian Reldamar, and I will cherish the day you no longer pester me."

Tyvian pointed at him. "Now that last one—*that* was a lie."

Carlo stood up, throwing his napkin down on the table. "Good day to you . . . to you both."

As he stormed out, Tyvian called after him, "Tomorrow night, Carlo! *Private* audience!"

Hool transferred herself to Carlo's seat and set about eating the rest of his lunch. "He doesn't like you."

"Nonsense—he loves me. He just can't stand that I'm better at his game than he is."

Hool stuffed a roll in her mouth and swallowed it with only two bites. "What about Hendrieux?"

Tyvian leaned back in his chair. "Just remember the plan and everything will work out. He'll be in trouble soon enough, I promise."

CHAPTER 17

TROUBLE IN DARK PLACES

Along the eastern edge of Freegate ran the narrow, swift waters of Arble Brook. It began as a waterfall flowing over the brim of Dain's Lake, the artificial reservoir that gave the rich folks of Angler Street their waterfront views and everybody else access to drinking water. After it fell from the steepest section of the Cliff District, past iron cargo elevators and winding covered walkways, it landed in a misty explosion of water vapor and poured in a torrent past the densely packed waterwheels of a great many industrial facilities—ore refineries, artifactories, mills of every size and description—until, finally, it reached a bend in its path and flowed under a series of covered stone bridges decorated with the decaying corpses of hanged people dangling through numerous trapdoors built into those bridges for exclusively this purpose.

In other nations of the world this would be where the local ruling authority displayed the fate of those who disturbed the social order. In Freegate, a city cheerily devoid of conventional notions of social order, the hangings were exclusively private affairs. Usually undertaken by the guilds against members who stepped out of line or, more often, against members of their assembly who refused to pay their dues, all one needed to do in order to hang someone legally and officially was to pay two bribes. One was to the city watch, of course, who would helpfully apprehend the offending party and hold them until their time of execution was due, and the other was to the Phantom Guild—the thieving guild of Freegate that administered the bridges, all of which fell entirely within their jurisdiction.

This area of town, immediately adjacent to the Blocks, was known as Corpse Alley. Nearby, within the highest room of the highest tower of a moss-encrusted, half-crumbling keep built along a thin stone jetty thrusting into the Arble, Zazlar Hendrieux was lying on a straw sleeping pallet and dipping ink.

Ink was a catchall term for a series of alchemical concoctions designed to stimulate the emotions and senses. The precise emotion or sense stimulated depended greatly upon the kind of ink taken. Some were soothing, like Cool Blue or Bright, while others were invigorating, like the Crimson. In any case, the effects of any vial of ink far outstripped those of mundane drugs like tooka, karfan, or alcohol. Vials of ink were also, all of them, highly addictive.

Hendrieux, at that moment, was dabbing his fingers into an open pot of Cool Blue, letting the sensation of supernatural calm trickle up his arm and spread through his body like rivulets of ice water through his veins. The Dweomer-based concoction was of a deep, navy blue color and had the consistency of thick oily paste. It stained the fingertips purple for days afterward, but the minor inconvenience was worth every moment of the calm it could give.

Hendrieux stared up at the flickering flame of the oil lamp above his head, his eyes unfocused, and let the terrors of the day slowly flake and chip off him like so much dead skin. The sight of the gnoll's blazing copper eyes and white fangs in the dark of the alley seemed like a distant, abstract image—something he saw in a picture book somewhere, or an old story told and retold by a close friend. Even the two men the gnoll had killed were gone from his mind.

Then there was Tyvian Reldamar. The famous smuggler wasn't dead, and he knew that Hendrieux had betrayed him. The thought alone would ordinarily be enough to keep the Akrallian awake and quivering all night. He would already have moved apartments, even though there was no way Reldamar could know he was here. He'd have a pair of his men watching his back at all times.

But so far as he was concerned, there was no reason to worry. So what if the two men he had sent failed? He had more men—he'd send four next time. Knowing Reldamar, he'd probably be too busy taking some expensive bath or having his toenails filed by some serving girl to realize he was in danger. That was always Tyvian's weakness—arrogance. He thought he was smarter than everybody.

He is smarter than everybody, a little voice whispered from deep inside Hendrieux's sedated mind. Hendrieux reflexively jabbed his middle finger deeper into the ink pot and let the magical concoction kill his concerns. The next time would succeed. Tyvian would die and he would be safe. It would all work out, and Sahand would never have to know.

Then there was the Phantom Guild. Taking Tupa Fat-Hands that morning had been an act of desperation. There would be consequences for it, that much was certain. The guild already disliked how Hendrieux had placed himself as head of their kidnapping operations. They wouldn't take kindly to his kidnapping useful black market alchemists. At other times the thought of Phantom assassins lurking in every alley, poisoned knives at the ready, would have driven him to paranoia, but the ink made it all better. There were no assassins. Even if there were, he could handle it. He was Zazlar Hendrieux, King of Thieves. They would all learn their place.

Sahand is getting impatient, the voice said again, and Hendrieux put three fingers in the pot and closed his eyes. Prince Sahand expected progress. He expected returns on his investment from him. That was the reason he nabbed Tupa in the first place.

"He'll get them," Hendrieux whispered to no one. "He'll see."

His increased intake of the Cool Blue ink put Hendrieux in a deep trance. He wasn't asleep. He could see the lantern flickering above him, he could hear the creaks of the rickety tower and the moans of the other ink-thralls on the couches and beds strewn across the floors in other rooms—many of them forced into addiction as a way of controlling them before being sent to serve Sahand. Hendrieux couldn't move—he was paralyzed with cold, numbing indifference and apathy. He was neither happy nor sad, but frozen perfectly between the two. Vaguely, in the distant recesses of his mind, were the stories about people who had dipped too far into Cool Blue and lost their capacity to feel anything. They were like the living dead, it was said, and soon starved, as they no longer saw the need to eat. Slowly, and with a monumental effort, Hendrieux withdrew his fingers from the ink pot, but then lay still and limp as a rag.

He didn't even move as Banric Sahand strode into the room and looked down at him.

Sahand's voice, even when echoing through the thick sheet of indifference provided by the ink, made Hendrieux's stomach quiver. "Take this wretch downstairs. I'll not discuss this in an attic like some squatting indigent."

Rough hands seized Hendrieux by the ankles and dragged his limp body down the stairs. He scarcely felt his head bounce off each step; he opened his mouth to protest but no sound came out. All he could do was fumble weakly for his pot of ink, knowing on some level that it was his only means of protection for what was to come.

The Great Hall of the Arble Keep, once the strongpoint of an ancient Galaspiner settlement, was now little more than a dusty, drafty room full of half-broken furniture and moldering tapestries. A good number of Delloran soldiers rose as Sahand entered at the head of his entourage.

Hendrieux was dragged into the center of the room and hoisted upright under each armpit by the gauntleted fists of Gallo, who held him before the prince like one might hold a puppy out to be inspected by a breeder. Hendrieux could only watch as Sahand slowly removed each of his gloves, one finger at a time. "Are you in there, Zazlar?" he asked, his voice seemingly miles distant. "I'm so glad to see you're enjoying your payment."

The prince nodded to one of his men, who stepped forward with a pot of bubbling red paste. "I'm afraid your little mental escape is going to be drawn to a close, however." Using a small brush, Sahand's man smeared some of the Crimson beneath Zazlar's nose and behind his ears.

Blazing hot panic lanced through every nerve in Hendrieux's body as the invigorating ink burned Cool Blue's effects straight out of his system. Hendrieux felt as though he had been plucked from a snowdrift and tossed in an oven. "Ohhh! Gods!" His muscles quivered and twitched, and he did his best to stand upright. "Th-Thank you, Your Highness."

Sahand smiled tightly. "Excellent. Are you back with us, Zazlar? Can you *feel* again?"

Hendrieux managed a haphazard bow. "Yes, Your Highness. I'm . . . I'm back."

"Good." Sahand kicked him in the stomach so hard, the Akrallian collapsed into a triangle on the floor, his face and knees pressed against the dirty ground as he struggled to take in air. Above him, he heard the steel-hard voice of the Mad Prince say, "*That* was for wasting my men."

Hendrieux rolled onto his back, his lungs trying to recover. His body still sang with the fiery effects of the Crimson, and his twitching muscles only made him flounder on the ground. "I . . . I am sorry, milord. Reldamar was a threat to our—"

"Reldamar is a threat to *you*, Zazlar, not *me*, and certainly not *us*." Sahand looked around at the dilapidated furniture and turned to one of his entourage of armored men. "Bring me a suitable chair."

A man bowed and left without comment.

"You told me Reldamar was dead," Sahand went on, fixing Hendrieux with his steel-hard glare. "Did you lie to me, Zazlar?"

Hendrieux struggled to his feet, still partially doubled over. "No! He was . . . or I thought he was. The spirit engine was destroyed, Your Highness, and I assumed—"

"You 'assumed.'" Sahand sneered. "Do you know why I am here?"

Hendrieux managed a weak smile. "I as-assumed that you wished to help me deal with—"

"There is that word again—'assume,'" Sahand interrupted. "Gallo, if Captain Hendrieux says the word 'assume' one more time, gut him."

Gallo, his breath gurgling rough assent, put a big hand on Hendrieux's shoulder and pressed a rondel dagger with a long triangular blade against the Akrallian's stomach. Hendrieux stood perfectly still.

Sahand's chair arrived, and the prince sat down. "Do you know why I hate the word 'assume,' Hendrieux?"

"I as— I don't know, Your Highness."

"I hate it because that implies that you, Zazlar Hendrieux, my hand here in Freegate, are *thinking*. I did not acquire your services because you were a *thinker*, Hendrieux. I acquired you because you had a knack for following complex *instructions*. Did my instructions involve sending a pair of my men to assassinate Reldamar in his home?"

"Well . . ."

Sahand's iron-hard glare narrowed. *"Did they?"*

Hendrieux shook his head. "No, milord . . . err . . . Your Highness."

"If I had wanted someone capable of thought, I would have hired Reldamar, not *you*, you insufferable dunce. I hired you because you were ruthless, cunning, addicted to ink, and able to follow *directions!*"

Hendrieux hazarded a glance at Gallo, whose scarred lips were blowing particles of spittle into his ear. "Yes . . . of course, Your Highness."

"I would like to share something with you, Zazlar, and afterward I would like your opinion on it." Sahand put out his hand to one of his men and a letter was placed in it. Sahand then handed it over to Hendrieux. "Read this."

Hendrieux unfolded it, and noticed the handwriting immediately. He began to tremble as his eyes scanned the page.

Your Highness,

Please find accompanying this note one of two packages shipped to me in error this past evening, the 29th of Ishmonth. The presence of these parcels in my abode caused a good deal of damage to my property. I am appending an invoice detailing the precise costs but, in brief, it asks for the replacement of or compensation for the following:

One (1) Window
One (1) Door, Pure Oak

One (1) Rug, Hand-woven, Hurnish
One (1) Candelabra, Crystal

One (1) Sleeping Draught, Ten-hour duration

Ordinarily, I would not seek to bother your esteemed person regarding matters of this nature, but as I must assume this was an error made by those in your employ, I thought it important that you be made personally aware of it. I regret any inconvenience this may cause you, and also regret that only one package is being returned. During its stay at my home, the other package was damaged beyond repair and not fit for additional use, and so I have taken the liberty to dispose of it for you.

As a gentleman of unparalleled reputation, I know you will take it upon yourself to resolve this unpleasant matter quickly and to the benefit of all.

Your Friend, in Spirit,

Tyvian Reldamar

P.S.: Please understand that shipping the parcel "cash on delivery" is not meant as a slight. I am but a poor smuggler who can ill afford to ship mislaid cargo.

When Hendrieux had finished, the color drained away from his face and he stood, shaking like a blade of grass in the wind before the murderous scowl of the Mad Prince of Dellor. "I . . . I—"

"Shut up!" Sahand snapped. "I received that note

early this morning, along with one of my men, who was tied up like a slab of *beef* and deposited in my personal supply tent by a courier djinn."

The prince paused, letting that information seep into Hendrieux's terrified brain. Hendrieux looked to his left and to his right, where each of Sahand's men were looking at him with deadpan expressions. Many of them had their hands on their swords. Gallo pressed the rondel harder against Hendrieux's stomach.

"Now," Sahand began, "what I would like from you, Hendrieux, is assurances that your feud with Reldamar is *over*. No further contact, do you understand? Avoid him—we are hopefully very near the end of our operations here, and I can't afford your simple, ink-addled brain getting distracted by petty vendettas."

"But . . . I haven't been . . . I mean I've been quite certain to . . ."

Sahand cocked an eyebrow at him. "I seem to recall you acquiring *three* gnolls for me some time ago, but then you seemed to have *misplaced* one, is that not correct?"

Hendrieux's heart sank. "Yes. But . . ."

Sahand ran a thick hand along the short silver stubble that adorned his chin. "You will be needed for another pickup from our supplier tomorrow night, Captain. Given your propensity to misuse my resources for your own personal reasons, I am leaving Gallo here as an advisor. I am *also* leaving more men to secure this tumble-down hovel of a slaver's prison you've acquired. I'll not have my operations compromised by some foolish thieving guild that gets angry over losing their favorite alchemist. Do you understand?"

Hendrieux, pale, bowed deeply. "Yes, Your Highness."

Sahand got up, his bodyguards falling into position around him. "One more thing, Captain—if I hear of you jeopardizing my aims to protect your worthless hide again, I'll have you staked out in a crow-cage with your eyes torn loose."

With a solemn nod to Gallo, Sahand turned and strode from the room, his cape swirling after him.

When he was gone, Hendrieux collapsed into a chair and let out a long, slow breath. His fingers twitched with a desire to go back into the tower and dive into another pot of Cool Blue. Gallo just stood there, watching him like a hangman on Traitor's Day.

CHAPTER 18

COVERT AFFAIRS

The Horse District occupied the northernmost corner of Freegate, clustering around Grand Avenue as it left the city and made for the Pass. Here, horses and livestock from the broad pastures of the North were brought for sale and trade. Accordingly, the district was a sprawling array of corrals, barns, stables, and racetracks, all of which were as full of vagabonds and fugitives looking for untended haystacks to sleep in as with horse traders and drovers. The wealthier members of the Drover's Guild paid the Watch to make regular sweeps of their property and pummel the ne'er-do-wells found there with sufficient savagery that they either died or deigned not to return. The rest of the guild, however, spoke of their unwanted guests with the same benighted resignation they reserved for rats and other vermin, and resolved not to leave anything of value out that wasn't securely bolted down.

It was in the hayloft of a barn owned by one such horse trader that Artus tried to get a good night's sleep. This was made inordinately difficult by the two other drifters present in the hayloft, who, together, snored loudly enough to make a spirit engine sound like a lullaby. Artus knew better than to ask them to keep it down—there was an unspoken pact of silence among barn-trespassers, born from the simple realization that one didn't know if the fellow sleeping next to you was in the barn just because he was broke or because he had just murdered his whole family and was on the run. If you didn't ask, you didn't find out, and everybody lived much longer, happier lives on the average.

Artus had been in this particular barn before, on his first trip through Freegate. He was just a few months older than twelve then and didn't know anything about the big cities of the West. Freegate had been a shocking experience—more people and more buildings than he had ever seen in one place. He'd been robbed of all his money on his first day, beaten on his second, and wound up in this barn on the night of his third. He had cried a lot then. He knew better than to cry now—you weren't supposed to weep and carry on in barns either.

It was cold in the hayloft, despite the piles of straw

under which he had burrowed. He could see his breath in the moonlight; it was a clear, cold night, and the thin mountain air left his throat dry and cracked. He wondered what Reldamar and Hool were up to. He hadn't seen Reldamar since he'd been ditched, and he hadn't seen Hool since this morning. They were probably up to something.

"Probably getting even with Hendrieux," Artus grumbled to himself. He thought he had at least as big a stake in getting back at Hendrieux as Tyvian or Hool—*he'd* been on that spirit engine, too, after all. Sure, he didn't have any children who were kidnapped or have any partners who'd betrayed him, but still . . .

Artus sat up. He was never going to get to sleep with his fellow vagrants' thunderous snores shaking the shingles off the barn anyway, and decided to see if the accommodations were any better under the grandstand at the racetrack down the road. He climbed down to the barn floor and crept outside, keeping a careful eye out for the trader's guard dog, though not because he was afraid of being attacked. The dog had been so consistently fed by various vagabonds through the years that it was fat and very friendly. It also happened to be quite insistent on *being* fed, and failure to do so meant it would bark its head off. This would, in turn, attract the trader who, though equally as fat as his dog, wasn't half as friendly and frequently had a poleaxe with him.

Since Artus had no food, he did his best to cross the yard to the gate without stirring so much as a clod of dirt. The dog, slumbering underneath the front stairs of the house, did not wake. At the gate, his eyes still fixed on the sleeping dog, Artus carefully moved to lift the hook . . . and stopped.

Someone was coming up the road beyond the yard, their steps jingling with the sound of armor and a sword. Not wishing to risk an encounter with a watchman, Artus peered through a crack in the gate to watch the person pass. It was not, as it happened, a city watchman at all.

It was Hacklar Jaevis.

The bounty hunter looked paler than before and even more weather-beaten, but was otherwise the same. He was walking in the middle of the street, which was strange given the quantity of mud there, and was wearing a purse openly on his hip, which was even stranger given the concentration of sneak thieves and muggers in the area. Granted there wouldn't be many who would challenge the likes of Jaevis, but it was still a risk. If nothing else, Artus was fairly certain that a talented cutpurse could nab the money and outrun the bounty hunter before having his throat slashed.

Every fiber of Artus's body shook with terror at the thought of Jaevis, here, alive. He knew this meant trouble for Tyvian and for Hool, too. How was he still alive? What could he be doing walking through the Horse District at this time of night? Watching Jaevis's silhouette recede into the dark of the winter night, Artus slipped silently out of the yard and began to shadow the bounty hunter through the muddy streets, ignoring the sound of his mother's voice in his head that told him, over and over, that this was the stupidest idea he had ever had.

Every step Jaevis took made a thick, sloshing noise in the mud—a sound that Artus used to cover the sound of him creeping along some ten paces behind. Every minute or so Jaevis would turn around and check behind him. Artus, who had picked up a talent as a tail when living on the streets of Ayventry, barely managed to dart into an alley or behind a cart before being seen each time. With each occurrence, however, his heart raced faster and faster. The gravity of his situation was becoming more and more clear—one trip, fall, or stumble, and Jaevis would see him. If Jaevis saw him, it would make the second night in a row where he was almost stabbed to death in a Freegate alley.

Still, it was Jaevis. It was crazy, but he just *had* to know what the bounty hunter was doing here.

There was a sudden thunder of hooves and a squeak of undergreased axles; a coach drawn by a pair of dun-colored draft horses rounded a corner and headed straight for Jaevis, who stopped walking and shielded his eyes from the glare of the large feylamps mounted on the coach's roof. The horses pulled up short at the coachman's guttural command right in front of the bounty hunter, and Artus prepared for a string of colorful, Illini expletives to be hurled at the driver. None came, however.

"Ozmar?" Jaevis asked.

"Jus' get in, dummy," the coachman returned.

Jaevis frowned and pointed at the coach. "They are in there?"

"Nah, I'm a bloody taxi come to pick your ugly self up!" the coachman sneered. " 'Course they're inside, ye bloody fool. Get *in*!"

Artus, still hidden at the edge of the road, was too confused to guess what was going on, but whatever it was clearly fell into the category of "strange and probably no good." He watched as Jaevis, apparently satisfied with the coachman's assurances, walked to the door of the coach and climbed inside. They were about to have some kind of secret meeting.

Whatever happened, Artus knew he had to get aboard that coach.

A man's voice—not Jaevis's—called from the curtained windows of the cab, "Ozmar, just drive us around—don't stop for anybody."

Artus stole out of the alley and crouched by the back wheel. There was no way to get in the cab, that was for sure. He heard Ozmar crack the whip and the coach lurched into motion and began to pick up speed. Artus trotted after it in the mud and noticed that the cargo rack at the back of the coach was completely empty. Doubling his pace into a full sprint, he nimbly leapt atop the empty rack and, clinging for dear life, was carried off with the coach as Ozmar gave the horses another crack of the whip. They soon were moving at a fast clip down the muddy, dark streets of the Horse District.

Artus took a moment climbing into a more comfortable position on the cargo rack, ensuring that he wouldn't fall with an errant bump or rut in the road, and then crept up to the rear wall of the cab and placed his ear just outside the small ovular window there. Over the thunder of the hooves and the rattle of the suspension, it took him a few seconds to fully distinguish the voices inside.

The first one he heard was Jaevis's, which was in mid-sentence. " . . . know you are who you say?"

The other man spoke again. It was more jocular and refined—the voice of a man who did not lead a hard life. "I assure you, Mr. Jaevis, that I vouch for my Galaspiner friend's honesty in this matter. You know my reputation—that should be good enough. I would like my fee, please."

Artus heard a faint jingle—the money purse. "You count. Hacklar Jaevis is no cheat."

A third person spoke—a young man's voice, healthy and with good humor. "That's a rather large fee for arranging a meeting, isn't it?"

"You are asking me to betray the friendship of a very dangerous man who happens to be in a very bad mood," the unidentified man said. "The price is fair considering the risks to my person."

"You want Reldamar. I will get him," Jaevis stated.

The young man chuckled. "Straightforward—I like that in a fellow. Yes, I want Tyvian Reldamar."

"Dead?"

"Tsk-tsk—bearing a grudge, are we? Alive, if you

please; no payment if the man dies. My esteemed colleagues and I wish to study him, not bury him."

The first man—the one who had set up the meeting, the one who knew Tyvian—chuckled lightly. "I should warn you both—Reldamar is seeing enemies everywhere at the moment. He's expecting poison in every teapot, for Hann's sake. He will be difficult to catch unawares, if at all." Artus's ears perked up at that. It sounded familiar somehow . . .

"I will catch," Jaevis grunted.

The first man snickered, "It is my understanding, sir, that the last time you went up against Reldamar ended with you at the bottom of a river with a blade through your guts. Use caution, or he'll unravel our whole little plot here, and then, my friends, *all* our geese are cooked." Where had Artus heard something about poisoned tea? Gods, it was right on the tip of his tongue!

"I've got an added stipulation," the young man said, "Mr. Jaevis, it is my understanding that you were recently contracted by the Defenders to apprehend Reldamar, is this not correct?"

"Yes."

"Well, I would like *my* contract to supersede that contract. Get him before the Defenders do, before Hendrieux does, and definitely before Sahand does. My Esteemed Colleagues would be most grateful."

"Jaevis will see it done," the bounty hunter said.

"If you are interested in paying an additional fee," the first man said, "I know where Reldamar will be, and I know that a *fourth* party is already interested in getting their hands on him—she is your chief competitor in this region, I believe."

The young man grunted. "I can't say I'm surprised—you can never trust the Kalsaaris." He laughed. "Listen to you—in bed with everybody. To think I once thought you and Reldamar were friends!"

"Of course we are," the man said, "This isn't personal, it is strictly professional. Reldamar will understand, I'm sure . . . well, eventually, at any rate."

The revelation hit Artus like a pitcher of cold water: the man was Carlo diCarlo, Tyvian's friend. Tyvian's friend who had just acted as a broker between Hacklar Jaevis and some creep who wanted to "study" Tyvian. Artus didn't know what that might entail, but it sounded pretty awful.

The coach hit a large bump, causing Artus to thump up against the back of the cab with an audible grunt. The three people inside immediately fell silent. Artus crouched down in the luggage rack, holding his breath.

There was a trio of thumps on the roof of the coach, and Carlo yelled out the window, "Stop the coach!"

Ozmar brought the coach to a halt, but even before it stopped moving, Jaevis opened the door and leapt out. Artus took a leap off the back and tumbled in the mud. Scrambling to his feet, he heard the bounty hunter draw his blade and bellow, "Spy!"

Artus ran full tilt down the road, his feet slipping and sinking in the mud. He heard the young man yelling, "Don't let him escape! Kill him!"

Artus darted sideways down a narrow street just as Jaevis made a quick slash where his ankles had been. This bought Artus another two paces on the angry Illini, but he didn't need to look back to know how close his pursuer was—he could hear the bounty hunter's armor jingle and could feel his massive frame barreling after him. Artus made another turn and another, and another, but Jaevis didn't fall behind; the weight of his armor didn't seem to be slowing him down by much.

Artus didn't know the layout of Freegate well—it was not a very logically planned city, and he had spent a collective six days here in his life. What he did know was that the coach had been skirting the edge of the city, where the Horse District had the room for its more space-intensive businesses. If he turned right, he figured it would take him closer to the center of town, where things were more congested and the chance of finding help or a place to hide would be greater.

Turning himself in the proper direction, Artus passed by a series of butcher shops, slaughterhouses, and abattoirs. The smell of blood and raw meat was thick in the air, but the road quality improved from mud to cobblestones. Behind him, Jaevis was puffing air like an angry beast. "You . . . will . . . die . . . boy . . ."

Artus ducked down an alley that dead-ended in a high fence. He leapt, caught the edge, and swung himself over just before the bounty hunter's sword embedded itself in the top beam. Jaevis's roar of rage was enough to keep Artus running, even though he felt safe.

It was a good instinct, since barely a moment later, Jaevis literally shouldered his way *through* the fence, the thin plywood splintering around his armored form. Artus gasped at this and picked up the pace again. At least, he reasoned, the guy's lost his sword.

He made another turn toward the center of the city, this time taking him down row after row of bakeries. This street was broader than the others, and clean, too, leaving him little to dodge around or throw in his path behind him. Jaevis was winded now, the weight of his armor finally taking its toll, and Artus began to pull away.

Then he heard Jaevis utter, "Enough," and the bounty hunter came to a stop.

Artus, smiling at his victory, looked over his shoulder . . .

. . . in time to see the Illini's dagger slam home in his back. Searing lances of pain radiated out from just below his left shoulder blade and he tripped, sprawling forward on the cobblestones. He tried quickly to rise, but the white-hot agony in his shoulder and arm made him swoon and fall back onto the ground.

Jaevis, breathing heavily, walked up to where he had fallen and put a boot in the center of his back. "End of road, boy." He yanked the dagger out with a savage twist, making Artus scream and almost pass out.

This prompted a grunt from Jaevis, who knelt next to him and cleaned his blade on Artus's shirt. "You are lucky, boy. If you did not look just now, dagger would have hit you in spine." He nodded solemnly. "Then you would be dead."

Artus tried rolling away, but Jaevis jammed a thumb in his open wound, making Artus again go pale with pain. "Hit bone. Boy should know that knife was poisoned. Jaevis could leave you here to bleed, and you would die. Maybe from blood you lose, maybe from poison, maybe from infection. Very painful death."

Artus tried to manage something pithy, or maybe just spit in the man's eye, but he couldn't get anything out. He wasn't Tyvian, after all—he was just a street rat.

Jaevis took a deep breath. "You are lucky boy, though. Jaevis has nephew, about your age. Would not want him to die so painfully. I will do you favor, for him."

Artus felt the tip of the dagger at the back of his skull. He said his good-byes to his family, and realized, with a profound sense of appropriateness, that he was just another son that wasn't coming home.

"Oi, you!" he heard a man yell, and felt the dagger withdraw.

"Boy is thief. I take my due," Jaevis said, standing up.

Through his tear-filled eyes, Artus could just make out a pair of men coming up the street, arm-length, spiked cudgels dangling from their hands. They were followed by the floating, glowing tattlers common to all watchmen. One of their tattlers flew over near

Artus's face and the other circled Jaevis. The second watchman whistled. "Lookee here, Martus—some Illini hick murdering a young boy in the street."

The first watchman nodded. "Shame what the world is comin' to, Toffer. 'Ere now, you—drop the pig-sticker, eh?"

Jaevis grumbled, "I pay three marks, you leave. Deal?"

"My my, Martus," Toffer said, "looks like this noble fellow has rid our fair city of another thieving soul."

"Hann bless his stalwart heart, Toffer," Martus replied, holding out his hand.

Artus, struggling through the pain, managed to wrestle his small purse from his belt and cast it on the street. "Seven marks," he gasped.

Martus and Toffer both whistled in unison. One of the tattlers illuminated the coins where they had spilled on the cobblestones. "Well now," said Toffer, "looks like we have a bit of a difference of opinion."

"He pays with my money," Jaevis growled. "He stole from me."

A tattler sank to Jaevis's large purse and illuminated it clearly for the watchmen. "And I suppose," said Martus, "that this thoughtful little pickpocket here took it upon hisself to leave you unrelieved of all that?"

"Do you happen to carry a small purse and a large purse at the same time, mate?" Toffer asked, grinning broadly.

Jaevis stewed for a moment and then said, "I give twenty-five marks—triple what boy is worth."

Artus tried to rise but was beaten down again by his injured shoulder. He instead rolled onto his good side. "You'll get . . . four times what I got if you . . . if you take me to Top Street."

"Why Martus," Toffer said, "how much did the little urchin just offer us?"

"Allow me a moment to make me calculations, Toffer," Martus said, and then added, "seven four times is twenty-eight, plus this seven here is thirty-five."

"He has not such money," the Illini countered.

"Tyvian—" Artus began, winced, and then started again. "Tyvian Reldamar's got it. He'll pay you."

Toffer and Martus exchanged glances. Martus whistled again and hissed, "Reldamar paid Captain Strayther *two hundred* today to stay clear of Imar's."

Toffer nodded. "So he's got the money, then."

Jaevis scowled. "Fools."

"What's *that*?" Martus thrust the end of his cudgel into Jaevis's gut, all traces of whimsy gone from his tone. "You want to be a toughie, eh? Think 'cause you got yourself some armor and a tough face you can just flap your gums at anyone you please?"

"Boy is good as dead. I will—"

Martus struck Jaevis in the solar plexus with the butt of his cudgel, causing the bounty hunter to stumble back. Toffer moved in and brandished his weapon in the Illini's face. "You listen here, you Kroth-spawned tit—I don't care if you work for the bloody Nine Queens of Kalsaar, Freegate belongs to *us*, and we don't take orders from nobody, got it?"

Artus knew Jaevis could kill both the men without much trouble—he'd seen him fight Tyvian on the barge. Still, the bounty hunter put up his hands and backed away, his coal-black eyes fixed on him. Even as the world began to spin, the eyes remained steady—the axis around which Artus's delirium rotated.

Martus helped Artus to his feet. "Well, lad," he said with a wink, "let's see if your friend Reldamar can pay up."

"Otherwise," Toffer chuckled, "we dump you in Arble Brook and see if you can swim with one arm, eh?"

The two watchmen laughed, and Artus saw their faces falling away from him. He found himself looking up at the black sky, and then remembered nothing else.

CHAPTER 19

MAN OF MERCY

"**F**orty bloody marks," Tyvian growled. He was sitting in a high-backed armchair and glaring at the fireplace in his second guest room. Behind him, his face ashen pale and slick with sweat, Artus lay facedown in the bed, a mass of bloody gauze pressed against his wound by a scowling Myreon Alafarr.

"This boy needs a doctor," Myreon stated simply as she set about changing the bandages. "The bleeding's stopped, but it's a deep wound."

"Should have left the runt on the doorstep to blee—Ow!" Tyvian grabbed his hand. "Bloody hell!"

Myreon chuckled to herself. "That ring is the best thing that ever happened to you, Reldamar."

Tyvian rolled his eyes. "Oh yes, what an improvement. I've gone from being a wealthy independent gentleman to a boarder for the inept."

Artus moaned. "Rel . . . Reldamar . . ."

Myreon touched his forehead. "He's burning up, suffering from shock, who knows what else."

"Can't you do some kind of Lumenal healing transmutation or something? We can't stay here for long, you know. I'm expecting more assassins at any moment."

"My fingers are still too weak, no thanks to you. If you don't do something, the lad is going to die."

"I already gave him a bloodpatch."

"I already told you that the bleeding isn't the problem—I think the wound is infected or possibly poisoned."

Tyvian scowled. "How long?"

Myreon shrugged, a look of disgust on her face. "Without treatment? A few hours, maybe. Are you so coldhearted that you'd let a boy die of infection in your own home?"

Tyvian didn't say anything, stuffing his hands in his armpits. He pursed his lips like a petulant child.

"Just call a bloody doctor!" Myreon snapped. "I know that ring of yours must be torturing you about it—just *do* it!"

"I won't let some trinket run my life," Tyvian snarled.

Myreon threw the spent gauze in a wastebasket and sat across from Tyvian. "Don't do it for the ring, you stunted human being! Do it for the *boy*!"

Tyvian's teeth were clenched. "What's the boy to me?"

"For the love of Hann, man! Have you no soul?" Myreon pointed to the suffering Artus. "This boy *needs* your help. He stuck with you all the way to Freegate, despite your treatment of him. He's the closest thing in this world you have to a bloody friend, and you're just going to let him *die*?"

"The boy's a street urchin, Myreon!" Tyvian shot back, his face red. "He's like a stray dog—he'll attach himself to anyone who feeds him! He doesn't give a damn about me. He stuck with me for the pay, and when he was injured and bleeding on the street, he thought he could just show up and I'd keep paying his way. If it weren't for *this*," he held out his ring hand, which was contorted in agony, "I'd have ditched the little freeloader weeks ago!"

Myreon shook her head and leaned back in her chair. "You're a monster. I don't know why I expected any different from you."

"Neither do I. Are you done with him?"

Myreon nodded, not looking at the smuggler.

"Back to your cell with you, then." Tyvian clapped his hands and the house specters seized Myreon by the elbows and escorted her back to her own room.

As soon as the door closed, Tyvian stood up and screamed. The fire in his hand was unbearable. Just like in the river-inn, he felt like the skin was blistering and peeling off his fingers, exposing the bone to the white-hot fire of the ring. Holding his hand by the wrist, he slammed it against the mantel, the end-tables, the walls—anything in reach in an attempt to stop the horrible pain. He doused it in the basin of water Myreon had brought for Artus, but no relief was to be had. He scratched and pulled at the ring in the water, but as ever, it didn't move.

"I won't do it, you bloody ring! Not now, not *ever*! *YOU DON'T CONTROL ME!*"

The pain intensified even more, and Tyvian fell to his knees, tears streaming down his face. He hissed at his hand. "No . . . bloody . . . way . . . in hell!"

Not knowing how he did it, nor remembering why, Tyvian found himself on the street, a heavy red cloak wrapped around him to fight the cold mountain winds. He had Chance at his side, at least, and the sun was rising over the Dragonspine, bathing the streets of the Cliff District in equal parts golden light and blue shadow. His hand still blazed with unbearable pain, but he had the wherewithal to check to see if he was being followed—he wasn't, or at least not by anyone he could spot.

He stopped walking. He had to be followed. He couldn't conceive of a circumstance where he *wouldn't* be followed. He shook his head, trying to clear it of the fiery pain that still crippled him. Ducking into the shadows of a restaurant doorway, he pretended to peer through the windows as though inspecting the place. From his angle, the reflection in the frosted glass of the door gave him a foggy glimpse of the street behind him—nothing but silhouettes and amorphous blobs of light, but it would be enough to detect movement.

A shadow shifted from one side of the street to another and vanished in a distant alley: his follower.

The ring burned him, making his eyes water. "Not now, damn you! Not . . . bloody . . . now!"

Tyvian's instincts dictated getting off the street—perhaps breaking into this restaurant and maybe ducking out the back. The ring wouldn't permit it, though. The agony overcame his better judgment, forcing him from the doorway and back along the street, his feet dragging.

He tried to think, but all the ring wanted was for him to press on, to stagger forward to whatever nonsensical mercy mission it had in mind for him. The experience was not unlike that of being drunk, except instead of the pleasant, numbing cobwebs of alcohol, he was afflicted with mind-blanking agony.

He looked behind him, blinking away tears. Nothing. Whoever was back there was good—it was no mean feat to shadow a man on an empty street at dawn, especially a street so clean and so sunny. Pleasant three-story town houses built in the stone-and-plaster Saldorian style lined both sides, each one with a small plot of lawn or a squat little tree out front. Between these were commercial properties of the highest caliber—hotels with flower-rimmed balconies and bars with rooftop decks that overlooked the entire city. The watch was paid well to make regular sweeps in this part of town, and anybody who didn't "belong" would be summarily tossed headfirst down the Stair Market and into the Chamber Pot.

People in dark cloaks darting from alley to alley certainly didn't belong, and tattlers were very hard to hide from. This fellow was either a recent arrival in this area or he had a special talent for avoiding notice. Or both.

Tyvian kept onward, clutching his hand to his chest but keeping his cloak over his shoulders to conceal his weakness—his tail was being wary, and he wanted the tail to stay that way until he could think of a plan for shaking him or her while being dispatched on a damned errand by a piece of cheap jewelry.

There was a break in the street—a canyon had been dug out by water cascading over the lip of Dain's Lake, splitting the Cliff District in two before vanishing into a dark crevasse some thirty feet below. There was an elegant bridge of gleaming birch railings and mageglass supports arching over the gap, and some ten or fifteen feet to Tyvian's right, twenty feet lower, another bridge spanning it for the next road down. The upper bridge, where Tyvian now found himself, was lined with tall wooden flagpoles flying the colors of the various guild members and wealthy merchants who paid to have the bridge maintained—advertising to the rich was worth more than any toll income.

Tyvian paused, trying to clear his head enough to

do some very crucial calculus. Behind him, he caught a glimpse of his shadow—getting closer, so much closer.

"Kroth," he growled to himself, "dying would be better than this nonsense anyway."

He drew Chance with his left hand and cut down a flagpole. He forced himself to catch it with both hands, though he practically passed out from the ring's objections. Then, holding one end, he began to run.

Tyvian heard his shadow break cover, coming at him at a dead sprint from behind. He angled himself toward the edge of the bridge, planted the flagpole, and vaulted.

Behind him, he heard someone swear in Illini (Illini?) over the rush of air past his ears. He pulled for all his worth with his arms, propelling himself through space. He had no idea if he'd cleared enough distance, no idea if he'd cleared too much. He dropped through the air, feet first . . .

. . . and struck the edge of the lower bridge, but only barely. Something in his leg cracked, but he had the presence of mind to roll forward. It was an ugly roll—he flopped across the bridge like he had been poleaxed. He banged his head and arms pretty badly. New pain joined the old tortures of the ring, and they did not harmonize well.

Tyvian tried getting up, but his leg and arm were now howling together. He groaned and almost passed out.

No! he cursed at himself. If he passed out, his tail won—the fellow was already circling around, mostly likely, and trying to get down to where he was before he disappeared. He imagined he could hear the slap of his boots against the cobbles.

The world swirled and pitched. Tyvian vaguely recalled grabbing something to pull himself up but then falling down again. After that all he could see, hear, or recall were the sounds of his own cries of pain and the curses on his lips.

When he came again to his senses, he was standing on the street he had just leapt from. On his left was a respectable home sporting a sign advertising the medicinal and alchemical services of a Doctor Wich. The ring's assault upon him had abated somewhat, but his lower left leg was taking up the slack. He found he couldn't put weight on it.

Remembering the Wandering Fountain, Tyvian glared down at the ring. "Think you're tricking me this time, eh? You almost kill me and you expect me to go along with your little plot? I know what you're up to—"

The ring flared as he turned away from the doctor's office. Across the street was a well-appointed gambling house, catering to "Persons of Breeding," according to the lettering in the window. Dragging his broken leg, Tyvian forced himself inside. It was empty, the morning light casting dusty beams of sunlight across the finely appointed room. Most of the chairs were set atop the gaming tables, but the bar stools were out and ready.

Tyvian shambled over to one and slapped his good hand on the bar-top. "Whiskey!"

A serving specter poured him a tumbler, but Tyvian made it a double. Grimacing, he knocked it back in one swallow and demanded another.

"A bit early for you, isn't it Mr. Reldamar?" The voice came from the shadows. Tyvian tried to grasp Chance, but the ring had paralyzed his hand too much with pain. The voice chuckled. "There's no need for that."

"Show yourself!" Tyvian growled.

Eddereon stepped into the light. His graying beard had been combed and his clothes were somewhat less rustic, but he was still every bit the barrel-chested mountain man Tyvian had met on the banks of the river all those weeks ago.

"You son of a bitch!" Tyvian pulled a knife with his good hand. "I'll kill you now, ring or not."

Eddereon brushed back his cloak to reveal the jeweled hilt of a longsword. "You are in no condition to murder me, Tyvian, and I would hate to kill you. May I sit down?"

Tyvian said nothing. He only knocked back his second double-shot. Between the alcohol and the ring-induced agony, he knew Eddereon was right.

The big man pulled up a stool beside him. "You are fighting the ring even now, eh?"

"I . . . refuse . . . to let you . . . control me," Tyvian grunted.

Eddereon shook his head and smiled. "I am not controlling you, Tyvian. The ring is not making you into a trained animal. It is waking you up."

"Kroth take you."

"We don't grant the ring to just anyone, Tyvian. If we did, we would have put one on Banric Sahand ages ago, as well as any other monstrous villain you could name. Every cutthroat, blackmailer, thief, and rapist in this miserable city would be carrying the ring about."

Tyvian snorted, trying to pry his pain-soaked fingers out of a fist. "Yes . . . wolf among sheep. I remember this lecture."

"The ring only punishes you for that which you know is wrong. If you are wracked with pain, it is not brought on by the ring, but by your own soul."

"Nonsense."

"Is it?" Eddereon cocked an eyebrow. "Can you remember the first time you killed, Tyvian?"

Tyvian scowled. He had been fifteen. A boy his age had challenged him to a duel for something stupid and childish—some adolescent idea of honor, he supposed; Tyvian had run him through the neck. He remembered clearly how the boy had gurgled bubbles of blood as he died, a look of painful surprise on his face. "What of it?"

"How did you feel?"

Tyvian remembered weeping. He remembered going to his mother and demanding she use her considerable sorcery to bring the boy back. When she refused, she had laughed at him for his repeated pleas. *Really, Tyvian*, she had scoffed. *Anyone so stupid as to challenge you to a fight deserves what he gets. As soon as you stop that unseemly blubbering, you'll realize the little fool killed himself.*

"You felt terribly, didn't you?"

"Go . . . to . . . hell."

Eddereon smiled and shook his head. "Stop fighting yourself, Tyvian. The easy way is not the only way, nor is it the best of ways. If you follow your heart, you will find the ring as much a help as it is a hindrance."

Tyvian pushed himself to his feet. "Mark my words, Eddereon—this isn't over."

Eddereon smiled. "Of course not. Allow me to pay for the drinks."

Tyvian fished a few silvers from his purse and slapped them on the counter, glaring at the mountain man. He then left the gaming house, stumbled across the street and pounded on the door to the doctor's office. There was no answer.

Eddereon came into the street. "Doctor Wich went missing five months ago. No doubt kidnapped, like so many other such professionals of late."

Tyvian glared at Eddereon. "Is that your angle, then? Did you rig this ring to bring me here to unravel a mystery you were too dense to solve yourself? Am I supposed to save the practitioners of the Low Arts all across Freegate and then earn my freedom?"

Eddereon shook his head. "Noble of you, but that is not the ring's intent. It wishes only to make you whole."

He reached out and touched Tyvian's broken leg. Tyvian would have jerked away but was exhausted, hurt, and foggy with lack of sleep to manage it. Incredible warmth spread throughout his body, but then pooled in his broken bone. In an instant the feeling had passed.

Tyvian's leg felt fine. "How . . . how did you . . ."

Eddereon smiled. "The ring, Tyvian. You, too, have this power. You must merely have the true and honest goodwill to use it."

"And buy into this entire 'goodness' charade? Is that it?" Tyvian snorted. "I either do it your way or Artus dies, eh? That's moral extortion."

Eddereon nodded. "How clever of you to identify it."

Tyvian backed away from him, his eyes wide, his legs wooden. "Kroth take you, you infernal bastard. I won't do it, do you hear me? Tyvian Reldamar is nobody's slave!"

Eddereon watched him go, his bearded face grim. "Then Artus will die. It is your choice, but there is only one right path. This, whether you admit it or not, is something you already know."

Tyvian turned around and left. He did not look back.

CHAPTER 20

DEATH'S DOOR

"That wretched boy," Tyvian growled. He was seated in his living room, a cup of bitter tea in his hand that he sipped in sharp, sudden movements. His hand throbbed. Over the crackle of a fire, he could sometimes hear the desperate moans of Artus, deep in the throes of fever's delirium.

He had summoned Myreon Alafarr from her room. The Mage Defender sat with her arms crossed, scowling at the floor. She appeared to have been brushing her hair—it glittered like gold wire in the rays of early morning sunshine. "Did you call me out here just to complain?"

"Yes."

"You won't get any sympathy from me. You know that."

Tyvian set down his teacup. "Myreon, am I an evil man?"

Myreon looked up and blinked. "Is that a trick question?"

"Just answer it, dammit."

"Yes, you are an evil man."

"There, you see! Ha!"

"I fail to see what I have just proven."

Tyvian held up the ring. "I contend that this little trinket does *not* make me a good person. Do you agree?"

"Agreed." Myreon nodded cautiously. "It merely constrains you to act as a good person."

"You will note that it is not hurting me now as much." Tyvian twiddled his fingers to illustrate. "It feels that, by torturing me into trying to find a doctor, it has somehow improved me."

Myreon shrugged. "It has."

"Nonsense."

"Believe me, Tyvian, were it not for that ring, a great many terrible things would have already been done by the hand it occupies. From my own perspective, my murder stands out as the foremost among them. I thank Hann that it remains in place, as with each passing day the swelling and pain in my fingers subsides, and one of these days I will be able to work a Binding spell on you in the midst of one of these chats, drag you back to Galaspin or even *Saldor*, and the entire world will be better for it. My only regret is that it will not be soon enough to save that boy's life."

"Your delusions aside, Myreon, what you have described is not an improvement upon me, per se, but a change in behavior dictated *for* me. There is a difference. I do not think or feel any differently with it attached than I did without it."

Myreon narrowed her eyes. "What are you driving at?"

Tyvian sipped his tea and tried not to cast a glance at the closed door to Artus's room. "You are a woman of education and a student of human nature, of sorts, and so I am curious about your opinion on the following: given prolonged exposure to this ring, would I actually change, or would I simply submit to an exterior will greater than my own?"

"I think, in the end, they are the same."

"No, they aren't." Tyvian waggled a finger. "Allow me to produce an analogy appropriate to your expertise. Suppose you capture a criminal and he is sentenced to one week's petrification. While petrified, he is and does exactly as you say—he is a model citizen of sorts. You even place him in an area where he will do good, like educating children or providing shade or some such tripe. While thusly constrained, can he be considered reformed?"

Myreon sighed. "I suppose not."

"And when he is released, will he be changed by his experience, or will he revert to his old ways?"

"I think that depends greatly on the type of person the criminal is. On the one hand, if the man was a criminal out of desperation, ignorance, or constraint, it seems unlikely he will continue on his former path, given that he has seen the results of his actions. On the other, if the man is a criminal by way of philosophical choice or inherent mental depravity, he will undoubtedly revert to his old ways, as the consequences of his actions are of little concern to him—he is either consciously aware of them and finds the risks they represent acceptable, or he simply does not care what happens to him."

Tyvian nodded. "Well said—I agree entirely. Now, which of those two kinds of criminal am I?"

"The second," Myreon stated.

"You have no doubts about that?"

The Defender looked Tyvian in the eye. She was about to speak but then stopped. "Why are we having this conversation?"

Tyvian shrugged. "What difference does it make? Just answer the question, please."

Myreon shook her head. "No. This is all part of some kind of plot, isn't it? You're trying to manipulate me."

Tyvian chuckled. "I assure you, Myreon, that if I were trying to manipulate you, you would never realize it until too late."

"No, no—I see what you're up to. Very clever, of course." Myreon stood up. "This line of questioning is meant to provoke in me the suspicion that you, Tyvian Reldamar, smuggler and blackhearted villain, are supposedly having some kind of profound change of heart due to that contraption affixed to your hand."

Tyvian stiffened. "That's ridiculous—"

Myreon shook her head, her voice rising almost to a yell. *"It is not!* You bring me out here and ask me questions about your moral caliber, as though *you yourself* were holding such things in doubt. You want me to think you are reluctantly facing the possibility that you are not, in fact, a soulless monster who, not more than a few hours ago, was going to let a young boy bleed to death on his front doorstep had he not been controlled by a magical device. I'll tell you one thing, though: *it isn't going to work!* I know you too well, Tyvian Reldamar! You are a wretched blight upon the good peoples of the West, and I will not rest until you are installed in a statuary garden for the rest of eternity!"

With that, the mage spun on her heel and, with a flip of her hair, stormed back to her cell-room. Tyvian sat on the couch, watching her go, and picked up his teacup again. He murmured quietly to himself, "Well, that's all I wanted to know, thank you."

Quiet descended. The crackle of the fire, the muffled moans of Artus. The ring pulsed and raged. *Do something,* it seemed to say. *Try.*

"I don't care about him. I don't," Tyvian hissed.

The ring flared. He felt as though his hand had been

thrust in the fire now for hours. He could scarcely think about anything other than the pain and the ring and himself.

And the boy.

Tyvian found himself on the threshold of Artus's room. The boy's face was a sickly shade of gray, glistening with sweat. He moaned but did not move. Tyvian watched him suffer, his hand blazing.

Eddereon's letter sprung to mind. Sentimental garbage, of course. It called him embittered and angry, as though his whole life and personality could be explained by some kind of petulant grudge. It claimed he needed friends, though he had many friends scattered across the West. He knew pirates and smugglers, rogues and thieves, tyrants and rogue wizards and . . .

. . . well, perhaps not friends, per se. Tyvian had never felt he needed friendship in its traditional sense. He didn't need others to enjoy his company—he enjoyed his *own* company well enough, thank you.

Artus let out a low, sobbing sound. "Ma . . . Ma . . . no . . . lemme stay . . . lemme stay . . ."

Tyvian had watched a man die like this before—in Illin. He'd been tagging along with a caravan coming back from Tasis when they were ambushed by bandits. It was a quick hit-and-run. They had shot a few arrows and injured a few camels, not trying to kill. The weapons had been poisoned, and within a few hours anyone who was wounded dropped into a deadly fever.

The caravan master had known the tactic—the idea was to slow them down, weaken them, empty their already flagging water supplies. It hadn't worked. The caravan master had ordered all the ill to be left behind with all the sick camels. All except his son, who had been among the wounded. He was carried to the master's private wagon, and there he cooked himself into an early grave. Tyvian, who had been posing as a doctor at the time, was forced to watch. It had taken less than a day.

This was the same poison, this was that same terrible death. This situation was different now, though. Then, Tyvian had an obligation to save the boy but could not, whereas now he supposedly had the ability to save the boy but not the obligation.

"Kroth take the boy," Tyvian snarled, but he could not leave the room. The ring burned him and burned him, but he did not advance.

Eddereon had said he had a good heart, that the ring was bringing out the best in him, but Tyvian knew it was a lie. All he needed to do to prove it was walk away, close the door, and have some dinner. Maybe take a nap.

But he did not budge.

He took a deep breath, his eyes watering with the torture being inflicted on him. He knew there was another option—he could stay here, by Artus's side, and watch him die. It would only take a few hours, and then the pain would be gone, simple as that. By doing nothing, he could beat the ring. He could endure it.

And then Artus would die.

Tyvian wiped sweat from his forehead with his

good hand. "You force me to do it, you miserable trinket."

The ring did not answer; it merely burned, oven-hot, between the tender flesh of his fingers. Tyvian hated that he was speaking to it again.

"I'll beat you," he said. "I swear by every god, named and unnamed, I will beat you." He closed the door behind him and sat beside Artus's bed. The boy did not stir save for his chest rising and falling with increasing difficulty. The room was hot.

"Tyv . . . Tyvian . . ." Artus mumbled.

His name struck him as a blow. He stood up, turned his chair around and sat back down. He stared into the fire and let the ring burn.

He was no one's slave. He would prove it. It was merely a matter of time.

INTERLUDE

A TASTE OF THINGS TO COME

Sahand stood in the midst of what had been a sumptuous feast hall in the sleepy hills of northwestern Eretheria. A land of pretty castles and picturesque villages, this place had been the perfect storybook image of a rustic hunting lodge on the edges of a great black forest. Deer, elk, and wood-drake heads were mounted against thick oak pillars. These pillars supported delicate wooden arches carved to look like the boughs of trees, and the ceiling was painted with pictures of leaves and forest animals where it wasn't stained black by centuries of wood- and pipe-smoke. Just before

Sahand had arrived, the long table had been strewn with tray upon tray of roast quail and cured ham as well as pitchers of cider and bowls of candied fruits. Men and women in the house of Viscountess Renia Elons had been laughing and talking about the day's entertainments, stuffing their faces with all the pleasant foods that their puffy cheeks could accommodate.

Sahand now stood on the table so that he was eye-to-eye with the Viscountess herself, who dangled by the wrists from the rafters of her own dining hall like a chicken trussed up for plucking. Joining the smell of roast meat and delicate soup was the smell of blood, now coating most of the floor and soaking the tablecloth crimson. As Sahand paced down the length of the table, he kicked the body of a man out of his way and sent the corpse toppling to the floor. "I find it hard to believe that I need to say this, Renia, but spying on me was not in your best interest."

Of all the methods of torture devised by man, strappado was perhaps the easiest and most portable. All the torturer needed was a rope, a beam, and a strong man. The victim's hands would be tied behind the back, the rope thrown over the beam, and then the strong man would hoist them up by the wrists, pulling their arms painfully out of their sockets from behind, tearing ligaments, mashing nerves, and, if the man were strong enough, you could drop them suddenly and then stop them with a jerk, breaking bones and ripping muscles to shreds. If they kicked and struggled, the pain only got worse. For someone who wanted to torture their enemies while on the go, there really was no substitute.

At the moment, Banric Sahand was just such a man.

"Again." He nodded to Gallo, who wordlessly loosened his grip on the rope so it slipped a few inches before jamming down on it again with his heavy armored boot. The Viscountess shrieked as the sudden stop dislocated one shoulder. She flailed and kicked, spitting and howling like a mad cat, as Gallo slowly hoisted her back to her starting elevation.

Renia Elons was young and vital for a woman of seventy, which was a keen indication of just how much money she had and what manner of sorceries she tended to spend it on. Her face was pale as parchment. "You can't do this . . . you can't!"

"Is that so?" Sahand's mail jingled softly as he looked about at the carnage he and Gallo had wrought of Renia Elons's retainers. It had been a simple matter, really—hardly an effort. Once he knew where to find her, the only complication was how best to travel here quickly and without being observed. Ironically, the Black Hall had served as an admirably convenient shortcut. "Do you have additional retainers I need to worry about? I must say, this array of overweight farmers was something of a disappointment. I fear it's true what they say: the flower of Eretherian chivalry perished with Perwynnon."

The Viscountess hazarded a glance over at the passionless, fish-eye stare of Gallo. Her voice rose an octave. "My cousins! My sons! The Defenders! They will know this was you! I will be avenged!"

Sahand's face was still as a stone carving. "Again."

Gallo let her drop and caught her again. This time the Viscountess screamed for almost an entire minute, tears streaming down her face. Sahand waited for her to fall silent before seizing her by the laces of her bodice and pulling her so close to his face that he could see the tiny webwork of wrinkles at the edges of her eyes. "Your simpering cousins? Your elderly sons, likewise fat from too much beef and beer? The Defenders, stretched thin and chasing down common thieves like constables? *These* are your threats? Listen to me, Renia, and understand: twenty-seven years ago I had the world in the palm of my hand. I was poised to conquer the West, and none of you mewling idiots seemed able to stop me. All I needed to do was to sack one simple town . . ."

"Calassa? This is about Calassa?" Renia moaned.

Sahand thrust her away and let her swing, the motion causing the old woman to howl in pain. "*Everything* is about Calassa! Every waking hour since that time has been dedicated to undoing my indignities at Calassa. You, Renia, have endangered that plan."

"What you're doing is madness, Sahand!" Renia sobbed. "Madness. All those people . . ."

Sahand had to hand it to the old sorceress—she, over and above anyone else in the League, had actually figured it out. He wondered, in that moment, if

Lyrelle Reldamar knew. No—she couldn't. If she did, she would have stopped him somehow.

And there was simply no one who could stop him. Not now.

The Mad Prince thought about explaining this to Renia Elons, but couldn't see the advantage in it. "Again."

Gallo dropped her so sharply that a bright bloom of red blood appeared at the shoulder of the Viscountess's fine white dress. She was weeping and gasping with pain all at once; Sahand figured her arms were just about ready to pop out of their sockets for good.

"Wh-What do you want from me?" the Viscountess moaned, "Anything! I'll give you anything! Please don't drop me again. For Hann's sake, mercy!"

Sahand showed his teeth. "And what would you offer me, Renia? Gold? Titles? What, exactly, would I want from a withered old wench in an expensive gown who's too old to tumble and too young to bury?"

Renia Elons drew a shuddering breath. "Then why torture me? Why, gods, why do this? I'm . . . I'm just an old woman . . ." Gallo began to hoist Renia up again; she began to scream. "Oh gods, Sahand! You don't have to do this!"

Sahand reached up and wiped a tear from the Viscountess's cheek. "I have some good news, Renia: I am not going to kill you tonight."

Renia Elons shuddered with sobs of relief.

"No, you see, Renia, if I were to kill you at this moment, it might look as though I were trying to keep you from talking, and I know I am being watched, and I must keep up certain appearances."

Renia gasped, "Oh thank—"

Sahand held up a finger and shook his head. "I hadn't finished, Renia: I can't kill you now, because it will look like *you* learned something about *me*. I *can*, however, slowly torture you to death because then it will look like *I* was trying to learn something from *you*."

Renia's eyes seemed likely to pop out of her head and roll around. "Wh . . . what?"

"Don't worry—I'll see to it that you last until morning. I am a man of my word."

Renia struggled weakly against the ropes. "No . . . no, please . . . no!"

Sahand looked at Gallo and nodded.

"Again."

To be continued in Iron and Blood: Part 2 of the Saga of the Redeemed . . .

Part 2

IRON AND BLOOD

Do I contradict myself?
Very well then I contradict myself,
(I am large, I contain multitudes.)

WALT WHITMAN

CHAPTER 1

THE SEMI-INVITED

"**W**ell, you are certainly dismal today. You look like the walking dead," Carlo diCarlo observed.

Tyvian didn't bother scowling, but he did manage a snort. "I was up well past dawn, that's all."

Carlo moved to signal his coachman. "We *could* stop for some karfan. There's a little place—"

Tyvian held up his hand. "No! I'll not attend a party with brown teeth. Bags under my eyes are preferable. Drive on."

A coach was a relatively rare form of transport in Freegate, given that a significant portion of the city streets featured stairs, but Tyvian was glad of the novelty as they jostled over the cobblestones toward the diplomatic quarter of the city. Directly adjacent to the sprawling Beggar's Market, it was there that the various governments of the world had once kept their embassies before the Municipal Council of Freegate had cut all formal diplomatic ties with everyone.

At the time they had done it because the Illini Wars and the conquests of the Mad Prince Sahand forced the traditionally neutral city to become entangled in a worldwide conflict. Kalsaari assassins and undercover Defenders killed each other in the streets, Dellor forcibly garrisoned troops within the city limits, and Alliance High General Conrad Varner had even entertained sacking it in order to cut off Sahand's supply routes. When Sahand and Kalsaar were finally defeated, Freegate had enough and kicked all the diplomats out. Everybody had assumed the Council and Lord Mayor would allow the embassies to be reestablished after a while, but the merchants of Freegate soon found the absence of various armed parties holed up in fortresses within their city limits to be quite pleasant, and no embassies were ever allowed to be rebuilt.

This didn't mean foreign powers weren't present in Freegate—far from it. It simply meant they needed to keep their numbers down, couldn't operate openly, and weren't allowed to send ambassadors to harangue the Council or Lord Mayor for any reason whatsoever. As for the fortresslike embassies that dominated the Castle District—as the diplomatic quarter was called—they either fell into disrepair when nobody bought them or had fallen into the possession of private owners with sufficient funds who needed to possess a large, fortified complex in the center of Freegate. One of these owners was none other than a Hanim of the Imperial Kalsaari House of Theliara. It was there that Tyvian and Carlo were bound.

"I'm rather surprised you managed to secure this meeting, Carlo," Tyvian remarked, examining his hair in a pocket mirror. He was dressed in his finest clothes—white linen shirt with flaring, embroidered collar, purple vest with gold piping, a mink-lined half-cape, and enough rings and jewels to show he meant business, but not so many that he looked like he was trying too hard. He hadn't brought his rapier Chance, of course—doing so would be a grave insult—but he did have a stiletto hidden in his right boot. The boot, of course, had antiscrying runes etched into its interior, just in case.

"The Hanim is celebrating her thirtieth birthday, and a very select group of five hundred people have been invited. As I implied yesterday, one of them owed me a small favor, so I was able to get us on the guest list."

Tyvian frowned. "Did you bring her a gift?"

Carlo chuckled. "Yes—you."

"Charming."

"It will be, I promise."

"How much do you know about this Hanim?" Tyvian asked, peering out the window. In the gray light of early evening the stylized minarets of the The-liara compound—an architectural oddity even in the eclectic, hodgepodge environment of Freegate—could be seen looming over the lower buildings around them like a trio of ivory lighthouses on a rocky shore. "How long has she been in town, did you say?"

"About two months. Her full name is Angharad tin'Theliara Hanim, that last bit being her title as a lady of the Kalsaari Imperial Court."

"I am well aware of her *name* and the meaning of her *title*. Tell me about the woman."

Carlo threw up his hands. "Who can tell with Kalsaari nobility? Lies and illusions everywhere, as always, and I haven't been able to pick out the true bits. She has taken no husband, which makes her a very valuable political ally among the beys of her family and beyond. She is no doubt a viper and an enchantress, doubly as dangerous as any woman you are likely to meet in the West, your sainted mother excluded. She is also supposed to be very beautiful, but you can take that with a grain of salt—these Kalsaaris use so many glamours and Shrouds that they could make an old man look like a sixteen-year-old girl, and you'd never know without a true-seer or mage-compass. For all we know, this is her ninetieth birthday, and she has four husbands and a gaggle of children back in her home country."

"So, in other words, you know she is a Kalsaari Hanim, who may or may not be married and who may or may not be female. Really, Carlo, I'm disappointed."

Carlo frowned and rearranged his robes to try and

hide his gut. "She has done a very good job of giving my regular rumormongers the runaround, and no one outside of her household seems to know anything about her for certain, other than the fact that she's been importing all manner of exotic beasts from around the world to display in her menagerie. Selling them, too, to whatever rich dimwit wants a purple man-eating parrot or an albino gorgon or whatnot. As I said at lunch yesterday, I try not to do business with the queenies except in emergencies, Tyvian. I'm afraid of them—I admit it! Some of the things I saw in Kalsaari camps during the war would curl your toes."

Tyvian rolled his eyes. "Spare me stories, Carlo. That was twenty-five years ago in another country during a war. This is a bloody *birthday party*."

"Hmph," Carlo grunted. "Don't say I didn't warn you. I hope your little proposal is worth the risk."

Tyvian didn't look at the iron ring, but he felt it tingle on his finger. "It is. Don't worry."

They were met at the gates by a pair of turban-wearing Kalsaari mark-slaves, each stripped to the waist to reveal their stupendously muscular, tattooed torsos. They seemed to take no notice of the freezing winter air as they inspected Carlo's invitation. Tyvian marveled at the sophistication and artistry of the enchantments inscribed in their tattoos, and noted the ease with which they wore the heavy scimitars at their hips. While Tyvian had no doubt that the mark-slaves would be extremely dangerous opponents in a fight, he was reassured that their enchantments in no way enhanced their mental faculties. Their search of he and Carlo was straightforward, mundane, and so poor that even a common thief could have smuggled a dagger or two past them. The only thing objectionable about the search was the sheer amount of awkward pawing Tyvian was forced to endure. By the time they were let past, he had to spend another few minutes rearranging his hair and clothing to restore them to presearch standards.

"Come on—we'll be late," Carlo hissed in the grand domed antechamber beyond the gate. The acoustics of the room were such that his whisper echoed off the far wall and back again.

Tyvian looked around and noted that, apart from the pairs of mark-slaves posted at various intervals throughout the massive hall, they were alone. No one else was making their way across the oceanic floor of polished marble toward the ten-foot-tall double doors that were thrown open. He frowned. "Do you mean to tell me, Carlo, that we were invited to a party and we showed up *on time*?"

"What? Should we have been early?"

Tyvian rolled his eyes. "We're not going in yet."

"Where will we go, then? We can't leave and come back—the Hanim would hear of it! They would think it suspicious."

Tyvian whispered into Carlo's ear so that the sound did not travel. "Pretend to be sick."

"Are you mad?"

He squeezed Carlo's upper arm. "I will *not* be the first person to arrive at an exclusive party. It will paint us as either fawning sycophants or unsophisticated rubes, and I won't allow it. Now, either summon up some vomit or, so help me Hann, I will slug it out of you."

Carlo shook his head and sighed. He then, through some trick of bodily control that Tyvian wished he possessed, became very green and nauseous looking. His cheeks bulged and his good eye became as glassy as his crystal one.

Tyvian smiled. "That's more like it." He escorted the queasy Verisi pirate to one of the many doors leading out of the antechamber that wasn't the main one heading toward the party. The mark-slaves drew their scimitars and crossed them before the door.

"You don't understand," Tyvian said pleasantly, not knowing whether he was understood or not. "My friend here is ill, and would like somewhere to lie down for a while."

"Are there some difficulties I may be improving upon?" The smooth, unctuous voice came from behind them. Tyvian and Carlo turned to see a slight, thin man in an ankle-length red robe and jeweled turban—no doubt a steward of some kind. His beard was oiled and fashioned into the shape of a particularly sharp garden trowel, and only his thin red lips were smiling. His eyes were giving off an even mix of anger and terror.

Tyvian nodded. "Ah, yes. I was just telling your slaves here that—"

The steward executed a short half-bow. "My endless pardons, sirs, but your repetition is not necessary. I, Fariq the slavemaster, hear all that the marked hear."

Tyvian smirked. "That must get rather noisy sometimes."

"Ha ha." Fariq laughed like a mechanical clock. "Truly you are the most amusing man I have met."

Carlo wretched, placing his hands on his knees. Tyvian patted his back. "As you can see, my friend could use a private spot to relax. Motion sickness, you know?"

Fariq's nostrils flared. "Such a thing is regrettably impossible. Her Beauteousness, the Hanim, in her immortal wisdom, has forbidden foreign visitors from all but the approved places. If you will follow me, please." He motioned toward the tall doors.

Carlo hacked and gagged up a string of saliva that drooped, slowly, toward the spotless floor. Tyvian saw Fariq stiffen at the sight. "Look, Farroo, if my friend doesn't get a chaise and a chamber pot, pretty soon he is going to baptize Her Beauteousness's floor with the contents of his stomach. Just a room, man—you may lock us in if you like."

Fariq, stiff as a board, made a hasty and terrified decision. "You will come with me. Do not stray from the path, for not all of the passages in the Hanim's sumptuous and impeccable abode are safe."

Looking over his shoulder every five seconds to

ensure they were behind him (and that no one else saw), Fariq hastily ushered Tyvian and Carlo to a different door than the one they stood before and up a plush-carpeted staircase that led to what Tyvian guessed would be the third floor of the compound. Then they traveled through a series of winding halls and interlocking doors that were as labyrinthine as they were impressive. Colorful mosaics adorned the walls, each room tastefully decorated with porcelain vases and intricately woven rugs, and each door uniquely carved wood with gold inlay. Finally, Fariq led them into an airy enclosed veranda filled with expensive cushions, glowing feylamps clad in brass, and one chamber pot, also of brass, which had been placed prominently at the center of the room. Before Tyvian could compliment Fariq on his choice for their repose, the slavemaster had closed the door behind them. He heard it lock with a heavy clunk—a mechanical lock, and a heavy-duty one at that.

Carlo immediately recovered and threw himself down on a pile of cushions. "I really hate doing that, you know. Inducing nausea isn't like faking a blush."

Tyvian went to the wooden lattice that enclosed their veranda from the air beyond. He found himself looking down at a long rectangular courtyard. He could tell immediately from the green grass and the vibrant flowers resting along the banks of a reflecting pool that it was sorcerously abjured against the cold. In it he saw a pair of mark-slaves standing guard on either side of a large door, just as impressive and stationary as all the others they had seen since arriving. It looked as though this door led to the street outside. He grunted. "The Hanim certainly takes her security seriously."

Carlo waved off Tyvian's comment. "Bah—at least half of those slaves are illusions. Possibly two-thirds. I don't know how much you look into the slave markets—"

"Not at all," Tyvian spat.

Carlo raised an eyebrow. "Well pardon me—I didn't realize you were clad in all white tonight, Your Holiness. In any case, a true mark-slave, especially the bodyguard types you see around here, costs more than your whole flat. Even an Imperial House like the Theliaras are unlikely to own more than a couple dozen of them. Some of those chaps might just be regular slaves but painted up to look like they are marked."

"That eye of yours see anything interesting around here?"

Carlo shrugged. "Wards and illusions are all over the place, so it's difficult to tell—you didn't think this place *naturally* looks like some queenie pleasure palace, did you? Suffice to say that the clearest thing I can see is the layout at the party you have delayed us from. The food looks scrumptious, and it's getting cold. How long do we have to wait?"

"At least fifteen minutes. Who else is at the party?"

"A couple guildsmen who look terrified, a brace of Eretherian ladies with a young knight escorting, a couple turbaned Kalsaari merchants—nothing exceptional."

"The Hanim?"

"Has yet to appear."

"Good. She wants to make an entrance. Let's just make sure to make one just before her."

Carlo snorted. "How will we know when that is?"

"You will have to rely on my years of fine breeding, Carlo. Trust me—we'll be fine."

Carlo sighed and rearranged himself among the cushions. He eyed the chamber pot. "I imagine I should vomit in that, just to keep up appearances."

"Nonsense. I'll not appear at an exclusive party with a fat Verisi stinking of vomit."

Carlo scowled. "It was your story, remember?"

"That ruse was designed to fool Fariq, not anybody else. I don't give a damn if he finds out we were lying. If anything, that ought to enhance our reputation with the Hanim."

"I thought you didn't know very much about her," Carlo smirked.

"I don't, but I have dealt with Kalsaaris before—more often than you, it seems." Tyvian peered at the courtyard. "Though my contacts tend to be less powerful than this, and certainly less wealthy."

"Smugglers."

"For all the sophistication of their sorcery, the use of magic in Kalsaar is restricted as the sole province of the nobility. If you aren't a pasha or a sultan or an emir or some such, you have no business touching the stuff. The penalty is . . ."

Carlo rolled his eyes. "Death, I know. That's the bastards' punishment for everything." He sighed. "Varner was right—we should have kept going. We had them by the balls at Tasis, and that damned Prince Marik had to—"

"Carlo, are you waxing historical again?"

Carlo grunted. "History is important."

"That may be, but it is also most unbecoming. It shows your age."

Carlo opened his mouth to reply but closed it again when a series of stomach-shaking booms came from the courtyard below. Tyvian's eyes darted immediately to their source, and he called Carlo over, gesturing that he should remain quiet. The Verisi crept closer, and they both looked down at the grand door in the courtyard that led to the street. Someone was knocking—someone very insistent.

BOOM BOOM BOOM. Tyvian concluded that whoever or whatever was knocking had to be as strong as a draft horse to get that kind of reverberation out of a door that big. A few moments later Fariq appeared, wringing his hands, a small party of slaves with him. He ordered the door opened.

An armed party of men in the black-and-silver livery of Dellor loped across the threshold like a pack of hungry dogs. They were led by an armored giant of a man in a wolf's-head helm who was holding an iron maul that had to weigh at least thirty pounds. The final member of their party swept through the door with, Tyvian noted, his usual mix of flippancy and nervous energy. It was Zazlar Hendrieux, dressed in his best, a great cape of black fur draped from his sloping shoulders.

"This means trouble," Carlo whispered. "We should leave *now*."

Tyvian tsked through his teeth. "I'm disappointed again, Carlo. Don't you want to get some information firsthand for a change? What happened to your sense of adventure?"

"If by 'adventure' you mean 'do I want to witness you *murder* Hendrieux in the house of a Kalsaari Hanim,' then I can assure you my appetite for such things is quite sated, thank you."

"Shhh!" Tyvian hissed, and leaned his ear as close to the lattice of the veranda as he could. "You've got the magic eye—read some lips. What are they saying?"

"The slimy little stooge is offering the apologies of his mistress for not personally meeting Hendrieux . . ."

"The *other* slimy little stooge . . ."

" . . . for their business tonight—apparently they have some kind of arrangement. Fariq is . . . Great gods . . ."

"What?" Tyvian prodded.

"He's offering them the Hanim's hospitality for the evening. Bloody Hendrieux and his henchmen are coming to the party!"

"*Really?*" Tyvian couldn't help but gasp. "That's incredible!"

"We ought to get out of here." Carlo stepped back from the lattice and knocked on the door. "We can just tell them I'm too sick to stay."

"Not on your life! Miss a chance to parade myself before Hendrieux? You're mad!"

"Tyvian, I—"

Tyvian held up the empty chamber pot. "Besides, you forgot to vomit in here."

The door opened, revealing a veiled female slave in diaphanous clothing who bowed deeply. Carlo cleared his throat. "Yes, I—"

Tyvian shouldered past him. "He is feeling much better. Which way to the party?"

The party was held in an expansive indoor garden that lay spread out beneath a domed canopy of pure mageglass construction. Among the exotic tropical plants and pleasantly bubbling brooks and ponds were scattered about three dozen cages containing a wide variety of exotic animals, from winged, rainbow-tailed coatl serpents to one-eyed, bat-faced cavern trolls, their thick, black-nailed claws clutching the bars as though they understood the meaning of their imprisonment. Wandering among this menagerie were five hundred guests showcasing the finest fashions from a half-dozen nations. Tyvian found it consistent with what Carlo had said about the local obsession with Her Opulence that the majority of the Hanim's guests were from the West, outnumbering the Kalsaari guests at a ratio of three-to-one. Eretherians, Akrallians, and even countrymen from his native Saldor gathered in loose clumps around the firepits, all of them trying to find dignified ways to eat chunks of grilled meat and sautéed vegetables off skewers without getting sauce all over their fingers. Slaves, as it turned out, were usually necessary for this process, and it seemed that everybody had some half-naked Kalsaari stuffing food down their throats for them. Tyvian watched this and supposed that when this much pampering was being offered, deep-seeded political and ethnic rivalries could be temporarily forgotten. Either that or the whole place was crawling with spies. Or both.

Yes, probably both.

He let Carlo go mingle—by which Carlo meant "eat"—but kept himself to the periphery of the party, largely unnoticed, until he could find the key players. The Hanim had yet to appear, that was certain, but Fariq could be seen bustling around and socializing in his mechanical fashion, serving in his apparent capacity as the Hanim's public face. There were a few prominent guild members and the Lord Mayor was in attendance, the latter seated on a fat cushion that just managed to eclipse the size of his prodigious rear end and was flanked by a half-dozen city watchmen. Tyvian, though, couldn't have cared less about the city's ostensible "rulers," since the only real ruler in this city didn't speak and was parsed out in little disks of precious metal. That really only left three people at the party he was at all interested in: Hendrieux and the two bald, tattooed old Kalsaaris chatting with him around a firepit placed discreetly behind a copse of palm trees. It was a less central location than he would have wanted, but it would have to do.

Tyvian made a direct line through the crowd toward Hendrieux's secluded conference, brushing past Eretherian ladies in massive gowns and brushing aside Saldorian lords in their capes and velvet waist-coats. He picked a few pockets, collecting a half-dozen heavy gold marks in the palm of one hand, and then wrapped them tightly in a bit of wide silk ribbon he deftly pulled out of an Akrallian lady's elaborate whalebone bustle. Each time he nabbed a trinket from another half-drunk party guest, the ring cut into his flesh, making him grimace. He had to remember to play his cards right tonight—the Iron Ring could ruin everything if he wasn't careful.

As he got closer to Hendrieux, he saw one of the Akrallian's Delloran guards standing at the edge of the meeting, keeping watch and making sure no one eavesdropped or interfered. The man had sharp eyes and picked Tyvian out at thirty paces. Good—what he had planned would be easier if the bodyguard were facing him directly.

Carlo was standing next to him. "What do you think you're doing?"

"I'm going to talk with Hendrieux."

"Do you really think his man there is going to let you?"

Tyvian grinned. "Don't worry, Carlo—he's been disarmed."

Carlo snorted. "He's six feet tall and probably

weighs two hundred pounds. He doesn't *need* weapons."

"You never have faith in my abilities, do you?"

They moved together through the crowd. As they got closer, Carlo let the distance between them grow. "Your abilities are *exactly* what I'm worried about. Remember our deal!"

"Don't worry—I remember," Tyvian hissed, mostly under his breath. He was only about five paces from the guard.

The Delloran put up a gauntleted hand. "Private discussion. Move along."

Tyvian hefted the ribbon-wrapped pound of gold and threw it as hard as he could into the Delloran man's eye. It struck home with a satisfying smack and the guard reflexively put his hands up to his bruised eyeball. In that instant, Tyvian kicked him in the groin so hard the man could only produce a whistling moan as he fell on his side. The ring throbbed with displeasure, but not enough to break Tyvian's stride.

He stepped over the bodyguard's moaning form and plopped himself on a cushion right next to his former partner. He popped his most winning grin. "Hello, Zaz."

Hendrieux's mouth dropped open as though it were unhinged. He sputtered but no coherent words formed.

Tyvian decided to fill the silence. "Turns out your men don't actually know what I look like. Rather sloppy of you, I must say." He sighed at Hendrieux's ink-stained fingers. "Then again, you always did have poor judgment."

Hendrieux looked at the armored giant of a man who had led the party into the Hanim's palace. "Gallo! Get him out of here!"

Tyvian held up a hand. "Now now—I've no intention of disrupting your little meeting." Tyvian looked at the two bald Kalsaaris. "Hello. My name's Tyvian, and Zaz here was an old business partner of mine. On a related note, I should warn you that he has a tendency to betray his business partners."

If the two Kalsaaris were bothered by this, they didn't show it. Their eyes, Tyvian noted, were almost reptilian in color and shape, and their skin was brown, dry, and creased, like sun-baked leather. Their fingers were long, thin, and covered in the small scars and stains of artisans who worked in delicate, dangerous crafts.

Hendrieux gave Tyvian a weak grin that did little to hide the panic in his eyes. "Tyv, I realize you must be angry, but—"

Tyvian shook his head. "You're trying to explain yourself, but the simple fact is, Zaz, I don't care why you stabbed me in the back. I don't care what riches Sahand offered to pay you or why—all I care about is that you double-crossed me when I had been nothing but straight with you. We made a lot of money together, you and I. We built names for each other. I was even fair with the profits. Your forty percent was more than sufficient to sustain your . . ." Tyvian sneered at

Hendrieux's fur cape and out-of-fashion boots. " . . . lifestyle."

The two Kalsaaris exchanged glances and muttered to one another in their language. One of them rose as if to leave. Hendrieux leapt to his feet. "No, wait!"

Tyvian got up more slowly. "Yes, please stay; I'll be on my way. I just wanted to pass along a little message." He put an arm around Hendrieux and pulled him close so he could whisper in his ear. "*Run*, you little weasel. Flee like the mincing coward you are. Cower in dirty corners. Surround yourself with Sahand's best troops, if you must, but I *will* find you and I *will* destroy you, and when I am finished the whole world will pass by your crushed remains and know what happens to cheap thugs when they try to dupe their betters."

Hendrieux laughed faintly. "Well . . . we'll see."

Tyvian executed a smart half-bow. "See you tomorrow, Zaz."

A heavy gauntlet fell on Tyvian's shoulder and he was spun around to see the hard face and blackened eye of the guard he had taken down moments before, his fist cocked back to throw a punch that would level a cow. Even as Tyvian winced to take the blow, he found himself most disappointed that the Delloran's quick recovery had spoiled such a fine exit.

The punch, though, never fell. Gongs were sounding and horns were blowing, and suddenly the Delloran was standing at attention. Tyvian saw that all of the assembled guests were coming to their feet and turning their attention to the same place. Losing no time slipping away from the angry guard, he found Carlo and took up position beside him.

"I trust that went well?" Carlo snarled.

Tyvian nodded. "I still have all my teeth."

Carlo rolled his good eye. "You're ridiculous."

"This is a party, Carlo—we're supposed to be having fun."

Carlo snorted. "No, we're supposed to be making a deal. Focus now—the Hanim approaches."

Massive gilded doors at one end of the hall were pulled open, revealing a hallway beyond plated in pure gold and lit by ebony lanterns in the shape of the Imperial Raptor of Kalsaar. At the center of this hall, carried aloft in a sedan chair, was Angharad tin'Theliara Hanim of the Imperial House of Theliara.

Tyvian immediately forgot the little confrontation with Hendrieux as his mind was overridden with other, more pressing thoughts. The Hanim possessed a kind of beauty he had never seen before—dusky, intense, *powerful*. She sat with the bearing of a queen in her thronelike chair, carried by four burly slaves who strained under the weight of its jeweled frame. Her face was thin and angular, with high cheekbones and full lips, her black hair spilling freely across her delicate shoulders in gleaming waves. Her eyes were yellow, like gold, and they swept across her guests as though she were a raptor herself, looking for a likely mouse to snatch up. Her hands and wrists dripped with rubies and gold that matched her long silk gown, and her fingers each had a bloodred fingernail two inches long—the sign of a woman who never needed to work.

Carlo elbowed Tyvian in the ribs. "Stop staring at her."

"The hell I will," Tyvian breathed. "She's *incredible*."

"She can have us tortured and *killed* with a flick of her eyelash," Carlo hissed in his ear.

Tyvian cocked an eyebrow. "What kind of torture, do you suppose?"

The slaves set the Hanim's throne down, and somewhere in the garden a heavy staff was slammed against the floor. A voice yelled, "All kneel before Her Immortal Grace, Angharad tin'Theliara Hanim!"

The Kalsaaris fell on their faces instantly, the Westerners bowed and curtsied deeply, but Tyvian did not budge. The Hanim's golden gaze fixed on him immediately. "You do not kneel?" she said coolly, her eyelids drooping as though bored.

He shrugged and sighed. "Sorry, but I'm afraid I don't do that."

"You are a guest in the Hanim's home!" Fariq appeared from behind a pillar, his face red and beard twitching. "You insult her!"

Tyvian shook his head. "I assure you, Fooka, no insult is intended, but I would also hasten to add that I am not a guest."

"I am *Fariq*!" The slavemaster stomped his foot.

"If you are not a guest, then what are you?" the Hanim asked, her face impassive.

"A gift, it seems. Accept me with the compliments

of Carlo diCarlo." Tyvian made a short bow that was more head-nod than anything else.

The Hanim's strange eyes bored into Tyvian's for a long moment, but he did not look away. Finally, he thought he saw the barest hint of a smile playing around the edges of her mouth. "Slaves, take this gift to my suite, where I will inspect it later."

Two mark-slaves grabbed Tyvian by the elbows and shoulders and dragged him off. They were not gentle.

"You may rise." The Hanim clapped her hands. "Let the party continue."

CHAPTER 2

TROUBLE WEARS SILK

The mark-slaves heaved Tyvian headlong onto a pile of silk cushions. The irislike portal through which he had been tossed swiveled closed with a grinding metallic sound, and then there was silence.

Digging his way out of the pillow-pile, Tyvian checked his person for any permanent damage. Aside from a few bruises he would be feeling for the next several days and a couple tears in his clothing that would need the attention of a good tailor, he was unharmed. He also noted that they had not found nor relieved him of the dagger in his boot. He doubted it would be necessary or even effective in securing his goals that evening, but still, it never hurt to be prepared.

The room in which he found himself was beyond even his expectations. Occupying the whole top floor of one of the Theliara compound's many minarets, Astral enchantments had been used to more than double the available space inside the circular room, including a broad terrace with arching windows showing panoramic views of the city around him. These windows, Tyvian noted, opened onto a long stone balcony that ran around the circumference of the room. Within the luxurious room there was a titanic bath carved from black granite that bubbled with hot water, a bed of such proportions that it could sleep ten people, and its own slave, who stood quietly next to the one entrance.

Tyvian got up and straightened his clothing. "I say, my good fellow, would it be possible for me to get a glass of wine?"

The slave produced a glass of wine from behind his back, already poured and on a tray. Even Tyvian, accustomed as he was to magical amenities, was taken aback. "Were you *expecting* me to ask for red wine?"

The slave bowed his head low. "Your wine, saab."

Tyvian took the glass from the tray. "On second thought, I'd rather have white—chilled, please."

The slave put the tray behind him and brought it back, this time with a glass of white wine. Tyvian took it and noted that it was cool to the touch. "Great gods, that's incredible! How do you do that?"

The slave bowed low again but did not answer.

Tyvian shrugged. "Of course you don't know—silly of me to ask. So, what's your name?"

"I am Walid."

"Worked here long?"

"Since my birth, saab."

"Does the Hanim treat her slaves well?"

Walid bowed low. "She is our star in the heavens."

Tyvian snorted. "That does not answer the question, you know. Never mind, no need to get you in trouble."

Tyvian knew he would be there awhile. The Hanim would spend at least some time among her guests, accepting their birthday wishes and gifts. Even if the unexpected presence of Hendrieux and his cronies was enough to cut her public appearance short, he figured he had at least an hour. He spent it asking Walid to acquire for him various objects from thin air, most of which he discarded when he tired of them—a leg of lamb, a tennis racket, a live chicken, a diamond-studded bracelet, chocolates, and so on—until there was a pile of junk three feet high and he had eaten his fill of every delicacy he could think of. Then he arranged the most comfortable cushions in the room in front of the self-lighting firepit and reclined on them, noting for the first time the skylights in the ceiling. The fatigue of the past few weeks caught up to him at once, and he dozed off.

When he dreamed, the images were discordant and nonsensical. The only face he could make out was of that hairy Northron oaf, Eddereon—the man who had cursed him with the ring. The bearded mountain man spoke to him in a language he didn't understand. Tyvian threw eggs at him until he went away, and he laughed. *I'll show you!*

He awoke suddenly. He was looking up into the golden eyes of the Hanim, his head on her lap, her long fingernails running through his hair. He stiffened, and she smiled, her teeth gleaming in the firelight. "Well, it seems my present is finally awake."

Tyvian consciously attempted to relax. The Hanim smelled of lavender, and her touch on his scalp was enough to make any man squirm, but he forced himself to take a deep breath. "I hope there has been no misunderstanding, my lady—I am not your slave."

"Bosh." She smirked. "A few simple enchantments and you wouldn't even remember your name."

"Ah, yes, but then I also wouldn't remember the business transaction I came here to conduct."

The Hanim ran a fingernail across Tyvian's forehead and down his nose. Suddenly, she vanished from beneath him, and Tyvian fell back onto the cushion where she had been sitting. He leapt onto his feet, saw her standing across the room, Walid at her side, and looked back to where she had been. *Had she really been there at all?*

The Hanim chuckled softly, clearly amused. "That is right—illusion, Mr. Reldamar. A demonstration of my power, if you will, so you will know—or *not* know, if you follow my meaning—what you are dealing with if you seek to swindle me." The Hanim's face dropped the smile and gazed at him with deadly seriousness.

Tyvian smiled. "Fortunately, I have neither the desire nor motivation to do so, milady. I simply wish to make a trade."

"You have a staff in your possession."

"If by 'staff' you mean the colloquial term for mage, then yes, I have. What's more, she is a Mage Defender."

"Such a woman is worth a lot of gold, Mr. Reldamar, but not just to me. You could have easily sold her to some pretty criminal organization. Why go to all the trouble?"

It was Tyvian's turn to be deadly serious. "Because I am not interested in gold. I want a favor."

The Hanim grinned. "The Verisi, diCarlo, seems to think it is money."

"As I said, milady, I am not swindling *you*."

"Favors can be more expensive than money. You might do better to behave as your friend thinks you ought to."

"With respect, Hanim, I don't *need* money."

"What is your favor, then?" She fished a sardine from a tray Walid had produced and ate it with a single rapid bite. Tyvian tried not to stare at her lips.

Having gotten to his feet, he came closer, stopping little more than an arm's length from the Kalsaari noblewoman. "I need to meet with an Artificer."

She smirked. "The Artificers do not meet with Westerners, and certainly not with thieves of rare magical goods such as yourself."

Tyvian returned the smirk. "I saw a pair of them meeting with my former partner this very evening."

The Hanim's eyes narrowed. "Call me a liar and I'll have your tongue."

"I am merely illLumenating Your Grace to unforeseen possibilities. Artificers, it seems, *may* meet with Westerners, if the price is right."

"What do I offer them?"

Tyvian held up his right hand. *"This."*

The Hanim's gaze snapped to the Iron Ring immediately. She leaned in closer, blinking. "What is it?"

Why don't you tell me? Tyvian wanted to ask, but held his tongue. The Hanim clearly recognized the ring but didn't wish to let on. That was fine by him. He cleared his throat. "An inconvenient artifact I need removed, and will not trust to any bumbling Freegate talismancer. It is quite sophisticated, I assure you."

The Hanim reached out and took Tyvian's hand, pulling it closer to her and turning it over. Walid dangled a piece of illumite over her for additional light. "Have you tried antispell?" she asked.

"Not without knowing what will happen. It is bound to my hand, and I don't want it stuck there."

"You could simply cut the finger off," the Hanim said, running her fingers over the smooth edges of the ring.

Tyvian grimaced. "I happen to like that finger."

She smiled at him. "Yet you risk your entire body by meeting with me."

"If I am dead, I don't need fingers. While living, I

would prefer to keep all of them. Can you do what I ask?"

The Hanim pulled Tyvian closer by his hand, until his knuckles rested against her chest. Her fingers stroked his forearm in a way Tyvian thought beyond the bounds of professional decorum. "What does it do, this ring? Why do you hate it so much?"

He met the golden gaze of the Kalsaari noble-woman and did his best to act as though his body was molested by dangerous enchantresses on a regular basis and found the whole affair quite boring. "Did I say I hated it, milady?"

"I can see it in your eyes. When you speak of it, your hatred flares up like fuel thrown on a distant fire. Why?"

Tyvian permitted himself to smirk. "Perhaps I'll tell you, but I only trade secrets for secrets."

The Hanim released his hand. "What do you want to know?"

"You do not, by any chance, have a professional relationship with Banric Sahand, have you?"

The Hanim sighed dramatically, as though she were on a stage and wanted the back rows to hear her. "A slight one. Sahand was once an ally of my family—during the wars—but not since then. At the moment, his vassals have expressed an interest in purchasing animals from my menagerie—the wilder and more frightening, the better. I do not know why."

Tyvian nodded. "Logical enough." To himself, he added, *Even though you're obviously lying.*

"And now your turn for secrets. What does the ring do?"

"I'd rather not say," Tyvian said.

The Hanim hissed like a cat. "Perfidious wretch! Is this how you do business?"

"Come now, milady, do you really think I am so stupid as to fall for the whole 'information trade' nonsense. It's among the oldest swindles in the book. What you told me was at least half a lie, and you would never believe what I told you either. Let's at least be frank with one another, shall we?"

The Hanim assumed a stately posture. "We will consider your offer and contact you tomorrow should it be possible."

Tyvian nodded. "I look forward to seeing you again, Hanim."

She snorted softly. "Still you do not bow."

"Don't take it personally," he said. "I've spent my life snubbing those with power, no matter how beautiful they are."

"Walid," the Hanim said, "put him out."

Walid clapped his hands and the floor fell away from beneath Tyvian's feet. He fell through the dark, cursing Kalsaari sorcery the whole way down, until the abyss through which he fell became a flume full of foul-smelling water and trash. It wound and dipped through some dark system of tunnels and at last ejected him with a whoosh into a gutter. He landed flat on his back, knocking the wind out of him and covering him with freezing muck.

Pulling himself out of the stink and grime, Tyvian wheezed until his lungs remembered how to breathe air, then spent several moments cursing the Hanim. "The wretched witch could have *at least* tossed me out a side door."

His clothes were a complete loss. Even if he had them magically cleaned, they would never quite be the same. He tossed his jacket in the gutter and used his scarf to wipe off the larger patches of refuse and slime from his breeches and shirt. For all his aggravation, however, he had to admit that the loss of a suit of clothes was a small price to pay for the deal he had secured.

Tyvian had complete confidence that the Hanim would accept his offer, because he knew that what he'd suggested was of immeasurable worth to Theliara and the Kalsaari Empire as a whole. A Mage Defender like Myreon was a walking secret weapon, trained in doctrines and disciplines the Kalsaaris would kill to know. For ages the Arcanostrum of Saldor had trained the world's finest magi, bar none, and the Kalsaaris knew it. But the presence of sorcery among the nobles in Kalsaar spoke less to their talent than to their tolerance of it. The overuse of magical power was still somewhat taboo in the nations of the West, and all magi were trained to use only the barest fraction of their power in any given situation. In those rare instances when they did use the sum total of their arts to tackle a problem, the very fabric of the earth shook. Tyvian knew this better than most: his mother, Lyrelle Reldamar, was one of the most powerful sorcerers alive, and when she worked a spell, the world trembled.

Myreon Alafarr was, of course, not anything close to Lyrelle. Tyvian knew that, Myreon knew that, but the Kalsaaris likely did not. Their magic was focused upon invocation—the most ephemeral discipline of sorcery, which created effects and simulations that lacked real substance. Myreon's skill in augury, enchantment, and transmutation would no doubt thrill them. Indeed, what enchantment, transmutation, and even conjuration the Kalsaaris had devised were all based on the confessions and interrogations of Western magi they had captured or who had defected to them over the years.

The exceptions to all of this were the Artificers. A secretive monastic order that devoted itself to a mixture of the Low and High Arts, they were the creators of magical artifacts beyond compare. It was said that their skill exceeded even those of the magi of the Arcanostrum or the Builders of Eretheria. Tyvian knew that if he could get them to take a look at the ring, not only could they likely remove it, but there was also a distinct chance they could tell him where and how it was made.

Of course, his deal with the Hanim would not put him *directly* closer to meeting with an Artificer. For as much as Tyvian thought the Hanim would accept his deal, he was twice as confident that she would double-cross him at her first opportunity. Not only was deception part of her nature, but he had gone out of his way to insult her pride this evening, and he knew she couldn't accept that without getting some kind of satisfaction for that injury at his expense. Betrayal seemed the easiest, most straightforward option.

The deal with the Hanim was one facet of a plot that, if it worked, would serve to relieve him of the ring, attain his vengeance on Hendrieux, fulfill his "deal" with Hool the gnoll and get the Defenders off of his back for a long, long time. His plot had been growing in complexity with every passing day, but with Hendrieux's fortuitous appearance at the party this evening, things just got a little bit simpler. Of course, he had to hurry.

Tyvian ran around the periphery of the Hanim's palace until he was reasonably certain he had catalogued all the visible exits. Doing a little mental geography, he calculated the most obvious route one would take from the palace to the Blocks, and placed himself in an alley a quarter mile distant that gave him a good view of the area. The problem, however, would be how to make a move on Hendrieux's party without getting killed.

"Hmmmm . . ." he said, trying to beat warmth into his arms. "If only I had a sword with me."

It was then that Hacklar Jaevis jumped from the rooftops onto Tyvian's back.

CHAPTER 3

JUST ANOTHER STREET FIGHT

The first thing that happened was Jaevis broke Tyvian's nose by slamming him into the wall of the alley. Then came a swift kick in the guts, which sent Tyvian's breath whistling through his teeth. Jaevis then picked the smuggler up like a sack of flour and threw him on the ground. All of this transpired in approximately two and a half seconds.

The alley spun in the darkness. Tyvian's nose was throbbing and clogged with what he guessed was a lot of blood; he couldn't breathe, see, or hear anything over the pounding in his ears and the white hot pain in his face. He felt Jaevis plant a knee on his breastbone, pinning him in place, and then Tyvian's world exploded again as the bounty hunter began to pound his head with his fists as though it were a lump of dough on a baker's counter. Dimly, Tyvian could hear the Illini muttering a single word, over and over: "*Vendetta.*"

After the third punch in the face, Tyvian managed to pull his knee to his chest and draw the dagger from his boot. Jaevis was so focused on pounding Tyvian's head flat as a coin that he very nearly didn't notice the flash of steel until it was too late. As it was, the Illini twisted at the last moment so the point of the dagger pierced his arm rather than his heart. Jaevis snarled with a mixture of rage and pain, clutching at the deep wound with his free hand and leaping up before Tyvian could stick him again.

Unpinned, Tyvian rolled away and into the street, which was really more stairs than street, and bounced down several icy stone steps before he managed to stop himself. Jaevis charged after him, his arm pumping blood but his mind apparently too filled with anger to care. Tyvian tried to rise with the aid of a lamppost, but the bounty hunter kicked him in the chest and sent him sprawling onto his back and tumbling down another half-dozen unforgiving steps. Air wheezing into his lungs, blood dripping into his mouth, Tyvian pointed his dagger at Jaevis to keep himself from being tackled again.

He didn't kill me—he needs me alive.

Jaevis drew one of his long, curved sabers with his good arm and adjusted his cloak. "Not so full of jokes now, eh?"

Tyvian, trying not to fall down any more stairs, scuttled away from him until he had room to pull himself into a crouch. "You're early, Jaevis."

The bounty hunter advanced slowly, leaving drops of blood in his wake. "You were not expecting Jaevis. Jaevis was expecting you."

Tyvian retreated, wracking his brain for a plan. "Must we debate semantics? I mean, let's be honest, you *barely* speak Trade. Shouldn't you just defer to me in linguistic matters?"

Jaevis grunted. "Still with jokes. I will cut out tongue, Reldamar."

Dagger against saber was no contest, even if Jaevis *was* short an arm. Tyvian had stabbed him deep, but the wound wasn't fatal. Thanks to the studded leathers Jaevis wore on his torso, the odds of getting a fatal blow in there were extremely slim. There was only one way out of this.

"Well, good-bye, then!"

Tyvian turned tail and ran.

Jaevis roared and pursued.

The bounty hunter was swift, and Tyvian had just gotten his face pounded in for a few moments, so his balance wasn't perfect; his flight was more of a controlled fall down the steep, stair-lined street. There was little doubt in his mind that he would be caught in a matter of seconds. Fortunately, a matter of seconds was all he needed.

Tyvian made a sharp right turn and ran, full bore, into the arms of two of Hendrieux's men. He made a show of struggling, but in all honesty he could not have been happier to see them. They had just come from the Hanim's party, as Tyvian had anticipated, and their group included eight soldiers in livery, as before, as well as the hulking Gallo, the fur-caped Hendrieux, and two men in rust-red robes and hoods. *Artificers, I presume.* Tyvian tried not to smile.

"Look what we 'ave 'ere!" One of the Dellorans held a tiny bead of illumite close to Tyvian's face. In the pale light, Tyvian could see the man had a black eye—great, it was the guard from the party. "It's Tyvian bleedin' Reldamar, and he's got his fine clothes all mussed."

Tyvian nodded. "Well identified, sir—and with only one eye, too! Hendrieux should give you a raise."

The man kneed Tyvian in the groin, which, he had to admit, was fair enough. He fell to his knees, nauseous with pain, but the two Dellorans hoisted him back up.

Hendrieux's face split into a genuine smile. "Tyvian! Now, what has you running scared, hmmm?"

Tyvian heard the cock of a crossbow and, between gasps of agony, managed to make introductions. "Gentlemen . . . I . . . give you . . . Hacklar Jaevis."

It turned out that Jaevis didn't have a crossbow, but rather a close relative. It was a hurlant—a crossbow-like device designed to throw spheres rather than bolts—and this hurlant was loaded with a smooth, fist-sized stone that popped and sizzled in the cool night air. "You give me Reldamar now."

The Dellorans all drew their swords; Gallo hefted his heavy maul. Hendrieux moved so he could leap behind Gallo, should it become necessary, and smiled. "Now now, friend—we've no love for this wretch, do we? We were just about to slit his throat ourselves."

"I take him alive." Jaevis's aim with the hurlant never wavered from Gallo's massive form. "I take him now."

"There are ten of us and one of you." Hendrieux said. "I don't think you are in a position to give orders."

Jaevis nodded at his weapon. "Thunder-orb gives me position. Give Reldamar *now*."

"One thunder-orb won't kill us all, Mr. Jaevis. Let's be reasonable—I have personal business with Mr. Reldamar here that will end in his death. You're a bounty hunter, aren't you? Why don't I pay whatever you're being paid plus, say, ten percent, and we call it even, hmmmm?"

Tyvian saw an opportunity to jump in. "He's bluffing, Jaevis. He's a coward—he's soiling his breeches at the thought of you firing that thunder-orb at him."

Hendrieux gave Tyvian a withering glance. "I am *not* bluffing."

"That's exactly what you'd say if you *were* bluffing."

Black Eye gave Tyvian an ear-boxing that sent his

head spinning. He let himself fall to the ground and pretended to whimper.

"Enough talk!" Jaevis's finger trembled over the trigger. "Back away!"

Hendrieux, his face a bit paler than before, began to back up. "Very well, very well—no need to—"

Gallo charged, heavy maul held high. He made no cry, bellowed no challenge—he was like a war machine with its switch thrown, sudden and inexorable. The next few seconds were complete mayhem. Jaevis fired at Gallo, and the magical stone detonated on the huge man's breastplate with thunderclap force, blowing everyone off their feet. Everyone, that was, besides Tyvian, who had sensibly gotten down earlier. The heat and crackling energy of the blast was still coursing through Tyvian's body; he was deafened by the sound, disoriented by the concussion. Still, he had the wherewithal to sit up.

Gallo, impossibly, wasn't dead. He had lost his maul and the loose wool cape he had draped over his shoulders, and his armor smoked and crackled like something stuffed in a furnace, but he stood up without so much as flinching. He backhanded Jaevis as the bounty hunter tried to rise, spinning the Illini around and knocking him back over. Tyvian grinned at this, but stopped grinning when, out of the corner of his eye, he saw Hendrieux coming at him with a drawn sword. Thinking quickly, Tyvian scooped a handful of gravel from the road and hurled it at Hendrieux's eyes.

The Akrallian flinched, buying Tyvian enough time to stand up and snatch a sword from one of the dazed Dellorans.

The Dellorans—the ones not blown to pieces by the thunder-orb, anyway—were getting up, too. Sounds were coming back to Tyvian's ears; they were fuzzy and indistinct, but they were definitely sounds. He took heart that, at the very least, he wasn't deaf.

Five of the eight Dellorans were left. Tyvian tried to stab one of them before he rose, but the ring shot a lightning bolt of pain up his arm and he was forced to drop his sword. The Delloran in question—Black Eye himself—tackled him by the legs, and the two men were left to rolling down those damned cobblestone stairs in an awkward wrestling match. Black Eye had strength and size, but Tyvian knew a few dirty tricks. Chief among these was biting, and he dug his teeth into Black Eye's nose as though it were a massive wedge of Leventry cheese. The guard responded with a few kidney punches that made Tyvian let go, but not before he took a chunk of nose with him. "Kroth-spawned tit," the Delloran growled. "Messin' up my face."

Another thunder-orb went off, blowing Black Eye and Tyvian up against the front stairs of a house. Tyvian felt his shoulder pop out of joint, and Black Eye cracked his own head on a stone and fell unconscious on top of him. Between his wounded shoulder and Black Eye's bulk, Tyvian was trapped. From his vantage point underneath Black Eye, he could see that the battle, such as it was, was nearly over.

Hacklar Jaevis had lost his hurlant and was fighting against the monstrous Gallo with nothing but his thin, curved saber. Gallo had a weapon that looked like a cross between spiked brass knuckles and a machete, and he used it in much the same manner. All of Jaevis's artistry with his curved blades was irrelevant against the hacking, driving blows Gallo delivered to the bounty hunter's guard with mechanical rhythm. Each block Jaevis made seemed to drive him back half a pace and sent shockwaves of force through his body to the point where he looked scarcely able to defend himself. Gallo pressed on until, eventually, Jaevis was forced to his knees. Gallo's armored paw seized the bounty hunter by the hair, hauled his head back, and laid his blade against Jaevis's throat.

"Say good-bye to your bounty hunter, Tyv," Hendrieux said softly. He was crouching next to Tyvian's pinned body, a long thin dagger in one hand. "I just want you to see this last ridiculous ruse of yours fail before I stuff a knife in your eye myself."

Gallo looked over to Hendrieux. His ruined voice betrayed no sign of fatigue or pain. "Now?"

Hendrieux held up his hand. "I'm glad it will end this way, Tyv—your body found beaten, dead, and dirty, pinned by a stinking oaf in some dirty Freegate side street. I bet they'll think you were mugged. Won't that be funny?"

It was then that Gallo was knocked across the street and slammed into the second story of a carpenter's workshop by some unseen force. Hendrieux stood up bolt straight. "What the—"

Tyvian had never heard Hool roar before. It was, in a word, terrifying. The volume and timbre of the bellow that escaped her lips was sufficient to make Tyvian's bowels watery, and he at least knew Hool had no intention of killing *him*.

The two Dellorans closest to Hool saw her copper eyes glinting in the dark and watched, open-mouthed, as she rose to her full height. Her bulky silhouette towered over them in the dim light of the street. In her hands was Gallo's heavy maul, which she had just used to propel the massive man through the air like a croquet ball.

Sahand was said to pay well, but apparently didn't pay *that* well. The men dropped their swords and fled into the night.

The last remaining Delloran stood quavering before the mighty gnoll's advance, longsword extended. He called to Hendrieux, "Orders, captain?" Hendrieux, though, was long gone. The lone Delloran glanced around him, saw he was alone, and then ran off in the direction the others had gone. Hool dropped the heavy maul as the man vanished from sight and began to sniff the air carefully, her ears rigid and upright.

"Hey!" Tyvian yelled. "Hey! Help me up!"

Hool vanished from sight, darting down an alley at

the speed of a galloping horse. Tyvian was left pinned and alone in the cold and dark. "Hool? HOOOL! Dammit, gnoll! I'm stuck!"

A minute or two later saw the weight of Black Eye suddenly lifted from Tyvian's body. The smuggler looked up to see Hool standing over him. "Hool!" He coughed, "It's about bloody time! What are you doing here anyway—you were supposed to be in the Blocks."

Hool ignored the question and skipped straight to criticism. "You are very stupid, Tyvian Reldamar. You are lucky other humans are also stupid, or you would be dead."

Tyvian crawled painfully to his feet. "Yes, Hool, thank you for the valuable critique."

"Hendrieux got away again—*another* magic door. You said those things were expensive, but he has three of them now."

Tyvian tried blowing his nose, but all that came out was blood. He reasoned that, at the very least, the shirt he was wearing couldn't get any *more* ruined. "He hasn't got three, just one—a door that magically connects to other doors. It's called an anygate."

"Where is it?"

"I'm not sure yet," Tyvian said, but the ring pinched him for it, and hard. Fortunately, the rest of him was in enough pain that the effect was largely masked. "Where's Jaevis?"

Hool pointed toward a different alley. "He snuck away when I hit the big man with his hammer. I can track *him*. He doesn't use filthy cheater magic."

"Not now, Hool, thank you," Tyvian said, limping over to the piles of bodies now littered around the street. "Speaking of the big man, what *did* happen to Gallo, anyway?"

"He should be dead but he isn't. I don't know why," Hool observed, cocking her head and listening. "He is close, but he's leaving."

Tyvian nodded. The man *had* to be life-warded beyond any life ward Tyvian had ever heard of—nobody survived a thunder-orb to the *face* and walked away, *particularly* not when they were knocked through a building immediately afterward. He made a note to avoid frontal confrontations with Gallo for the foreseeable future.

Tyvian found the second Artificer lying underneath one of the Dellorans killed by the initial thunder-orb. "Here—is this one alive?"

Hool nodded. "He is bleeding, but he will probably live if nothing catches and eats him before he gets home."

Tyvian sighed, which made his bruised ribs complain. "Ugh . . . well, that's something. Here, pick him up and bring him to my flat."

Hool's ears flattened against her head. "Why?"

Tyvian shrugged; the gesture made his dislocated shoulder scream, but he kept his desire to wince to himself. He doubted Hool was sympathetic to physical pain. "I want to make sure he isn't caught and eaten, of course. Now hurry, or all this will have been for nothing."

Hool hoisted the unconscious Kalsaari onto her back while Tyvian snatched up the hurlant where Jaevis had dropped it, then they both headed for home. Altogether, Tyvian decided it had been a rather productive evening.

He tried not to think about how much of it had relied on pure, dumb luck.

CHAPTER 4

CONSCIENTIOUS OBJECTOR

Myreon did not sleep, yet she was too tired to do
much of anything else. She lay on the plush mattress
with the downy quilts bunched around her and stared
at the ceiling.

Artus was almost certainly dead by now. The
thought of it made her want to cry, but no tears came.
The poor young fool—came this far, followed Reldamar every step of the way, only to be cast out and
murdered in some Freegate alley for no discernible
reason.

He had been a good person, too—Myreon could

tell just by looking at him. In her time, she'd seen a lot of bitter, desperate children gathered in the wretched alleys of Saldor and Galaspin, eyes dull and hard as shale. They were the progeny of ink-thralls and prostitutes, raised with the lash and taught to expect nothing. Artus hadn't been like them, though. He had an easy smile and an honest way about him. He spoke like a boy who had been loved once and perhaps still was somewhere. He could have made something of himself, if not for Reldamar's meddling. The tragedy of it chilled her bones.

Myreon wondered how many people like that— good, innocent fools—had their lives ruined by Tyvian Reldamar. She thought of a flower girl in Ihyn who Tyvian had employed as a lookout for his safe house, killed by accident when she threw herself in front of the Defenders advancing to capture him. She remembered a young Akrallian enchanter who had trusted Reldamar with sensitive documents and, as a result, was rotting in an Akrallian dungeon to this day. Everywhere the man went, people suffered.

And yet . . . *no*. There was no "and yet." Tyvian Reldamar was a spinefish—colorful, interesting, even beautiful, but if you touched him you wound up dead or hurt. To him, there was nothing beyond himself. That ring could torture him all it wanted, but it couldn't torture him into believing in something good or noble. It couldn't force him to be selfless. Myreon suspected that Tyvian believed that Good and Evil were arbitrary distinctions made by those who wished to control other individuals through the creation of some kind of moral code. To him, they had no more true meaning than any other baseless superstition. He thought of them as the crutches leaned upon by the stupid, the ignorant, and the weak.

He was wrong, though. She knew what true nobility and true selflessness was. She had seen it in her father. She had even seen it in Lyrelle, Tyvian's mother—a woman so selfless that, though she had it in her power to seize her son and bind him to her will, she did not do so. As Magus Lyrelle had often remarked, "Each of us must be allowed to make ourselves as we intend. For others to fashion you in their image—even with the best of intentions—is the commission of a grave violation."

Myreon dragged her thoughts away from the Reldamars and back to herself for a moment. Her room had no spirit clock, no way to judge time. It was late, at any rate. A storm was rolling in, blotting out the moonlight and dropping a pall of fog over the dirty Freegate streets. Assuming her message had been received, how soon could she expect a rescue attempt? She tried to estimate timetables—how long it would take to verify the veracity of the rescue message, how long it would take to get a team together, how to sneak it into Freegate without the city watch noticing? "Gods," she grumbled, "a long time."

The best she could hope for, she realized, was for a rescue party to be on the midday spirit engine tomorrow. If she had to do it, she would bring ten men disguised as guild apprentices and journeymen. Watchmen would be all over the spirit-engine berth, tattlers and all, but if the Defenders scattered to various sections of town while disguised, no one would likely notice or care. Equipment would have to be shipped separately, as parcels—crates to be delivered to whichever warehouse would serve as a rally point. The operation required to muster them all would take hours. Tomorrow night, then. She could be rescued from here as early as tomorrow night.

She had the sinking feeling that wouldn't be soon enough.

Thump!

A sound through the wall, muffled but clearly audible. Myreon bolted upright in bed and cocked an ear.

It had come from Artus's room. Gods, she thought, the specters are removing the body. She felt ill. Her tongue, dry and sour, seemed to swell in her mouth. Her eyes watered. "Reldamar, I am going to . . ." She couldn't summon a curse suitable enough, so she just let the dead silence swallow her rage for a moment. She shook her head, thinking of the smuggler's mocking smile. "Somehow."

Another thump and then a crash. The sound of broken porcelain—it had to be the blue-and-white Hurnish vase on an end table by the door in Artus's room. The specters must have knocked it over as they carried out the corpse.

Except that serving specters never did anything like that. They were existentially *incapable* of breaking household objects or anything in general—you had to get specially constructed ones that were able to break eggs, let alone accidentally break vases. So, if they didn't break it, then that meant somebody else was in Tyvian's flat. But who?

Myreon stood up and went to the wall, pressing her ear against it.

Silence for a long moment—only her breath and racing heart to mark the time.

"*Unnnhhhhh . . .*" It was the faintest of moans, barely verbal, but Myreon heard it. It was like a spike of fire in her spine.

Artus was still alive.

Myreon was numb with shock. She kept listening, her face pressed so hard against the wallpaper it was probably making a permanent imprint.

"*H-Help . . .*"

"Oh Gods!" Myreon leapt to the door, trying the handle though she knew it was locked. "Hey!" She pounded on the door. "Let me out! Let me help him! He's fallen out of bed! Please!"

It was pointless. One did not argue with specters—they were not intelligent beings. They did what they were supposed to and nothing more. Reldamar had them set as housekeepers and cooks and improvised jailors—nothing else interested them. They were probably cleaning up the broken vase around Artus's fever-wracked body at that very moment, never imagining they might help . . .

Wait.

"That's it!" Myreon snapped her fingers. She cast her glance around the room, looking for something to spill. Her water pitcher was empty and had been for hours and no other liquid given to her. That liquid, however, hadn't just vanished entirely; the chamber pot sat in the corner, not yet emptied.

With the specters' cleaning function in mind, Myreon tore off the lid and hefted the heavy porcelain bowl in both hands, the stink of her own urine burning her nostrils. She aimed at the door to her cell and dumped the contents on the floor so it would leak under the door and into the living room. She didn't have to wait long.

The door was flung open and a floating towel dropped on the puddle on the threshold of her cell. Myreon leapt over it, brushing past something invisible. The specter did not grab hold—it was cleaning the filth from the floor first, and its companion was busy cleaning the mess Artus had made. She had a few seconds to dart into the living room, up the short corridor, and duck into Artus's room.

Artus was facedown on the floor, sweat-soaked and panting. On his back, the bandages Myreon had placed were black with dried blood. She immediately crouched and grabbed him under the armpits. "I've got you! Are you all right?"

Artus's head rolled back. His eyes were bloodshot but surprisingly clear. "Hey . . . how'd I get on the floor?"

Myreon lifted him—he was heavier than he

looked—and dragged him back into the bed. She was out of breath by the time she was done. "You're . . . you're alive!"

Artus lay back weakly on his pillow. "Yeah . . . sure . . . Tyvian saved me . . ."

"No he . . ." Myreon frowned and felt his forehead. He was cool to the touch. She felt around to his back and pulled the bandage away—the wound was healed. Practically gone. "How in hell's blazes did Reldamar—"

"Oh Saints! That's right!" Artus's eyes popped open wide. He moved as if to get up again, but Myreon pushed him back down. "Lemme go! I gotta talk to Reldamar!"

Myreon still couldn't quite figure out what had happened. She found herself staring at the boy for a moment before finally gathering her wits. "Artus, you nearly died—you have to stay in bed!"

He nodded slowly. "Okay, Ma. Sure . . . sure thing . . ."

Myreon felt a force seize her by one arm and begin dragging her out of the room. She struggled against it. "Artus, what do you mean Reldamar saved you? What did he do?"

Artus, though, seemed to be drifting away again. "Saints, this is a swank place, huh? Nice . . . nice curtains . . ."

Another specter had its hooks in now, and Myreon felt her feet sliding on the floor. "No! Somebody needs to take care of him! He needs water! He needs something to eat!"

The specters made no comment. She was slowly dragged from the room and into the hall, cursing the whole way. She considered trying to dispel them—a relatively simple maneuver, typically—but that would tip her hand early. She was saving what little energy and strength she had regained for the moment when it would be most necessary. So instead she wove a small portion of her power into a small telekinetic push that knocked a vase off the mantelpiece in the living room. This prompted one specter to release her immediately and, moving faster than Myreon might have believed, catch the vase before it hit the floor.

It was the opening she needed, however. She yanked against the other specter, and though it didn't lose its grip, it did slide across the floor with her, unable to find purchase with whatever eldritch process gave the thing traction. Dragging it along, if slowly, might be enough—she only needed to make it to the front door of the flat. Once she crossed the threshold, the things would have no further power over her.

Her heart pounded in her chest as she forced herself against the living room floor, step by labored step. The specter had replaced the vase on the mantel and again she felt the cold, formless force of the thing join its companion by grabbing her under her other arm. She was stopped in her tracks and dragged backward half as far as she had come. It was only by propping herself against a pillar that she managed to stop her backward progress. "Dammit!"

She created a bigger distraction then—this time a telekinetic burst at the fireplace, stirring ash, soot, and fiery sparks across the floor. One spark landed softly on the armrest of great, high-backed chair. The specters released her immediately, fetching brushes and dustpans from distant closets and flying to the rescue of Tyvian's upholstery with all the speed of falcons in flight.

"Ha!" Myreon bolted for the front door. She had no staff, but she was strong enough to possibly work a few spells to get her to safety. Any reward she could offer the city watch for her safe return would probably outstrip whatever funds Tyvian could offer to bribe them. She had to hope.

She flung open a closet in the front hall and fished out a heavy purple cape with a hood. For that split second, she wondered about Artus. If she left now, what would become of him? Could she leave the boy in Reldamar's care?

And yet . . . Artus had been saved. By Reldamar. Somehow.

Maybe, against all reason, Reldamar would take care of him. Maybe the ring would make him. Maybe . . . maybe he even *wanted* to.

Myreon shook her head. She couldn't wait any longer. She turned and threw open the door.

Reldamar stood on the threshold in front of her, key in hand. He looked at her with a kind of resignation. "I thought as much." He was filthy, bloodied, and seemed to sag under his own weight. His nose was broken, and it made his voice sound oddly high-pitched. Hool towered behind him, an unconscious man across her shoulders.

Myreon raised her hands for a spell, but the specters seized her from each side and dragged her off-balance.

Tyvian shook his head and entered his home. "Purple really isn't your color, Myreon. You're too pale."

There were a lot of things Myreon wanted to yell at him at that moment, but only one came out. "You saved him. How?"

Reldamar didn't meet her gaze. "None of your business."

The specters kept pulling her along. She scrambled to get purchase on the smooth floor. "You aren't fooling anybody, Tyvian Reldamar! You aren't fooling me for a second!"

Reldamar scowled at her as he followed her into the living room. "Get back in your cell, go to sleep, save your strength—tomorrow is a big day."

Myreon was pushed over the threshold of her cell. "Why? What's tomorrow?"

Reldamar said nothing. He merely gave her a cold, steady look as he slammed the door in her face.

CHAPTER 5

BAD DEALS

Sahand watched the Artificer's face carefully, waiting for any sign of deceit or evasion. Instead, the leathery-faced monk merely nodded. His Trade was surprisingly unaccented. "I will do it."

They were standing on a wooden platform erected over a circular pool about ten yards in diameter. The water, originally clear as a mountain spring, was now murky and crimson—the color of blood. The underground chamber in which the pool lay reeked of death so strongly that the men who worked here wore kerchiefs treated with pungent oils over their noses and mouths to keep from retching. Sahand had made it very clear that any man vomiting in or near his pool would pay with his life. This rule had resulted in one elderly alchemist with a weak stomach and whiny voice being suspended upside down from this very platform, his wrists slit, and left to drain until empty. No one else had vomited.

In retrospect, Sahand rather regretted exsanguinating the alchemist. It had been relatively early in the process, and he hadn't fully anticipated how complicated the preparations would be. Not only was the man talented, but the addition of his blood to the pool had caused a number of problems that set back the entire project by weeks.

A trio of soldiers wrestled a cage with a snarling baboon up to the platform as Sahand and the Artificer watched. Sahand motioned to his men as they worked. "I came up with the idea of utilizing vicious animals to enhance the effect some time ago, but full implementation took longer than I expected. Too many of the same kind would calm the energies in the waters by too much, as would collecting the animals in any kind of predictable pattern. I've needed to employ an individual with a wide range of contacts to acquire the beasts almost at random. This baboon comes from the jungles south of Hurn—very aggressive, I'm told."

The baboon snarled and whooped as the soldiers positioned its cage over an iron grate, beneath which swirled the deep red waters of the pool. The men looked to Sahand, and the Mad Prince nodded. In unison, the three men drew iron skewers about three feet long and stabbed the beast over and over until its screams turned to wails of pain, then whimpers, then deathly silence. The beast's blood ran in rivers down its ruined corpse, raining into the pool below.

With each drop, Sahand could feel the burning power in the pool grow stronger. The cavernous chamber, though located high in the mountains in the depths of winter, grew hot. Sahand's hair stood on end with the sheer amount of the Fey pulsing through the room. He did his best to suppress a smile. "I have been giving this project a great deal of my personal attention, but my duties are many and I have need of another skilled hand to take over certain final preparations."

He started down the ramps the led up to the platform. The Artificer followed, his head bowed. "You are having difficulty releasing the energy?" the old monk asked.

"Yes, in a manner of speaking. We can siphon out some of the energy held therein—the ancient warlock kings who built this place were masters of such power sinks, and the release of a measured amount of energy has not been a problem. I am not interested in a measured release of energy, however. I want to release it all at once. I want to tap it in its entirety."

Sahand waited for the shocked reaction from the Artificer as the gravity of what he had said sunk in. Again the Mad Prince was pleasantly surprised—the old monk only nodded slowly. "I see. This is to be a weapon."

Sahand grinned and put a finger to his lips. "The reputation of your noble order is not exaggerated, sahib. You are one of only two human beings besides myself to figure that out. The other one is dead. We had . . . a difference of opinion."

The Artificer bowed deeply. "We of the Artificers are seekers of knowledge only. We are not blinded by the West's notions of propriety or custom."

Sahand pointed to the hunched, gaunt form of Hortense the thaumaturge. The man had been working practically nonstop all week, and the elaborate systems of focusing crystals, channeling rods, and power funnels he had erected around the edges of the pool looked like the work of some desperate madman. "There is my lead warlock. He is a thaumaturge by trade and has skill with the Low Arts, but he lacks the knowledge of the High Arts to complete the preparations. He is highly motivated, as you can see, but he will require your assistance to complete his work."

The Artificer's sharp eyes narrowed at the frantic activity of the warlock. "What is his motivation?"

"His daughter's virginity. I trust you needn't be motivated in a similar fashion?"

The Artificer looked back at the vast, ancient power sink. "No. To see this thing done and to carry the tale back to my order will be enough."

Sahand nodded. "A simple enough price to pay, sahib. I will leave you to your tasks."

The Artificer bowed again and made directly for Hortense. Sahand watched him for a few moments more and then nodded to one of his men. The man ran up and saluted. "Keep an eye on the Kalsaari," the prince said, pointing to the soldier's crossbow. "If he makes any move to leave this place, shoot him in the leg. Don't let him bleed out, though, or I'll have your balls."

"Yes sire!" The man clicked his heels and returned to his post.

Satisfied, Sahand took his leave and wound his way through the icy tunnels and crumbling galleries of the ancient ruined palace to return to his tent overlooking the slumbering city of Freegate below. It was snowing more heavily than before, and a squad of soldiers were clearing the snow away from their tents and defensive positions, building snowbanks that would slow down potential attackers, not that any were likely. Sahand had full confidence now that nothing could stop him.

Inside his tent, Carlo diCarlo was waiting for him. Sahand knew better than to act surprised that the old master thief was able to steal past his guards, but the intrusion hadn't been expected. His hand flew to the hilt of his dagger—a dagger infused with a particularly brutal enchantment. Carlo, though, had already leveled a wand at the Mad Prince.

"I didn't come here to kill or be killed, Your Highness," Carlo said, his crystal eye reflecting the firelight in circular patterns. "I have things to discuss."

Sahand removed his hand from his dagger and shrugged off his cloak on the rack beside the pavilion entrance. "Out with it."

Carlo settled his bulk into a chair—not *Sahand's* chair, sensibly enough—but one close enough to the brazier to heat his hands. "You were right—both of your League associates are in the city or will be shortly. One of them used me to hire Hacklar Jaevis to nab Reldamar for his own purposes, and the other is—"

"Angharad tin'Theliara Hanim. I know; I'm not an idiot. Her whole reason for being here is to provide me with the animals I need, and now the Artificers—this is hardly useful news."

Carlo shrugged and removed his crystal eye to polish it with a cloth he produced from a pocket somewhere. "Your little pissing match with the city watch isn't winning you any favors either. Hendrieux is extremely unpopular in the Phantom Guild and the Guildmaster is making plans to destroy him."

Sahand sat behind his desk and poured himself a drink of straight oggra from a genuine ogre horn. He didn't offer Carlo any—the harsh liquor would probably kill the fat swine. "How do you know that?"

Carlo grinned. "Because I *am* the Phantom Guildmaster, obviously."

Sahand nodded. "Hmph. That explains a great deal about your resources; why the confession?"

"Because I want you to know that I have to act a certain way in the next few days that will result in your operation in Freegate being shut down. There is a troop of Defenders on their way here on the next spirit engine that Reldamar is going to play like puppets, mark my words, and I will aid him. Furthermore, neither Theliara nor your other conspirator believes you are working on Rhadnost's Elixir anymore—"

Sahand nearly choked on his oggra.

Carlo held up a hand, "Don't ask how I know—I just do. I don't know what you *are* working on, and neither do they. Even if I did, I wouldn't tell them, since you are an enemy I don't relish having. I'm only here to tell you that trouble is coming, and whatever happens, I don't want to be held responsible for it. Understand?"

"Perfectly." Sahand nodded. "I won't forget this, Carlo. You can rest assured that I will pay you exactly what I owe you." The Mad Prince swirled the harsh, clear alcohol in his mouth. "I will pay you with interest, even."

Carlo bowed and slipped out. It was amazing how stealthy a fat man could be.

Tyvian watched the Artificer's face carefully, waiting for any sign the old Kalsaari was trying to dupe him. The old monk met his eyes firmly and nodded. "I will do it." His Trade bore no trace of accent. Tyvian wondered if that had anything to do with the bone talisman the Artificer wore around his leathery neck.

Tyvian grinned. "Excellent. Believe me when I tell you that you will be well compensated for this, Mr . . ."

"I am called Dohas." The Artificer's dark eyes scanned Tyvian's dining room, noting the mageglass chairs and table, the fine chandelier lit by the warm glow of tiny feylamps, the lush embroidered rugs. He nodded again. "I will have the mage's staff."

Tyvian snapped his fingers. "Done. How long will it take you to remove it?" He held his right hand out and pointed to the plain iron ring. "There's the bastard. Work your arts, sir, and be quick. Time is of the essence."

Dohas removed a small flat stone from some hidden pocket in his robes and waved it over the ring. Tyvian felt a slight tug in his innards, as though somebody had just yanked a string running from the stone through his arm and tied around his liver. He grimaced.

The Artificer looked at him. "You felt that?"

"Just a mild tug. Is that good or bad?"

"Ah." Dohas put the stone away and turned Tyvian's hand over and back again, his delicate fingers stroking the ring as though cleaning it.

Tyvian drummed the fingers of his free hand on the table and tried to keep from tapping his foot. He took a glance at the spirit clock—three in the morning. He face was still throbbing from Jaevis's attentions earlier, despite the salves he had applied. Hool had been "kind" enough to pop his shoulder back into joint with a savage tug, but his left arm still felt as though it might fall off. He ached, stank, and had no doubt he looked like an Illini mud-barker during monsoon season. He also guessed he only had a matter of hours to get everything ready for tomorrow.

He tried to catch Dohas's gaze, but the Kalsaari now

had a different stone out. This one was on a string, the old monk dangling it over the palm of Tyvian's hand and watching as it jerked from side to side or up and down, depending on how close it was to the ring. "I'm sorry, but did I mention I was in a bit of a rush."

"The Art will not be rushed."

"The Art doesn't realize there will be a troop of Defenders of the Balance kicking in that door in a matter of hours."

The Artificer stared at Tyvian, his whole body suddenly rigid.

Tyvian forced a laugh. "Sorry, sorry—forget that last. I spoke out of turn. Please, continue at your leisure, sir."

"Ah." Dohas returned to his work, but this time he seemed to be bobbing his string-on-a-stone a bit more urgently.

Hool lumbered into the room, a tub of beef jerky under one hairy arm. Dohas froze again, his eyes locked on the gnoll. She ignored him. "Artus is waking up. I think he is feeling much better."

Tyvian looked over his shoulder at the gnoll. "Hool, I'm busy."

Hool sniffed the tub of jerky. "Is this for eating or wearing?"

"Whichever you please. You didn't sit on the couch, did you?"

"No, that is where I put your dirty clothes."

Tyvian heaved a sigh and did his best imitation of Dohas. "Ah."

A weak voice called from the guest room. "Reldamar . . ."

One of Hool's ears swiveled to listen, but her copper eyes stayed fixed on Tyvian. "I told you. He needs to tell you important things."

Tyvian looked at Dohas. "Can you do this while we walk?" The monk frowned, and Tyvian jerked his free thumb toward the front door. "Defenders, remember?"

"Ah. As you say." The Artificer rose, his hands cradling Tyvian's hand as though it were fashioned from glass. They walked in this way to just outside Artus's room and Tyvian poked his head in the door.

Artus had propped himself up in bed. The boy was pale, his eyes only half open, but he still looked worlds better than he had yesterday. "You . . . you took me in."

Tyvian stepped inside the room and stood at the bedside, the Artificer trailing along like some sort of tattooed manicurist. Tyvian shrugged, "The least I could do."

"I . . . I didn't know if you would . . ."

Tyvian took a deep breath. "Yes . . . well . . . I did, didn't I?"

Artus smiled at him. "I knew you weren't such a bad guy . . . knew it . . ."

"Look, let's stop talking about me. What happened to you?"

Artus frowned at the Artificer. "Who's that guy?"

"Focus, Artus—what happened to you?"

"What happened to your face?"

"Hann's boots, boy! Tell me what *happened*!"

Artus blinked for a moment, as though dredging his memories. Then his eyes flew open. "Saints! I almost forgot! I've got a lot to tell you—somebody is trying to capture you! They hired Jaevis—he's not dead, you know—and there was some younger guy and your friend Carlo . . ."

Tyvian pulled up a stool and sat down. "All right, slow down. Give me the whole story, and don't leave anything out." Tyvian thought about that for a second. "Let me amend that statement—leave out any of your own commentary on the events in question. Just give me the facts."

Artus reported. It took a while, since Hool kept interrupting with critiques of Artus's decisions and Artus took to defending those decisions, starting a gnoll-on-boy argument that Tyvian would have to break up. Still, Tyvian was pleased with the level of detail Artus could supply, and made a mental note to add this skill to the list of things the boy could do if properly focused. It then occurred to him that he was beginning to think of Artus in terms of a working assistant.

Was he? Tyvian felt there was a distinction between using someone for personal gain and employing someone as an assistant. He was certainly planning on the former—Artus was indispensable to his plan, somewhat regrettably. Was the boy worth keeping around, though? He certainly seemed loyal, if Artus had risked his life just to find out information regarding Tyvian's own problems. That was something he could certainly *exploit*, if nothing else. It was half the reason he had saved the boy's life, after all.

Right?

While Tyvian listened and mulled this over, Dohas continued to work on the ring. He now held a fine-tipped ink brush and was painting delicate runes all over Tyvian's ring finger in neat little circles and meandering rows. Tyvian tried to figure out what the fellow was doing but couldn't follow it all—the complexity of the monk's work was far beyond his own working knowledge of magecraft. Myreon could probably explain it to him, but he had made sure she was secured in her room before waking the Artificer up. He didn't want the two of them to meet.

Whatever Dohas was doing, he could feel alternating pulses of cold and heat coursing through his hand and halfway up his arm. There was a faint odor in the air, too—something Tyvian couldn't identify but that immediately caught Hool's attention.

"Someone is doing magic in here," she announced, glaring at the Artificer.

"Hey! I was just getting to the part where Jaevis was going to stab me in the back of the head!" Artus had a bowl of soup in his lap, brought by the serving specters. The color had returned to his cheeks.

Dohas, who had frozen at Hool's statement about magic, now sat staring at the gnoll, his ink brush shaking gently in one hand. Tyvian nodded at him. "Don't worry about her. She hasn't eaten a sorcerer since I've known her—please continue."

"What is that little man doing to your hand?" Hool asked, her hackles raised.

Artus threw up his hands. "Does *anybody* care about Jaevis almost stabbing me?"

Tyvian sighed. "Artus: we know Jaevis didn't stab you in the head, and the important parts of your story are over. In fact, I'll tell you how it ended: just before Jaevis killed you, the city watchmen found you, Jaevis backed off—not wanting to make an enemy of the Watch—and you got brought here where I had to pay them an exorbitant sum of money—which, by the way, you owe me."

Tyvian turned to the gnoll. "Hool, this 'little man' is an Artificer who is trying to remove the ring from my finger so that I can more effectively help you recover your pups from the clutches of Hendrieux and, probably, Banric Sahand." He looked at the Dohas. "You, sir, had better keep up whatever it is you're doing because if you stop again, so help me, I will feed you to the gnoll. There! Is everybody clear, now?"

Hool grumbled to herself and lay down on the floor, one eye trained on Dohas, who immediately began work again. Artus sat there open-mouthed. "How'd you know how the story ended?"

Tyvian rolled his eyes. "Hann save me."

Dohas put his ink brush away. "It is ready now."

Tyvian regarded his rune-covered hand. "Ready for what, exactly?"

"I will enact the spell. We will need space; it will

hurt a great deal and I am uncertain exactly what will happen."

"You're really taking off the ring?" Artus asked, pulling himself out of bed.

"Yes," Tyvian said, and looked at the Artificer. "Let's go out on the terrace."

They walked through the flat, toward the open-air terrace overlooking the length of Top Street to the south. It was snowing lightly, coating the oak planks in a thin layer of silver dust that seemed to glow in the dark. Tyvian opened the glass door and went outside, shivering against the cold. Dohas followed, as did Artus.

Tyvian stuck out his hand, taking a deep breath and blowing it out in a cloud of condensation. "Let's get this over with."

"But if you take off the ring, won't you be a bad person again?" Artus hugged himself against the winter air, the snowflakes resting lightly on his eyelashes.

"Don't be ridiculous, Artus—I'll be the same person I've *always* been, just without something biting me every time I—"

"But you would have *killed* me. You would have left me to Hool. You would have—"

Tyvian cut him off. "I also saved your life, remember? I picked you out of that burning spirit engine and *saved your life*. I saved your damned life *last night*, too! I didn't have to do that, did I? Doesn't that count for something? I've also fed you, dragged you along to Freegate, put up with your incessant questions, and—"

"You threw me out!" Artus snarled, pushing Tyvian's sore shoulder. The smuggler fell back a pace, wincing in pain. "You left me to rot on the streets again! If you didn't have that ring, I bet you'd've let me die on your doorstep rather than shell out your precious *money!*"

"Dammit, Artus, I—" The door to the terrace slammed behind the boy as he stormed inside. Tyvian's mind raced. What if he left? What if Artus ran away, just when he most needed him?

"The spell must be done now, before the ink fades," Dohas cautioned. The Artificer cast off his robes, revealing his wiry, taut body to the winter air. His skin was covered with tattoos, all drawn in flowing, arabesque patterns and glowing with power. Tyvian could feel the hair on his arms standing up—the leathery Kalsaari monk was drawing in power through his tattoos even as they spoke.

Tyvian pushed thoughts of Artus away—this was more important. This first, then deal with Artus later. The ring throbbed dully against his finger, hurting him, no doubt, for not going to the boy. He sneered at it. "You've pinched your last, trinket." He nodded to Dohas. "Do it."

The skinny monk drew himself to his full height and chanted in a reedy voice, increasing his volume gradually until he was shrieking at the top of his lungs. Then, just as Tyvian began to wonder what the neighbors might think about the noise, Dohas slammed both his hands atop Tyvian's outstretched one.

There was a rush of hot air and an ear-splitting bang—had the Artificer not been clutching Tyvian's hand with both of his, he would have fallen over from the force of it. Then came the pain—white hot, blinding. It fell upon Tyvian's entire body at once, as though his bones were growing barbed thorns in unison. He screamed . . . and screamed and screamed. It seemed to last forever; his entire life flashing by in an instant. He saw the face of every person he had stolen from, conned, cheated, or killed. All of them cried out his name, each voice piercing him to the quick, burning his mind like hot needles thrust through his eyes.

Then, as suddenly as it had begun, the pain stopped. The cold rushed back to embrace his body; he was on his knees on the terrace, his right hand cradled in his lap. He blinked the tears away from his eyes and looked down.

The ring sat where it always had, as black and hard as an iron manacle.

Dohas was also on his knees, his body smoldering with the heat of the ritual. "It . . . it . . . cannot be done . . ."

Tyvian struggled to his feet. "What? What did you say?"

"It is not fused to your body." The Artificer's eyes

were closed, his body shivering. "It does not meld itself to flesh or bone or blood."

Tyvian's heart seemed to stop. "What does it attach to, then?"

"It is fused with your soul, Tyvian Reldamar." Dohas opened his eyes, meeting Tyvian's gaze. "You and the ring are one."

"I can still cut it off," Tyvian said, half asking.

The Artificer nodded. "At the price of fracturing your own self. This is an artifact beyond my arts."

Tyvian grabbed the wiry monk by the necklace and hoisted him to his feet. "I don't *accept* it! Your order is among the finest in the world at this sort of thing, and you're telling me you don't know how to remove it? Someone must! Someone else among the Artificers, perhaps? Surely you aren't the best they can offer!"

Dohas's voice never wavered. "I have never seen nor heard of anything fashioned by mortals that can do what this ring does. My order and my Arts can offer you nothing."

"Who can?"

"I will not name them; they are creatures of legend, not to be trafficked with by mortals."

"Tell me!"

"No. For your sake, no."

Tyvian clenched his teeth to keep from screaming in the old Kalsaari's face. He wanted to throw the worthless charlatan off the roof, to beat him bloody, to hear him *apologize* for his utter failure. Instead, he only dragged Dohas inside and threw him at the feet of Hool, who was waiting for them. "Tie him up. Get him out of my sight."

Hool put a foot on the Artificer's chest, but thrust a thick finger in Tyvian's face. "You go talk to Artus now. You have made him *very* upset because you are stupid."

"I am not in the mood." Tyvian scowled at the gnoll. To think that this beast presumed to order him about in his own home!

Hool bared her teeth. This close, they looked like they were as long as Tyvian's fingers. "You go and talk to him or I will *make* you."

Tyvian sighed. "Sometimes, Hool, you remind me of a nanny I once had."

"Good," Hool announced, and threw Dohas over her shoulder. The Kalsaari appeared to be frozen with terror at the gnoll's proximity. Tyvian hardly blamed him.

"You . . ." Dohas hissed, "You leave me for the Defenders?"

Tyvian groaned and rubbed his eyes. "Spare me the blubbering—I have quite enough of it on my hands already."

The Artificer, though, didn't look like he was going to beg. His eyes hardened instead. "The Yldd. They are known as the Yldd."

"The . . . the creatures of myth who can help me?"

Tyvian blinked. "Wait, why tell me? Why do me the favor?"

Dohas grinned mirthlessly. "I have done you no favor, Tyvian Reldamar. No favor at all."

Hool carried him away, muttering to herself about wizards and nonsense. Tyvian sighed and left to speak with Artus.

Tyvian found the boy dragging a knife across the bedsheets in his bedroom. He couldn't help but notice there were tears in his eyes. Feathers were floating through the room, and Tyvian spied a set of fine goose-down pillows that had been savagely murdered not moments before. Tyvian knew he should have felt angry—he *wanted* to be angry—but he found himself only standing there and watching. Eventually, Artus noticed him in the doorway. "What? What're you gonna do about it, huh?"

"Nothing." Tyvian held up his right hand. The ring gleamed dully in the lamplight.

Artus straightened. "You didn't take it off?"

"The Artificer failed. Why are you destroying my bed?"

Artus jutted out his lower lip. "'Cause you're a jerk and you deserve it. You gonna kick me out?"

"Are you going to leave?" Tyvian asked. The question hung in the air. Both of them looked at the floor.

"I *should* leave," Artus said, sitting on the ruined bed.

"I *should* throw you out."

Neither of them spoke for a few moments. Tyvian

sat in a chair Artus hadn't gotten around to destroying. Artus looked at him. "What's this? What's going on?"

Tyvian didn't say anything. He didn't know how to put it; he wasn't sure he *wanted* to know how to put it. "How . . . how would you like another job?"

"What, carrying your stuff again? No thanks."

"No, this time you'd be working on your own. I'd be relying on you to complete a very dangerous task; my life would be in your hands."

Artus leaned back on the bed. "How much?"

Tyvian almost said, *The forty marks you owe me for buying you off the Watch,* but didn't. He sighed. "Name your price."

"Five hundred."

Tyvian coughed. "I'll give it to you, boy—you aren't shy."

"Take it or leave it, jerk." Artus smiled.

Tyvian found himself smiling back. "Fine—it's a deal. You'll need some equipment before I give you instructions, though. Go in the back of my closet—you'll find a chest there with a bottle of perfume. Bring it out here."

Artus frowned. "I'm not gonna have to wear perfume, am I?"

"It's not really perfume."

Artus went into the walk-in closet and started rummaging around. "Well, what's it do, then?"

"It makes you look like me."

Artus's head popped out of the closet like a rabbit from a hole. "*What?*"

Tyvian smiled. "After you find it, I need to teach you how to use a seekwand."

Artus came out with the perfume bottle in one hand, holding it up to the light. "Who am I going to find?"

Tyvian produced a handkerchief from inside his shirt and threw it on the end table under the lamp. The monogram read TR. Artus looked at it, face blank with incomprehension. Tyvian rolled his eyes. "I forgot you can't read—me, Artus. You're going to find *me*."

CHAPTER 6

CAGE FOR A SMUGGLER

Tyvian shifted from side to side among the plush cushions of Carlo's coach, his hands clenched into fists on his knees.

"Now who's nervous?" Carlo snickered. "I told you she accepted the deal."

Tyvian scowled at the Verisi. "She's going to double-cross us, Carlo. You must know that."

Carlo shook his head. "No, no—not for that she won't." He pointed at the drugged form of Myreon Alafarr, who was leaning against a wall of the coach, snoring through an open mouth.

Tyvian snorted. "Don't say I didn't warn you."

"If you are so certain, then why are you going?" Carlo asked, pulling out his crystal eye and polishing it.

"A calculated risk, Carlo. Besides, I have a backup plan."

"Oh?" Carlo chuckled. "Do tell!"

Tyvian produced a pair of thunder-orbs from up his sleeve. "Courtesy of Hacklar Jaevis. Not the most elegant of emergency plans, but certainly effective."

Carlo shook his head, replacing his eye. "Great gods, Tyvian, you are losing your flair for the sophisticated, I'm afraid."

"And you are losing your keen wit. That was a wholly pedestrian insult."

"What happened to your face, anyway—you look like you've been kicked by a horse."

Tyvian scowled and made a conscious effort not to touch his sore nose. The swelling had gone down, but he knew his eyes were still black and blue and his cheeks puffy. "Are we critiquing each other's appearance now? Shall I inquire how your quest to become the world's first spherical man is going?"

Carlo shrugged. Then, peering through the wall of the coach, he banged on the ceiling. "Here! This is the place!"

Tyvian climbed out and saw that they had crossed the city to the Cloth Market. Here, concentric circles of colorful awnings spread out from the broad and ornate stone fountain at the market's center, which frothed with magically heated water. In this fountain—the Bathsfont—local launderers washed their clients' clothing by the ton every day. It was late afternoon and a light snow was falling from a quiet gray sky, muffling the sounds of clothiers and seamstresses haggling price underneath heated canvas. They were situated at the market's southern edge, and a variety of porters, couriers, and laborers lounged about the entrances to several taverns, watching them.

Carlo emerged from the coach as well and nodded happily to the bystanders. "There, you see, Tyvian? Very public, very safe."

In the distance Tyvian heard the moan of a spirit engine pulling into the depot. Right on time. So long as Artus was in position . . .

Tyvian frowned and resisted the urge to scan the streets for the boy. He knew Artus would have no trouble tailing the coach through the city, particularly with the seekwand, but he still felt the need to double-check. He was relying a great deal on that boy to come through with his end of the plan, and it made him uncomfortable. He never liked relying on people whom he couldn't entirely control, and Artus, as an adolescent, was permanently in that category. Suspicious, he allowed himself a brief look around but saw nothing. That was either good or very, very bad.

Carlo clapped his hands and his two coachmen dragged the snoring Myreon out of the coach and put her in a wheelbarrow, which they then piled high with bolts of linen to conceal her. When they were ready, he motioned for Tyvian to follow him. "Right this way."

The Cloth Market was a good choice for a public meeting regarding an illicit transaction, as it was simultaneously crowded and private at the same time. Once within its winding, steam-choked maze of awnings, clotheslines, and pavilions, one could seldom see more than a few yards ahead while, at the same time, being no more than a few feet from dozens of other people. The smell of clean, pressed cotton and the freshness of the falling snow was invigorating to Tyvian, as were the vibrant wares being hawked by effete Akrallian tailors, swarthy Rhondian cobblers, and burly Galaspin furriers. He took a moment to inspect some particularly impressive leather gloves before Carlo hastened him on with a scowl. Tyvian permitted himself a smile; some of his anxiety regarding the upcoming meeting faded. *You know what is going to happen*, he told himself. *Just relax.*

"Here," Carlo said, stopping before a pavilion of brilliant yellow and white stripes. Tyvian looked up and saw the black-and-gold pennant of the Kalsaari Empire hanging limply from its central pole.

Tyvian bowed and gestured at the tent flap. "After you, Master diCarlo."

Carlo shook his head. "You're paranoid." He flipped the tent flap open and stepped inside. Tyvian followed.

Inside, the tent was heated by a brazier of glowing hearthstones set to one side of the hexagonal pavilion as well as four armed mark-slaves. The floor was thickly carpeted with hand-woven rugs, and there were four piles of cushions that Tyvian had come to identify as the Kalsaari equivalent to chairs. Two of these piles were occupied already. One held the slavemaster, Fariq, dressed in his official bloodred robes with jeweled turban and sporting the same nonsmile as he had when they first met, the night before. The other supported a man wearing an ankle-length skirt of sorts but no shirt. He looked withered, sandy, and old—like a piece of fruit left in the desert sun too long. His head was shaved bald and was covered with tattoos—another Artificer, virtually identical to the one tied up in Tyvian's living room. What a coincidence . . .

Fariq stood and bowed low. "Many stupendous welcomes, most intelligent and magnanimous sirs. The most gracious Hanim offers her apologies for her lack of attendance, but assures you that I, the humble Fariq, may execute our dealings with faith and efficiency. Please sit."

Carlo sat, but Tyvian did not. "Ah, Frumar—excellent. I was hoping we would meet again."

Fariq's pointed beard twitched slightly at the mangling of his name. "I am, likewise, most pleased. To business?"

Carlo opened his mouth to speak, but Tyvian cut him off. "That's what I like about you, Famak—no small talk. Let's to brass tacks, then. I imagine this man on your right is the Artificer I requested to see?"

Fariq nodded. "He is."

"Does he speak for himself?"

The Artificer was staring at Tyvian, no visible expression on his weathered face. Fariq answered for him. "My infinite apologies, sir. He does not deign to speak to Westerners."

Tyvian snorted. "Puts a bit of a crimp in our deal, doesn't it?"

Fariq shook his head rapidly. "No, no—of course not! He will speak to my humble person, and I will of course relay his words with accuracy."

Tyvian scowled, and Carlo cut in. "What is he talking about, Tyvian? Why is there an Artificer here? Where's the money?"

Fariq blinked. "Money? A million pardons, my good sir, but there was—"

Tyvian interrupted. "There is no money, Carlo—that wasn't the deal I made."

Carlo sprang to his feet faster than a man of his age and girth had a right to. "What? You said there would be money!"

"No, I merely *implied* there would be money, Carlo. Not the same thing at all."

Carlo's mouth popped open and he sputtered, ineffectually grasping at curses. Tyvian thought the performance was quite impressive, really.

"See," Tyvian said, "I told you your wits were failing."

Fariq looked over at the wheelbarrow that had been brought into the room. "Is that the mage?"

Tyvian nodded. "It is."

"Just a moment!" Carlo barked. "I demand to speak to the Hanim!"

Fariq bowed. "I regret to inform the gentleman that nobody may demand anything of the immovable Angharad tin'Theliara Hanim, may She live forever."

Carlo snorted. "As though I give a damn about your queenie pride, you dirty little sand-gobbler! The Hanim assured me I would receive—"

"One hundred percent of the value of Master Reldamar's deal," Fariq interjected, his lips curling back into a cruel smile. "And that is what you shall receive." He jerked his head in Tyvian's direction, and two markslaves immediately seized the smuggler by the elbows.

Tyvian glared at Carlo—his turn to perform. "You rat. I should have known."

"Don't give me that, Tyvian." Carlo's face was red with artificial—well, perhaps genuine—anger. Tyvian reflected that he really *had* lied to Carlo about the money, and it's possible the old Verisi was expecting some actual remuneration for this charade. "You planned to cheat me, too. The Hanim wasn't just interested in the mage, you know."

"Enough!" Fariq clapped his hands, which caused the Artificer to evaporate.

Tyvian shook his head, burying his mirth deep, deep inside. "A simulacrum. I'm an idiot."

Fariq pointed a finger at Carlo. "You! Pull back the laundry to show me the wizard you have brought."

Carlo folded his arms. "You pull it back yourself.

I didn't bleed the soil of Rhond red to take orders from some slave. *Especially* not one who just cheated me."

Fariq maintained his ugly leer. "You ought to be more polite, Carlo diCarlo. You pretend offense and yet the glorious Hanim knows very well that you are being paid by many parties to deliver Reldamar into their clutches. Did you really expect to be paid twice for the same job?"

Carlo stiffened. "That's *exactly* what I expected, actually."

Tyvian's eyebrows shot up. "Multiple parties? How many people want me anyway? Hendrieux, obviously, and the Defenders, and the Hanim, but . . . who have I missed, Carlo? I should at *least* get to know who you've been working for!"

Tyvian's performance was convincing enough that all eyes were now on the rotund Verisi pirate. Carlo shifted from foot to foot, his face boiling with a volatile mixture of anger, frustration, and embarrassment. He then took a deep breath, forced his hands down to his sides, and said, "Very well, then. Since I haven't any choice . . ." He walked over to the wheelbarrow and grabbed a fistful of laundry. "Here's your bloody mage."

When Myreon was revealed, Fariq and his two marked bodyguards leaned forward to see. There was Myreon Alafarr, Mage Defender of the Balance, just where she was supposed to be. The only thing amiss was that Myreon was *awake*.

Tyvian felt the hair on the back of his neck stand on end, and shut his eyes just in time for Myreon to unleash a bolt of pure white energy that sizzled the air like bacon in a pan. Tyvian's captors released him immediately to tend to their seared retinas, and he ducked away from them. Opening his eyes, he saw everyone but himself and Myreon clutching their hands to their faces. Fariq, who had been the focus of the sunblast, screamed and writhed on the ground, his turban, robe, and beard all burning.

Two mark-slaves rushed the mage, but Myreon held up her hand, her first and fourth fingers curled tightly alongside the erect second and third, her thumb flat against her palm—the fifteenth position for minor enchantment, if Tyvian remembered correctly—and spoke in a thunderous voice. *"STOP!"*

The mark-slaves stopped dead in their tracks, suddenly rigid and motionless like wooden practice dummies, their faces wild with confusion and fear. No doubt knowing such an enchantment had only bought her a handful of seconds, Myreon darted out the tent flap. Tyvian followed close on her heels.

Once among the tents and stands of the Cloth Market, Myreon looked around, unsure where to go. Tyvian yanked her by the arm. "This way!"

Myreon pulled her arm free. "Follow you? Are you mad?"

"Who do you think cut your dose of that sleeping draught in half? Look, it's me or them—you choose." Tyvian pointed—three mark-slaves barrelled out of the tent, their ensorcelled tattoos glowing in the cold winter daylight.

Myreon planted her feet, spread her arms wide, and brought her hands together in a standard Gathering maneuver. A cold blue orb of light formed in her palms, and with the utterance of a word wholly lacking in vowels, Myreon released it at the mark-slaves. It struck the first of them on his chest, exploding into a riot of white light and deep cold, freezing the nearby tents solid and sending sheets of icicles hurtling in all directions. Tyvian knew a lode-bolt like that would ordinarily be enough to kill any three men dead, freezing them as solid as rocks, but when the spell faded the three mark-slaves were still coming, only a glistening sheen of ice coating their rippling muscles.

Tyvian shook his head. "They're warded—this way, come on!"

Grimacing, Myreon followed. They ran like rabbits, skipping in and out of tents and ducking under clotheslines as they wound their way through the labyrinthine tangle of clothing displays and fabric salesmen. Behind them the mark-slaves did a good job of playing the part of hounds, bellowing to each other in their foreign tongue and smashing their way through tents and people alike.

"Can you cast something to slow them down?" Tyvian asked. Despite his best efforts, the mark-slaves were still on their trail.

Myreon shrugged, panting with exhaustion. "Like what?"

"Conjure up a wall or something!"

"I don't *know* any conjurations," Myreon countered.

A mark-slave tore through the back of a tent, ripping the canvas apart like paper. He saw the two of them and shouted for his friends. Tyvian grabbed Myreon by the collar and ducked inside another tent, then another, and another, until finally they dove underneath an untended wagon loaded with straw being sold for mattresses.

"What if we call a watchman?" Myreon offered.

"How much money have you got on you?" Tyvian asked.

"Nothing, why would . . . oh . . . ." Myreon frowned. "I hate this cursed city."

Tyvian fished in his pockets and brought out the two thunder-orbs. "I've got these."

Myreon scowled. "It won't work on them—they're warded!"

"Then I won't throw it *at* them. Gods, am I the *only* one who displays any ingenuity in these matters?"

The bellows of the mark-slaves got closer, and Myreon cursed. "They must have a seekwand."

"Kalsaaris lack the know-how," Tyvian corrected. "They've just got enhanced senses—like bloodhounds. Let's move."

They kept running, this time toward the edge of the market itself. "Where's that gnoll of yours when you need her?" Myreon gasped. Her pace was slowing.

Tyvian grabbed her by the collar and dragged her into an alley just outside the market, his sore shoulder groaning in pain. "You need to get out of the saddle more often, Myreon. You're soft."

Myreon leaned back against the wall, hands on her knees as she struggled to catch her breath. "I'm . . . usually . . . the one doing the chasing. This . . . is a different experience altogether."

The mark-slaves voices came echoing up the street—they were closing in.

Myreon turned and looked at the back of the alley—a narrow passage between two brick buildings led through to a street on the other side. "Here—this way!"

"Not so fast!" Tyvian pulled Myreon back and threw the two thunder-orbs at the gap. They exploded in spectacular fashion, causing the corners of the two buildings to collapse into a pile of impassible rubble.

Myreon stared at their blocked escape, aghast. "What . . . why did you *do* that?"

The mark-slaves appeared at the entrance to the alley, their faces grim. Tyvian looked at them and sighed. "I'm sorry, Myreon, but my plan calls for us to be captured."

"Plan?"

"Well, yes—I always have a plan." Tyvian nodded. "You'll be delighted to know that your regaining the ability to cast spells will be most useful to its successful execution."

Myreon shook her head, backing away from the tattooed brutes as they came ever closer. "You *purposely* led us to this alley. I can't believe it!"

"I know this sounds ridiculous, but you're going to have to trust me," Tyvian said, getting down on his knees. "Oh, and I'd curl into a ball if I were you—I'm pretty sure we're in for some savage kicking."

Nobody noticed the column of mageglass-clad soldiers marching through the Stair Market. The fact that it was snowing rather harder now, the flakes drifting down in heavy clumps that hit the cobblestones with an audible *thwick* and gradually building, was part of the reason. Another reason was that most of the merchants, knowing a heavy snowstorm when they saw one, were packing up shop and heading indoors, so there were fewer eyes on the street anyway. But the main reason that the column of twenty armored men went unnoticed was because they were, all of them, concealed with sorceries so powerful that few wizards outside of Saldor could have even dared attempt them.

The Aura of the Ordinary was a personal favorite of Master Defender Ultan Tarlyth—something of a specialty of his, actually. The spell was a mixture of the orderly power of the Dweomer and the calming, soothing power of the Lumen, making those who were under its protection appear essentially, totally unremarkable and disinteresting. Back in the war, Tarlyth, as a young mage, had used this same spell to ambush a whole supply train of Sahand's army before the battle of Calassa. In his most arrogant moments he liked to tell himself that he was at least partially responsible for the Mad Prince's final defeat.

The spell was difficult to maintain, though, particularly in a place as full of suspicious eyes as Freegate. At the front of the column, a heavy gray cloak thrown over his mirrored armor, Tarlyth held his staff aloft, focusing as much of his attention as he could on maintaining the Aura as his Defenders marched in orderly fashion toward Top Street. To those they passed, they all appeared to be nothing more than a disorganized crowd of cloaked men moving in the same general direction—nothing to arouse more than a brief flicker of interest from even the most suspicious. The price of that, however, was Tarlyth's hands nearly freezing with the icy power of the Dweomer and huge yawns battling their way up through his chest from the soothing Lumenal energy filling his body. A nap before a warm fire sounded like the absolute most wonderful thing in the world to his old bones at that very moment. Dammit, he thought, were I only a younger man.

Tarlyth kept it up, however, and for several reasons. The primary need for the Aura was political—Freegate didn't want the Defenders in, and the Arcanostrum didn't want to aggravate Freegate. The city was sitting on one of the Western Alliance's most important trade routes, and the governments of Galaspin, Eretheria, and even Saldor would throw an apoplectic fit if a rash action by the Defenders caused Freegate to impose punitive tariffs. Though Tarlyth himself didn't find tariffs all that upsetting, he *did* enjoy his job and position within the Defender organization, and he didn't want to jeopardize it lightly. In all honesty, he shouldn't even be here.

That, of course, brought up the second reason: Tarlyth was and had been a member of the Sorcerous League for over a decade now. He initially joined with the exclusive intent of spying on them for Saldor and the Defenders, but as the years had taken their toll on his once-robust body and he found himself ever more restricted from field operations, his attitude toward the organization had changed. With the Arcanostrum of Saldor, even in this modern, progressive age, sorcerous research and expanding the uses of the High Arts was consistently met with skepticism, wariness, and reluctance. Tests had to be performed; there had to be approval from committees of the various colleges; funding had to be secured. The process could take years unless you had the political connections that Tarlyth lacked. He wasn't a research mage, anyway—he was a Defender, a practical user of the Art, not some skinny-wrist bookworm holed up in a laboratory.

The odds of Saldor finding a way to restore his youth while he was still alive were slim to none. There was always cherille, but the stuff could cost more per bottle than half a year's stipend. He was the son of a blacksmith, not some wealthy noble-born mage with his family's estate to help support him. No, Tarlyth knew that if he intended to become the young, virile ox of a man he had been in his youth, the Sorcerous League was the only way to do it.

They got things done. Irresponsibly sometimes, in-effectively often, but they went out and did it. They took risks. They invested in their members. They encouraged innovation and, what's more, shared results. Sahand aside, he had come to think of it as less a secret cabal of evil wizards and more of an exclusive club of like-minded, forward-thinking men and women devoted to the advancement of the Art. The fact that the Arcanostrum disavowed its existence merely reinforced for Tarlyth where his loyalties *ought* to lie. Saldor sought to control, while the League sought to *liberate*.

By the time the Defenders reached Top Street, the snow was coming down in sheets. Tarlyth let the Aura drop and planted his staff on the cobblestones as his men fanned out up and down the rows of expensive homes and elaborate hotels. Closing his eyes, he hummed to himself a slow, building tune—wordless and slightly off-key. The music brought Lumenal energies seeping from the houses' cheery decorations and caused the slumbering seeds of nearby flower beds to coalesce into an Augury of Distress. Tarlyth could feel tugging on his soul from a hundred different directions—manifestations of people's needs and wants, their troubles and secret calls for aid. He could feel babies crying like gentle tickles across his stomach; he could feel the sickening pangs of a drunk or ink-thrall in need of their next drink or dip; he could feel the thrumming beat of someone seeking something lost. Tarlyth blotted them out—what he needed to find was someone in need of rescue.

It only took him a moment to isolate it—like a screeching, painful abrasion across the chest and back, the feel of someone trapped against their will, hoping to be free. It had to be Myreon. "Sergeant!"

The Sergeant Defender stepped to the Master's side. "Sir!"

Tarlyth nodded down the street. "The seventh house on the left, penthouse flat; go with speed, but be careful. Reldamar is to be taken alive."

The sergeant saluted and called his men to him. They lit their firepikes, activated their wards and guards, and moved at a quick, efficient double-time to the base of the tastefully appointed grounds of a three-story apartment complex. When they had the place surrounded, Tarlyth scanned the building for traps or hexes—it was clean. Just some warding on one of the rooms in the penthouse; that was, presumably, where they'd find Myreon. He gave the sergeant the go-ahead.

The assault was quick and disciplined. Four blew open the front door with thunder-orbs and stormed the front stairs, supported by another five who began a floor-by-floor search. Another group of five activated their lightfoot charms and scaled the side of the building as though it were a ladder, making it to the roof and in through the skylights at about the same time as the front-door party were storming the penthouse. The remaining men secured the exits, making sure no one could get out without going through them. Tarlyth keyed his helmet to hear what his men heard—a simple enchantment placed on the mageglass helms of all staff-bearing Defenders.

"*First floor—clear!*"

"*Second floor—clear!*"

"*Third floor— Oof! Contact, contact! Isolate!*" Tarlyth heard a few explosions and the flash of a firepike or two—sounds of struggle. The voices came thrumming through the helmet in a jumble. "*Man down! One hostile, heading downstairs!*"

"*We got him!*"

More flashes from firepikes, a few more thumps and groans, then, "*Got him! Grab his arms! Watch it!*"

"*Third floor—clear!*"

The Sergeant Defender appeared at the front door. He had a bloody nose. "Sir, you can come up now."

Tarlyth smiled—so much for Tyvian Reldamar. Myreon's rescue operation was providing the perfect opportunity to apprehend him for the League; if he could have, he would award the girl a medal for her contribution. The secrets the Iron Ring possessed could be a major breakthrough in the ultimate goal of every League member—Rhadnost's Elixir.

Tarlyth found Reldamar on a landing between the third and second floor, flat on his face, a fur cape pulled over his head. Two Defenders were sitting on him—one on his back, one on his legs. His hands were being cuffed behind him. Tarlyth leaned down, looking at Reldamar's hands.

There was no ring.

Tarlyth felt his spine tingle. With a rapid flick of his

hand, he ripped the cape off the downed man with a simple spell. Looking up at him he saw the bearded, bloodied, filthy face of not Reldamar, but of Hacklar Jaevis. "What the . . . *Jaevis?*"

The Illini spat blood on the floor. "Why do you interfere with Jaevis? We are allies."

"Dammit!" Tarlyth groaned, skipping over the man and running to the third floor, ignoring the sharp pains of his arthritic joints as he pushed them. He found one Defender down, a knife in his stomach, being tended to by his fellows, and another two with obvious wounds. The flat—once finely appointed, no doubt—was a smoldering wreck after ten Defenders and one Illini bounty hunter fought a brief, desperate battle here with all the magical weaponry at their disposal. Tarlyth darted past them to where two more defenders were trying to open the locks on the warded room. "Blow it open!" he barked.

One defender pulled back his mirrored visor. "Sir, Magus Alafarr could be in—"

"Blow it!"

The two men didn't hesitate. They fell back from the door, drew antispell and thunder-orbs from their bandoliers, and threw one after the other. The door's wards winked out a split second before it was obliterated in a thunderous explosion of Fey energy. Tarlyth was through the door before the smoke cleared. There, tied to a chair, was a leathery old Kalsaari with a tattooed body. His dark eyes were wide with panic—this was the source of the need for rescue Tarlyth had sensed, drawing him and his Defenders right here. "Kroth's bloody teeth!" he swore.

How could Reldamar have known they were coming? Where else could he be? How was it possible Reldamar could have anticipated this? Had Myreon been compromised? Had one of Tarlyth's contacts betrayed him? He stomped from the warded room and kicked over an end table. "Dammit!"

"Sir! We found something!" A Defender called him into the dining room. When Tarlyth came in, he found the men puzzling over an envelope on a luxurious mageglass table.

Tarlyth snatched it up; it was addressed to "Commanding Officer, Defenders of the Balance Standing in my Dining Room." Tarlyth tore it open with a snarl.

Dear Sir or Madam,

Welcome to my humble abode. I have no doubt it is somewhat more humble now than before, since I am well aware of just how little care your organization gives to the furniture and, say, doors that appoint a would-be detainee's living quarters. In any event, I bid you to make yourself at home. There is a pretty good bottle of wine in the cupboard over the washbasin in the kitchen (just for you—I wouldn't waste it on the blunt palates of those thugs you employ).

As you probably have noticed by now, I am not at home. I don't anticipate coming back anytime soon, so don't get your hopes up. No, you should know that by the time you are likely to read this, I and your dear friend, Myreon Alafarr, have fallen into custody of one Angharad tin'Theliara Hanim, who no doubt wishes some kind of terrible fate upon us. Don't hold it against her—she's Kalsaari, after all.

Now, if you should be looking for dear Myreon and myself, I expect you should find us in the dungeons of the Hanim's little palace away from home. You can't miss it—it's the big thing with all the minarets in the Castle District. I rather doubt she'll be terribly welcoming, what with you Defenders being the sworn enemies of her people and all, but you're welcome to try and visit. I promise not to tell her you're coming.

Ta-ta for now,
Tyvian Reldamar

Tarlyth tore the letter in half when he had finished and threw himself in one of the dining room chairs. The Sergeant Defender appeared and saluted. "Sir, orders?"

Tarlyth sighed. "There's a bottle of wine over the washbasin in the kitchen. Fetch it for me, would you? Bring two glasses and the Illini—we need to have a talk."

CHAPTER 7

COMRADES IN CHAINS

"One day I'm going to write a book," Tyvian said casually, as though he were sipping tea among friends at a café in the Stair Market. Even under those circumstances this comment would have been odd, but in the depths of a bleak, frigid dungeon and standing on tiptoe so he could relieve the pressure on his wrists, which were manacled above his head by a chain hung on an iron hook ten feet up, Tyvian's confession was downright bizarre.

"What the hell are you talking about?" Myreon's

face was bright red, but not from anger. The color was due to the fact that she was suspended upside-down by her ankles, which were manacled in a manner identical to Tyvian's wrists. The Kalsaaris had tipped her upside-down, though, since they needed her hands to be in casterlocks.

"I'm talking about my book idea, Myreon—pay attention," Tyvian scolded. "I'm going to call it 'Dungeons of the World.' It will be my analysis of the various jails, prisons, dungeons, and oubliettes in which I have been incarcerated from time to time. I think it will be quite interesting."

"Shut up," Myreon answered. Groaning, she lifted herself up from the waist to bring herself somewhat upright, relieving the pressure on her head for a moment. The mage could only hold it for a few moments before falling back upside-down. She struck her head on the stone wall for her efforts. "Ow! Kroth damn it!"

"Stop acting the ninny," Tyvian said. "I'll need you rested for when we escape."

"What, *now* you want to escape? What the hell is wrong with you? *We could have escaped already!*"

"Yes, but that would have only been a temporary victory."

Myreon rolled her bloodshot eyes. "Are you going to tell me what the plan is?"

"No, I am not."

She grunted in incoherent frustration. "How am I supposed to help if I don't know what the plan is?"

"To be honest, I'm not sure I can trust you yet."

"*You* can't trust *me*?" She shook her head. "This is absurd."

Tyvian would have shrugged if his arms weren't already at their full vertical extension. "You have to admit that, up until a very short time ago, it was your stated personal goal to see me turned to stone. Save for the duress of our pursuit and incarceration, I somehow doubt you would be using the term 'we.'"

Myreon sighed. "The Kalsaaris are a common enemy to all Westerners. Even you can see that."

"Nonsense. I have done business with Kalsaaris quite a bit in my career and found them as amenable as any Western business partner—you should know, as you ruined several of my smuggling attempts by detaining and interrogating my Kalsaari contacts in Tasis."

"Those men were bigger criminals in the Empire than you are here. This Kalsaari is a Hanim of an Imperial House—there's a big difference."

Tyvian nodded. "Granted, but it still doesn't make you trustworthy."

"For the love of Hann . . ." Myreon grumbled, but fell silent.

Tyvian looked around. The dungeon was a simple affair—a cylinder of stone that sank fifty feet into the ground, with a narrow staircase winding along the edge from the door at the very top to the very bottom, where a number of iron hooks were pounded into the wall. From these hooks, manacled prisoners

could easily be suspended like so many slabs of beef. At the center of the floor there was a heavy wooden table complete with all the chains, manacles, and bloodstains necessary to indicate a vehicle for torture. As a final touch, some shallow pits were dug into the ground and covered with rusty iron gratings—crude cells for prisoners who somehow didn't rate being hung on the wall. Tyvian wondered if they were being treated better or worse than those thrown in a hole, but couldn't decide. Given the small windows at street level, high above them, he imagined that when it rained all the water would run down and fill the holes, which would be very cold and potentially dangerous over long periods of time. Then again, being hung from the wall was far more uncomfortable, even if the risk of drowning was smaller.

"This all has something to do with Hendrieux, doesn't it?" Myreon grumbled at last.

Tyvian smiled. "Now *there's* the Mage Defender I know and love."

The door at the top of the dungeon opened and two mark-slaves entered, bearing ornate golden feylamps fashioned in the shape of dragons. Behind them came another, particularly large mark-slave, who crouched to enter because, on one shoulder, he bore the elegant and slender form of the Hanim herself. The Hanim was then followed by Walid, who walked quietly behind the imposing procession with a blank expression, hands behind his back.

Tyvian looked at Myreon. "Time to prove how

much you're in the game, Myreon. Not a word—say nothing, understand?"

Myreon nodded, her face grim. "Even if they kill me."

"It's not *you* I'm worried about them killing," Tyvian said back, and then did his best to compose himself as the Hanim was brought down to the dungeon floor atop her slave.

Walid laid out a small, ornately woven rug before Tyvian, and the Hanim was set down upon it. Her golden eyes gleamed in the light of the feylamp. "We meet again, Tyvian Reldamar."

Tyvian smiled and nodded. "Forgive me if I fail to kneel again, but I am currently unable. Perhaps if you were to un-shackle my wrists . . ."

The Hanim grinned. "That smile won't work on me, smuggler." She knelt before Myreon and ran her long fingernails along the mage's cheek. "A Mage Defender, and pretty, too—such a prize. His Imperial Magnificence will be most pleased with me."

Myreon pulled back from her touch as much as possible, glaring at the Kalsaari through her swollen, bloodshot eyes.

The Hanim tsked at her through her teeth. "Now now—such anger will only make you easier to control, my prize. You will tell us your secrets, one way or another."

Tyvian cleared his throat. "A question, if I may?"

"Of course." The Hanim turned from Myreon and rose slowly.

Tyvian let his eyes wander down the front of her silk gown. He was not disappointed. "You've wanted me for the ring the whole time, haven't you? Our private meeting in your chambers was simply to stroke my ego. You wanted me to think myself more important than I was, making it easier to lure me into your trap, right?"

The Hanim permitted herself a smirk. "I also wanted to inspect you. If I'm to have you and your ring in my possession, I wanted to know if you were worth having."

"My apologies, then, for not allowing our meeting to progress that far." Tyvian smirked back.

"Oh, for the love of Hann . . ." Myreon blurted out, her eyes rolling.

The Hanim broke eye contact with Tyvian. "I understand that you are planning to escape."

Myreon's eyes bulged out of her head, but Tyvian grinned. "Ah, you were listening—I thought as much."

The Hanim looked around at her dungeon. "Tell me, Master Reldamar—"

"Please, call me Tyvian."

The Hanim glared at him. "Very well . . . tell me, *Tyvian*, I am clearly less well versed in the design of dungeons than yourself. However would you expect to escape a dungeon such as this one?"

"You will understand, Hanim, if I decline to explain it to you. Rule number one for escaping dungeons is to refrain from telling the jailor your plan."

The Hanim pulled herself to her full height and,

fixing her eyes on his, she spread her arms forcefully and intoned, *"You will tell me how you will break yourself out of this dungeon!"*

Tyvian felt the enchantment take his mind up like a wave. He was suddenly delirious, insensible, intoxicated with a mix of Lumenal and Dweomeric energy. Before he knew it, he was talking. He explained the weakness in the mortar due to years of water damage, which would allow him to slowly work the hook out of the wall. He described how the lack of guards in the dungeon itself would allow him to quickly free Myreon from her prison. Then, armed with the mage's Arts, they would soon overpower the two guards in the guard room beyond the stairs. From there it was a short run through the palace to the courtyard he had observed with Carlo on the night he visited. A quick lightfoot spell to aid their climbing, and they would be over the wall to freedom before any further guards could be summoned.

When he finally finished, he added, "It's all very simple, really."

The Hanim was clearly incensed as her enchantment ended. "Very clever, Tyvian, but you are still too arrogant. I am now tripling the men in the guardroom. There will be five guards here watching you at all times." She reached out and seized his chin in a viselike grip. "Understand, smuggler—you are *mine*. I would rather have you with your wits in place, but I can make just as much use of the ring and your body *without* a mind as with one."

She pushed Tyvian back against the wall. He permitted himself a laugh. "Really, Hanim—I'm *blushing*."

The Hanim's scowl softened into a flat-lipped look of consternation. "You are a challenge, Tyvian Reldamar. I wonder if your friend Carlo knows how much I am going to enjoy you."

"Carlo's a clever fellow. He'll figure it out."

The Hanim snapped her fingers and her slave picked her back up. Walid rolled up the rug, and the Kalsaari noblewoman and her procession climbed the stairs and left the smuggler and the mage in peace again.

When the door closed, Myreon began yelling. "You fool! You complete idiot! Do you know what you've done?"

Tyvian rolled his eyes and sighed. "No, Myreon, please explain it to me."

"Maybe you were too busy making moon-eyes at the witch to notice, but you just told that bloody devil-woman *exactly how* we planned to escape!"

"Indeed, it seems that way."

"Seems? *SEEMS?* I can't believe this! You've gone mad! I think you might actually *want* to be her consort!"

Tyvian nodded. "I must admit the job seems to have certain advantages."

Myreon howled in frustration. "Kroth damn you, you arrogant dunce! You've doomed us both! How in the name of all the gods are we going to get ourselves out *now?*"

"Well, Myreon, that's just the thing," Tyvian said calmly. "*We* aren't."

Hool crouched on the crest of a low hill, listening to the wind as it blew across the Taqar, stirring the plains of tall, blue-gray grass into waves and ripples as broad as the ocean. The sky was white and unblemished, and Hool could not see the sun, though she felt its burning weight upon her shoulders. The air smelled like rain.

She saw flocks of birds startle and fly out of the grass, twirling in the air as they fled, twittering their warnings to the others. Hool sank lower into the grass, watching. It could be a molecat, or perhaps a coyote, and she knew her pups were hungry. "Brana," she hissed, "pay attention."

Little Brana, her youngest, crouched next to his mother, a perfect mimic. His big yellow eyes, though, were fixed on his mother's powerful shoulders and sharp gaze. At her scolding, he refocused on where the birds had fled, his white-tufted ears swiveling to the task at hand. "Yes, Mama."

Hool sighed. This was a dream. She'd had it before, with her eldest, Api. She felt a horrible, cold, wrenching pain grow in her stomach. She knew how the dream ended.

"Mama loves you, Brana," Hool said quietly.

Brana wasn't listening. He had caught the scent— the sickly sweet odor of raw meat sweating in the sun. It was freshly skinned and enticing. Too enticing for him. The young pup was off, scurrying through the grass with lightning speed.

Hool howled after him, "No! It's a trap, Brana! Trap!"

She ran after him then, her heart pounding, her eyes and ears scanning the blades of grass to see the way they turned and hear as they brushed against Brana's cream-colored coat. The dream was a liar, though, and she saw nothing. The grass moved in the wrong directions, it led her in circles. All she could hear was the quiet scrape of Brana's paws against the dry earth. "Brana! Come back!"

Then, through a trick of her dream, Hool saw it in her mind's eye as clearly as though it were before her: a heavy iron jaw of serrated, sharpened teeth lying in the grass, the skinned hock of a calf atop its rusty touchplate. It was laid by a human cattleman to catch wolves, coyotes, and, sometimes, foolish gnoll pups. Brana, tongue lolling to one side, burst upon the scene and, nose wiggling with excitement, pounced upon the plate. Hool closed her eyes. She could never watch this.

She heard the rusty scrape of the springs and Brana yelp. He only yelped once.

"Mama loves you, Brana," she murmured, her heart screaming.

Only the wind answered.

Hool awoke with a start, her face pressed into a snowbank. She laid still, the pain of the dream still washing over her. Brana's scent still lingered in her nostrils. She moaned into the ground and breathed heavily. *"It's not real. Just a dream. Just a dream. They're alive."*

A door slammed closed, and the world snapped back into focus. Her ears shot up; she listened carefully. It was a woman; she smelled of sex and death. She was going to the outhouse to throw up the poison she had drunk. Hool was too far away to tell who the woman had been with inside the big riverhouse with the tall stone wall, and it was too risky to go and grab her. Reldamar had said this place was where humans sold other humans to each other as slaves, which seemed a ridiculous idea. He had told her terrible stories about how they would fill their blood with poisons to make the slaves loyal, and how the place had a magic door that let them take people from anywhere, make them slaves, and send them anywhere. Hendrieux, he said, had to be inside. She'd been watching the big house for over two hours now, taking short naps to save her strength, but there hadn't been a whiff of him.

Her hiding spot was an abandoned grain silo, its roof long since fallen in, its base ringed in thick snowbanks. It stood perhaps twenty yards from the walls of the fortress—close enough to smell what she needed to, but far enough that there was no way the poor eyesight of any human guards could spot her in the dark and snow, even if she hadn't been hiding.

Hool didn't want to hide. She was tired of stalking—she wanted to pounce. She wanted to kick the doors of the big house down and kill the men inside. She would rip them apart until they told her where Api and Brana were, and then she would go and get her pups. Then she would find Hendrieux, skin him alive, and make his flesh into a cape. She would wear it whenever humans came near, so they would know that she was not to be trifled with.

Tyvian Reldamar, however, had forbidden her from doing this. *Trust me, Hool*, he had said, *if you charge in there alone, you won't be saving anybody—these aren't half-drunk taverngoers, these are trained Delloran soldiers in armor. Even you can't kill all of them.*

Her job was to wait and watch. When she was *certain* she had found Hendrieux, she was supposed to send up a signal to tell Reldamar he was here. He had suggested a fire, which only proved how little the human knew about setting fires. It was snowing too hard and everything was wet—a fire was out of the question. Even if she could start one, Reldamar's half-blind human eyes couldn't see it anyway, nor could his tiny human nose smell it unless he was right next to it. Come to think of it, even their hearing was terrible. Sometimes Hool wondered how humans managed to survive at all.

The same door behind the walls opened again. It was a man this time—big, heavy, wearing mail that clanked as he walked. There was a smell of pipeweed about him that was concealing his personal scent. She stuck her nose higher in the air and breathed more deeply.

"Hey, girl! Where are you? We ain't finished, you and I!" the man called into the dark.

The woman was still vomiting, so she didn't answer. Hool couldn't understand what compelled humans to drink that much poison. On the Taqar, the gnolls only partook of such poisons during acts of penance or when testing resolve—such things weren't for *fun*. Maybe this woman was one of those they were forcing to take it. Hmmmm . . .

"Hey!" the man yelled. "You ain't sneakin' away, are you? Not after I was so nice!" His boots crunched through the snow in the courtyard beyond the wall, getting closer to the woman.

The woman took a deep breath and moaned. "Comin', milord. Jus' . . . jus' cleanin' meself up, is all."

Hool snarled softly; she found herself pitying this female who was too weak to claim her own mate. Hool had never let a male give her orders—she was always alpha, and any male who thought to challenge her would feel her teeth at his throat. This woman weighed less than Brana, and was weak and skinny as a stick. She would be claimed by any man who wanted her. She needed to eat more and get stronger.

"There you are!" the man said, pulling open the door of the outhouse. "Ugh . . . you smell like death."

The man was closer now, and Hool got a better taste of his scent—the sweat in his boots, the oil he used on his armor, the leather wrapping around the hilt of his sword. She'd encountered this man before, walking with Hendrieux when they had killed the beer-smelling men in the ugly house. He was one of Hendrieux's guards—if Hendrieux wasn't here, this man would know where he was.

"No more waiting," Hool muttered, and crept slowly out of the silo, the snow barely stirring as she passed. The streets were empty and dark, but she knew her silhouette would show up clearly against the new fallen snow if she were to head directly down the street, and she knew that eyes were watching the street from the fortress. She kept to the edges, blending in with the piles of trash and the run-down facades of the buildings—a shadow with gleaming, copper eyes.

The man was growing angry with the woman, and she was pleading with him. Hool didn't pay close attention, however—she was concentrating all her senses on moving quietly and not being seen. The air was still but for the falling snow and the gurgle of the narrow stream beyond the fortress—there was no tightening of a bowstring, no gasp of recognition to be heard from the catwalks or battlements.

The woman fell back. The man had struck her. "Foul bitch! You think I'll pay for you now? I've paid your worth already in the drinks you poured down your ugly mouth. Get inside!"

The woman screamed instead, which made the man angrier. Hool heard him kick her in the stomach, making her retch into the snow. Hool knew she didn't have much time—the weakling woman would go in the house soon, and the man would be gone. She darted across the last ten feet of snow and leapt to the top of the wall, balancing like a great cat atop the crumbling crenellations.

The man was beneath her, no more than five yards away, hauling the sobbing woman to her feet, his cheeks red from the cold. If he were to look up, he would see Hool's eyes—she knew they were glittering in the light from the windows of the house. She made a decision; she pounced.

She landed squarely on the woman's back, pinning her facedown in the snow. The man's eyes grew wide, but Hool had him by the throat and threw him down as well. She sat atop his chest, her teeth bared. "Where is Hen-droo?"

"Gods! It talks!" He struggled against Hool, but her weight and strength were too much.

Over her shoulder Hool heard the sentries on the second floor of the house moving to inspect the noise. Hool snarled and dragged the man by the mail shirt into the outhouse and slammed the door. The smell and sound of the filth-choked stream below filled the air, burning Hool's nostrils. Space was tight in the tiny outhouse; Hool's snout was pressed up so close to the man's face that she could feel his breath against her tongue. He, presumably, could also feel her hot, thick breath as she growled at him. "You will tell me where is Hen-droo or I will rip off your face."

The man quivered in her grasp. "Hann save me! A gnoll!"

Hool shook him, which in turn shook the entire outhouse. "Answer me!"

"Okay! Okay! Just don't kill me!" Tears were brimming in the man's eyes. Hool curled her lips at his cowardice. "Captain Hendrieux is inside—well guarded. You'll never get in alive!"

"You are lucky." Hool said.

"Wh-Why?"

"I am not going to kill you," Hool said, and then crumpled the man's body into a ball and shoved it down the vomit-ringed hole in the outhouse floor. He cried like a child, struggling weakly as he slid down the short tunnel and landed with a plop in the swift current of the stream below. It occurred to Hool that he would probably drown now, and she scolded herself for lying to him.

She slipped out of the outhouse and hid herself behind the woodpile. The woman she had tackled sat up, swaying from the effects of the poison in her blood. "Wh-What? Hello? Something hit me . . ."

"Go home, stupid weak girl!" Hool hissed at her, her ears cocked to hear the sentries above—they were elsewhere, but she could hear the footsteps of another one drawing close.

The woman looked at Hool, her bleary eyes trying to focus. "Hey . . . you're . . . you're one of those things."

"I am not a thing. Go home now!"

The woman got to her knees and shuffled across the snowy yard, reaching her hand out. "Wow—you're a lot bigger than the other one."

Hool froze. "Other one?"

The woman giggled and lay back in the snow.

"Yeah—they got one, just like you. Smaller though. In . . . the . . . storehouse." She closed her eyes.

Smaller one.

In the storehouse.

When the sentry passed, Hool crept up to the unconscious woman and sniffed her clothes. It was very faint, but the scent was there—a musky, woody sent, mixed with dry wildflowers.

It was Brana. He was here, and he was afraid.

Rage bubbling through her like molten iron, Hool turned her attention to the massive house.

Reldamar or no Reldamar, she was going in there, and she was getting her pup.

CHAPTER 8

JAEVIS EX MACHINA

Tyvian's wrists, arms, and shoulders were knotted with cramps and raw with pain thanks to his incarceration, but he refused to let it dampen his spirits. He had passed the interminable hours playing "I Spy" with Myreon. Myreon, unfortunately, was a very poor accomplice for this enterprise, since all the Mage Defender seemed intent on doing was brooding, moaning, and cursing him in every way she knew how. She also was a bad guesser.

Since their meeting with the Hanim, the scenery in the dungeon had become more interesting. True to her word, the Hanim had stationed five mark-slaves to watch them inside the dungeon itself. There were two at the top of the stairs to guard the exit and three more on the dungeon floor to keep watch over Tyvian and Myreon's persons. The mark-slaves, not the most imaginative fellows, took their orders quite literally, and stared directly at the two prisoners the entire time. Tyvian had been counting blinks for the past hour or so, and had concluded that the big one on the right was nervous, since he was blinking constantly, while the squat one in the middle was calm, and the tall one on the left wasn't even real, since he hadn't blinked at all.

"I'm telling you, Myreon, that tall one is a simulacrum."

"Who gives a bloody damn which one is a simulacrum or not?" she snapped.

"Myreon, I am trying to engage you in conversation to distract us from our predicament. The least you can do is play along."

She groaned. "I'm sorry, Tyvian, but no amount of inane small talk on your part is going to distract me from the fact that I am chained *upside-down* in a *Kalsaari dungeon!*"

"Stop yelling—I'm right next to you, you know. Besides, it could be worse—you could be wearing a skirt instead of breeches, and then you'd be upside-down *and* indecent."

"Go to hell," Myreon snarled, and thrashed in an apparent attempt to spit in Tyvian's direction.

"You are going to wear yourself out, you know."

"Wear myself out *for what,* you insufferable boob? Perhaps some physical demands might be made of *you* when you whore yourself out to Her Eminence, but I assure you they will not be asking *me* to perform calisthenics while they probe my brain for sorcerous information!"

"No one is going to probe your brain for Arcanostrum secrets, I assure you," Tyvian stated, standing on his tiptoes and flexing the blood back into his fingers.

Myreon rolled her eyes. "You've been saying that for hours now, and I am beginning to think I would prefer being cut in two during a botched escape attempt rather than endure your insinuations at the existence of a successful one."

"How's the headache?"

"I have been stuck upside-down for the better part of a day now, how do you *think* it is? I can hear my blood pumping in my ears more loudly than I can hear your babble, which, as it turns out, is the best part about this whole affair. Now, would you please leave me alone?"

"We've tried this already, Myreon—if I can't talk to you, I have to talk with our jailors here, and they are terrible conversationalists. Why, the short one there only smiles when I insult his parentage, and what fun is that, honestly?"

Myreon addressed the largest of the three slaves watching them. "Could you *please* send somebody down here to torture me? Having to listen to this man is worse than anything you lot could *possibly* dream up."

Tyvian grinned. "I daresay your wits are getting keener, Myreon—that one was pretty good. Perhaps you should hang upside-down more often."

Myreon said nothing, and Tyvian assumed she was glowering. He couldn't say he blamed her either—he was getting rather impatient himself. He had expected his plan to come to fruition at least an hour or two ago, at the latest. He might have given up hope had he not remembered his mother's first rule of manipulating others: *Always have faith in the capabilities of those you use. Like any workman, if you choose your tools well, they will perform their duties as expected.*

They'll be here, Tyvian assured himself, *it's just a matter of time.*

As if on cue, a series of bells began to clang with such rapidity that he knew it had to be the work of an alarm. His suspicion was confirmed when the two guards at the top of the stairs exchanged nervous looks and drew their scimitars.

Tyvian smiled. "Ah! Excellent—here they come."

"What? Here *who* comes?" Myreon asked, her voice losing the sardonic edge it had maintained for the past few hours.

"Our ticket out of here, of course."

"I thought you said we *weren't* escaping!"

"We aren't—we're *being broken* out. Semantics, I know, but they're important when being compelled to answer questions."

Myreon turned this over for a moment, and then asked, "By whom?"

"The Defenders, of course. And possibly Hacklar Jaevis, though I can't guarantee that."

"Wh-What? The Defenders? Here? How would they know—"

"I left a note for them, of course."

Myreon's mouth was hanging open, which Tyvian thought was peculiar, given that she was upside-down. "How did you—"

"You *told* me you were trying to escape. There are only a finite number of ways that can be done from that room with the resources I left at your disposal. Predicting this was really only a matter of reading spirit engine schedules."

"I *knew* it! I just *knew it!*" Myreon said, squeezing her eyes closed. "I *knew* you were playing me."

"Myreon, I'd thought you'd be pleased—your friends are here to rescue you. Doesn't that make you happy?"

She brightened for a moment, but then narrowed her eyes again at him. "Wait . . . how does this help you?"

"Well, I presume they'll take me along with you, seeing how I'm a wanted criminal and all."

Myreon snorted. "That's a tremendously large presumption."

"Maybe. I'm fairly confident in it, though."

"*I* wouldn't take you with me."

"Yes, you would."

"No, I wouldn't!"

"I don't see the point in us arguing about this—we'll know who's right soon enough."

Myreon let air hiss between her clenched teeth. "I hate you."

The two prisoners didn't speak to each other until, a few minutes later, Jaevis kicked in the door at the top of the dungeon stairs. The Illini bounty hunter's black eyes blazed over his blood-caked beard, and the twin sabers in his hands were crimson with gore. He killed the two slaves guarding the stairs with two vicious, disemboweling strokes—whose tattoos, as Tyvian had guessed some time ago, were imitations of the real things—and charged down the stairs toward the dungeon floor, shouting curses in his language with a hoarse voice.

"Jaevis!" Myreon yelled. "The tall one is a fake! He's a fake!"

"Will you shush!" Tyvian hissed. "No need to ruin the surprise!"

The simulacrum mark-slave was the first to meet Jaevis in battle at the foot of the stairs, but the phantasmal being's combat skills were somewhat lacking. It lifted its broad-bladed scimitar high over its head as though intending to cleave Jaevis into two neat halves, and Jaevis, using his higher position on the stairs to his advantage, cut the simulacrum's arms off just below the elbows and, as part of the same flowing movement, dragged both his blades along the thing's throat. Had it been a real person, the amount of blood would have been impressive, but as it was, the being simply vanished into a pink fog and Jaevis charged through it to meet the actual mark-slaves, whose magical tattoos were gleaming with red and purple light.

Each of the mark-slaves, even the shorter one, was bigger than Jaevis both in height and weight, and their magically augmented strength made their bare hands deadly weapons. This Jaevis clearly knew, and so he circled the two men beyond their grasp, forcing them to draw their scimitars against him.

Like the simulacrum before them, they were poor swordsmen, and they hacked wildly at the bounty hunter, each swing designed to kill. Jaevis elegantly evaded their attacks with a series of dodges, feints, and skillful parries. Tyvian, having fought Jaevis before, noticed a couple of the same moves being used again, but was impressed at how well the bounty hunter adapted to fighting multiple opponents—an advantage, Tyvian imagined, inherent to fighting with twinned slashing blades like the two short sabers.

Then both mark-slaves rushed Jaevis, hoping to overwhelm him. The bounty hunter, having little room to retreat, dove into a somersault that shot him between the two brutes. Coming up behind them on his feet, he thrust his blades backward into the spine of one of his opponents. This, by all accounts, ought to have killed the slave outright, but the protective signs upon his body were sufficient to allow him to turn around, still upright, with Jaevis's blades still firmly planted in his back.

Thusly disarmed, Jaevis retreated, drawing a stiletto from a sleeve. The mark-slaves discarded their scimitars and advanced on him with their bare hands, which glowed with murderous red light.

"Jaevis!" Tyvian shouted. "The keys! Throw me the keys!"

"Watch out for their hands!" Myreon added. "They have Fey enchantments on them!"

"Gods, Myreon—he can *see* that they're glowing! Don't distract the man!" Tyvian snapped.

Ignoring both of them, Jaevis put his stiletto in the eye of the injured mark-slave with a quick throw. This injury was enough to drop the brute, who wailed pathetically on the ground as blood spurted from his new wound.

"Well done!" Myreon cheered. "They can't put tattoos on their eyes, now can they. Ha!"

Jaevis moved to recover his swords but was met halfway by the other mark-slave, who delivered a left hook that exploded on his shoulder with a burst of flame and an audible pop. The blow threw Jaevis through the air and dropped him in a heap five paces away. He barely had time to recover before the slave was on him again, foot raised to stomp the bounty hunter into an early grave.

Jaevis rolled away at the last moment, drawing another knife and slashing at the slave's leg in the same motion. The slave's tattoos flashed and the blade failed to leave a mark.

"Where are the Defenders?" Myreon snarled, eyes following the fight with manic attention.

The mark-slave looked down at where Jaevis had attempted to cut him and laughed. Before the bounty hunter could scurry out of reach, he seized Jaevis by the scruff of the neck and threw him bodily against the stone wall between Myreon and Tyvian, who heard at least one bone break on impact and hoped it wasn't Jaevis's skull. The bounty hunter slumped against the wall, stunned.

"Jaevis! Jaevis, wake up!" Myreon prodded the Illini frantically with her casterlocked hands. The mark-slave, still chuckling, advanced slowly, cracking his knuckles in preparation for the final blow. Despite Myreon's prodding, Jaevis didn't stir. "Where the *hell* are the Defenders?"

"Kroth!" Tyvian swore. Jaevis dying would put a *serious* hole in his plan. There had to be something he could do . . . but what?

He noticed, then, that his right hand—his *ring* hand—was tingling. It wasn't pain, per se, but rather a feeling of *restlessness*, as though his hand needed to be wrung or swung around to get out some kind of stored energy. Tyvian yanked against his chains—nothing. He yanked again, this time as hard as he could. He felt something give. Could he actually . . . ?

It took one more pull to snap the chain that held Tyvian captive. Everyone—Myreon, the mark-slave, even himself—stared at what he had done. "Hann's boots," he whispered, looking at the broken chain in his hands.

This was the distraction Jaevis had been waiting for. The bounty hunter, evidently not as stunned as he had appeared, leapt from the ground, knife in hand, and slashed the blade along the one other place besides the eyes that mark-slaves didn't have tattoos. More blood than Tyvian had seen in some time spilled from between the slave's legs, and the man screamed at a pitch that seemed likely to shatter windows. Jaevis shoulder-checked the slave onto his back and watched him writhe in pain for a moment before recovering his sabers and turning to Myreon and Tyvian. "You will come with me now."

Tyvian fished the keys to Myreon's chains from one of the dead guards. "Nothing would give me more pleasure, Mr. Jaevis."

A pair of Defenders—breathless, wounded, with their firepikes gleaming—appeared at the top of the stairs. "Hurry up, bounty hunter! We've got trouble!"

When Myreon was freed, Jaevis pointed to some spare shackles on the wall and said, "Put those on Reldamar. He is prisoner."

Myreon grinned, rubbing the feeling back into her hands. "Nothing would give *me* more pleasure."

Tyvian grinned back. "I *told* you you'd take me with you."

CHAPTER 9

THE OL' SWITCHEROO, REDUX

The cavernous halls of the Theliara Palace were
strangely silent as Artus darted from column to
column, his soft-soled boots barely creating a whisper of sound over the lush carpets and smooth marble
floors. It had been about ten minutes since he had followed the Defenders and Jaevis through the knocked-
open doors, and he had become irrevocably lost. The
galleries seemed to run in circles, the stairways never
seemed to bring him where he thought they would,
and the corridors all looked precisely the same. The
halls seemed to change when he looked away, too. If

Tyvian hadn't warned him that the place was awash in illusion, he would have thought he was losing his mind.

It had been some time since he'd seen anybody. Artus pulled out the seekwand to check if he was going the right direction. The swirling pool of shadow that enveloped the wand's tip jerked and flickered, which Artus *thought* was a good sign, but he wasn't sure. For the tenth time that day, he wished he had paid closer attention when Tyvian was telling him how it worked.

An alarm bell sound somewhere deeper within the palace (or farther out, depending on whether Artus was deep inside the place or not, of which he couldn't be sure). Guessing that the Defenders had finally triggered some attention, Artus resolved to go in the direction of the alarm, as stupid as that seemed to be on the face of things.

His instincts proved to be accurate. At the foot of a narrow spiral staircase, Artus found a pair of bodies—a mark-slave with his throat cut and a Defender with his head tilted at an unnatural angle, his mirrored armor spattered with gore. Holding back a wretch at the sight of it, he moved on, trying to remain as stealthy as possible.

Before long he heard the sound of fighting and the screams of injured men. Several female slaves fled past him in the corridor, so hurried that they didn't even recognize he was there. Artus wondered whether *they* were an illusion, too, but couldn't figure out why you would have your illusory servants run away.

Creeping along the edge of the corridor in the direction from which the slaves had fled, Artus poked his head through a doorway that led to a balcony. Keeping himself low so as not to garner much attention, he stepped onto the balcony, to find himself situated above an extravagant indoor garden, featuring geometrically precise rows of fountains, topiary, ponds, and flowers that stretched off seemingly into the horizon. He found himself staring, bug-eyed, at the scale of the opulence before him—an *indoor* garden? Saints, it was the size of his family farm, and it was warm as springtime!

Another clash of steel on steel refocused his attention on what was happening in the garden. There, not too far from him and near a jewel-encrusted gazebo, he saw Hacklar Jaevis cutting down a slave armed with spear and shield while Myreon Alafarr dragged a shackled Tyvian Reldamar along behind her. Three mirror men were covering their backs, their firepikes occasionally spitting bolts of white flame into distant galleries and down corridors, discouraging any pursuers from taking a shot at them. Artus shook his head—the scene was exactly as Tyvian had described it would be. How in blazes did the man *do* that?

Artus kept himself hidden as the trio passed, heading for the opposite end of the massive garden complex, where an arched exit yawned. With his inherent sense of direction he could have sworn that particular direction led farther *into* the palace, but it didn't matter— Tyvian had told him just to follow and not do anything until "the time was right." Though he didn't have any clear idea of what the right time would be, Artus was confident that *now* wasn't it. Grabbing a silk banner hanging off the front of the balcony, he slid down its length, dropped into the garden, and stole after Tyvian and his captors.

Once in the garden, following them was easy enough, but remaining unseen was far more worrying. Just before they reached the edge of the garden area, Artus's arm brushed a neatly trimmed bush. The sound made Jaevis to stop short and spin around. Artus barely had enough time to drop to his face and hope the cluster of flowers in front of him were enough to conceal him. His shoulder throbbed, as though remembering what Jaevis had done to it not so long ago, and he held his breath. It was a full minute before badgering from both Myreon and Tyvian got the bounty hunter to move on.

When they left the garden and began to roam the long, broad corridors, things became even more complicated. The keenly honed senses of Hacklar Jaevis, professional bounty hunter, and the disciplined formation of the Defenders, far exceeded the shadowing skills of an adolescent street urchin and erstwhile farmboy. After another close call involving his toe scraping along a polished marble floor tile, Artus was forced to extend his following distance to almost the length of whatever chamber or hallway through which Jaevis and company were moving. He found himself listening at doors and catching the barest glimpses of his "quarry" from yards distant, just to avoid detection. He held the seekwand up from time to time, just to check if he was going the right way.

The alarm that had been clamoring about Tyvian and Myreon's escape had ceased, and an eerie silence again descended on the Theliara palace. No guards challenged their passage through the corridors and not a soul showed themselves as the escapees, with Artus still behind them, sought a way out. It did not seem forthcoming. Finally, as Artus skulked in the shadows behind a circular door frame, he heard Myreon call a halt to the procession.

"This is ridiculous. We are clearly walking around in circles—that witch Theliara is probably leading us back to the bloody dungeon!"

"We need window only," Jaevis grumbled. Artus noted that he sounded tired and his words were labored.

"When was the last time you saw a window?" Myreon countered.

"Cast spell, then. See the way out."

"And how, exactly, would you have me do that? Perhaps if I had a Truthlens I could pull that off, but I don't and I don't know of any auguries that will make the illusory things glow and the real things whistle. Then there's the problem of phantasms—they are half real, so they aren't as easy to detect. If I start pitching counterspells around, I might vaporize a load-bearing phantasmal pillar or something and the whole bloody roof will come down!"

"Ma'am," one of the Defenders said, his breathing labored, "we could try to contact outside again."

Myreon sighed. "By all means, Sergeant, but I doubt the sending stone will start working all of a sudden."

Jaevis grunted. "Is problem."

"Would anyone like to hear what I think?" Tyvian offered.

Jaevis and Myreon responded in unison. "No!"

"Fine. Suit yourself."

Silence followed for a few moments, and Artus thought they might have moved on. He almost poked his head out, but then Myreon said, "Fine, since you are the one with all the jailbreak experience, what would you do?"

Artus could almost *hear* Tyvian's grin. "Jaevis, Sergeant—how many guards, marked or otherwise, have your company killed this evening?"

"Twenty-three," Jaevis said.

"I'll confirm that," the sergeant said. "Twenty, at the least. We've lost five, though," he added.

Tyvian whistled. "That's quite impressive—my congratulations. I daresay that is the majority of armed guards at the Hanim's disposal. She is, after all, only one member of an Imperial Kalsaari House living in a foreign city, and an unmarried one at that. This means she probably isn't all that popular—I imagine all the good little girls live closer to Daddy and the Emperor and have for themselves important husbands whom they can order about. So, by the standards of Imperial Kalsaari Houses, she is relatively poor—she can't afford more than a dozen or so mark-slaves, most of whom Jaevis here has so aptly dispatched. I'm guessing her last few—her most important ones—she is saving to do two things."

"Which are?" Myreon asked.

"The first is obvious—bodyguard herself. The second is almost as obvious—set a trap for us. She can't have us escaping, after all—think of the embarrassment! Think of the slight to Kalsaari Imperial power! No—a trap is awaiting us, and all of our wandering around has been to buy time for her to set it."

"And your plan is?" Myreon prompted.

"Well, trip the trap, of course. It's the only thing we *can* do."

"This is bad plan," Jaevis announced.

Tyvian sighed. "I don't expect you lot to understand, but let me put it to you this way: Myreon, remember Akral, a year ago?"

"I had you right were I wanted you," Myreon growled.

"And what did I do?"

"You escaped."

"I promise you, my ever-graceful Saldorian nemesis, that we will do the same thing here that I did there."

Myreon sighed. "He's right, Jaevis. Let's spring the trap."

When they left the room, Artus followed again, but

this time he was more than nervous—he was terrified. Trap? What else can I do? Artus thought. Just keep following them, stupid!

When the trap was sprung, Artus didn't see it so much as *hear* it.

Tyvian, Myreon, the Defenders, and Jaevis had just descended a broad staircase that passed through a wide, arched portal. Artus, from the opposite end of the corridor leading to that portal, heard them yelling in excitement, but only managed to make out Myreon's voice say, "We're out!" Then there was the ear-splitting screech of metal grinding against stone and the bellows and shouts of dozens of Kalsaari voices.

When Artus peeked at where the six of them had gone, he saw a brass gate blocking the portal. He could only guess that similar gates had risen or been dropped into place, barring all the exits from where Tyvian and company were trapped. Seeing nobody between him and the gate, he quickly crept closer so he could see what was going on.

He was looking down from a gallery that ran around the edge of a wide, circular rotunda. Tyvian, Jaevis, Myreon, and the mirror men stood back-to-back-to-back at the center of the floor below, surrounded by about forty slaves who had all leveled spears to form a perfect circle of sharpened steel around the would-be escapees. The two other exits to the room—one of which seemed to lead outside—were barred with similar brass gates as the one at the top of the stairs.

"I must say I am impressed, Master Reldamar," a

woman's voice said with a sultry air. Peering from his hiding spot to the opposite side of the gallery, Artus saw a beautiful, dark-haired and olive-skinned woman dressed in golden silks standing between a pair of burly mark-slaves.

Tyvian bowed deeply. "I am happy to have been so impressive, milady. I only regret that I could not impress you just a *bit* more."

The Hanim's lips curled into a smirk. "Amusing, as always. Tell the Illini and the Saldorian stooges to drop their weapons."

Tyvian held up his chained wrists. "I think you will find that said Illini and stooges don't take orders from me."

"Your business is with me, witch!" Myreon said firmly, pulling herself to her full height. Her blond hair, wild and ragged from her treatment in the dungeons, seemed to whip and writhe, as though tousled on some phantasmal breeze. "This attempt at kidnapping is a violation of the Tasis Accords. You risk war by holding me here!"

The Hanim's laughter was dissonant music. "May I point out, Magus, that the invasion of my palace by these . . ." she sneered at the mirrored armor of the Defenders. " . . . 'soldiers' is likewise a violation of the Tasis Accords? You are as guilty of starting a war as I."

Tyvian nodded. "She's got you there, Myreon. Your Master Tarlyth is acting with surprising recklessness to save little old you. Do you happen to owe him money or something?"

Myreon shot Tyvian a baleful look. "You give me no choice but to invoke destruction upon this place. Release us at once and spare yourselves my wrath!"

"Look around you, mage!" the Hanim countered. "This room has been warded against your magical bolts and blasts. My mark-slaves are immune to any attack you could possibly muster. Come come—this needn't end in violence. Surrender and be handled gently."

"Death before surrender," Jaevis barked.

The Hanim glared at him. "That offer does not extend to *you*, Illini. Whatever you do, your agony will not cease until the Eye of Ishar boils the oceans dry."

Myreon cast a brief look at Tyvian. "Well? What about Akral?"

Tyvian shrugged. "Oh, this is *nothing* like Akral."

"Enough," the Hanim said, and spreading her arms and crooking her fingers into positions of power, she spoke in a thundering voice, *"DROP YOUR WEAPONS AND SURRENDER AT ONCE!"*

The enchantment caused the air to tremble, but it was met by Myreon, who crossed her fists before her face and pushed outward while uttering a single eldritch syllable. This caused the temperature in the room to spike to a nearly unbearable degree for a brief moment and then the two mark-slaves on either side of the Hanim dropped their weapons and put their hands on their heads. The Hanim stared at them, dumbfounded.

"You'll not be winning any sorcerous duels against

me, Kalsaari," Myreon announced. Even from his hiding place, Artus could see how her blue-gray eyes flashed.

"Now," she added, cupping her hands at her breast-bone in a Gathering maneuver, "try *this.*" The Mage Defender released a lode-bolt that screamed through the air, but rather than freezing the Hanim dead, it passed directly through her to strike a wall on the other side.

The Hanim laughed. "You might be a better wizard, Defender, but I am the smarter opponent."

"Idiot," Tyvian growled, "she's an illusion. She wouldn't risk herself like this."

"Then she has to be nearby," Myreon snapped back. "A simulacrum can't cast enchantments!"

The slaves took a threatening step forward, Jaevis began to weave his blades in anticipation of the fight, and the Defender's firepikes glowed fiercely with burning energy. Tyvian gathered up his chains in his hands to form an improvised weapon. "Well," the smuggler shouted, "perhaps if we had the leisure to search all the adjoining rooms, that piece of information would be worthwhile!"

Tyvian's words jolted Artus from his horrified observation. *She was somewhere nearby!* A moment ago he had been wondering just how long he'd last while chained to an oar in a Kalsaari galley, and now, burning through his terror like hot sunlight, came a plan. A crazy, harebrained, hopeless plan, but if he was going to do something, the time was right now.

Slipping back from the edge of the gallery into the shadows along the wall, Artus crept carefully, drawing Jaevis's hurlant out from under his cloak. It only took him a minute to spot her, dressed in a long black robe, half hidden behind a pillar and shrouded in darkness—the *actual* Hanim. He could see her long, bloodred fingernails curling into complicated patterns as she wove the spells that made the illusory "her" dance. Artus heard her mutter something under her breath, and then heard the illusion say, "This is your last chance. Surrender now, or suffer my wrath."

From behind her, he advanced, placing each foot carefully on the hard stone floor. If she turned around . . . if he so much as made a single, solitary sound, she would hear him, and he was dead. He held his breath, his heart thumping hard enough to bruise his ribs. Step after step, inch after inch, and then he was there, right behind Angharad tin'Theliara Hanim, Kalsaari enchantress. This, Artus realized, would be his finest mugging yet.

He pressed the hurlant against her back and growled. "Twitch and yer dead, sweets."

She stiffened, and Artus wrapped his hand over her mouth. The words tumbled out of his mouth automatically, pitched low and gravely to hide his age, all of it part of a routine he had made second nature on the streets of Ayventry. "You scream, you blink, you say one bloody word, and I'll have you laid out for the priests, unnerstand?"

The Hanim was very still. Artus pressed the hurlant harder against her back. "Trigger's getting itchy, love!"

The Hanim nodded.

"Walk," Artus growled.

From the rotunda floor below there was a sudden quiet. "Why isn't anybody moving?" Myreon asked.

"Something's wrong," Jaevis said.

"Yes, very good Jaevis, thank you," Tyvian sneered.

Artus maneuvered the Hanim to the stairs, one arm still wrapped over her mouth, the other pressing the hurlant into her kidneys. "Open the gate, love."

The Hanim flicked a finger and the gate sank out of view. Artus pushed her into the light, and the entire rotunda was suddenly struck speechless. All of it except, of course, Tyvian. "Ah, Artus—it's about time."

The two mark-slaves flanking the fake Hanim, having regained their senses from the enchantment, bellowed in dismay at the sight of their mistress being thusly waylaid, but Artus shouted back at them. "You hold fast, boys, or I airs out her guts!" He pulled her closer, so his hand slipped from her mouth to her neck.

"Who sent you, assassin?" the Hanim screeched, her voice suddenly hoarse. "I'll double your price!"

Tyvian grinned broadly. "That is not an assassin, Hanim, but my young associate. He's really more of a thug and a murderer."

The two mark-slaves were moving around the gallery, closing in on Artus. They hadn't stopped! He had a moment of panic—should he shoot her? *Could* he shoot her? Why didn't she tell them to stop? Oh Saints, he was doomed! He saw Myreon's face fall—another few seconds and they'd be on top of him. How could he make her stop them without killing her?

Suddenly Artus remembered his sisters, and he knew exactly what to do. He grabbed a big handful of the Hanim's long, thick hair, right down by the roots, and gave it a twist and a yank that used to make Kestra squeal like a pig. To his surprise and amazement, the mighty Angharad tin'Theliara Hanim did the exact same thing. She even fell to her knees. Artus pressed the hurlant to the side of her neck. "What, you fink I'm kiddin' or some such?"

At the sound of their mistress in pain, the mark-slaves slowed. When the Hanim held up her hand, they stopped cold. "Ah! Let go! Let go, you horrible—"

Artus gave her hair another good yank, bringing tears to her eyes. "You ain't running this show no more, sweets. You gimme what I want and we all walks away, right?"

Myreon leaned over to Tyvian. "What's with the phony accent?"

Tyvian shook his head. "Don't ruin it now." He then turned back to the Hanim and moved to go up the stairs. The slaves pressed spears against his chest. "Can we dispense with these now?"

"What are you talking about?" the Hanim growled through clenched teeth.

Artus increased the torsion on her hair by wrapping it around his fingers. "Do what he says!"

The Hanim waved her hand and four out of every

five slaves vanished in a puff of smoke. Tyvian then stepped between two of the eight or nine remaining and came up the stairs. "Well, now, Hanim—we have ourselves a predicament, don't we?"

"I will hunt you to the ends of the earth, smuggler! I'll see you all suffer before you die!"

Tyvian tsked and shook his head. "Let me be more clear. My associate here has a particularly nasty enchanted rock pointed at your lovely neck and seems likely to tear your scalp clean off in another few moments—bad for you. You, on the other hand, have us lost in this lovely maze of a palace and still, no doubt, have a couple more dangerous tricks up your well-tailored sleeves—bad for us. It seems to me that we ought to cut a deal."

"No deal!" Jaevis growled, eyeing the remaining slaves like a dog eyeing meat. "Cut her ugly throat."

"Stay out of this, Jaevis," Tyvian snapped. "So, can we deal?"

"Ma'am?" The Sergeant Defender glanced at Myreon.

Myreon held up a hand. "Steady . . ."

The Hanim's face was twisted in a dirty scowl. "Release me first?"

Tyvian shook his head and smiled at Artus. "Not a chance in hell. Deal first, then we talk about releasing people. Here's what I want—you show all three of us the way out. Once we are breathing real, actual night air, Artus here lets you go."

"Tyvian," Myreon said, "there are seven of us. And

why are you making deals anyway? You are *my* prisoner!"

Jaevis snorted. "No, he is *my* prisoner."

Myreon rolled her eyes. "Who you will be turning over to me as soon as I furnish the proper reward. Need we be this technical?"

"I do not turn Reldamar over to you. There is higher bidder."

Myreon's mouth dropped open. "What! Who?"

The Hanim, tears marring her mascara, snickered softly. "The red-haired young man, isn't it?"

Myreon looked at the Hanim. "Who is that?"

Artus saw Tyvian's mouth pop open for a split second, but then the smuggler closed it and composed himself. "Look, it really doesn't *matter* who Jaevis works for, since I'm not bargaining for *his* release at all, so he won't be getting paid." He faced the Hanim. "When I said 'all three of us' I meant Artus, myself, and Myreon here. You can keep the Illini and the Defenders, for all I care. They're exhausted and injured, and I doubt that those firepikes have much more than a charge or two left in them—those two mark-slaves and your remaining retainers can handle them, I'm sure."

"You dog!" Jaevis screamed, "Death to you!" He rushed the stairs, but the mark-slaves intercepted, pushing him back with casual ease.

"Reldamar, you scum!" Myreon snarled. "I'll not let you abandon my men here!"

Tyvian nodded. "Thank you, Myreon—right on cue. I, as it turns out, am not entirely heartless. I am *willing* to negotiate the release of your mirrored co-horts, provided you do one thing for me."

Artus watched the Mage Defender stew for a second, then she heaved a heavy sigh. "What is it?"

Tyvian held up his wrists. "Take these shackles off of me, please."

Myreon's face screwed itself up into a bitter grimace. "Done." She waved her hand and Tyvian's shackles fell to the floor.

Tyvian nodded, rubbing his wrists, and looked to the Hanim. "Well? The use of your scalp and the continuation of your life in exchange for the release of myself, Artus here, Myreon, and her three flunkies. Deal?"

"You have a deal, Reldamar," the Hanim growled. "Tell your brat to let me up."

"Artus, help the lady up."

Artus yanked her up by her hair, causing her to scream again.

"When this is over, your time will be short, Reldamar. I'll see to it that every knife from here to distant Sandris will be hunting you."

Tyvian gave the Hanim a kiss on the lips. "Until then, my desert flower. Come Myreon, Artus, stooges—let's get out of here."

The Hanim waved a hand to open a hidden door-way, and the awkward party moved through, a few slaves following them at a respectful distance. The last things Artus heard as the door slammed closed behind him were the screams of Hacklar Jaevis as the mark-slaves broke his bones.

CHAPTER 10

REWARDS DUE

The storehouse was a short tower in the far corner of the keep, built on a narrow strip of land that jutted out into Arble Brook. It had only one entrance—a door on the ground floor that opened into the courtyard. Pressing her ear against this door, Hool heard Brana's whine. Several minutes later she could still hear it, echoing in her head: a pathetic whimper in Hool's native tongue, squeaking out through an echoing chamber, quavering as though barely strong enough to speak.

"*Mama? Come get me, Mama. Please . . . come get me . . .*"

At that sound, Tyvian's plan had been erased in a holocaust of maternal rage. Breathlessly, tears running down her snout, Hool softly called back to her long-lost pup. *"Mama's coming, Brana. Mama loves you."*

The Dellorans inside the keep were drinking and celebrating, so they did not hear her kill the courtyard guards or capture the one inside. The guard inside the tower had been watching the river when she came upon him in the dark and broke his hip. She hung him upside down from the rafters.

She found Brana in a small cage of wire and steel, held in a deep, dark room full of animal cages that had been his prison for months. It stank of blood, fear, and filth and she tore it apart with her bare, bleeding hands. They had injured her pup. They had filled him with foul magicks. They had shaved patches of his fur away so they could burn him with horrible devices. They had made him howl with pain and threw him in a dark hole alone. They had left him to starve and taunted him when he was sleeping or awake. All this Brana had told her when he was, at last, nestled in her arms again.

Hool's heart felt as though it were being ripped, stretched to the breaking point between two extremes. One of her pups, one of her babies, was back with her and safe. Brana clung to her chest, just as he had when he was brand new and still suckling at her breasts. Still whimpering, he nuzzled his fuzzy snout against her warmth. Her love was like a sunrise, setting her world afire. But the hatred was there, too—hatred for the beasts who had done this to her pup. Where her love was bright and hot, the hatred was dark and hard and cold as the ice of deep winter.

She would make them pay. The guard hanging from the rafters would be first.

Even before Hool began, the man wept and begged and called out for his mother. The irony of it filled Hool with a blinding, white-hot anger that could only be released by dragging the man's own knife across his naked skin, peeling him like a grape. Hool pressed the bloody edge of it against the meaty inside part of his thigh, and the guard shrieked. "Sweet Hann's mercy! Don't don't don't . . ." His voice melted into a garbled howl as she stripped a section of skin three inches wide off his body.

Taking her time, Hool methodically stripped him of his skin. Listening to him plead for mercy produced a deep satisfaction that could not be accurately measured, all while his comrades drank poison and rutted with dirty women no more than a few dozen yards away.

The guard eventually died, and Hool completed dressing the corpse like a hunting kill, hanging the hides from the rafters to dry. She tossed Brana parts that looked good to eat—meatier parts like the arms and buttocks—so he could gain back some strength. She had left his organs in the courtyard to be found—those contained his spirits, his wretched essence, and she wanted no part of such a foul and tainted soul.

There were more Dellorans, though. There was

more vengeance to visit upon them. There was her other pup—her darling Api, brave and daring—to find. She wanted them to know she was coming for them. She wanted to fill them with the same terror they had filled her pups with all this time. At the top of the tower, her fur stained maroon from the blood of the skinned Delloran, she poured herself into a howl that would freeze fire and blacken the sun itself.

Hendrieux was sitting on a chair set atop a table, two slave girls at his feet, competing for attention by removing more and more of their clothing, while around him Sahand's Delloran soldiers drank and whored their way through their lord's reward. Hendrieux flipped each of the women a half-mark apiece, and smiled. "Keep it up, ladies. Winner gets a very *special* present."

Sahand's appreciation for acquiring the Artificer from the Kalsaaris and not screwing it up overly much had come in the form of a massive chest of gold coins and the orders to simply "lay low" for a couple of days while the final touches on the prince's plan were put in place. To Hendrieux and the men, that meant being cooped up in a fortified keep that no one but the Phantoms knew they occupied. It also meant being cooped up in a fortified keep full of slaves placed there for their exclusive use. Things couldn't have been better if Tyvian Reldamar's head had been delivered on a silver plate

The slave girls grinned weakly at him—one of them was missing a tooth—and pawed at their bodice laces. Hendrieux watched with heavy-lidded eyes and dipped his little finger into the pot of Cool Blue in his lap. He had done it. He, Zazlar Hendrieux, had earned the respect and praise of the most powerful, most dangerous ruler in the West. He would be a rich man. Leaping up from his seat, he raised his hands above his head and shouted to gain his men's attention. "Lads! Lads! Let's have a toast, shall we?"

Tankards were immediately raised as the wine and ale was passed around. Hendrieux, smiling more broadly than he had in weeks, snatched a cup from another man and said, "To Prince Sahand, long may he live, and to all the bloody gold he's gonna rain on our heads! To riches, lads! To riches!"

The men met the toast with cheers. Hendrieux was declared the man of the hour, hoisted atop their shoulders and carried about in triumph. After a score of minutes and two cups of ale, he was dancing on a table when Gallo appeared at the door to the hall, a cold wind entering with him.

The revelry died immediately, and all eyes went to Gallo and what he had in his hand.

"What have you got there, Gallo?" Hendrieux asked, trying to keep the levity from dying down. "More meat for the fire?"

Gallo held up a bloody lump of flesh and threw it onto the floor. "All I could find of Jenner."

"He was the guard at the storage tower." Hendrieux said, his voice calm only from the ink he'd taken. Silence blanketed the hall, and men reached for their swords. Hendrieux looked at the bloody pile of flesh on the floor and felt suddenly queasy. "Who . . . who . . ."

Just then, a bestial howl echoed from somewhere outside. It persisted for several seconds before finally wearing away to nothing, but the sound left a mark that remained long after it was gone. Hendrieux looked around and saw every face as drained of color as his own.

Every face, that was, except Gallo's. "The gnoll's here," the fish-eyed man rasped. "She's not happy."

There was no escape from the storage tower without being exposed to fire from the sentries atop the keep. Hool knew they were inattentive for now but would not be for long, and then she would have to figure out how to get them without being shot. From the top of the tower, now sticky with the drying blood of Brana's torturer, Hool could easily see the catwalks atop other parts of the curtain wall surrounding the fortress, but those catwalks did not connect to the tower itself. She could make the leap and escape, but not with Brana, and she could not leave him. The space from the storage tower to the main building was shorter—ten yards maybe—but not short enough for a leap with her pup. The closest door at the back was thick oak studded with iron, and had been barred against her. They knew she was here now. She wanted them to know. Nothing would save them.

"Mama," Brana whimpered, nestling closer to her bosom, "Can we leave now? I don't like it here."

"We need to find your sister, Brana. Hush," Hool told him, running a hand gently through his fluffy cream-colored mane. It was tangled with mats and she could feel the scars beneath it. Again her heart exploded with the feelings of rage and elation. Her baby was safe, but she had another pup. Another pup these monsters were hurting somewhere at that very moment.

"They took Api away, Mama." Brana said softly. "They said I would never see her again."

"They were liars, Brana. Hush, now." She laid a hand along the top of his head and scratched his ears the way he liked, and Brana let loose a deep sigh.

The sound of human voices came from within the fortress building and from the turrets that overlooked the tower Hool controlled. They were doing something. The strong one, Gallo, must have returned. They must be regrouping. This was bad. Hool could take any four of them at a time, but she needed them to be disorganized. She needed them to be afraid. She cursed herself for howling—that had been foolish. She was acting stupid, like a human.

Gathering up the clothing of the dead guards, Hool painstakingly crafted a nest for her pup. Setting him gently within it and covering him so he would not be seen, she whispered. "Brana, I have to go find your sister now."

"I want to come, Mama. I can help."

"Rabbits don't help wolves, little one."

Brana nodded, understanding. "I'm the rabbit."

"And what do rabbits do?"

"Hide in their holes."

Hool scratched his ears. "Good boy, and what else?"

"Run like the wind."

"You be a good rabbit, Brana. Mama has to be a wolf."

"Will you come back?" Brana asked, big yellow eyes gleaming in the lamplight.

"Always," Hool said, her voice trembling.

"Don't cry, Mama."

Hool licked him on the nose. "Mama loves you, Brana."

Turning away from her pup, her precious Brana, Hool ran and took a flying leap from the top of the tower, sailing across the thirty feet of open air between it and the keep, and landed against the rough stone wall. Gaining purchase in an arrow slit, she began to climb.

CHAPTER 11

TWO STEPS AHEAD

"I don't get it." Artus said, his eyes crossed so he could focus on the glowing tip of a firepike that floated no more than six inches from his nose. "*How* is this better than where we just were?"

"Don't worry, Artus. Everything is under control." Tyvian kept his smile pinned to his face, more for everyone else's benefit than his own. He hadn't *quite* anticipated this part of the plan going this way. They hadn't gone halfway across the plaza that lay before the gates of the Theliara compound when about ten Defenders had popped out of nowhere, ordering Tyvian and Artus to their knees, their firepikes tucked under their arms and blazing with power. They acquiesced, of course, and Myreon had given the smuggler a smug little grin as she reapplied the same shackles she had removed just moments before. They were now surrounded, kneeling in the snow with their hands on their heads. They took away Jaevis's hurlant from Artus—their only weapon—and patted them down for anything else. Artus, it turned out, had nicked the Hanim's gold necklace (for which Tyvian made a mental note to congratulate the lad later—he was a real talent in the thievery department, that was for sure), but they had nothing else of value, besides a pretty ordinary-looking bottle of perfume with a glamour enchanted upon it—fairly standard fare for perfume.

Myreon crouched in front of Tyvian, grinning broadly. "So, Reldamar, did you have a contingency plan for this?"

Tyvian decided only to give the mage a wink and a smile. "You'll see."

Myreon's smile dropped into a sneer. "I am really going to enjoy putting you away."

"Myreon! I see you've made it out in one piece—well done!" The voice was a full, deep baritone, frayed slightly with age and fatigue. A tall, broad-shouldered Mage Defender strode through the snow with the confidence of a man long used to being invulnerable.

Upon seeing the mage, Myreon dropped to one knee. "Master! I . . . I didn't expect to see *you* here."

Tyvian blinked, unable to contain his surprise. "Master *Tarlyth*? Of Galaspin Tower?"

The old mage pulled himself to his full height—Tyvian noted a bit of a gut pushing out under his mage-glass breastplate. "And you must be Tyvian Reldamar. You're a shame to your family name, boy."

"That's very kind of you." Tyvian nodded. "And may I say that *you*, sir, are about to cause a diplomatic incident."

Myreon rose and made a show of brushing off her filthy robes and smoothing her ragged hair. "He's right, sir. You shouldn't be here. We've got to get out of Freegate before the Watch spots us. I imagine the Hanim is calling them . . ."

Tyvian snorted out a laugh. "Oh, I doubt it. A wealthy, powerful enchantress being waylaid by a thirteen-year-old ragamuffin with a talent for hair-pulling? I imagine she will prefer it if no one ever speaks of this event again. There isn't enough *real* gold in that entire palace to keep the Watch from gossiping about *that* one."

Myreon looked like she wanted to kick Tyvian in the face, but the presence of the venerable Master Tarlyth was enough to keep her anger bottled into a single, withering glare. "Well then, good for us," she said to Tyvian. "We'll be out of here with you in chains in no time at all."

Tarlyth nodded. "I have taken care to conceal our arrival from prying eyes. No one knows we are here. You, Master Reldamar, better get used to those chains—your little tricks have run their course."

A frown crossed Myreon's face. No, Tyvian corrected himself, a different *timbre* of frown crossed Myreon's face. "Forgive me, sir, but why did you come *personally?*"

Tarlyth held up a hand, "I'll explain later, Myreon— for now, we've got a spirit engine to catch."

Tyvian peered between the cordon of Defenders toward the streets and alleys feeding into the plaza. It was dark, the snow was falling, and the light from the firepikes was enough to virtually blind him. He could see no sign of movement, but that didn't mean there wasn't any.

A pair of Defenders grabbed him by each arm and hoisted him to his feet. Two others did the same for Artus, and the rest of them began to form a column to march out of the city. Tyvian's mind raced for a way to stall them. "Wait!"

Tarlyth and Myreon looked at him with dour faces. "What?"

"There's one thing you didn't anticipate—I've hidden Magus Alafarr's staff. If you don't release me, it will be handed over to the Lord Mayor's office at sunrise! They'll *know* you were here, in violation of Freegate's neutrality ordinance."

Tarlyth nodded. "Ah—that reminds me." He

reached into his cloak and, by some trick of Astral transmutation, pulled Myreon's magestaff out of it. "Here you are."

Tyvian was genuinely surprised. "Wh . . . but I . . ."

Tarlyth delivered Tyvian a small grin that he probably used on his grandchildren when explaining how he knew they'd been raiding the cookie jar. "You don't become a Master Defender, sir, without knowing a few tricks yourself. That was quite an impressive hidden compartment, by the way—just not impressive enough."

Tyvian sighed. "Well, worth a try."

Artus groaned. "Is that all we got, Reldamar?"

The Sergeant Defender tapped the butt of his firepike against the snowy earth—it didn't make the sharp crack that he probably wanted. "Company . . . move *out!*"

Then Tyvian heard it—harness bells, jingling closer. He grinned. "No, Artus—it seems I've got a bit more, after all."

Tarlyth raised his staff and spoke a few words under his breath. The light from the distant streetlamps dimmed a bit, and the snow appeared to lose its midnight luster. All of them—everyone in the party— seemed to fade from notice. Tyvian had trouble focusing on the back of the Defender in front of him, as though he was just too boring to look at. He knew of this spell, of course—his older brother had used it all the time when he was an apprentice and wanted to sneak out of the house—but he'd never seen it used on such a large scale before.

Myreon was beside him, whispering, "Whoever it is, Tyvian, they're just going to ride right by us. They'll never notice us under this spell, in the dark, in the snow."

Tyvian spoke at a normal volume. "If this is you gloating, Myreon, I have two things to point out. First, you again fail to understand the nuance required to deliver a proper gloat . . ."

Carlo's coach, its wheels replaced with sleigh runners, slid into the plaza, pulled by a quartet of heavy draft horses, sweat steaming off their flanks. Behind it were trotting about two dozen figures, their padded leather caps and heavy blue cloaks illumenated by the darting spheres of light that followed them—the Freegate city watch, accompanied by their tattlers.

" . . . and, second, your gloating is once again premature."

Tarlyth and Myreon sprang into action then, working sorceries to confuse the simple tattlers or dispel them altogether. But it was too late. The magical constructs, insatiably curious and devoid of any notions or expectations of "ordinariness," were immune to the Aura of the Ordinary, and quickly flitted over to shine their bright lights on the glittering helmets and glowing weapons of the Defenders of the Balance. The watchmen spotted them immediately.

"Company!" the Sergeant Defender bellowed. "Defensive formation, double-quick!"

Tyvian found himself dumped on his back as the Defenders rushed to form into a double line, the first line kneeling, their firepikes set against the ground, the second line standing, their pikes braced under their arms, prepared to fire. The watchmen barked orders of their own, and brandished a variety of maces, spiked cudgels, and mourning stars. They wore small target shields etched with some basic magical guards, and most of them were wearing two or three talismans of various sizes and descriptions around their necks. They encircled the Defenders on three sides, standing about ten paces away, shouting and jeering at the invaders of their city. The Defenders shouted back, so that the result was a cacophonous mess of men screaming various threats and commands.

Carlo's coach-turned-sleigh pulled up just behind the line of watchmen and the door popped open, revealing the squat, fur-wrapped form of Carlo himself, his crystal eye twinkling in the light of the firepikes. His coachman hopped down, fished him out a stool with a silk cushion, and Carlo slid out of the coach and deposited his backside on the stool, his hands folded neatly into a fox-fur muff. 'Well, well, well—what have we here?"

"Let me handle this. You don't need to be involved," Myreon said to Tarlyth, and stepped forward. "I am Mage Defender Myreon Alafarr on special assignment from Master Tarlyth of Galaspin Tower. This man,

Tyvian Reldamar, is in my custody. Saldor will make it worth your while to assist me in keeping him captured until we can get aboard a spirit engine and leave you in peace."

A giggle escaped Carlo's lips, gradually building to a gut-splitting guffaw that rocked him back and forth on his stool until he nearly fell off. He was joined by the snickers and jeers of the watchmen, who twirled their assortment of spiked, blunt instruments menacingly. Through it all, Myreon and her Defenders stood rigid and erect, their eyes never flinching, as though they were openly mocked every day of the week where they came from.

When they had all calmed down, Carlo steadied himself on his perch and called to Tyvian, "What do you say, Tyvian? Should the fellows here toss you in a dungeon?"

Tyvian pressed past the Defenders and stood next to Myreon. "Carlo, enough charade. Could you please remove these shackles from my hands? They are chafing me horribly."

Carlo's jeweled eye sparkled in the tattler-light, his face an unreadable mask. He snapped his fingers, and a watchman stepped forth with a set of skeleton keys and an assortment of enchanted oils for undoing magical locks. "Sorry I'm a bit late—had to put the runners on the coach, blasted snow," Carlo said, his face breaking into a grin.

Myreon thrust her staff at the advancing watchman, knocking him sprawling with a blast of invisible force. "I'm afraid I didn't make myself clear—this man is my *prisoner*." Behind her the Defenders advanced a pace in unison. "Any act of force on your part would be foolish. You are not our equals, even if you do out-number us."

Tyvian was pulled back behind the Defender's lines by the collar, but he didn't struggle. He had what he needed—the perfume bottle, lifted off Myreon and concealed in his hands. He caught Artus's attention and nodded. *Get ready.*

Carlo chuckled, shaking his head. "Magus, with all due respect, do you *really* intend to attack the city watch of Freegate to arrest a *smuggler*? Do you have any idea the political mudslide you'd cause? Saldor, Galaspin, Eretheria—they'd lose millions to trade tariffs. Traffic between the West and the North would get choked to a trickle until your governments paid reparations; the Defenders would get labeled as 'mavericks' and 'irre-sponsible prosecutors' and lose the reputation they've worked so *hard* to build. Then, of course, there's you— you'd get yourself stationed in the dustiest, dirtiest outpost the Western Wastes can offer, left to dodge scorpions and dump sand out of your slippers until the queenies finally come to take Illin back and mash you under the foot of some ten-ton manticore. Now, tell me madam, does that sound like a good trade?"

As Carlo talked, Tyvian began spraying Defenders with the perfume. Its magic was simple enough, but worked wonderfully if the individual wasn't warded against the ether. Defenders, as it happened, almost never were—such wards interfered with seekwands and made their concealing magicks harder to use. One by one the back row of Defenders fell victim to the simple illusion contained in the bottle. When they looked back at him (which they did every few seconds), Tyvian did his best to look nervous.

Tarlyth stepped forward, facing Carlo. "I am Master Defender Tarlyth of Galaspin Tower. While Magus Alafarr might not be enough to impress you, I should be. You make a compelling argument, but allow me to make a counterargument: I can, with a few words, obliterate every one of you gentlemen, wards or no wards. I can bake your bones inside your skin; I can freeze you until you will shatter at a touch; I can call down lightning from the sky to smite you. All we ask is safe passage out of Freegate and an agreement to not make an incident of this. Do this, and not only will we pay you handsomely, but you will get to keep your lives as well. Now, I ask *you*, Master diCarlo, is *that* a good trade?"

The watchmen grumbled at that, looking to Carlo and muttering to themselves. Tyvian wondered how much money the fat Verisi had to pay them to show up. It was probably an enormous sum, and he knew it didn't cover getting into an *actual* scrap with Defenders of the Balance.

Myreon suddenly cocked her head. She turned to face Tarlyth and pointed at Carlo. "Wait a minute—how did you know his name?"

If Tyvian and Artus were going to make a move, it had to be now. "Artus, *RUN!*"

They ran in opposite directions, making certain to conceal their shackles under their shirts. The back row of Defenders lost no time in turning around and splitting up in an attempt to run them down. Tyvian and Artus began to dart back and forth among them, dodging errant grabs and failed tackles as they leapt and dove through the snow.

And everybody—Defenders and Artus included—was the spitting image of Tyvian Reldamar.

Myreon and Master Tarlyth froze, temporarily stunned, as they saw seven snow-covered Tyvians wrestling and chasing one another around the plaza. "Don't let 'em get away!" the Sergeant Defender barked, leaping atop the closest Reldamar and putting him in a hammerlock. The rest of the men leapt into action, but hesitantly, not sure who to tackle.

The disguised men kept yelling, "I'm not him! I'm not him!" and Tyvian and Artus yelled the exact same thing, of course. It was sheer pandemonium.

"How the . . ." Myreon gasped, and then started throwing dispels as best she could, but it was dark, she was tired, and her aim was off. She missed the first few. Tarlyth was better, dispelling two of the Shrouds in short order (the two Defenders were in the process of wrestling each other), but it provided all the time Tyvian and Artus needed to slip into an alley and vanish from sight.

By the time Myreon and Tarlyth had everything sorted out, they found themselves alone in the plaza with their ten men—their prisoners, the sleigh, Carlo diCarlo, and the watch had all melted back into the night. All they had to show for it was a single, empty perfume bottle.

Carlo picked Artus and Tyvian up a block away and sped off. Artus had managed to snatch back the hurlant while wrestling with a Tyvian Defender. He was giggling uncontrollably. "Hot damn, that was *incredible!*" He slapped his knee.

Tyvian sighed. It was distinctly disconcerting to see "himself" behaving in such a manner. "Carlo, the shackles, if you please."

"Yes, yes—not even a thank-you, though? I mean, look at all the snow you're traipsing into the coach?"

"Sleigh," Tyvian corrected.

"Whatever. It's not even mine," Carlo grumbled, producing an enchanted oil and a pair of lock picks and getting to work. "What kind of idiot would bring a coach to Freegate—you can't even get to half the city. I just hold onto the thing and use it in the wintertime for private conversations that I don't want eavesdropped."

Tyvian noticed Artus's expression suddenly change; it was as though something had just occurred to him, a storm building just behind his face. Well, behind *Tyvian's* face, but still . . . "What's the matter, Artus?"

"Tell ya in a minute," the boy said, holding out his shackles.

Carlo nodded. "Ah—so *you're* Artus and *that's* the

real Tyvian. Good. I'll know which one will get my dirty jokes now."

As soon as Artus's shackles popped off and hit the floor, he snatched up the hurlant and stuffed it in Carlo's face. "Don't move or I blow off your head!"

Carlo put his hands up. "Fine, fine—I'll tell you all the dirty jokes you want, boy! Gods!"

Tyvian frowned. "Artus, what the hell are you doing?"

"Reldamar!" Artus said, his voice cracking, "I told you already! That's the man that betrayed you, remember? He's the guy in the coach with Jaevis and that other guy—the young guy."

Carlo groaned. "This is ridiculous."

"Tell him! Tell him what you done!" Artus pressed the hurlant harder against Carlo's cheek.

"Boy, that hurlant's broken." Carlo pointed to the firing mechanism, "It looks like somebody fell on it."

Tyvian watched his own expression change to doubtful on Artus's shrouded face. "Artus, *did* you fall on that hurlant?"

"I . . . uhhh . . . I had to dive to the ground a couple times, if that counts."

Tyvian grabbed the hurlant and pulled it away. "Yes, that counts."

Artus folded his arms. "He betrayed you, though—I wouldn't trust him."

"Don't be ridiculous, Artus. Carlo has been helping me the whole time."

"What?" Artus sat up. "How?"

Carlo shrugged. "Well, we haven't been exactly conspiring, but I've been dropping Tyvian plenty of hints. We work together well—our minds work in a similar way—and I certainly have no love for that thug Sahand or that louse Hendrieux. I have to say, though, Tyvian, this particular plot has even me lost. What are we doing again?"

Tyvian sighed. "Myreon is going to keep hunting me—she can't help it. I left her the perfume bottle so she could track us."

Artus said, "But she doesn't have the seekwand—I have . . . oh. Right, she took it back."

Tyvian nodded, smirking. "Even if she didn't, she's with a pile of Defenders and they probably have a spare. Hell, we're in a sleigh in the snow—they could just follow our tracks. Anyway, with Myreon on our tail, it's an opportune time to pay Hendrieux a little visit."

"What? Why?" Artus asked, but Carlo was laughing. "What's so funny?"

"I love it, Tyvian. You're using them the same way you used them against that Kalsaari witch—a wrecking crew. In chasing you, they'll be forced to attack the Dellorans when they find them, which, of course, will be exactly when and where they spot you."

"Whoa," Artus breathed. "But we don't know where Hendrieux is."

Carlo snorted. "Of course I do—he's in Arble Keep, along with a lot of heavily armed Delloran soldiers. Who do you think is renting the damned place to them?"

Artus blinked. "But . . . if you knew the whole time, why didn't you just tell . . ."

"As much as I appreciate young Tyvian's friendship, my boy, I've no desire to die for him. I wasn't going to tell him because I didn't want to be the one who he found out from. That kind of information could have cost me a lot of very important organs I've come to rely on for breathing and such."

"Besides," Tyvian said, "I've known where Hendrieux was, more or less, for a little while now. There are only so many anygates in Freegate, after all, and Hendrieux has always had contacts with the slavers in the Phantom Guild."

"Shhhh!" Carlo waved his arms

"Carlo," Tyvian said, grimacing, "I appreciate your fine performance earlier this evening, but I don't think that entitles you to—"

"I said *shut up!*" Carlo shouted.

Tyvian, taken aback, fell silent, as did everyone else. They listened to the jingle of the horse harnesses through snow-muted air for a moment before they heard it, faint but not too distant. It was the mournful, slow howl of a great beast. It was Hool.

Tyvian looked at Carlo. "Can you see her with that eye of yours?"

Carlo shuddered. "She's starting early, Tyvian. The Dellorans will have their guard up."

Tyvian nodded. "More fun for Myreon and her friends, then—let's go."

CHAPTER 12

PAYBACK

Had Sergeant Tillick Nord of the Delloran army been in charge, he would have burned the stupid tower to the ground rather than wait for whatever was in there to come out. Of course, Nord was not in charge, and "Captain" Hendrieux had told them they needed to keep a low profile. So, that meant that Nord and a dozen of his men had to crouch behind the frigid, wind-worn battlements on the top of this godforsaken fortress, crossbows loaded and cocked, and hope the gnoll or whatever was in the tower would be dumb enough to come out the door they had their weapons trained on. He was too much of a Delloran to admit he was freezing, and too much a professional to complain openly about anything, but he could still taste the pipe smoke on his lips and the warm ale in his belly, and he hoped to all the gods that this ridiculous gnoll-thing would show itself quick so he and his men could feather it and go back inside to party.

Nord passed a pouch down the line after picking out some of the dried leaves inside—wakeroot, the soldier's best friend, guaranteed to sober a man up in a minute or less. "Everybody takes a chew. You can get yerself nice and drunk again once this is over." Nord stuffed the wad of pungent black leaves in his mouth and held it in one cheek, the fiery juices bubbling on his tongue and tickling as they ran down his throat. When it hit his stomach, it was like somebody had lit a firebomb in his innards. Nord's eyes watered as the world was brought into stark focus at the same time as a raging headache assaulted his temples. Wakeroot got rid of the drunk by, essentially, skipping straight to the hangover. Still, he found he could see straighter, once he squinted past the pain behind his eyes. Down the line, men were coughing and groaning as their own hangovers hit them. Nord cursed Hendrieux under his breath; they were in for an unpleasant evening.

Just *how* unpleasant, however, wasn't made clear until a few minutes later. Such clarification came in the form of a pack of angry people gathering outside the stockade gate. This struck Nord as odd simply because nobody ever used the gate—all transport was conducted through the anygate in the fortress's dungeon—and that, as far as the outside world was concerned, this particular ruin was nothing but a run-down brothel and ink den. Nord walked over to the side of the battlements that faced the gate, which was opposite from the side facing the storage tower, and kept an eye on things, just in case. He couldn't see who was out there, thanks to the height of the walls, but he guessed it was some kind of bizarre domestic disturbance . . . in the middle of the night . . . in the winter. Right.

A magically amplified voice thundered over the walls. *"Attention, occupants of the Arble Keep; you are harboring a fugitive and are hereby commanded to open your gates by the authority of the Defenders of the Balance. You have two minutes to comply."*

"Damn," Nord hissed, and began issuing orders. "Matcher, report to Hendrieux and Gallo, ask them to advise. Keeler, Verins—you two stay on the tower. Everybody else form up here. We're gonna have visitors in a minute, and I want 'em welcomed. Go!"

The men instantly set to their tasks, and Nord had nine crossbows set up to rain quarrels on anybody coming through the gate just before it blew inward with a white flash. A pair of Defenders were the first through, crouching by the edges of the wall and pointing their firepikes up toward the battlements to cover the rest of their party. They sent a few white-hot blasts of enchanted fire up toward Nord's men, but they had cover, and firepikes were notoriously inaccurate weapons anyway.

"Take'em down—aim for any part of 'em not glitterin'!" Nord barked, and two crossbows clacked, sending a bolt through one Defender's thigh and one through the other's hip. Nord grinned—fancy magecraft was nice, but good shots were better.

An instant later a full squadron of Defenders, armored and angry, were storming through the gate. The first four were taken down by Nord's men, but the next few shots were deflected by the mage they had with them, who threw various guards and wards over the Defenders' heads as they made their way toward the keep's entrance. Firepike bolts hissing and spitting past his position, Nord stayed calm, noting that the mage seemed to have forgotten to ward herself and *wasn't* wearing the standard mageglass breastplate or helm.

Spitting to test the wind, Nord raised his own crossbow to his shoulder and took aim at the wizard's bright yellow hair. "Say good-bye, girlie."

"Good-bye, girlie." A deep, rumbling voice said from behind him.

His hair suddenly standing on end, Nord twisted to look over his shoulder. In the dim evening light all he could see was a huge, hairy bulk and a set of gleaming white fangs protruding from a bloody maw. "What . . . the . . ."

"Keeler and Verins missed me," the gnoll growled.

These were the last words Nord ever heard.

Before the Defenders arrived, Tyvian, with Carlo's help, had mimicked a set of tracks in the snow indicating that they had gone inside Arble Keep, leaving Carlo's sleigh and horses tended by his coachman beside an empty water trough. Carlo produced a warding taper of bloodred wax and lit it, the magic in the candle shielding them from magical detection for a brief time as they waited in the coach.

Predictably, Myreon and the Defenders were so incensed by his recent escape they didn't take the time to investigate further than seeing the tracks and questioning the coachman, who quietly indicated the massive, walled-in ink-den as the fugitives' current location. The siege of the place followed no more than a few seconds later.

Tyvian noted that Tarlyth wasn't present. He wondered why the Master Defender would have come all this way—it was definitely not standard operating procedure, and, as much as Tyvian liked to flatter himself as being at the top of the Defenders' most wanted list, there was simply no reason a man of that stature would leave his warm office in Galaspin and come here, a city where he was expressly forbidden to enter by international law.

Unless it was something he needed to do personally because he couldn't afford his colleagues back at the Tower knowing about. Because it was illegal. And had something to do with Tyvian himself. And Sahand.

And maybe even Theliara. And involved him meeting with or otherwise knowing Carlo.

Tyvian sat in the coach, eyes wide, as giant puzzle pieces thudded into place in his brain. "Gods . . ."

"C'mon!" Artus said, jumping out of the coach once the last of the Defenders was through the door. "What're we waiting for?"

Snapping himself out of his revelation, Tyvian snagged Artus by the collar before he had gone too far. "Not so fast now."

The boy stopped in his tracks, blinking at the smuggler and the old pirate. "C'mon! We're going to get them, right? The Dellorans, Hendrieux, the Defenders—everybody!"

"Not we, *I*. You, my young friend, have better things to do than be gutted by a Delloran soldier during some delusion of grandeur."

Carlo produced a few items from a sleeve and passed them through the coach window. "Your effects, Tyvian. Is there something wrong with your hand?"

Tyvian looked down to see his ring hand contorted in pain. Apparently he was getting used to its bite, or perhaps his good deed of stopping Artus was mitigating the bad deed of allowing Myreon and company to run into what was probably some kind of cross fire. "It's nothing. I didn't escape the Hanim entirely unscathed, is all."

Carlo grinned. "Why don't I believe you?"

"Because you are a mistrustful, miserable old man, that's why," Tyvian countered, taking *Chance*, the throwing knives, and the illumite shard Carlo was offering and stuffing them into the appropriate pockets.

Artus's voice broke into a whine. "Why can't I go? I can fight!"

Tyvian shook his head. "No, you can't. You only think you can—there is a major difference. The men in there are trained soldiers in armor with swords. This is no amateur back-alley knife fight in Ayventry. This is for your own good."

"Since when do you care what happens to me?" Artus countered.

Tyvian scowled. "Are all children at your age so petulant? I care what happens to you because I have a use for you, stupid. I need you to use those sprightly legs of yours to run around back and keep an eye out."

Artus blinked. "Why?"

Carlo cuffed Artus on the back of the head. "In case Hendrieux tries to slip out the back! Gods, Tyvian—is he always this dense?"

Tyvian thought back to the Hanim's palace, no more than a half hour ago, and smiled. "No, Carlo, I daresay the boy is sometimes quite clever."

Artus's face split into a huge smile. "Really?"

"Why are you still here? Run, Artus, RUN!" Tyvian clapped, and Artus took to his heels.

"He won't get past me!" he said as he sprinted out of sight. "You'll see!"

Carlo watched him go. "Never thought I'd see the day."

Tyvian groaned inwardly. "Dare I ask?"

"He reminds me of you, when you were that age. He's taller, though."

Tyvian scowled. "I won't dignify that with a response. Good-bye, Carlo. I'd lay low until the day after tomorrow, at the earliest. Plausible deniability and all that."

Carlo clasped Tyvian's hand in a warm, firm handshake. "If I were you, as soon as I left here I would lay low for the next decade. You're making a lot of enemies tonight, you know."

An explosion shook the fortress wall, and the two men immediately separated. "That's Myreon breeching the main keep—my cue. I've got a revenge to secure, Carlo."

"Good-bye, Tyvian. Look me up sometime when we aren't both embroiled in some kind of international espionage." And with that, Carlo clapped his hands and the coachman leapt to his place. With a crack of a whip and a jingle of sleigh bells, the Verisi pirate and his borrowed sleigh vanished from sight.

Tyvian shook the cramps out of his ring hand, drew out and activated *Chance*, and darted through the open gate. Stepping over the injured bodies of the Defenders, he crossed the courtyard, climbed the narrow stair, and ducked inside Arble Keep. *Tonight*, he told himself, *Hendrieux runs out of places to hide.*

Hool hoisted a screaming Delloran over her head and threw him down the narrow spiral stairs into his fellows. They collapsed under his weight, rolling down into a heap of arms, armor, and weapons. Hool took up the battle-axe of the man she just threw and hacked the three Delloran soldiers apart as they struggled to rise. When they stopped moving, she moved on.

At the foot of the stairs the door stood open. She sniffed the air beyond—there were two men, one behind the door and the other a bit farther in. He probably had a crossbow. Fishing a shield from the heap of slaughtered men, Hool held it out with her left hand and went in, kicking the door so it slammed into the man behind it hard enough to stun him for a moment. The man with the crossbow fired from behind an overturned table, hitting the shield. Hool dropped it and covered the distance between herself and the table in one bound, splitting it and the man behind it in two with a titanic, two-handed swing of the axe. She swung so hard that it embedded itself deep in the floor, so she left it to face the other man, who had recovered from the door slam.

This one had a sword and shield and was circling her cautiously. Hool roared at him, causing him to back away, but she was unarmed, so he quickly advanced again. Hool decided to hold still and wait for him to do something stupid. She didn't have to wait long. The man advanced to striking distance with his sword, assuming his reach exceeded her own, and made a conservative overhand cut with his blade. What he failed to realize was that while she couldn't reach his body from that distance, she *could* reach his hand. Darting past his swing, she seized him by the wrist and yanked him close, bringing her knee into his groin. After that, as he wheezing with pain beneath her, and with his one weapon in her control, killing him was easier than breathing.

There was another explosion; Hool knew that the other attackers of this place were now inside. She also knew Myreon was with them, which meant Reldamar would be nearby. He wasn't as stupid as the wizard, though, so Hool knew he would probably be sneaking in rather than just running around and blowing things up. He would be hunting Hendrieux, just like she was. She had to hurry if she wanted to catch Hendrieux first.

The room she was in now had several exits. Like most buildings she had encountered, everything was needlessly confused by doors and stairs and corridors. Gnoll yurts had one room, as that was all you needed. This place was like a rodent's warren—Hendrieux could be holed up just about anywhere. Reldamar probably already knew where Hendrieux was hiding and was headed directly there. But where?

Hool opened up all the doors in the room, letting the air from the adjoining corridors and rooms flow inside. She breathed deeply, hunting for a scent. In the open air, when she was downwind, she could pick up the trail of a particular person from miles away. Here, however, her sensitive nose was assaulted with the pungent odors of fire, blood, and magic, making a trail almost impossible to pick up without spending a lot of time she didn't have. She needed some kind of marker—something to follow that was distinctive enough to be found through the scent-filled air and that would be found with Hendrieux.

Then she smelled it—the smell of the magic door Hendrieux had used all those times to escape her. Even at this distance the metallic, cold smell burned her nose. It was stronger this time, so Hool knew this door was very important. Hendrieux would be close to it. Yanking her axe free from the floor, she rushed out of the room to track them down.

The keep was in total disarray as Hool passed through it. She saw dead and dying men all over the place, and even more fighting for their lives. Doors were bashed in, tapestries were on fire, and she even saw several Dellorans frozen stiff, their skin white with frost. These smelled like magic. Slaves and miserable humans filled with poisons screamed and stumbled around, getting in the way, dying, fleeing, and adding to the chaos.

Shutting it all out, Hool darted across contested corridors and edged around desperate hand-to-hand battles, her nose leading her deeper and deeper into the aging keep. Finally, when she knew she was beneath the earth, in the dank, cobweb-strewn dungeons and all sounds of battle had faded, she heard Hendrieux speak.

"Hurry," he said, his voice breathless. No one answered.

The smell of magic was so overpowering, Hool

could scarcely get a whiff of Hendrieux, let alone who he was talking to. Crouching in the darkness and letting her ears guide her, she crept closer, her padded hands and feet scarcely disturbing the dust that lay in thick layers around her.

"Why are you stopping?" Hendrieux asked his companion. "They could be just behind us! Come on!"

Hool slipped around a corner and saw him, his blade-thin silhouette clearly ilLumenated by the flickering red light of an oil lantern he held in his left hand, a slender rapier in his right. Next to Hendrieux, resting on the floor, was a chest, its lid partially open. The gold inside produced an orange glow in the lamplight.

Hendrieux ignored the chest and spun around on his heel, searching the dark recesses of the cellar. "Where are you?"

Hool let her growl escape, rumbling up from the depths of her broad chest until it seemed to shake the walls. The color drained from Hendrieux's face, and his whole body trembled as he looked frantically left and right, waving the guttering lamp before him like a holy symbol. "Oh gods! She's here! She's coming for me! Help! Gallo!"

Hool pounced, aiming to knock Hendrieux on his back. He glimpsed her for a brief second, illuminated by his lamp, and screamed. In that instant, she saw the terror in his eyes and her heart leapt at her victory. She would make his skull a trophy, and wear his fingers in a necklace as a warning. His wicked blood would be sweet.

. . . And then Gallo rammed her in the side with an armored shoulder. The force of the blow was enough to knock the air out of Hool's lungs and send her spinning across the room to smash into a wall. Others might have lain there, stunned, but Hool's instincts told her to roll to her feet and draw her axe. Her lungs screamed for air, and she took several, gulping breaths, but didn't take her eyes off the huge armored form of Gallo.

He drew out a heavy bladed falchion with a wickedly spiked hilt, his dead black eyes fixed on the gnoll. "Go," he said to Hendrieux, "Take your gold and flee." His voice betrayed no evidence of emotion.

Hendrieux nodded. "Right. Be careful."

Hool moved to intercept Hendrieux as he hoisted the chest on his shoulder, but Gallo was there to meet her. He slashed his falchion at her in a savage arc, causing her to leap back. He recovered his swing quickly, his armor seeming to have no effect on the smoothness of his movement. More magic, she thought, sourly. It was from Gallo that some of the heavy magic stink was emanating, she was sure.

Hool tried twice more to evade the huge warrior, but there was nothing for it—she would have to go through him to get to Hendrieux. It was dark now, and her sensitive eyes could make out the gleam of his armor. He couldn't see as much—probably only her eyes, which would glow in the distant torchlight.

So Hool closed her eyes. She could hear Gallo's demeanor change as he lost sight of her. He became still, so his armor would not give away his position, but she could still hear his labored breaths, each of which was like a flare in the dark. Silently, she moved to hit him in the flank, aiming to put the iron spike at the back of the battle-axe straight through his breast plate. Then she charged, opening her eyes only at the last moment. Gallo spun to face her but it was too late. Her strike with the axe was perfect—the armor-piercing spike punched straight through the center of his armored chest, no doubt puncturing his heart beneath.

Gallo, though, did not fall. His scarred, masklike face registered no injury. He merely looked at the gnoll before him, clenched his left gauntlet so that some mechanism caused a short, stabbing blade to thrust out from his knuckles, and drove it into her stomach.

Hool lurched away before Gallo could twist the blade, and a hot, searing pain contorted her abdominal muscles. Before she could recover, Gallo followed up his attack with a brutal kick to her wounded midsection, sending the gnoll rolling to one corner of the room. As she panted for breath, whimpering against the pain, the huge warrior yanked the axe out of his chest and broke its thick, oaken handle over one knee like a piece of kindling. "Now you die, dog."

Hool gathered herself and backed away from him, her growls mixing with wheezes of pain. He was wrong. No human was going to kill her. No human was her equal.

The troubling thing, though, was that she wasn't

sure that Gallo was entirely human—not anymore anyway.

Tyvian could see that the Dellorans didn't have much hope of holding out against the onslaught he had arranged against them, but he knew it had very little to do with the average Defender. Certainly, a dozen mageglass-armored men with firepikes helped, but it was the Mage Defender in their midst that was the tipping point.

Mage Defenders were not primarily trained to use magic as an offensive weapon, but Saldor's involvement in the Illini Wars had showed them the worth of giving all of their magi—Defenders especially—certain basic instruction in the more martial aspects of sorcery. Myreon, it seemed, was living proof of how a little training could go a long way.

As Tyvian made his way behind the main body of those storming the keep, he saw numerous examples of Myreon's handiwork. Lode-bolts that had frozen Dellorans solid were only the most obvious signs; there were also a number of Defenders who were untouchable behind numerous blade- and bow-wards, making them into human siege engines behind which their fellows could shelter from the better-trained Dellorans, or all the barred and locked doors that had been casually blasted apart from Myreon's liberal use of The Shattering, which shook the whole keep with its every invocation. Tyvian caught a glimpse of her once,

charging with a pair of Defenders at yet another Delloran strong point, her hair wild and her hands steaming from the power she was channeling, yelling battle
cries that would have been more fitting in the mouths
of historical characters like Finn Cadogan or Conrad
Varner.

Tyvian shook his head as he watched Myreon break
through the Delloran barricade without missing a
stride. *Say what you will about the woman, but don't question her patriotism.*

The ring throbbed with the kind of steady, uncomfortable pain that usually indicated he was being irresponsible and shallow but not precisely evil. Tyvian
shut it out as he went deeper into the keep, in the exact
opposite direction from the fighting. If he were Hendrieux, he thought, that was exactly where he would
go to make his escape. The anygate Hendrieux had
been using was down there, for one thing. Anygates
weren't the kind of thing you would put in the living
room of a castle—dungeons and other internally de-
fensible positions were usually the best.

Tyvian knew he was on the right track when he
heard Hendrieux scream in terror. He doubled his pace
into the dungeon, pulling out the illumite shard and
hanging it on a lanyard around his neck to light his
way. Hool, he guessed, had beaten him to the prey. He
only hoped he could get there before she finished torturing him to death.

He met Hool as she stumbled backward through a
door. Her lips were foaming pink with blood and she

had numerous vicious wounds on her shoulders and arms, plus a serious gut wound that was pouring blood down her hind legs. She spared him barely a glance as she backed away from where she had come from. Tyvian, likewise, backed up—whatever was doing that to Hool was not something he wanted to tackle without some strategic forethought.

Emerging from the doorway came Gallo, clad in the same dirty plate mail, blood likewise pooling at his feet from several wounds, most obviously a massive puncture in his chest that *should* have killed him already, were it not for the incredible life-warding the man had evidently been . . . given? Afflicted with? Tyvian wasn't entirely sure if living with those kinds of injuries forever qualified as a boon. Gallo, an arahk-style falchion in his hand, was apparently unperturbed by his injuries, and his black, flinty eyes never strayed from the gnoll. If he noticed Tyvian, he gave no sign.

"Reldamar!" Hool managed, her voice rough with pain and exhaustion. "Get Hendrieux!"

The ring twinged, making Tyvian pause. "You need help, don't you?"

Hool, growling, dodged a pair of two-handed swings from the giant man, waved him off. "No time! He's running!"

Tyvian's feet tried moving away, but every step led the ring to squeeze tighter on his hand. "Dammit!" he shouted, and produced his two throwing knives. They were long thin blades, and razor sharp—perfect for armor. The first he put through Gallo's sword hand, which was enough to make the beast drop the falchion. The second he slid across the floor to Hool, who snatched it up. "I want those back!" he yelled, and disappeared through the door from which the two combatants had come. The ring complained, but not as strongly as it might have.

Beyond, a long, winding stair led him even more deeply into the old keep's dungeons. He choked on the dust that had been kicked up by Hool's desperate battle with the Delloran giant and followed their trail of destruction until he found what he assumed to be its point of inception. It was an old wine cellar appended to the dungeon, with only a few empty casks remaining. Beyond that, Tyvian could see the reflection of lamplight on the walls of an adjoining room: Hendrieux.

Straightening his tattered shirt and wishing he'd had the forethought to ask Carlo to bring a clean set of clothes with him tonight, Tyvian pulled himself to his full height and walked through the door. Hendrieux was crouching against the far wall, rapier across his knees. His eyes were glazed with a kind of sleepy calm—ink, no doubt—and he grinned faintly as Tyvian entered. "Ah," he said, "I thought this was your doing."

On the wall stood what had to be an anygate, judging from the Astral script etched around the door. Tyvian snorted. "Can't remember the right combination of runes to link to where you want to, can you? I keep telling you, Zaz—ink will rot your brain."

Hendrieux stood up, rapier out, and assumed the en garde position. "The idiots didn't listen to me. They didn't know just how dangerous you are, and they didn't listen."

Tyvian drew *Chance* and mirrored Hendrieux's stance. "You stabbed me in the back, Zazlar. I'm here to return the favor."

"You won't get to see my back, Tyvian! When Gallo finishes with your pet, he'll come back here and the two of us will see you dead, once and for all."

"What makes you think you'll live that long?" Tyvian countered, advancing a pace.

Hendrieux circled away from the wall, changing his blade position, shifting smoothly through a number of Akrallian fencing styles. Tyvian had to remind himself that Hendrieux was no slouch with a blade—it was so easy to underestimate someone as underwhelming as Hendrieux. Tyvian matched him, style for style. "What's the matter, Zaz, can't decide?"

"What about this?" Hendrieux opened with a feint that Tyvian saw coming, but only barely. He batted away a thrust at the last second that would have pierced his liver. The Cool Blue Hendrieux had in his system was dulling the Akrallian's facial expressions, making him hard to read.

Taking note of this, Tyvian pressed back with a series of feints and aggressive beats to knock Hendrieux off-balance. It worked well enough to cause him to stumble back two paces until his back was almost against the anygate. He recovered his defense and grinned. "Barrister? I didn't think you liked Eddonish styles."

Tyvian permitted himself a shrug. "Usually too thuggish for my tastes, but since I'm fencing a thug—"

Hendrieux lunged, Tyvian parried and riposted, injuring the Akrallian in the shoulder. Snarling, Hendrieux locked blades and closed into corps à corps. Instinctively, Tyvian reached for a knife, only to remember too late he had given it to Hool. Grinning with only his teeth, Hendrieux swept Tyvian's forward leg, knocking the smuggler to his knees. Their blades still locked together, Hendrieux pressed down with all his weight, crushing Tyvian to the floor. "What," he hissed. "No knife, Tyvian?"

"What, no sword, Hendieux?" Tyvian countered, and with a twist of his wrist, the unyielding mage-glass blade of *Chance* cut straight through Hendrieux's rapier, leaving him with a broken end.

Eyes wide with shock, Hendrieux fell backward. Tyvian hopped to his feet and lunged, but Hendrieux had already turned his back and fled straight to the anygate. Before Tyvian could intercept him, the Akrallian vanished through the magical doorway.

"Kroth's teeth!" Tyvian swore, and dove through the door after him.

CHAPTER 13

A BITTER END

Hool spat blood and tried to keep her tongue from lolling out as she backed away from Gallo. The slender stiletto Tyvian had given her was dark with the giant warrior's blood, but nothing she did to him seemed to have an effect. She had pierced his body a dozen times—in the armpit, the knees, the abdomen, and the face—and Gallo was just as strong as when the fight began, an eternity before. With every lunge and attack came a price. Gallo's falchion was gone, but his gauntlet-blade was still there, and his fists and feet were each armored bludgeons that had broken her bones and bruised her body.

The bloody, scarred mask of Gallo's face regarded her like a death specter, his hooded, lifeless eyes boring into her. His breath came evenly, if ragged, as though the deadly battle were all part of his ghoulish routine. Hool, meanwhile, was gasping for air, every dodge and step agony on her exhausted body.

She knew now that she could not win. She could not kill this man. She needed only to keep him busy until Tyvian could win. She needed to last a bit longer.

Gallo charged, swinging his blade-hand in an arc intended to cut above Hool's eyes. She ducked low and thrust the stiletto in another chink in his armor. She struck flesh and drew blood, but again there was no benefit for her. Gallo kneed her in the jaw and she fell backward.

Exhausted, her roll back to her feet was too slow, and Gallo's mail-clad boot slammed down on her chest. He leaned his mountainous weight down on her, pushing all the air from her lungs as he drove his gauntlet blade toward her face. Hool caught it with her hands and pushed it away. Gallo, expressionless, went at her again, steadily and inexorably, like a machine pressing grapes. Hool's arms quivered and the blade grew closer and closer to slamming home in her throat.

In a last, desperate ruse, she released his arm, letting the blade slam forward, but twisted her head away at the last instant. It cut along her jowl but hit the stone floor with such force that it shattered. Gallo lost his balance, and Hool placed both of her hind legs against his chest and pushed him off. This time she rolled to her feet quickly, but afterward was dizzy from the exertion.

By then Gallo was up again and met Hool's desperate lunge with a straight arm jab that broke her nose. He put another two uppercuts into her already broken ribs and, grabbing her by the ear, threw her headlong into a musty storage closet. "No more time for you." he announced, and slammed the door closed before she could get back out.

Hool heard the door barred against her as she battered it in the dark, but she was too tired. She sank back against the sacks, bags, and blankets in the closet. Her broken nose twitched at the musty odor that assaulted her, and then, recognizing the scent, she sat bolt upright.

Frantically, she dug through the piles of cloaks and clothing until she found it, her fingers trembling with horror. The world fell away from her and she began to howl with a pain far deeper than any blade of Gallo's could have inflicted.

Tyvian tripped on his way out of the anygate. He was in a woodcutter's yard, probably near the South Inn District, near the edge of Freegate along the road south. The snow had built up to shin-deep, and he hadn't been ready for the shift as he rushed through the door.

Hendrieux was on him in an instant, knocking

Chance away with a frozen log and leaping on his chest. Pressing his thumbs into Tyvian's windpipe, he giggled, the cold winter air puffing out his nostrils like smoke. "Got you! Got you! Ha!"

Tyvian grabbed a heavy handful of the wet snow and stuffed it in Hendrieux's nose and mouth. The Akrallian inhaled some of it and, coughing, loosened his grip long enough for the smuggler to slug him in the solar plexus and roll out from under him.

Casting around for *Chance*, Tyvian suddenly realized an unusual drawback of mageglass weapons—their icelike appearance blended perfectly with the snow on a winter night. "Kroth's bloody goddamned teeth!"

Roaring, Hendrieux bull-charged him, but Tyvian met the attack with a right cross to the jaw that spun the Akrallian around and dumped him on his face.

He took the second he had to recover to scan for a weapon. There, across the yard and half smothered in snow, he saw the unmistakable outline of an axe buried in a chunk of wood. He ran toward it, snow churning around his legs, and wrenched the weapon free. Spinning around, he expected to see Hendrieux right behind him, but he wasn't.

"Look what *I* found." Hendrieux giggled. He had *Chance*.

"Of all the bloody . . ." Tyvian groaned and took a step closer.

Hendrieux twirled the mageglass blade and tossed it from hand to hand. "My goodness, I knew the balance on a blade like this was good, but I never dreamed it was like this! Tyvian, how thoughtful of you to bring me a souvenir to remember your demise by."

Tyvian grimaced and considered tactics. Hendrieux's footwork would be slowed by the snow, but the same went for him. *Chance* would make toothpicks out of the top-heavy wood axe without even trying, and the odds that he could cut past Hendrieux's guard with it were slim to none. This was bad . . . very bad.

Hendrieux advanced, *Chance* at full extension. It was a lure, and Tyvian wasn't stupid enough to take the bait. "You never did tell me why you did it, Hendrieux. Was the money that good?"

Hendrieux performed a lightning quick cut that beheaded Tyvian's axe. "Oh, Sahand pays well, don't you worry. That isn't why I did it, though. I would have done you for half what he offered. Want to know why?"

"Not especially." Tyvian circled Hendrieux and vice versa. The Akrallian could take him at any moment, and they both knew it. They were postponing the inevitable.

"You think you're so smart! You think you're Hann's gift to the human race, with your superior attitude and your fancy education and your refined tastes. That bothered me, but what bothered me more is that everybody else buys it! Next to you, I was the dull sidekick, the fool, the monkey you send on errands! Sahand made me a captain! He gave me respect! When I walk down a street wearing his coat of arms, people back away."

"Are you sure it isn't in disgust?" Tyvian offered. He had an idea. A long shot, but worth a try. He advanced on Hendrieux as though about to strike.

Hendrieux held *Chance* against Tyvian's throat, stopping him cold. "I'm disgusting, am I? Not so disgusting as you'll be when they find you come thaw. Good-bye, Tyvian Reldamar."

Tyvian shrugged. *"Bon chance!"*

The triggering enchantment on the hilt heard the activation words and the blade of the mageglass rapier vanished. Hendrieux's ink-laden expression opened up into genuine shock an instant before Tyvian slammed the heavy axe-handle into the side of his head. He dropped to the ground, spitting teeth and blood.

Tyvian fished *Chance*'s hilt from the snow, reconjured the blade, and pressed it against Hendrieux's chest. "Funny thing just occurred to me—conjurations from a trigger item require the owner to be touching the item in question to make and unmake it. Nothing specifies what *end* you need to be touching. Isn't that fascinating, Zazlar?"

Hendrieux's lips quivered. "Tyvian . . . Tyvian, please, don't do it! Don't kill me, please!"

"What, and miss my one chance to show the world what a captain's post in the Delloran military gets you?" Tyvian grinned and pressed a little harder against Hendrieux's chest.

Hendrieux scrambled backward through the snow. "I'm sorry! I'm sorry! I . . . I'm an idiot! I didn't mean what I said back there . . . about . . ."

"You don't need to tell me you're a liar, Zaz. I'm the fellow you betrayed, remember?"

Tears welled up in the Akrallian's eyes. "I just wanted to make good for myself! I . . . I . . . I didn't mean to betray you. It was the only way! You gotta understand! Please! I'm begging!"

"I know exactly what you're doing. It is quite amusing—please continue." Tyvian raised *Chance*'s tip to his throat. One flick of the wrist and Zazlar would end his days bleeding out in a dirty snowbank in some Freegate slum. Very fitting, Tyvian thought.

Hendrieux began to weep then, shaking his head and mouthing the word "no" over and over, his hands held up in surrender.

"Well," Tyvian sighed, "this is just embarrassing. Good-bye, Zaz."

Tyvian willed his hand to draw the tip of the lethal mageglass blade along Zazlar's throat, but instead a white-hot pain seared his whole sword arm. Screaming, he dropped *Chance*, clutching his arm to his chest. "NOOO! NOT NOW!"

The ring had passed its verdict, and the punishment was severe.

Hendrieux lay on his back for a brief moment, a stunned look on his face. He got up slowly as Tyvian writhed against the ring, expecting a trap. When none came, he laughed.

Picking up *Chance*, he thrust it through Tyvian's thigh, putting the smuggler on his back and in even more pain.

Standing over Tyvian, Hendrieux spat in the smuggler's face. "My lucky day, eh, Tyv?"

Then he was gone, leaving Tyvian to scream in agony and anger both.

Myreon was all alone. She didn't know where the rest of the Defenders had gone, but she knew that most of them had been injured or killed. The warriors of Dellor were rightly feared—their defense had been organized and fierce, even when caught by surprise. Were it not for her own talents with the High Arts, they likely wouldn't have won. As it stood, she hadn't seen another living Delloran for some minutes, but she was performing a room-by-room search, working her way from the roof down. Her body ached and her skull was throbbing from channeling so much energy that she doubted she had the concentration or stamina to invoke another lode-bolt; she resolved to cross that bridge when she came to it.

She had found her way into the basements and subbasements of the old ink-den when she heard the sound—a slow, keening wail, muffled somehow into a barely audible moan. Holding her staff in two hands, Myreon sought out the source of the noise. Was it a Delloran? Was it one of the slaves who hadn't run away? She hoped, whatever it was, her basic grasp of staff fighting would be sufficient to defend herself, if necessary.

She entered a storage cellar that had been ravaged

by an intense brawl. Shelves were smashed, chests thrown about, and blood covered the floor, forming a thick red paste with the ever-present dust. The sound was coming from what was probably a closet, barred from the outside. The wailing, Myreon could tell, was in no way from a human throat.

Hool! She was injured and locked in a closet. Would it be safe to open it? The gnoll had never liked or trusted her. The feeling was certainly mutual, and she had no real desire to surprise an injured monster.

Before she could decide, she heard a crash above her and the organized, heavy tread of what were either more Dellorans or . . .

Myreon backed away from the stairs she had come down just before a trio of Defenders, looking grim and exhausted, tromped into the room. They were led by none other than Tyvian.

"Magus! Come on!" His voice was strangely high-pitched, and he wore an open, honest expression that didn't suit him. Of course—the Shrouding spell.

"Artus?" Myreon made a snap decision and unlocked the closet door, then followed the boy down the stairs. "What are you doing here? You men, why are you following him?"

"Well, Tyvian sent me to guard the back door. Thing is, though, there ain't no back door—just a dirty river—so's I figured that he was just trying to keep me outta trouble, right?" Artus explained as he ran, his adolescent lungs somehow able to breathe while chattering. "Then, I figured, I can help nab Hendrieux. Then

I ran into these fellows, and well, once I convinced 'em that I'm not Reldamar—"

"That's all very well, but why are you coming with us?"

Artus shot her an incredulous look. "I wanna see how this turns out, don't you?"

They charged deeper and deeper into the winding, dark dungeon, their every step moving them closer to their goal. Artus began to lose them, the Defenders and Myreon too exhausted to match the boy's boundless energy. Still, Myreon and her men could follow his footprints in the dust, which eventually brought them to the anygate.

The first thing Myreon noticed was a giant, horrifying monster of a man who could be none other than Sahand's infamous agent, Gallo, easily recognized because of the various warrants the Defenders had issued for him. He was facing the anygate, prodding the runes around the edges in a complex code pattern. Behind him was the comparatively diminutive figure of Zazlar Hendrieux, his face a ruin of bruises and blood. Between the two men she saw a chest of gold coins, half open.

Gallo reacted to the arrival of the Defenders as though he had expected their appearance all along. A quick flick of his wrist saw a tiny, glasslike sphere of antispell strike the first man on the chest. Even as his mageglass armor disappeared, Gallo kicked the chest of gold across the floor so it hit the man in the knees, toppling him.

Gallo was stopped by a blazing firepike blast to the chest by one of the other Defenders. The hit rendered his breastplate concave and smashed him against the far wall of the chamber but, impossibly, Gallo seemed otherwise unfazed by the attack. His ruined voice could be heard over the roar of churning air kicked up by the magic blast. "Hendrieux, get through!"

Hendrieux, though, found himself flanked by the two other Defenders. He immediately dropped the mageglass rapier in his hand and raised his arms over his head. "I surrender! Mercy! Mercy!"

Gallo was not so docile. Recovered from the blow he received, he darted for the anygate, snagging Hendrieux by the arm as he ran past.

"Stop!" Artus put himself in Gallo's path, a sword in his hand, but the Delloran let the boy's blade clatter harmlessly off his armor and straight-armed him into the ground without breaking stride. Before Artus could recover, Gallo had dragged Hendrieux and himself through the anygate and vanished from sight.

"Dammit!" Artus said, wiping the blood from his nose and standing up. "They're getting away, Myreon! Come on!"

She held up her hands, "Not so fast, boy! You don't know where that goes!"

"But they're escaping!" Artus countered, and leapt through the half-open door.

"Artus!" But he was gone. Myreon stared at the gate, face grim. If the boy was walking into a trap and if they thought he was Tyvian . . .

"Ma'am," one of the Defenders said, grabbing her arm. "Let him go."

Myreon shook her head. "If Sahand gets his hands on him . . . he's just a boy."

"No ma'am," the Defender countered. "He's a criminal."

Myreon gave the man a long, hard look. Then, holding her breath, she stepped through the anygate before any of the other Defenders could move to stop her.

Body aching, blood running down his legs, Tyvian crawled back to the door in the woodcutters yard and opened it. Within was a simple storage room, filled with icicles formed from a leaky roof. "What? Dammit!"

He closed the door and opened it again—nothing. He opened it a third time—still the damned storage room. Somebody had reset the gate. Tyvian lay back in the snow, staring at the sky, and had to laugh. He held up his ring hand. "You've really done it now. See what your moralistic nonsense has earned us? We're bleeding to death in a snowbank. Congratulations, ring."

Tyvian knew he was as good as dead. Though his free hand pressed feebly against the deep leg wound, he could feel the blood spurting out too quickly to be stopped entirely. "Kroth. Kroth's bloody teeth."

He imagined Eddereon *was* there, standing over him in the snow, that odd, warm expression on his face, like a father watching his son learn to ride. The big Northron pressed his broad hand to Tyvian's leg, and it was filled with the most incredible warmth. Tyvian felt suddenly stronger, better. He managed to sit up.

Eddereon was there. Eddereon *was* wearing that ridiculous expression. Tyvian scowled at him. "So, you can bring people back to life?"

Eddereon nodded. "So could you, if you felt something strong enough."

"Aren't you even the least bit disappointed in my recent attempted murder of a former friend?"

Eddereon nodded, snowflakes shaking loose from his beard. "Yes, I am. I understand, though. Accepting the ring takes a long time."

Tyvian frowned. "Did you heal me entirely?"

"Your nose is still broken, your leg will bleed a bit, and your shoulder is . . . well, how does it feel?"

"Like hell."

Eddereon nodded. "There you are. I could heal you all the way, but some pain will do you good for what is to come."

"Are you an augur now? You can tell the future?"

"The boy, Artus, is in danger. As is the mage, Myreon Alafarr."

Tyvian snorted, pulling himself unsteadily to his feet. "Hang the mage. She wants to make me into public art."

Eddereon sat on the woodpile. "She is a good woman doing what she thinks is right. You can't fault her for that."

"I can, have, and will."

"Hool needs you, too." Eddereon added. "She is in a great deal of pain."

"Well, can you call me a coach, too? Because I don't see myself limping through a snowy night to find them."

Eddereon pointed at the anygate. "The Defenders and their Master will be coming through there soon enough. Don't trust him, Tyvian. He isn't who he says he is."

Tyvian watched as the Northron stood up to leave. "Do you know who he's working for?"

"He is a member of the Sorcerous League. They want you for the ring on your finger, just as they wanted me in the past. Don't let them have you. The ring's secrets are not for them to know." With that, Eddereon hopped the fence of the woodcutter's yard and was gone.

Tyvian scowled after him, fiddling with the immovable ring, when he heard a soft *whump* behind him—the anygate had connected. He limped to it and threw it open before the Defenders on the other side could come through.

He emerged into the same room he had been before, deep below Arble Keep. Master Tarlyth with a quartet of Defenders stood there, their firepikes pointed at his face. The Master Defender's tone was dry. "I take it your revenge didn't go as planned?"

Tyvian looked down at his wet, bloodstained body.

He was careful not to touch his ring. "Did the bastard get away, then?"

Tarlyth nodded. "Yes. Yes he did. Magus Alafarr and your . . . associate went after him."

Tyvian noted *Chance* where it lay on the floor and was thinking about how to grab it before the facts hit him. "What . . . Artus? Artus *went after them?*"

"I somehow doubt you will ever see them again, Master Reldamar," Tarlyth remarked, and snapping his fingers, called *Chance* into his open hand. "You are hereby under arrest."

Tyvian's shoulders slumped—that was it. There was no way out of this one. He extended his hands to be shackled. The Defenders weren't gentle.

As they led him up and out of the cellar, limping and exhausted, he heard Hool howling. The long, mournful sound slid down the stairs and through the winding corridors of the cellar, and Tyvian felt a chill leak through his bones like something greasy and foul. This was not a howl of pain . . . at least, not of physical pain.

They found her lying in the middle of the courtyard, facedown, a small, fuzzy creature nestled next to her, which whimpered in a staccato rhythm to mirror its mother's long, grief-stoked wails. Tyvian, seeing the weeping wounds and foul injuries inflicted on the tiny pup, felt his heart fill with something unfamiliar—something painful and hard, as though fluid were pumped inside until the pressure couldn't bear it. He looked for a word for the feeling and he found it—sorrow.

Tarlyth regarded her and grunted. "She's found one of her pups," he said.

Tyvian's voice was hollow. "Not just one."

Hool arched her back, head pointed to the sky, and howled for all her worth. They could now all see what was in her lap.

It was a fur pelt.

CHAPTER 14

THE WAGES OF GALLANTRY

Myreon stepped out of the anygate and into ankle-deep snow and air so frigid it made her gasp. This chill, however, was nothing compared to the one that ran up her spine a split second after she looked around and saw where she was: an armed Delloran camp pitched beneath the soaring domes and cracked arches of ancient ruins. She could see out past the pickets and over the whole of the narrow valley in which Freegate sprawled—they had to be thousands of feet up, well beyond the notice of anybody in the city. The Dellorans could have been here for years and nobody would know.

A cry of pain ripped Myreon out of her shock and brought her back into the present. She saw a group of six men, armored and wearing heavy wool and fur cloaks, standing in a circle around the prone form of a man who looked, for all the world, like a bruised and battered Tyvian Reldamar, except it wasn't. It was Artus, and the Dellorans were beating him to death.

The boy's voice, incongruous in Tyvian's lips, was frayed and hoarse, "No, please . . . I surrend—" A Delloran boot hit him in the throat, causing him to gag.

The owner of the boot was a man twice Reldamar's weight wielding a wicked dagger with a serrated blade. He knelt down as the other men kept kicking Artus and pressed its blade to the boy's face. "Payback time."

Myreon's heart was pounding—six men, many more nearby. As she stood there, the wind fluttering the strips of her tattered, patched cloak like streamers behind her, her golden hair wild, her staff glowing with power, she knew time was of the essence. Slamming her staff into the snowy ground, she released as much anger as she could into the Shattering. The big Delloran's dagger disintegrated with a fiery pop, sending blazing shrapnel in every direction. It scorched Artus's face, but that was better than having his throat cut, and it got the soldiers' attention. *All* of them.

Tents opened, men rushed for their weapons, orders were issued. Myreon heard them saying, "Staff at the gate!" and "Activate your wards!"

Myreon spread her arms, thrust out her chest, and hoped her voice wouldn't crack. She channeled the tiny amount of Lumenal energy given off by all the living bodies nearby into a blazing flare of light that burst from the end of her staff. The shadowy camp was bathed in a harsh white glow, causing many men to shield their eyes. "By authority of the Defenders of the Balance, I hereby order you to drop your weapons and release your prisoner or face the full weight of my Art."

The Dellorans wasted no time in parley. Four of them advanced on her at a near sprint, weapons drawn. They planned to take her simultaneously from either side, and the plan was a good one. Myreon only had an instant to react, and she did by capitalizing on the Lumenal ley her staff flare had established to release a sunblast at one group of men. The blazing white bolt again lit the camp as bright as noon, and the two men struck recoiled in horror, their cloaks aflame and their faces seared.

The second pair lost a man as well, who fell to his knees clutching his eyes and screaming. The second man, though temporarily blinded by the flash, had the discipline to follow through with a lunge, his short blade barely missing Myreon as she retreated out of reach. He retracted into a defensive stance, but she could see that his eyes were still unfocused and blind, making him vulnerable. She quickly swept the man's forward foot with her staff, knocking him off balance, and then followed the attack with a hard, overhand chop with the full length of the magestaff. The man put his arms up reflexively to guard his head, and My-reon's strike shattered his forearm just below his sword guard. The man screamed, but not before the butt of her staff hit him in the groin, felling him.

Adrenaline surging through her veins, Myreon strode toward the two remaining Dellorans standing over the whimpering body of Artus. She channeled the Lumen again into a simple glow-glamour, caus-ing white light to pour from her eyes and an unearthly Aura to surround her like a shield. She shouted at the two men and the platoons of armed allies behind them, trying to hide the weakness in her knees and the tremor in her arms. "Cease and desist—this is your final warning!"

The assembled Delloran host paused. Crossbows were shouldered, spears were leveled, but nobody ad-vanced and nobody shot her. They hadn't called her bluff. A tense silence, broken only by the moan of the wind cutting through the broken tunnels and empty galleries of the ancient ruins, fell over the camp.

A booming voice rose from the assembled guards. "My congratulations to your trainers, girl. In my expe-rience, courage is the hardest thing to teach." A broad-shouldered man in a hood moved through the cordon of spears surrounding Myreon.

Myreon pointed her staff at him. "Stand back!"

The man barked a harsh laugh and pulled back the hood, revealing a slablike face, pinched and cracked with a mixture of anger and disgust. Myreon didn't need to see the iron circlet on his brow to recognize him—Banric Sahand, Mad Prince of Dellor. "Are you sure you know what you're doing, girl? I've bested much better magi than you." Myreon backed away from Artus as the Mad Prince came to face her from a few dozen paces away. "Is Reldamar worth that much to you?"

She took a deep breath, trying to still her panicking heart. She felt like her entire body was quivering with a peculiar mix of fear and elation. "You are far from home, Your Grace, and in violation of the treaty of Calassa."

"I didn't sign that treaty; I was freezing on a mountainside at the time." Sahand stomped a foot and, with a violent, brutish series of arm motions, cast a blazing ball of Fey energy at Myreon, forcing the mage to throw herself to the ground to dodge it. The fireball struck an ancient statue behind her, which burst into an ear-shattering explosion that obliterated a half-dozen tents nearby and set the whole area aflame. Roaring, Sahand came at her like a bull.

Myreon climbed to her feet in time to meet his charge. She put her staff up to parry what she assumed would be a physical blow, but Sahand's fist stopped just short of her and then opened as he uttered the harsh word, "AKRKH!" A blossom of orange flame burst from the Mad Prince's palm and struck her in the chest. She felt the air pummeled from her lungs as she was sent hurtling through space. She crashed through the burning doorway of a tent and slammed upside-down against a rack of pots and pans. She collapsed on the floor in a heap, the world a spinning, burning sea of red fire, black smoke, and white pain.

Myreon found, to her surprise, that her staff was still in her hand. Struggling to her feet, the smoke and fire stinging her eyes and choking her nostrils, she focused her attention on drawing a perfect circle on the dirt floor and then striking the exact center with the butt of her staff. The icy-cold Dweomeric blast boomed outward, extinguishing the fire and blowing what was left of the tent into the air. Breathing clean, cold air again with grateful gasps, Myreon came again to stand before Sahand.

The Mad Prince was still there, waiting for her. "Hmph. Not a quitter. I like that in a woman."

Myreon gathered as much Dweomeric energy as she could from the cold, wintry mountain air and sent a lode-bolt at Sahand so large it left icicles on the ends of the mage's fingers. Sahand spun himself in a quick circle and reflected the bolt back at her. She did the same, this time sending it back with enough speed that Sahand was forced to duck out of its way. Behind him the assembled masses of Delloran soldiers threw themselves to the ground in a panic. Myreon permitted herself a tight smile. "You forget that we Defenders have been trained to duel."

"I don't forget things, girl," Sahand grumbled, and struck the earth with another Fey invocation that caused the ground to shake and gouts of flame to shoot toward Myreon. She braced herself and worked a Dweomeric dispel that would counter it, but the sheer power of Sahand's casting was such that she was seared and smoking even after the spell had been dissipated.

Sahand followed that spell up with another, and another, each of them such violently powerful Fey spells that Myreon could barely shield them with Dweomeric energy, even though they were fighting on a cold winter mountain slope—ideal Dweomeric conditions. Exhausted from her efforts to dispel the spells, her breath came in ragged, gasping bursts and she had her hands on her knees. Sahand, she noted, had barely broken a sweat.

"Trained to duel, eh?" he said with a chuckle. "You, girl, are a sorry excuse for a mage. Look at you— panting like a dog, waiting, no doubt, for some kind of opening or mistake." Behind him at a healthy distance, his men chuckled in kind. They made lewd gestures and catcalls.

Myreon threw a weak lode-bolt at Sahand, but the Mad Prince batted it away contemptuously. "That's *it*? This is what they taught you in Saldor? Ha! Get over here, kneel, and beg me to spare your life."

The jeers doubled at the prospect of Myreon kneeling. The laughter seemed to press in on her from all sides. She realized she was surrounded now—no way to get back toward the anygate. Trapped.

"You . . . really are . . . mad . . ." she said between breaths, and used her staff to pull herself to her feet. "Let . . . Reldamar . . . go . . ."

Sahand drew a knife and seized Artus by the hair, dragging him to his knees in front of her. "You want him so badly, I'll give him to you. What part do you want first? The ear? The eye?" He let the tip of his blade waver from spot to spot on Artus's disguised face.

"Leave him be," Myreon growled, and did her best to cast a fireball, but she was so exhausted the spell barely made enough heat to light a candle.

Sahand gave her a cruel grin. "I don't take orders, girlie." He slid the blade of his knife along Artus's face, sending a rivulet of blood running down his cheek. Artus screamed himself awake.

"Tyvian!" Myreon shouted. "Tyvian, stay calm! I've . . . I've got things under control. I'll save you."

Sahand's guards leveled spears and advanced on Myreon from all sides. Sahand held his knife up so it caught the light of the burning tents. The blade was slick with blood. "I'm not a patient man, Defender. Surrender or I cut off something that won't grow back."

Artus's voice blubbered between Tyvian's swollen lips. "D-D-Don't do it. Don't . . . please . . ."

Myreon felt sick; he was just a boy. Her pride wasn't worth his death. "O-Okay. Leave him be. I . . . I surrender."

Sahand grinned, and Myreon could have sworn his teeth were pointed, like a beast's. "Kneel, Defender."

Myreon was flanked by two Dellorans, and she threw down her staff and knelt. "I give up."

"Not fast enough," Sahand sneered, and with a quick, savage motion of his knife, cut off Artus's left earlobe. Artus screamed and fainted.

Myreon struggled to stand, "You . . ."

Sahand shook his head and laughed. "For a girl who likes to quote the Treaty of Calassa at me, you don't know your history, do you? I'm not to be trusted." He looked at his men and nodded.

Myreon felt the white-hot pain of a blade entering her back and the blood bubble to her lips. She then pitched forward onto the icy cobblestones and passed out.

Sahand kicked the unconscious Defender onto her back and snorted. "That's got to be Alafarr."

One of his men put his sword on Myreon's breastbone and prepared to thrust. "Finish her, milord?"

Sahand thought about it—much as he liked the idea of killing the Defender here and now, there might be uses for her if she survived the knife wound . . . and uses for her if she didn't, come to think of it. "Pick them both up and throw them in the dungeon."

"Both, milord?" one of the men asked.

"Question an order again and you're dead," Sahand snapped, and added, "Clean up the camp and prepare for an attack. The Defenders know we're here."

CHAPTER 15

CONSCIENCE MAKES A COMEBACK

By dawn, the snow stopped but Hool had not. She would not be moved from her place of mourning and the new Defenders that arrived with the break in the storm were not inclined to try. Her howls were hoarse and pitiful, each one as filled with raw pain as the first had been. It gave a strange, tragic air to the dirty work that had to be done. Bodies were loaded onto carts, fires extinguished before they could spread, blood washed from the halls. The Defenders who had fallen in the siege were laid in the yard alongside the grieving Hool. Tyvian wondered if their surviving Defenders had done this to appropriate some of Hool's grief for their own purposes. It was a strange thought, for him. He was having a lot of strange thoughts that morning.

His leg bandaged, Tyvian sat on the back of a cart, watching the cleanup, his wrists and ankles in shackles. He had his back to where Hool sat, her living pup still by her side, pouring her mother's agony out on all to hear. With every howl, he felt himself wince. To his surprise, the ring had nothing to do with it.

Is it my fault Hool's pup was killed? He found himself wondering. The answer should have been obvious—how could it have been? He had no knowledge of Sahand's plan for them—he still didn't have that knowledge—so he couldn't be held responsible.

Then why did he feel like this?

Another howl caused him to stiffen, and he tried to focus his attention on the designs embroidered into the shawl worn by his guard—a Defender disguised, just as the rest of the reinforcements had been, in simple clothing that wouldn't have stuck out in the Blocks or Corpse Alley. It had worked thus far only because it was the Blocks and Corpse Alley, and no watchmen would come down here anyway unless directly bribed to do so. Hendrieux had chosen Sahand's urban hideout well.

Tyvian found himself, bizarrely, wishing Myreon were there for him to talk to. She was a good sounding board, if nothing else. He could tell her that he was feeling empathy for a gnoll, and she would inform him that he was a lying, cheating, scheming monster who was making it all up. Somehow that would have helped pull the stitch out of his guts that had rested there ever since he saw the dirty fur pelt in Hool's trembling hands. Somehow.

The idea of her seeking out her children was never real to me, Myreon. It was an abstraction—a foothold on her personality that allowed me to use her, just like I use you or Artus or . . . well, everybody.

Another howl, another bucket of ice water poured down Tyvian's spine. It hardly mattered what Myreon thought anymore; she was almost certainly dead. Artus was dead, too, the poor fool. Running through an anygate and probably straight into Sahand's camp— typical Artus. More heart than brains. To think the boy died at the hands of Banric Sahand . . .

"Dammit," Tyvian snarled to himself. Wasn't he going to let Hendrieux kill the boy no more than a month or so ago? Gods, that seemed a long time past. Had he become so attached to Artus? To Hool? To even Myreon?

He had to be. Why else would he be sitting here, moping over how sad Hool looked and how terrible Artus's death had likely been and how much he actually seemed to miss bantering with Myreon. The damned ring had addled his brains. It had taken the calculating, cold, efficient man of the world he had been and made him into a . . . a . . . a what?

Tyvian leaned back and looked at the sky, wincing again at another one of Hool's wails. He let all his plotting and scheming of the last few weeks unfold in his mind's eye. How had he come here? How had it changed him? Was he different?

The revelations of last night came back to him with full force; he lay, half paralyzed with thought, running the scenario through his head. The ring had wound up on his finger because Eddereon wanted it there. Eddereon thought he was "worthy" of it, whatever that meant. It was Eddereon who tipped off the Defenders of Galaspin Tower to his own and Hendrieux's spirit-engine operation—easy enough. Galaspin Tower meant Tarlyth, and Tarlyth meant two things: first, that Myreon was the Defender dispatched, and second, that Tarlyth had given this information to the Sorcerous League. That would explain how Hendrieux knew, since Sahand was known in underworld circles to be a member of the League, even if most people didn't believe the rumors. Tarlyth informed Sahand of the Defender attack, and Sahand told Hendrieux to stay away. Being the dunce that he is, Hendrieux set Tyvian up for a bigger fall than it would have been otherwise.

Where did that leave him? Tyvian wondered. He wasn't sure, but something else was forming in the back of his mind, along with Sahand, Tarlyth, Theliara— all members of the Sorcerous League. Sahand was in Freegate messing with something in the old ruins of Daer Trondor—probably the old power sink sitting on the Saldor/Galaspin/Freegate ley line. To do this, he needed a lot of help. He got Hendrieux to kidnap alchemists, thaumaturges, and the like; he used Theliara and her menagerie to supply him with wild animals, for some reason. Tarlyth was probably involved in keeping the Defenders off Sahand's back while he did all this.

Enter Tyvian himself and the damned ring. Tarlyth and Theliara wanted *him* and the ring on his finger. What did Sahand want with that power sink, though? What was the Mad Prince's piece in all of this? How did it fit, and why had the three members started to pit their resources against one another? What did it mean for himself, wounded on a cart, with no friends left but a devastated gnoll?

Everything suddenly clicked. It happened so quickly that it made Tyvian gasp. "Gods . . . I've been blind!"

Sahand was a monster. He was a colossal, horrifying tyrant who ruled his miserable, winter-locked principality with a brutality unmatched by modern rulers. Just over a quarter century ago, shortly after wresting control of Dellor by way of a bloody coup, Sahand had waited for the Duke of Galaspin and his armies to be called across the sea to defend Illin from the Kalsaaris, and then he invaded the defenseless Galaspin countryside. Villages that hadn't surrendered were burned. Men who would not kneel were executed, often in sight of their children, and then the women were ordered raped. It was said that the Mad Prince, as he quickly became known, wrote a letter to the Duke of Galaspin, assuring him that if he or his bannermen ever set foot in their home country again, he would catapult the duke's newborn grandchildren from the walls of the city. When the duke sent General Conrad Varner to free his suffering land, the Mad Prince did exactly as he promised. A memorial stood to the young princess to this day—an obelisk of granite, surrounded by gardens, standing six hundred yards from the walls of Galaspin. Tyvian's face twisted in disgust just thinking about it.

Tyvian knew he was many things, but he was *not* Sahand. He was not the kind of person who tortured people for fun. He did not seek to master perverse sorcery. He did not starve a whole country just so he could horde gold for another war attempt. He did not hurl infants from catapults. He did not torture, murder, and skin what were, for all intents and purposes, someone's *children*. He, Tyvian Reldamar, might be a criminal, but he had *standards* . . .

. . . *which was precisely why he hadn't been thinking clearly on this matter.*

He hit the muddy ground of the courtyard at a limping, half run, half hop, his guard trailing behind. "Hey! Where do you think you're going, mate?"

The smuggler was surprised at how angry he was, suddenly. His hands shook so badly he had to ball them into fists. He planted himself in front of Hool and pointed at her forcefully. "Snap out of it, dammit!"

Hool's pup growled at him, its hackles raised, and stepped between Tyvian and his mother.

Tyvian ignored it and kept addressing Hool. "Are you going to sit here and weep for the rest of your life, or what?"

"Leave the beast alone, Reldamar!" The Defender who had followed him across the courtyard grabbed Tyvian by the shoulder.

Tyvian pushed him flat on his back in the mud. "Unhand me! You think I'm a monster? You think Sahand and I are the same, eh? Well we *aren't*. I am *not* that man, and I will *not* be bested by him."

The Defender stared at him, open-mouthed, and then climbed to his feet, calling for backup. "The bloody smuggler's lost his marbles!"

Tyvian grabbed Hool by the ears and pulled her face so he could look her in the eyes. They had lost their usual, predatory luster—they were dull, like tarnished coins. "Is this it for you, then, Hool? You're going to give up? *Snap out of it!*"

Tyvian could hear the mud sloshing as the guards closed in. Hool blinked, her eyes focusing on Tyvian as though he had just appeared. "Brana . . . Brana needs medicine. He is hurt."

"Hool, in eight seconds I'm going to be dragged away by these men. After that happens, get some medicine in my flat—top shelf in the kitchen cupboard—and then head for the old ruins in the mountains. Sahand is there, Hool. He *killed* your pup, do you understand? He is planning on killing many, many more."

Two men wrapped their arms through Tyvian's armpits while a third hit him in the back of the knees. After he collapsed, they dragged him off. Hool watched, her ears alert. Tyvian smiled at her, said, "We haven't lost yet!"

In his youth, Tyvian concluded, Master Tarlyth had probably been a mountain of muscle. He had hands like garden rakes, each finger thicker than most people's thumbs. Tyvian wondered how a man with hands like that could achieve the rank of Master in the Arcanostrum, let alone Master Defender.

Let alone while being a traitor.

"Tea, Master Reldamar?" Tarlyth asked quietly. They were sitting in a private room in Arble Keep, a flimsy card table between them. The scent of blood and ash still hung in the air, despite the shutters of the narrow window having been thrown open. The floor had splinters of broken furniture and a few bloodstains, and Tyvian thought the presence of Tarlyth's silver tea set in the midst of all this was marvelous. It was just the kind of irony he was coming to associate with the Master Defender.

"No thank you," he said, "I've no interest in what you consider to be good tea."

"You're in quite a lot of trouble, son. I'd expect a bit more deference." Tarlyth considered Tyvian with his heavy lidded eyes.

Tyvian met his stare evenly. "I don't really think I'm in half as much trouble as you pretend, actually."

"You stand accused of murder, smuggling, and dealing in proscribed magical texts. This doesn't seem like a lot of trouble to you?"

"It's odd, you know, sending Myreon 'Magus Errant' and then you showing up personally to rescue her. I mean, the whole point of Magus Errant is so the Arcanostrum coffers don't have to pay for the long-shot activities of its agents. Yet here you are, risking a diplomatic incident, getting your men killed in combat—not to mention committing career suicide—just so you can rescue a junior mage Defender and capture a smuggler."

Tarlyth sat back in his rickety chair. "I don't see why it's any of your business what I do or why. Especially not now."

Tyvian smirked. "What *are* you doing here, Tarlyth? What's the *real* reason?"

"I brought you here to discuss what is about to happen to you, Reldamar, not indulge your petty inquiries." Tarlyth frowned.

"Forgive me, Master Tarlyth, but I *know* what is going to happen to me already."

Tarlyth's frown deepened. "Oh?"

Tyvian snorted. "Shall we dispense with the charade—I'm finding myself in an impatient mood and, while I would ordinarily enjoy our little parry-riposte of innuendo and veiled threats, let me be explicit. I know you have no intention of handing me over to Saldor for punishment; I know that you and Sahand, along with Angharad tin'Theliara Hanim and who knows *who* else, are in collusion on some grand project Sahand is heading up. I know this because you, Master Ultan Tarlyth of Galaspin Tower, are secretly a member of the Sorcerous League."

The teacup fell out of Tarlyth's hand and shattered

on the floor. Tyvian watched the big wizard visibly compose himself, locking his jaw and clamping his hands on the flimsy armrests of his chair as though restraining his body from some kind of emotional detonation. When he finally spoke, it was with a calm so artificial that Tyvian could practically smell the fiery rage burning just underneath. "You claim to know quite a lot."

Tyvian didn't so much smile as show his teeth. "Let's not pretend all that I have thus far presented is inaccurate. Your reaction to my accusations alone confirms it—for a man living a double life, you really are an atrocious liar. Now, let's see—getting back to what you intend to do with me: you can't kill me, because you want *this*." Tyvian held up his ring hand and noted how Tarlyth's eyes lingered on the plain iron band. "And you can't hand me over to the authorities because the *League* wants the ring, too, and the Arcanostrum will discover the presence of this rather sophisticated sorcerous artifact the very *moment* I am processed for incarceration preceding my trial. Obviously, once Saldor gets its hands on me, you and your League cronies won't."

Tarlyth's face was boiling like a thundercloud, but still his voice kept its artificial calm. "That's what I can't do, but have you considered what it is I *can* do?"

"Yes, I was just getting to that. Sahand's behavior has been the primary clue to the whole affair, actually. He *isn't* interested in me; quite the opposite, in fact—he's been trying to keep me out of his hair this entire time. He's had Hendrieux purchasing exotic wild animals, kidnapping thaumaturges and warlocks, and he's been using some very expensive magical hardware. Brymm, biomancy, and the bribes necessary to obtain exclusive use of the Phantoms' own private slaving anygate are, none of them, inexpensive enterprises. When we couple that with the secrecy he's been laboring under, one can only presume that his project, whatever it is, is both very important to the League as a whole and to him personally.

"Sahand simply doesn't have the contacts in Freegate to pull this off alone—his occupation of the city earned him a permanently bloody reputation, and he'd need assistance from the League to get started. So, you help him. Why? Well, because what he's creating, as I said, is important to all of you. Important enough that one of your number—Theliara—has gone so far as to set up shop here in Freegate and *bring along a menagerie of wild animals and a few Artificers*. Am I to believe she would just hand them over to Sahand's agents if there *weren't* some kind of connection between the two of them? Nonsense."

Tarlyth's massive, marble-sized knuckles were turning white on the armrests. "You're rambling."

"All the more reason to not interrupt. Now, all this brings us to your presence here with a pack of Defenders. On the one hand, Myreon and I gave you the perfect excuse to come—no doubt this might end up looking quite heroic of you if you pull it off—but you're *also* here because you have questions for Sahand, questions probably along the lines of, 'Are you really doing what we think you're doing?' These are questions, you feel, probably best asked over the blazing tip of a firepike. Am I right?"

Tarlyth's nostrils were flaring so widely, Tyvian was fairly certain he could stuff his arm up to the elbow inside them. "Sahand can't be trusted. I've said so all along."

Tyvian nodded. "A wise stratagem, and one no doubt reinforced by your experience as both a League member *and* a Master Defender."

"Well deduced, Master Reldamar—I see your reputation for intelligence is not exaggerated. That still doesn't explain what it is I intend to do with you." Tyvian opened his mouth, but Tarlyth held up a hand. "No, please—allow me to confess, as you have said enough already. I intend to place you in Astral stasis in this room, where you will remain until it is convenient for one of my colleagues to collect you later, after I and my Defenders have dealt with Sahand and quietly left the city. You, of course, will seem to have managed another miraculous escape from this room—your reputation for elusiveness has it's drawbacks for you, you see—so you will be in the League's possession with no one being the wiser. If you were to clear away some of this debris on the floor, you would find the veta already drawn and ready to receive you—I need only incant the spell. So, as charming as this conversation has been, I see no reason to continue it."

Tarlyth stood up and spread his arms. His staff materialized in his hand with a snap of his fingers.

Tyvian frowned at him. "I really wouldn't do that, if I were you."

A cold wind blew in from the window as Tarlyth's staff began to glow. The first syllables of the incantation began to slither past his lips—ugly, confusing sounds that seemed to bend the mind and hurt the ears. Tyvian stood as well. "Are you familiar with the concept of blackmail, Magus?"

Tarlyth froze in place; the power he was channeling was sucked from the room with an audible pop. "What?"

"An associate of mine—you remember the fellow in the sleigh with the watchmen from last night, of course—well, he is a rumormonger of sorts; not only does he know you are here, but I informed him about your collusion with the League before entering this place. I furthermore told him that were I not to return to his office by tomorrow morning, he should send a letter detailing all of this to the Lord Defender in Saldor. I imagine you'll deny it, of course, but I think you'll find Carlo is quite good at acquiring corroborating evidence if it suits his need. He *is* the secret Guild-master of the Phantoms, after all."

"You're bluffing." Tarlyth said, his polite tone slipping, replaced with an almost canine growl.

Tyvian shrugged. "Unlike the rest of the rubes in your organization, I know for a fact that magi—even *Masters*—have no ability to detect lies. Feel free to call my bluff, if you are so convinced. It would seem to me, however, that you have a great deal more to lose than I do if you wind up being wrong."

A vein bulged in Tarlyth's forehead. His jaw was clenched so tight, Tyvian was concerned his teeth might crack. "I should kill you right now."

"No, you really shouldn't. Allow me to inform you, instead, of what we're *going* to do."

"What?"

Tyvian smiled. "You are going to call a meeting of the Sorcerous League and *I* am going to attend it with you."

CHAPTER 16

IN THE ICY CLUTCHES

Artus didn't want to open his eyes. As long as he kept them closed, he could keep on imagining that this was all a nightmare. If he opened them, he knew that he'd start crying, and he didn't want to cry. He had to be strong and clever, like Tyvian. That was, after all, who they thought he was.

His whole body was bruised and battered, but if he didn't move, he felt all right. The only thing that hurt then was his face—the places where Sahand had cut him burned in the frigid air. He was lying on his back, his arms splayed out to his sides, on a floor so hard and cold that it had to be solid ice. He knew Myreon was in the cell, too, which was another reason he didn't open his eyes—he didn't think he was ready to see her dead eyes staring at him.

Artus had no concrete idea of how long it had been since his arrival, since he was fairly certain he had passed out at least twice during the whole thing. In any event, it seemed a long time. Though he did his best to keep his breathing slow, his heart was pounding in his chest so loudly that he swore he heard it echo off the walls. Something terrible was about to happen to him. Something more terrible than anything that had ever happened before. He kept imagining what that might be, despite his best efforts not to, and that only made his heart race faster and his stomach churn more fiercely. He wanted to vomit with terror.

The gate to the dungeon or prison or wherever he was rumbled open suddenly, the sound making him jump. His body screamed in protest at the movement and he couldn't help but cry out. From beyond the gate, he heard a man's voice grumble, "Sounds like he's awake."

The second voice was higher pitched and sharper. "Well then he gets a show, don't he? C'mon, gimme a hand with this one."

Artus squeezed his eyes shut. He didn't want them to see the terror in his face. He didn't want them to talk to him. Instead, he lay very still as he listened to the two Dellorans drag some kind of wheelbarrow or cart closer and closer until, at last, they stopped no more than a few feet away. He then heard the sound of the men grunting and groaning as they maneuvered some kind of large load somewhere, and then one said, "Steady, now—first nail's the hardest, right?"

A hammer pinged off the end of a metal spike, and a new voice joined the chorus—a weak, rattling moan that escalated with each strike of the hammer until it became a steady, wailing gasp of agony. "Shut up, you," one of the men growled. "Or I'll put one through your feet, eh?"

The wailing voice deflated into a low, barely audible sob until another spike was hammered home, and then the wailing intensified again. The Dellorans cursed the wailer with threats and vivid profanity before they went away. When the gate closed again, all Artus could hear was the slow, hiccuping sobs of the newcomer.

Artus swallowed hard and then opened his eyes. He was looking up at vaulted stonework no more than seven feet up at its highest point. Icicles dripped from cracks between the stones, and he could barely see his breath in the flickering white light of a nearly dead illumite shard dangling in the hall beyond his cell. This light was freely admitted, since his cell was caged off from the corridor by a metal grate bolted into the stonework, and in the grate a sliding door was mounted, a heavy iron padlock holding it closed. The corridor beyond was narrow and gradually sloped up towards where the guards had entered and left. Artus knew it was that direction, though he couldn't see the gate, thanks to the curve of the corridor as it wound up and away from him. He noted that it also went down as well—there were apparently deeper and darker cells than the one he was in.

As Artus sat up with a groan, the thing that grabbed his attention, though, wasn't the hall or the illumite or the existence of deeper cells—it was the man nailed to the wall of the corridor immediately opposite his cell. A square iron spike had been driven through each of the wretch's wrists, at once crucifying him and displaying the brutal attention his barely clad body had received. His skin was a spiderweb of cuts and scabbed-over scars, and the spaces between were discolored with deep, ugly bruises. One hand had its fingers broken and bent at terrible angles, while the other had no fingers at all. Blood dripped from his ruined, toothless mouth, and his face was swollen and purple, but he was still alive, and Artus recognized him. The man was Zazlar Hendrieux.

"Saints . . ." Artus gasped.

Hendrieux lifted his chin from his chest slowly, moaning as he did so, and fixed the black slit of one bruised eye at Artus. He hacked out a thin, weak laugh. "S-Sur . . . surprised?"

Artus rolled onto his hands and knees and crawled to the metal grating. "I thought you was on their side, Hendrieux! What'd they do?"

The corner of Hendrieux's mouth tugged into what might have been a smirk before, but now merely showed off the bloody scabs of his gums. "S-Sahand was displeased with me. Very dis . . . displeased. Don't act so surprised, you son of a b-bitch. You . . . you knew. You knew this would happen. Should've killed you . . . when I had the . . ."

Artus felt weak with horror and disgust. He knew why Sahand had ordered Hendrieux nailed there—it was a promise. It was to show Artus—whom he probably thought was Tyvian, because of the shrouding spell—what he could expect for himself. Artus turned away from Hendrieux and his eyes fell on the heap of bloodstained cloth that was Myreon. "Myreon! Myreon, are you alive? Saints save me, I *need* you to be alive. Don't be dead! Don't be dead!"

Artus shook the unconscious Defender, rolling her over on her back. His heart leapt when he heard her groan weakly, but it fell again when he saw the mage's face and the pool of blood she had been lying in. Her lips were blue and her skin was ice cold.

"Kroth," Artus swore, and wrung his hands. What to do? What to do? He had to stop the bleeding somehow. With his bruised body screaming its protests, he rolled Myreon around until he found the knife wounds in her back. Pulling back the mage's tattered robes, he saw that the wounds had already stopped bleeding, after a fashion, and were now just sticky, black gashes that seemed to swell out of Myreon's back. Looking at them made his own shoulder twinge from the knife wound he'd received there. Though it had only been a few days ago, the injury seemed a lifetime away now.

He did his best dabbing at Myreon's injuries with a

shirt he had borrowed from Tyvian. He could practically hear Tyvian's snide remarks about how he was ruining a fine piece of clothing, but he didn't care. He needed Myreon to live. She was the one who could figure all this out. Tyvian's instructions hadn't gone so far as to tell him how to deal with being Sahand's prisoner—he had no idea what to do now, other than quake in terror, and he knew that wasn't going to help him survive, and he *had* to do that. He couldn't die. He'd promised his ma as much.

"You've ch-changed, Tyv—" Hendrieux coughed weakly. "Not like y-you to b-be saving some staff."

Artus looked at the ruined man nailed to the wall, and suddenly knew that the more he acted like Artus, the worse things might get. What would happen if Hendrieux figured out he wasn't really Tyvian? The smuggler had told Artus that the shroud would last until he was either subjected to "concentrated Lumenal energy" or until anyone trained in the High Arts found out it was there and dispelled it. If Sahand knew he was just some kid and not Tyvian Reldamar . . .

"Nothing to s-say, Tyv . . . not even to an old friend?" Hendrieux said weakly, his ruined body trembling and shaking.

Artus tried to think of something witty, but only came up with, "Shut up, Hendrieux!"

Hendrieux began to undergo some kind of seizure, so he stopped talking, though Artus doubted it was at his behest. He had seen tremors like that before in Ayventry—withdrawal from ink addiction. It looked like a kind of mental torture, and he couldn't imagine the agony one would feel if *physically* tortured at the same time. A wave of pity welled up in him for Tyvian's ex-partner, but he quashed it by bringing to mind when Hendrieux tried to have him murdered in an alley.

The gate to the dungeon rumbled open again, and this time there was only one set of boots echoing off the cold flagstones. Artus's stomach leapt into his mouth. He wanted to play dead again but stopped himself. *Tyvian* wouldn't cower, and he had to be Tyvian—his life depended on it. Using the grate to help himself to his feet, Artus swallowed his fear as best he could and planned to meet the gaze of whoever came around the corner. This meant, a few seconds later, he was staring into the flint-gray eyes of a man who had to be Banric Sahand himself. Artus couldn't help but blink and step away from the grate.

"Awake, I see," Sahand remarked. He was dressed in an ankle-length fur cloak joined with a golden chain at his collar, and wore an ornamental mail shirt that gleamed in the dim light. In the cramped quarters of the dungeon, he looked like a giant.

"I couldn't sleep. The cell here is real uncomfortable," Artus said, trying to mimic Tyvian's wry grin.

Sahand snorted. "Enjoy it while you can. As Zazlar can tell you, it's all downhill from here. That is, of course, unless you are of some use to me."

Artus racked his brain for what use Tyvian could

possibly be to Sahand. He came up with a stock answer. "I guess you want those secrets of mine, huh?"

"Of the ring, specifically. Provide them, and I'll let you go with just a slap on the wrist," Sahand said, fixing Artus with his hard eyes, "But I'll know if you're lying."

Artus's heart was pounding. He dared not look, but he wondered if the shroud he wore mimicked him having the ring, too. Casually as possible, he moved his right hand behind his back—just in case. "Nobody knows when I'm lying."

"I wouldn't try to swindle me, Reldamar." Sahand said, reaching into a pocket sewn into his cape to produce a small glass vial. "Those who do wind up very miserable indeed. Don't they, Zazlar?"

Hendrieux whimpered softly through his parched lips, "Yes, milord."

"Good answer." Sahand grinned and clapped a gloved hand on Hendrieux's shoulder, causing the wretch to scream. "I suppose you know why I've brought Zazlar down here to see you."

"You're trying to intimidate me," Artus said softly, swallowing hard.

Sahand frowned. "Oh no—hardly, though I can see how you would think that. Actually, I brought Zaz down here as a bit of a peace offering. We are enemies, Master Reldamar, only because Zazlar here saw fit to betray you. Now, Zaz, what did I say about betraying Master Reldamar?"

Hendrieux's voice was barely audible, "You t-told me to leave him alone."

"Yes, I did, didn't I?" Sahand said, patting Hendrieux's cheek, which caused blood to leak out of the man's mouth. "I would have been content if your spirit-engine operation had simply been called off, but Hendrieux wanted to ruin you. He had some kind of personal score to settle—he resents you, Reldamar, despite everything you've done for him. He, of course, didn't have the guts to do it on his own, but once he had *my* treasury to exploit, he lost no time in double-crossing you, didn't you, Zazlar?"

Hendrieux let out a low sob, and Artus again felt his stomach tie in knots. Sahand was about to kill him, and Artus knew he would have to watch. The scariest thing about it was that Sahand thought Tyvian would actually *want* to watch.

"You and I are not so very different, Reldamar." Sahand said, holding up the small glass vial before the light. Though the glass was clear, whatever was in it was of the purest black. "Both of us," Sahand continued, "are above the normal rules that apply to the average fool. The primary difference is that, while you merely seek to exploit them, I intend to rule them. I am, at my core, a philanthropist—I realize that humanity is too stupid to conduct its own affairs, and so I plan on forcing them to do as I say, as is only sensible."

"I'll tell you what you want to know if you give Myreon medical attention," Artus blurted.

Sahand gave him a steady, cold look. "You are in no

position to negotiate. Since when are you so concerned with the welfare of some staff?"

"She has her uses," Artus said quickly.

"Not anymore," Sahand deadpanned. He held the glass vial just beyond Artus's grasp. "Do you know what this is, Reldamar?"

Artus stared at the vial, knowing full well that Tyvian *would* know. "That's a stupid question."

Sahand scowled. "If I were you, I'd mind my tone. Point taken, however—stands to reason you'd recognize it. Do you know what they call Black Cloud in Kalsaar? They call it *kabuslar bir seyler*—'the stuff of nightmares'—poetic, yes? It's quite expensive, as you know, so you will appreciate my expenditure of some for your benefit."

Artus wracked his mind for the term Black Cloud, trying to remember all the conversations he overheard in the slums of Ayventry about dark and illegal things. All he could recall were some ink-thralls musing on it while numb with Cool Blue, and he hazarded a guess. "Why would you need ink?"

At the word "ink," Hendrieux's swollen eye opened a crack, and it focused immediately on the vial in Sahand's hand. Impossibly, his beaten, broken body went rigid and he pulled his head back and away from Sahand. He began to emit a steady, high-pitched whine. "Noooo . . . n-noooo . . . pleeease noooo . . ."

Sahand grinned. "So you've never seen it used, then? Well, as it is pure Etheric energy, Black Cloud is essentially bottled despair and concentrated terror.

Take just a tiny bit, and they say you will have visions and nightmares to keep you awake for months on end. Take too much and, well . . ." Sahand gripped Hendrieux by the chin and wrenched his head around to face him.

Artus, his eyes wide, held up his hands. "No, wait— you don't gotta do this!"

Sahand's laugh was flat and passionless. "I don't *have* to do anything, Reldamar. I *want* to do this. Take it as my gift to you."

Sahand pulled the stopper out with his teeth and spat it out. His other hand then closed like a vice on Hendrieux's cheeks, forcing his mouth open. "Down the hatch, Zaz."

Tears ran out of Hendrieux's swollen eyes as Sahand poured the tarlike Black Cloud down his throat. When it was gone, Sahand released him and stood back. For a moment all Hendrieux did was suck in long, wheezing breaths, coughing up some of the dark, magical liquid as he did. Then he began to scream in a way that made Artus shut his eyes and nearly double over in horror. Hendrieux's beaten, swollen eyes popped open, bloodshot and wild, and his whole body went rigid with his screams. His toothless, bloody mouth stretched into a perfect O as he produced such a horrible, overwhelming sound that Artus couldn't stop it from invading every part of his body, until he himself felt like he was dying from terror. Blood flowed from Hendrieux's nose as he shook and quaked with whatever horrible effect the ink was having on him. He convulsed, his back arching violently, his head striking the wall, his arms tearing at the spikes that held him in place. Then, finally, just when Artus began to scream himself, Hendrieux suddenly stopped and went limp.

Sahand was laughing softly. Removing a glove, he clamped a hand around Hendrieux's bloody wrist. He left it there for a moment, checking for a pulse, and when satisfied, put his glove back on and shook his head. "And so ends Zazlar Hendrieux." The Mad Prince looked at Artus and noted the tears running down his face. "Well, Master Reldamar, it seems me and you are a bit different, after all."

"You and I," Artus corrected quietly.

Sahand's smile vanished. "I'll leave you to collect your thoughts. Be ready to deliver in one hour, or suffer my displeasure."

When the dungeon gate again slammed closed, Artus slumped to the floor and wept.

CHAPTER 17

ASSEMBLED FRUSTRATION

The Artificer did good work, that much was certain. Sahand stood at the edge of the bloodred pool, hair standing on end as he felt the Fey radiating out from its depths in pulsing waves, like the beating of some massive, disembodied heart. The smell of death and the musk of wild animals mixed in the air with the faint, sour taste of brimstone. Sahand let it burn on his tongue and savored the sensation.

It was the taste of revenge.

The apparatus suspended over the pool had been removed, and no one, not even Gallo, was permitted this close to the ancient power sink. It was Sahand's and Sahand's alone to approach—the creation to which he had devoted much of the past two decades. His triumph, his final victory, was so close. It only had to work once—just once—and he would have achieved what all his armies and spies had failed to do all those years ago.

"Let's see Varner stop me now," he growled under his breath. It was a foolish thing to say, though—Varner was gone, back across the mountains to the north to fight for his cousin, the King of Benethor. Finn Cadogan was gone; the Falcon King, Perwynnon, had long since been murdered by his own retainers in a fit of their own cowardice; Prince Marik the Holy, Shield of Illin, vanished without a trace. Even old Keeper Astrian X was dead and gone. Of the coalition that had handed Sahand defeat at Calassa, none remained except perhaps old Lyrelle Reldamar, the old bat retired and sipping tea on her country estate. To the west, the wars of a quarter century ago were dead and gone; a new age had dawned, and they thought he, Banric Sahand, was just a boogeyman left to mope in icy Dellor for the rest of his life.

The fools were all in for a surprise.

"Dread Prince." Sahand didn't need to turn around to know it was the Artificer. He was the only one besides Gallo who would willingly enter this chamber, and Gallo had been ordered elsewhere.

"Yes?" Sahand held his hands out over the crimson waters. Where his shadow struck the surface, the liquid boiled and frothed, as though eager to leap out and consume him.

"The focusing apparatuses are in their final positions and the ley is sufficiently unstable. The task is done."

Sahand nodded—right on schedule. He turned to face the weathered old Kalsaari, noting the fierce glow in his eyes; the Artificer wanted to see this as much as he did. "I will begin to draw the veta in one hour."

"As the Dread Prince wishes," the Artificer said, bowing low to the ground before withdrawing.

Sahand lingered for a few moments longer before following him out. Around him, the ancient frescoes of the Warlock Kings who once strode these same halls looked with empty eyes on the complex sorcerous constructions that now filled most of the available space leading to and from the power sink. There were those, even among the League, who said desecrating the ancient homes of those godlike sorcerers of old was a recipe for disaster. To tap into their ancient power was to flirt with catastrophe, they said, and that some of the lores they had devised were best forgotten.

"They will see," Sahand muttered again. "When the dust settles, everything will be clear."

Back in his tent, he fetched a hardwood case from a shelf and opened it. Inside were a half dozen *sha*, specially made for the ritual Sahand was about to perform. He ran his fingers over them carefully—they were rough and irregular on the surface, just as they should be, and hard as chalk. His fingers tingled from touching them.

Sahand threw off his cloak and began to unbuckle his armor—the ritual needed to be performed nude, and his body needed to treated with . . .

Snick.

The letterbox. Sahand whipped his head around to glare at it. A message? *Now?* He considered ignoring it, weighing the pros and cons of arousing the League's suspicion. Had that redheaded twit or that Kalsaari brat got them in a panic over his intentions? Possibly, though it would take more than the say-so of a couple junior members to get that band of sorcerous ninnies to come after him. More importantly, did it even matter? His triumph would be complete well before the time it would take them to meet, quarrel over a plan, and then pursue him. No, best to ignore the letter and proceed with his own plans. Who cared what the message said? There was nothing that interested him more than the ritual at hand, and there was nothing anyone could do to stop him now.

Nothing whatsoever.

"Hello, my name is Tyvian Reldamar, and I'm delighted to be invited into your . . . whatever this place is." Tyvian smiled and waved at the assembled host of Shrouded sorcerers. There were scores of them lining the terraces of the Black Hall, stretching upward in every direction, their black robes and impassive faces making them look like the world's largest assembly of judges, jurists, and hangmen. Tyvian tried not to think about how apt that analogy might be in the end.

His shoulder still hurt from the fight in the alley with Jaevis, his leg still throbbed from the wound Hendrieux had given him, his every square inch was bruised, battered, and exhausted beyond all limits. He couldn't even *remember* the last decent sleep he'd had, and yet here he was, in some alternate dimension, surrounded on all sides by sorcerers who probably wanted to dissect him like some kind of exotic toad, trying to talk his way out of this mess and into another one. Oh, for the simple life of international smuggling . . .

"Where is our Esteemed Colleague from Dellor?" Tarlyth asked. The Master Defender, whose Shroud looked an awful lot like a younger Tarlyth might have—big, red-haired, and burly—stood beside Tyvian, his hands clamped firmly on Tyvian's chains, which he had steadfastly refused to remove. Tyvian thought this ridiculous—wherever did the man expect him to run?

One of the fellows with a scepter, standing at the bottom of the hall along with Tyvian and Tarlyth— some kind of officer, Tyvian thought—shook his head at the Master Defender. "He has not come. Such is his right."

"To business!" someone yelled from above. The call was echoed by others, and staves, canes, and feet were pounded on the black stone floor. "Yes! Explain this!"

and "Why is an outsider among us!" and even "Blasphemy! Betrayal of the League!"

Tyvian smiled up at them all, waving like a local hero might in the midst of a parade. He whispered to Tarlyth, "I say, is the turnout usually this good, or am I just that much of a draw?"

Tarlyth was not amused. "No games here, Reldamar. One misstep and this is the last place you'll ever see."

Tyvian winked at him and gave the crowd a perfunctory bow. "Esteemed black sorcerers, hedge wizards, and eccentric recluses: it has been brought to my attention that you lot have an interest in *this*." He held his ring hand up, and the gallery fell silent. He nodded to them all. "Good to see I was not misinformed. Now, I wanted to come here in person because, as it happens, I believe we can help each other."

One of the officers—a short man with an eye patch and a long white beard—snorted at this. "The League needs no help from the likes of you, smuggler. We are only entertaining your presence as a favor to our Esteemed Colleague from Galaspin." He nodded to Tarlyth, who nodded his thanks in return.

Tyvian shrugged. "I see. Well, here's how this is going to work—I'll answer one of your questions if you lot will answer one of mine. Sound fair?"

The one-eyed fat wizard shook his head. "We do not give up our secrets lightly, Reldamar."

Tyvian couldn't help but smile. "I promise not to ask anything too personal. I give you my word as a Reldamar." The ring bit into his hand as he said that, but he was in so much pain everywhere else, he barely felt it. "Shall we begin?"

A hand rose from halfway up the gallery. It was a woman, or at least it appeared to be, in her middle age, gray streaks running through her hair. The one-eyed fellow pointed to her with his scepter. "The Chairman recognizes our Esteemed Colleague from Eretheria."

The woman had a man's voice, deep and powerful. The effect was unnerving. "Tell us what you know about the order that placed the ring upon you." General murmurs of assent rippled through the crowd—a popular question, it seemed.

Tyvian shrugged. "Almost nothing, I'm afraid. They work as a cell-structured organization, I'd imagine. I have met only one other person with the ring, and he has said virtually nothing about the rest of the organization, assuming there even is one."

Groans of disappointment and accusations of deception roared from the gallery. Some of the sorcerers shouted threats and brandished wands and orbs of various descriptions. Tyvian stared at them calmly, watching them work themselves up as they saw how little he seemed to fear them. The honest truth was that he hadn't felt this frightened in ages—any one of these people could reduce him to ashes in a matter of seconds and he had no way to escape without their help. The feeling was exhilarating, actually, and served to deaden the exhaustion weighing him down.

The Chairman—apparently old one-eye's rank—tapped his scepter against the edge of the wide black well that formed the exact center of the hall until everyone quieted down. "May I remind the gallery that there can be no lies spoken that the Well of Secrets does not reveal. Observe." He motioned to the still, ink-black waters of the Well. "The waters are dark."

The sorcerers collectively grumbled at this. A couple walked out of the hall entirely. When they had settled themselves, the Chairman nodded to Tyvian. "Ask, Master Reldamar, but ask carefully. Your very soul is at risk."

"Don't worry—my first question is very simple, really." He addressed the crowd. "How do you fellows feel about being betrayed and robbed by one of your number?"

Dead silence. The Chairman's voice was grave. "Our policies for traitors are swift and severe, Reldamar. Why do you ask?"

Tyvian cocked his head to the side. "I'm sorry, was that your next official question for me, or was that follow-up of some kind? Hmmm . . . perhaps we ought to have ironed out the question-asking rules a little more clearly before we started to—"

"Answer him!" somebody yelled from the back. She was joined by a chorus of others, and then more, until the entire hall was howling for Tyvian to explain himself. He hazarded a look over his shoulder at Tarlyth. The youthful, handsome face of the Shrouded

Defender was frozen into a masklike scowl. His eyes were staring at the smuggler so hard, Tyvian thought it amazing they weren't drawing blood.

When the Chairman had calmed everybody down, he pointed his scepter at Tyvian. "You had better explain yourself."

"And if I say I was merely curious?"

As Tyvian spoke, a glimmer of light flickered from the center of the Well of Secrets and then was gone. One of the other officers—a tall, bald man—leaned over the pool and shook his head. When he spoke, it was the voice of an old woman. "Not much time to see, but it was a lie, for certain." He (she?) glared at Tyvian. "He knows something."

Tyvian smiled. He had them now—they were all staring at him, hanging on his every word. "So, tell me, what is it that Banric Sahand has told you he's working on?"

Silence. The air seemed to thicken with anxiety.

Tyvian laughed softly to himself. "Never mind—allow me to guess. Hmm . . ." He rubbed his chin, pretending to think; pretending that he hadn't figured this out hours ago. "Rhadnost's Elixir, isn't it?"

No one said a word. Every last one of them was frozen solid, as though caught with their hands in the cookie jar.

Tyvian paced around the Well, trying to make eye contact with as many of the assembled sorcerers as possible. Tarlyth was forced to follow him, carrying his chains like some kind of lady-in-waiting holding her mistress's train. "See, the trouble with having a magic well that detects lies is that you can't lie when you need to. For instance, I can infer from your collective silence that I hit the nail on the head just now—Rhadnost's infamous Elixir. The long-lost formula for eternal life; I can see why you'd all want it, obviously. Sahand, of course, was never really interested."

A voice of protest rose from the gallery. "Why wouldn't he be? Who *wouldn't* want to live forever?"

Tyvian shook his head, forcing a chuckle. He had their attention; now it was time for a little incitement. "Sahand doesn't care about living forever, and do you want to know why? It's because, unlike you lot, Sahand isn't a *loser.*"

Tyvian saw a few of the sorcerers stiffen at that, while a few others muttered darkly. He smiled and went on, "Come now—look at yourselves. Do you expect me to believe I'm in the presence of greatness? Please. You're a bunch of sad, bitter people whose antisocial beliefs have led them to hide under a rock and collude in secret with a series of other magical bottom-dwellers. Let's face it—if you lot were half as talented as you pretend, you would have overthrown the Arcanostrum ages ago. You are *just* the type of pathetic nobodies who'd sell their souls and bankrupt their fortunes to live forever. Why? Because you've collectively come to accept that the victory you savor and the success you long for won't happen in this lifetime. Maybe not even the next."

The grumbling rose to angry outbursts, more

threats, and a series of detailed descriptions of the kinds of curses one or another sorcerer might inflict upon him. This time the Chairman didn't intercede. He was watching Tyvian with his one good eye—it was of the clearest blue, and for a moment Tyvian thought he recognized it. He had more important things to do, though, than unravel the secret membership of the Sorcerous League.

He shouted over the gallery's jeers. "Sahand *knew* this about you all! He knew it and he *played* you, like the idiots you all are. Sahand doesn't need to live forever because, unlike the rest of you, he plans on achieving his goals *now*, while he is still *alive*. He tells you a plausible story—just plausible enough that your magic well here doesn't give him away—and all of you fill in the blanks for him, delighted to have somebody with some courage finally doing something to help the League. Eternal life for everybody, right? As the fellow up the back said, who wouldn't want it?"

The jeers fell silent again. Sorcerers were looking at their feet, some were shaking their heads. Others had their fists bunched up in their robes, fury contorting their faces to the point of nearly cracking through their Shrouds. "So what *is* he doing?" someone asked.

"Well, I can't say for certain." Tyvian cocked an eye at the Well, but it didn't glimmer. He immediately realized how easy it would have been for Sahand to half-truth himself into League support. "Also, seeing how all of you pitched in to transport Sahand and a small army of his soldiers *in secret* up in the *mountains* in the midst of an ancient *fortress,* it would be a rather suicidal prospect to go and ask. Take my friend here." Tyvian jerked a thumb over his shoulder at the glowering Tarlyth. "He's been suspicious of Sahand for some time now."

All eyes now turned to Tarlyth. The Chairman stroked his beard. "Really? And why didn't our Esteemed Colleague from Galaspin *inform* us of these suspicions?"

"Easy." Tyvian smirked at Tarlyth and gave him a wink. "He was probably planning on double-crossing all of you, too. He *is* a Master Defender, after all."

Everyone looked at the Well. It remained still, calm, and black as night. Tyvian marveled at what a rotten lie detector it was.

"Reldamaaaar!" Tarlyth screamed like a wild animal and thrust his hands toward the smuggler in a sorcerous gesture too subtle for Tyvian to follow. He felt a heavy, hot wind hit him in the chest and then he was sailing through the air, green fire all around him. A death-bolt? Maybe, but not focused enough to kill, since he wound up smashing into a collected group of black-robed wizards like a catapult stone, dizzy and smoldering, but not altogether fried.

The Black Hall erupted into sheer havoc a split second later. Most of the assembled fled, making for the thirteen exits like theatergoers fleeing a fire. They pushed, shoved, trampled one another underfoot; some of them used enchantments to leap through the air, climb along the ceiling, and one woman actually turned herself into a bat and tried flying. She didn't seem very good at it, though, as she kept slamming into the wall.

The rest of the gallery—perhaps a mere tenth of those assembled—devoted their attention to destroying Tarlyth. He was alone at the bottom of the hall—the officers had vanished in puffs of smoke, apparently—and was beset on all sides by a half-dozen black-robed wizards. The ley in the Black Hall was exclusively Etheric, to the point where other energies were almost impossible to channel, and so as Tyvian got his bearings, the combatants struggled with their magecraft to the point where there was more shouting and gesturing than actual invocations flying around.

Tarlyth, though, was Arcanostrum trained and a Master to boot. His spells did *not* fail—death-bolts struck down two of the assailants in bursts of green fire before the others could erect wards to shield themselves. When their spells finally took effect, Tarlyth showed his prowess once more. Black, thorny vines that burst from the floor to envelop him were dispelled into black smoke with ease; tiny imps conjured to poison him were banished with a single word; their own death-bolts were blocked with wards that blazed with power.

Tyvian steadied himself, getting to his feet as the last of the fleeing sorcerers pushed past him. Now what? His mind still spun in his head, unable to focus— there had been another part of this plan but he couldn't remember what.

Even for a Master Defender, though, four against one were long odds. Tarlyth missed with a spell, enabling one enemy to step *through* a shadow, only to emerge from another shadow behind the Master. Tarlyth turned, but was slashed with a jagged dagger across the chest and then struck in the back with a bolt of darkest purple energy, which caused him to scream in pain and fall to his knees.

Then Tyvian remembered. The last part of the plan was *save Tarlyth*.

He looked down at his chains, still clamped around wrists and ankles, and focused his attention on the ring. "C'mon, you little bastard. Now is the time." He pulled—nothing. The chains held.

He looked up to see the four remaining sorcerers closing in on the prone Tarlyth, snickering to themselves. Tyvian looked back at the ring. "Don't you *want* me to save him?" Then there it was again—that twitching, anxious feeling in his ring hand, just like in the Hanim's dungeon. Tyvian grabbed hold of the chains and pulled for all his worth.

They shattered off his wrists and ankles as though made of glass.

He hit the first sorcerer in the back of the head with the wadded-up remains of his chains, and the fellow dropped in a heap. The other three looked up, shocked.

One of them managed, "But you're . . ." before Tyvian broke his nose with a haymaker swing. The other two hastily prepared spells to stop him, but Tyvian was swinging the chain again, causing them both to hold their arms up to protect their faces. He hissed to Tarlyth, "Can you stand?"

Tarlyth got to all fours. "Y-Yes . . ."

Tyvian threw the chain at the two and kicked a third sorcerer in the face as he was trying to rise. "Then c'mon—let's get out of here before your cronies grow spines and come back for you."

Tarlyth glared at him through bloodshot eyes. "Why should I go *anywhere* with you?"

Tyvian had him under the arms and was guiding him as fast as possible toward the closest exit. "Because I'm your only ticket out of this mess."

"Where are we going?"

"To stop Sahand and save the world," Tyvian answered, and pushed Tarlyth out of the Black Hall.

CHAPTER 18

FARMBOY'S LUCK

Artus was shivering. He had laid his cloak over Myreon, who was still breathing, though the tiny wisps of white vapor coming from her blue lips grew smaller and smaller with every passing moment. Several times Artus considered taking back his cloak, but on every occasion he stopped himself. If he took it away, Myreon might die, and he didn't want her to die. He didn't want anybody to die.

Sahand had said he'd be back in an hour, but it felt a lot longer than that already. With no windows there was no way to really tell, and Artus knew that when your mind was racing—as his most certainly was—a few minutes could seem an eternity. He passed the time staring at the floor or ceiling, beating his hands and feet together to keep warm, and doing everything possible to not look at the haggard ruin of Hendrieux's body, still hanging on the wall.

When Sahand gets back, that's gonna be you, a little voice in Artus's head kept repeating. He shouted it down with various assurances—he'd think of something, Myreon would wake up, Tyvian would save him, and so on—but none of them were very convincing. The jig was up—Artus of Jondas Crossing, on the verge of fourteen years of age, was going to die forgotten and alone in some dark, icy prison while impersonating a criminal mastermind.

He laughed aloud, his voice echoing softly through the dungeon tunnels. Who would have thought the youngest son of a Northron farmer would have wound up here? If he ever made it back home (which he wouldn't, but still), he would be the most interesting man in the province. He could hear the old men at the Broken Wagon chatting to each other on the clapboard deck in the middle of a heavy, humid summer day. *Young Artus, Marta's boy, done come back over the mountains from the West—escaped Sahand's dungeon, they say, and has beasts and mages for company. Smart as a whip, that lad—shame about the family.*

Artus's empty stomach twisted and growled; he felt like it was mocking him. Who was he kidding? Escape Sahand's dungeons? He was dead and gone, and there was no point in saying otherwise, even to himself. He was done for—Tyvian had finally ditched him, selling him up the river for the smuggler's own gain, just like he always did. He shoulda turned down that ten marks on the streets of Ayventry, all those weeks ago. He probably would be sleeping under the stairs inside some smoky bar, picking the pockets of drunk patrons and dodging the constables. He wouldn't have been happy, but he would be warm and most certainly in less danger. "Kroth take that, Reldamar," he muttered.

The dungeon gate rumbled open and Artus pushed himself into the back corner of his cell. A Delloran soldier wearing a crude eye patch and rusty black mail stomped around the corner and peered into the gloom with his good eye until he spotted Artus. "'Ere, you— His Grace says to feed ye, so here it be. Come over and take it or I'll just pour it on the ground." The Delloran held up a wooden bowl with something wet and brown inside.

Artus pulled himself to his feet, his legs stiff with cold and bruises, and hobbled closer. The Delloran withdrew the bowl. "Listen 'ere—His Grace told me you was a tricky one, so no funny stuff, hear?"

Artus held up his hands. "Okay."

When Artus came to the iron grating, the one-eyed guard held out the bowl and Artus took it, but realized quickly that it wouldn't fit through the bars without turning it sideways and pouring out the gruel. The guard chuckled at him. "Now who's tricky, eh?"

Artus scowled at the man, wondering, and not

for the first time, from what horrible pool of bullies Sahand drew his men. The guard, still chuckling to himself, turned and left. When Artus heard the dungeon gate rumble closed again, he got down on his knees and saw if he couldn't pour the gruel into his mouth through the bars. His tongue could reach the edge of the bowl, but only if he pressed his face against the ice-cold bars so that they burned his skin. Sighing, he considered pouring the gruel on the ground in protest. A fairly significant debate arose between his rumbling stomach and his freezing hands. Somehow, he reflected, his situation had gotten worse.

"Tyvian wouldn't be stuck down here, I bet," Artus grumbled. "If it was him gone through the magic door, I bet he'd escape somehow—just as easy as if he had always been expecting it, because he *was* expecting it and— *Kroth take it!*" In the middle of his tirade, Artus realized that one of his fingers had frozen to the bowl as the gruel was starting to harden.

Something occurred to him at that moment— something that made him hold his breath for fear of somehow forgetting it or losing the thought before it had fully formed. He remembered one particularly cold winter when he was little, going in the barn with Marik and Conrad. All the cider jars had cracked because Marik had filled them too full and left the stoppers in, and Ma was angry. Artus remembered being surprised that water could do that—break jars—but Ma had just shaken her head. *Ice is bigger than water,*

Arty. If you keep water in too tight and it freezes, the ice will find a way out, even if it means cracking the jar.

Artus looked over at the rusty old padlock holding his cell door closed. Would it . . . could it work? He'd need a stopper, though . . . Sahand! Sahand had spit the stopper of that bottle of Black Cloud out on the floor. Where was it? There!

His hands trembling with cold and excitement, he broke the ice layer forming over the gruel and slowly passed it from hand to hand until he had moved the bowl along the grating to where the padlock rested. It was a fat, heavy piece of iron, crudely made with a gaping keyhole the size of his thumb—perfect. As carefully as he could, he held the padlock level with one hand while, with the other, he poured the watery gruel into the lock until it was overflowing. He then dropped the bowl of gruel and, with a foot stuck through the grating by the floor, he kicked the stopper over to himself. He then stuffed it into the keyhole so it filled the entire space. He knew that wouldn't be enough, though, so he tore off strips of his frilly shirt and tied them around the lock and stopper, holding it as tightly closed as he could manage. When this was done, he backed up, his fingers numb and his body throbbing with pain. He only had to wait.

And wait.

And wait.

And wait.

And wait . . .

Clink.

Artus's head shot up—had he nodded off asleep? No—yes—it didn't matter. Had he really heard what he thought he heard? Gingerly, he crawled over to the padlock. He could see frozen gruel spilling out of every little fissure in the old, heavy lock. The stopper was still in place, though, and when he tugged on the lock, he discovered that it wasn't as firmly attached as before. Not quite broken, but one of the pins holding the lock together had come loose. Wrapping his numb fingers around the iron lock, he yanked as hard as he could, putting every ounce of his adolescent frame into it. His bruised muscles and exhausted body screamed in protest, but he ignored them and kept on yanking, screaming as he did so. Finally, on the fifth or sixth pull, the padlock broke open. He was free of his cell.

"Yes! Yes, yes, yes, yes! I did it! I *did* it!" Artus whooped, but then stopped himself—he wasn't out of the dungeon yet. There was also Myreon to think about—the mage, incredibly, was still breathing.

Leave her. Artus heard Tyvian's voice clearly in his mind. He knew it was exactly what the smuggler would say, and he'd be right. There was no way he could drag Myreon—a grown woman, and a tall one, too—out of this dungeon, even if the doors were all open and the guards were waving him out. If he wanted to survive, he'd have to abandon the mage to her fate. It was the sensible thing to do.

It wasn't the *right* thing, though. Artus could hear Tyvian chuckling at his foolishness, but there it was—

it wouldn't be *right* to leave Myreon. He couldn't really say why that mattered so much, but it did. *Doing right*, as Ma always said, *don't mean doing easy*. Myreon was coming with him, or they were both staying. Maybe he wasn't as smart as Tyvian was, sure, but there wasn't anything he could do about it. He was who he was.

He would have to be smart, though, if he was going to survive the next few hours. "So, what would Tyvian do?" he said aloud.

As far as he could tell, Tyvian's great talent lay in predicting what other people would do in response to the things he did. Artus had watched him, time and time again, flawlessly predict other people's actions simply by judging their character and wants and all that. So, to be like Tyvian, all he needed to do was figure out what the other guys were going to do and then plan accordingly. So, how would that help him now?

"If I were one of them ugly Delloran jerks, what would I do if I found I had escaped?" Artus asked himself. The immediate answer was, *Put him back in the cell with a swift kick*. Pretty obvious and it didn't get him anywhere. Thinking a bit more, he expanded the possibilities. He found himself addressing the barely alive Myreon. "Okay, so what if, for argument's sake, I got us to escape out of the dungeon totally—like, them guards come down here and find the cell empty, right? What do they do then?"

Artus grunted—they'd probably throw a fit. Sahand didn't seem like the most understanding boss, and if the guards let who they thought was Tyvian Reldamar escape from the dungeon, Sahand would probably put a knife in them. So, they'd try and find him and Myreon as fast as possible, probably sound the alarm, and there'd be guards all over the place in minutes. Even supposing, then, that he *were* able to open the dungeon gate (which he doubted), he'd be caught again as soon as the guards saw he was gone, since he and Myreon weren't going anywhere quickly.

"But wait a second!" Artus exclaimed. "I'm *not* Tyvian Reldamar! They don't know who I am at all, do they? If I can get out of here and break the spell, then . . . well . . . then they won't know who they're looking for. They *wouldn't* find me!"

Breaking the spell, though, wasn't going to be easy. For starters, Artus didn't really know where one got a hold of "concentrated Lumenal energy," and he only had the vaguest of ideas what Lumenal energy was—"white magic" was all he could think of, even though he knew that wasn't entirely accurate. He thought back to the road to Freegate and how Tyvian had wanted them to walk in sevens and stay in the bright sunlight and so on to encourage a "Lumenal ley," but he didn't think that would be enough to cut it. Still, he had to try—it was his only chance.

Rolling Myreon onto his cloak, Artus dragged the half-dead mage out of the cell, and rather than go up to the gate, opted instead to go deeper into the shadows of the dungeon, until he was confident the both of them were concealed in the darkness of the lower cells.

Crouching in the dark, he prayed to Saint Handras for luck and Saint Ezeliar for bravery, and waited to see if his trick would work.

He only had to wait a few minutes before the gate rumbled open and a pair of guards came to his cell. Their reaction was immediate and extreme. "Gods, Matek, the bastard's gone!"

"I told you he was tricky! I told you!"

"Shut up and find him!"

One of them started toward where Artus was hiding, and he held his breath as his heart began to leap and jolt in his chest. The guard hadn't gone more than a few steps before the other one called to him. "Where you going?"

"Maybe he hid down here?"

"Why would he hide *in the bloody dungeon*?"

"I just thunk—"

"Stop thinking! He's trying to escape, stupid! He's probably on an upper level somewheres—Kroth, we probably walked right past him in the dark. C'mon!" With that, the two of them turned and ran up and out of the dungeon.

They did not close the gate, just as Artus had hoped they wouldn't. *Haste makes waste,* Ma always said.

"Hello, Reldamar . . ." A weak, thin, whisper of a voice came from behind Artus. He jumped at the sound of it.

In the dark, Artus could barely make out a pair of delicate, bony hands sticking out between crude bars. "Don't worry . . ." There was a long pause as the man seemed to be gathering breath. "I won't . . . sound the alarm."

"Who are you?" Artus asked.

"It's me . . . Hortense. The warlock from the Stair Market?" He wheezed a soft laugh. "You don't remember me, do you?"

Artus blinked—a warlock? "You mean . . . you work with magical trinkets and such? Spirit clocks and feylamps and—"

"Yes." The thin hands withdrew in to the pitch-black of the cell. A narrow, haggard face with a long nose pressed between the bars. The man's dark eyes were bloodshot and ringed by black circles. "You aren't Reldamar, are you?"

"Listen, do you know how to make a . . . a . . . Lumenal . . . something?"

The warlock's tired eyes closed and he nodded. "You're shrouded, of course."

"Can you help?"

"Only if . . . if you make me a promise."

Artus tried not to sigh—as if he didn't have enough to do. "Okay . . ."

"I have a daughter—Sahand took her from me, I don't know where. You . . ." Hortense's face trembled, tears welling under his eyes. ". . . you must find her for me. Save her. Tell her I'm dead."

"But you aren't dead," Artus said, shuffling from foot to foot as he glanced worriedly at the gate to the dungeon.

"Soon enough." Hortense smiled weakly, "Can you promise me that, whoever you are?"

Artus took a deep breath. What was one more woman to rescue, really? "Sure. I promise."

Hortense took a long hard look at Artus and nodded. "Bring me the shard of illumite and the wooden bowl you dropped."

Artus retrieved the bowl and pulled the illumite down from where it hung in the hall, trying very hard not to look at Hendrieux or notice how his blood was congealing on the icy floor. "Here," he said, pressing them through the bars. "Now what?"

The glow of the illumite lit the whole of Hortense's cell—it was tiny, cramped—not even enough room to lie down in. Hortense himself was wearing what must have once been fine clothing—the kind of thing gentlemen wore in Ayventry. Artus thought he might have picked his pocket once upon a time. Now Hortense was a gaunt specter of a man in fraying wool and linen, and he was doing him a favor. It felt strange.

Hortense pushed the items back into Artus's hands. "Place the illumite shard in the bowl . . . and smash it with something hard until . . . it shatters." Hortense wheezed out a weak cough. "Then, quick . . . quick as you can, breathe deeply . . . of the light that pours out."

Artus snatched up the remains of his padlock and did as Hortense asked. It took several blows—he was surprised at how hard the little shard of illumite was—but suddenly he heard it crack under the force of the heavy iron lock. The dungeon was suddenly lit with sun-bright light, pouring out of the bowl as though a piece of daylight had been broken off and somehow dropped in. Closing his eyes, he pressed his face into the bowl, breathing deeply. It smelled, bizarrely, like freshly cut hay and wildflowers. His body tingled with warmth and a bubble of giddiness bounced around in his stomach. He laughed, despite himself. He could do this. He was going to save Myreon and Hortense's daughter and—

"Why . . . you're just a boy." Hortense's voice sounded a bit stronger.

Artus looked at the warlock and noted the old man was standing up a bit straighter and his eyes were less bloodshot. "I'll come back for you if I can, and I swear on my father's honor that I'll find your daughter."

Artus then grabbed Myreon by the wrists and tried to pull her, but she barely moved. He pulled harder and harder until, at last, she budged a couple inches and his grip slipped. He fell on his back, panting and looking at the ceiling. "Say, Hortense," he said, catching his breath, "do you know where I can find a wheelbarrow?"

CHAPTER 19

THE DIRECT APPROACH

"You're a madman," Tarlyth shouted, clutching his white cloak tightly around his body as he staggered up the steep incline. The wind was howling so loudly, Tyvian could scarcely hear him.

"We could always go back!" Tyvian shouted back. "Arrest me, and then the letter goes to Saldor tomorrow morning. You'll be hunted by the League *and* the Defenders!"

"Damn your bloody eyes!"

The two of them were hiking up an icy scree slope, the city of Freegate displayed behind and beneath them like a poorly constructed model in a shop window, glazed with snow and hazy with soot. Squinting against the wind, Tyvian could see the yawning galleries and ruined atriums of Daer Trondor, the ancient mountain fortress of the long-dead Warlock Kings, a mile or two ahead of them. He tried to ignore the freezing air that cut through his thin shirt and tattered jacket, telling himself that, at the very least, he was too numb to feel all the pain he was likely in.

On his hand, the ring pulsed like a second heart, each pump like a shot of hot karfan to his veins, urging him onward, forbidding him rest. He had Tarlyth's arm over his shoulders and, despite his injuries, he was pulling the heavyset old mage up the mountain, one step at a time. Tyvian literally couldn't believe he was doing this—he kept checking behind him to confirm where he was; when he pinched himself, he felt nothing, and he couldn't decide whether it was because this was all a dream or his skin had lost feeling better than an hour ago.

"We—" Tarlyth started, but stumbled, and Tyvian had to help him up. "We could at *least* get the Defenders I've got down in the city! Then we'd have a chance!"

"And give you the opportunity to arrest me as soon as this is all finished?" Tyvian snorted. "Sounds like a terrible plan to me."

Tarlyth's lips were blue and his teeth were chattering. "And walking up to Sahand's front door is a *good* plan? We'll die out here!"

They made it to the top of the slope and a broad

ledge wide enough for two wagons to drive side by side. It was reasonably flat, but covered with several feet of heavy snow. "You know . . ." Tyvian said, dumping Tarlyth on his back in a drift and putting his hands on his hips, "I bet this was a road once."

Tarlyth was breathing heavily. "Gods, I can see why Myreon wanted you caught so badly. Listening to you blather is torture; if I had the energy I'd zap you dead and take my chances on the run."

"So you're saying you're of no use to me in a sorcerous capacity, is that it?" Tyvian crouched beside Tarlyth and ran a hand along his chin. He was due for a shave—funny how being in various forms of captivity for a few days made one forget the little things. "That's going to put a crimp in our plans."

"*Your* plan, you insufferable jackass. You've put me in this mess, but I'll be damned if I'm going to be considered a *conspirator*."

Tyvian shook his head. "You misunderstand me when I say 'our.' I'm not referring to you and I, sir."

Tarlyth rolled onto his side to look at him. "Who, then?"

Tyvian stood up and shaded his eyes, searching the surrounding slopes of the big mountain. Finally, he spotted her, or rather, *they*—two furry golden shapes, one large, one small, heading straight for them at an impossible speed. "I'm referring to *her*, actually."

Hool and Brana were upon them in a matter of minutes, bounding four-legged over the snowdrifts and sliding down the rocky slopes with the predatory agility he'd come to associate with gnolls. Hool's fur was still caked with blood and Brana was still missing patches of his mane, but it seemed the two of them were much better off than when he last saw them. "I see you found the bloodpatch elixirs in my flat."

Hool nodded, puffs of white steam pouring out of her flared snout. "Yes, but somebody has been there already and smashed all of your things."

Brana yipped in what Tyvian thought, presumably, was an expression of support for his mother. The little gnoll wasn't much more than a ball of golden-yellow fur with big eyes and a black nose. He shuffled behind Hool's haunches as Tyvian looked at him.

"Brana says for you to stop looking at him. He doesn't like people," Hool announced, and then looked at Tarlyth for the first time. "Who is this wizard?"

"I'll tell you in a minute. First, did you find Sahand?"

"I found a lot of soldiers in the old ruins, as you said. I don't know their names."

Tyvian nodded. "Sounds like the place. And?"

"We cannot get in without being shot with crossbows." Hool put her ears back and gestured toward the distant ruins. "They are good sentries and guard all the ways up well. I have been trying to find another way, but there isn't one. You say the one who killed my Api is inside?"

Tyvian nodded, remembering for a moment Hool's howls from that morning. He shivered, but not from the cold. The ring pulsed warmly. "He most assuredly is, Hool."

She thrust a finger into Tyvian's chest; he was so weak, it nearly knocked him over. "If we find him, you will let me kill him."

"You have my word."

"Ha!" Tarlyth snorted, still lying down. "You think you have a chance against *Sahand*? Two big dogs, a skinny smuggler, and a half-dead mage aren't enough to make him *sweat*, let alone defeat him. Maybe if I were well-rested, I could—"

Tyvian hit Tarlyth in the face with a snowball. "Shut up now—no more talking."

Hool picked Tarlyth up by the front of his robes and displayed her teeth. "I am no dog. You are more *monkey* than I am dog."

"Don't kill him, Hool—he's part of the plan."

Tarlyth and Hool asked in unison, "What plan?"

"When will you people realize that I *always* have a plan?" Tyvian sighed. "It just so happens that, in this instance, it isn't a very good one and subject to change as we go along. Follow me."

Tyvian started up the slope again, the ring pushing him harder along with each step.

It was almost dusk by the time they reached the final approach to the ruins. Hool had Tarlyth slumped across her shoulders, Brana bringing up the rear, sniffing the air nervously, his fuzzy ears swiveling wildly to and fro. Tyvian was in the lead, and he crouched behind a boulder so the sentries at the entrance to the camp couldn't see him. The guards were maybe fifty yards away, up an almost forty-five-degree slope, sitting behind a barrier of barrels and bails of hay. The two sentries Tyvian could see were erect, alert, and disciplined—they wore Sahand's silver wyvern on their black tabards, and their mail glittered in the fading daylight. Hool was right—no good way up. This was by far the easiest entryway to approach—the others were at the top of nearly sheer slopes or attended by even more guards. Sahand really *did* have a small army up there.

Tarlyth was looking over Tyvian's shoulder. "Well, what's this brilliant plan?"

Tyvian pointed at Tarlyth. "You're the diversion—start running."

Tarlyth's mouth popped open. "Wh . . . what? Is this a joke?"

Tyvian looked at the gnoll. "Hool, did I mention that this man assisted Sahand in acquiring you and your pups for his little experiments?"

The hair on the back of Hool's neck stood straight up and her lips drew back to reveal her teeth. Even after hearing it numerous times now, her growl still made Tyvian feel ill. Tarlyth looked as though he were actively wetting his pants. "Now . . . now . . . hold on . . . I didn't . . ."

The Master Defender backed away, hands weaving various defensive guards and wards, but the duel in the Black Hall, coupled with the grueling climb, had left the mage depleted and unable to channel enough energy to more than just fling sparks at the angry mother gnoll. Brana, too, was copying his mother, and while perhaps not as thunderously terrifying as Hool, he was still about fifty pounds of angry teeth and fur.

Tyvian shook his head at Tarlyth. "You should probably start running."

Tarlyth tried to step around Hool and Brana, but they blocked the way down. "Reldamar, you can't . . . you said . . ."

"I said I was your ticket out of this mess—I didn't tell you where that ticket was taking you instead. You choice, Tarlyth—get ripped apart by gnolls or see if Delloran crossbowmen can hit you in high wind at dusk at fifty paces." Tyvian looked at the gnolls. "I know what I'd choose."

Tarlyth turned and ran—not straight up the slope toward the guards, but at an angle, working his way across the cliff face to . . . well, Tyvian suspected Tarlyth hadn't thought that far ahead, yet. For a half-dead old man, he ran pretty well, but then the prospect of being devoured by a wild animal had that effect on a fellow.

The Dellorans spotted him almost immediately. An alarm was called, and the first sentry shouldered his crossbow and took a shot at Tarlyth. He missed by a mile, the wind taking his bolt and throwing it well off course. The second man, noting his partner's shot, adjusted, took careful aim . . .

Clack!

The black bolt flew in a wicked arc and hit Tarlyth

below the left knee, right through his calf. The Master Defender howled in pain and fell flat on his face. He began to tumble down the cliff face, end over end, each bounce producing more cries as bones were probably broken.

The ring clamped down on Tyvian's hand with a razor-sharp bite of pain. He clenched his teeth and hissed at it. *"Not now . . ."*

The Dellorans were reloading and one of them came over the front of the barricade, crossbow at his hip, heading down to investigate who it was they had just shot.

Tyvian didn't need to tell Hool when to take her opening. She growled something in her tongue to Brana and began to slink upward, circling away from the descending guard, her chin practically touching the ground. Tyvian followed her at a half crawl, half crouch, hoping the second guard kept his attention on where Tarlyth had gone and not where he had come from.

Hool covered the fifty yards between the boulder and the barricade before Tyvian was even a third of the way up. The guard there saw her at the last moment, but it was too late—he went down beneath her bulk and only managed a gurgling cry before Hool ended him. The descending guard spun around. "Hey!"

Hool stood up and threw Tyvian the dead man's loaded crossbow. Tyvian just managed to catch it before it sailed off into thin air, and he took aim at the remaining guard, who was aiming at Hool. They fired at the same time.

Clack. Clack.

The guard missed Hool by inches; Tyvian caught the guard in the hip. He fell backward, twisting from the force of the shot, and rolled down the hill in the same direction Tarlyth had gone, grunting and screaming as he went until he vanished from sight. Tyvian ran up the last of the slope and vaulted the barricade before anybody else could see.

He'd barely arrived when Hool slapped a helmet on his head. "Stand up and look around like a soldier, or the other guard posts will know!"

Tyvian obeyed, deferring to Hool's exemplary infiltration instincts. Sure enough, a few other guards from other posts along the edge of the old ruins had heard the commotion and were looking in his direction. Tyvian gave them a casual salute and then hunkered back down behind the bails of hay and barrels. "Well, so far, so good."

"Stop talking," Hool grumbled. "You're always talking."

"We should split up—you'd give me away."

Hool snorted. "You'd give *me* away. You move like a sick donkey."

Tyvian thought about inquiring after the metaphor, but remembered Hool's admonition regarding his tendency to chatter. "What about Brana?"

Hool looked at him like he had just grown wings

and tried to fly. "*He* is going to be a good rabbit and hide. He is too little for battle."

Tyvian nodded. "Makes sense—good luck, then."

"Do not die," Hool advised, and then, picking up a shield, darted deeper into the camp. Tyvian lost sight of her almost immediately behind a cluster of tents.

Tyvian stripped the dead guard of his mail shirt, trying not to think too hard about how the man had died—his face was little more than a mushy ruin of torn flesh and blood—and fished a long dagger from the man's belt. It wasn't an ideal weapon, but it was a damn sight better than nothing.

The camp was built beneath what had once been a grand gallery overlooking the Trell River Valley. Tree-like columns supported ancient vaulted ceilings as far as the eye could see. The "roof" of the gallery was a full thirty feet over Tyvian's head, and he marveled at the architects who could have designed such things to be built this high in the mountains and have them stand for almost three thousand years. Most of the architecture in Freegate was lucky to last half a century. Of course, that was as much due to the occasional riot and the famously lazy for-profit fire brigade as it was to any engineering concerns.

Between the columns and the piles of rubble where the ceiling had collapsed in places over the centuries, the military camp was laid out with typically military precision. Staked into the stone ground were rows upon rows of tents, arranged in ten-tent units that formed a regiment apiece—forty to fifty men, including command group, in each section. There were burning iron braziers every three or four tents or so, lighting the gloomy gallery and spilling heat into the frosty mountain air. Indeed, the presence of all the fires and the wind-blocking properties of the columns and rubble-piles served to raise the temperature in the ruins from bone-chilling to merely cold. Tyvian actually felt a tingling in his nose indicating that it was starting to defrost somewhat. This was a relief—he had begun to worry he was going to lose it to frostbite.

He crept up to a tent that was dark and looked still, and after listening long enough to determine it wasn't occupied, slipped inside. It was an armory containing racks of crossbows, assorted quivers of bolts, enchanted and otherwise, and a wide variety of swords, axes, shields, and helmets. He rummaged about for a rapier and came up with the next best thing—a cavalry saber, well-maintained if a trifle top-heavy, with a plain iron basket hilt and knuckle guard. He took a few practice swings—it would do.

A troop of men stomped by outside, their armor jingling. "Fan out!" an officer of some kind barked. "Reldamar may try and escape this way, and I'll whip every man-jack o' you raw if that happens. Move!"

The men knuckled their foreheads and scattered in teams of four, beginning a search pattern that reminded Reldamar eerily of a late night visit to his flat several days ago. Peering through the tent flap, he could see he had about another minute or so before he'd have to move or get caught. That gave him a minute to ask himself a very important question: *How can they be looking for me if they don't know I'm here yet?*

The answer leapt to his lips almost immediately. "Artus."

Artus was alive.

CHAPTER 20

DOWN DARK HALLS

"Who are you and where do you think yer goin'?" The Delloran soldier had Artus by the collar and was using it as a tourniquet for the boy's throat. Thanks to the helmet the man wore, Artus could only see the man's dirty beard and blazing eyes. It was enough to let him know the kind of fellow he was—a murderous thug, just like every other man in Sahand's service.

Artus didn't have any trouble sounding frightened. "They told me to ditch the body somewhere, so . . . so I'm ditching the body somewhere." He jerked a thumb at the corpselike Myreon in the wheelbarrow.

The soldier took a good look at Myreon and licked his lips with a red tongue. "Yeah?"

Artus noticed the soldier's grip loosen and tugged himself away. "Yeah, that's right."

The soldier stomped around the wheelbarrow, prodding Myreon with a mailed hand. "She were a looker, that's certain. Shame she's dead."

Artus did his best not to scowl. "Yeah, well can I go?"

The soldier pointed up a narrow passage half filled with rubble and ice. "Dump her over the side with the rest. Anygate's off limits since she came through."

Artus blinked. That was it? It was that easy?

As if reading his thoughts, the soldier grabbed him by the scruff of the neck. "How come I ain't seen you around before?"

"I used to work in Arble Keep, 'fore the mirror men showed up. I ran through with Captain Hendrieux and . . . and the big feller."

The soldier grunted and let him go. "Get outta here—don't let me see you down here again, or it'll be yer hide."

Artus saluted and pushed the wheelbarrow off in the direction the man indicated. When he was out of sight, he set the wheelbarrow down and let his breath run out in ragged gasps. Saints, he didn't know how long he could push this thing! His legs were quivering and his every pore seemed to ache with pain, and Myreon seemed to look even worse. He wanted to listen for her breath but didn't. He couldn't stomach the idea that she was dead, though he didn't know why, exactly. She wasn't a bad person, at any rate. She had come after him—she had tried to save him from Sahand, and that meant a lot. It was more than Reldamar was doing anyway. For the thousandth time he wondered where the smuggler was. He wondered if Tyvian were thinking about him.

Probably not.

So far, Artus's "disguise" as himself was working perfectly. Apparently there were or had been a cadre of adolescent boys—slaves and vagrants, probably—brought here by Hendrieux to do menial work, and nobody paid much attention to a kid pushing a wheelbarrow with a corpse around. That soldier had been the first one to take an interest—everybody else was running around in armed groups, looking for Reldamar.

Something occurred to Artus then. If everybody else was looking for Reldamar, what was *that* soldier doing? Peeking back around the corner, he saw that the man was still there, keeping watch. He was guarding something. What, though?

Artus looked around—he was still in the depths of the earth, or so it seemed. The halls and passages and rooms he passed through looked to be millennia old—the engravings on the wall showed things that he was fairly certain no longer existed and hadn't for ages. There were giant monsters ridden by glowing wizards, flying cities, armies of the walking dead . . .

. . . Well, at least he *hoped* things like that no longer

existed. His history wasn't very good. More accurately, his history was nonexistent beyond the stories of the Saints of the North, which he wasn't sure was exactly history anyway. Well, maybe it was, but . . .

Focus, Artus. Tyvian's voice seemed to echo in his head so clearly that Artus actually looked around to see if the smuggler had found him. No, just his brain playing tricks; it was a good point, though—focus. He needed to focus. Why would you need a guard way down here in the depths of this weird old maze?

"Prisoners," Artus muttered to himself. Obviously—he was guarding more prisoners. Maybe even Hortense's daughter.

"Okay Artus," he said under his breath, "what's the plan?"

The soldier wasn't a great deal taller than Artus, but about twice as broad. He was armored, and armed with a broadsword and dagger at his hip, whereas Artus had nothing. There was also the little problem that he had never killed anybody in his life, and wasn't sure if he could if he wanted to. As a final point, he noted that, aside from his beard, the man had no hair to pull, and even if he had, Artus somehow doubted a little hair pulling would work as well against a brutish Delloran soldier as it would against a spoiled Kalsaari Hanim.

Running through his options, Artus came up with the best plan he felt he had at his disposal. He began to scream, "Help! Help! It's Reldamar! I'm being attacked! Help!" His voice echoed through the icy corridors. In the distance he heard shouting and the crashing jingle of mail and weapons coming closer at a run.

Artus picked up a rock and peeked around the corner, expecting the soldier to be almost upon him. He wasn't, though—the soldier was looking in his direction but hadn't left his post. Where was the jingling coming from, then?

Artus looked behind him. A troop of four Dellorans were at the opposite end of the corridor where he had stopped to rest, and they were jogging in his direction, scanning the surrounding passageways. Their sergeant's voice echoed, *"It came from this way. Look sharp, boys."*

"Kroth's teeth!" Artus swore, and put his back into pushing the wheelbarrow back toward the lone sentry. One Delloran, he figured, was better than four.

When the bearded soldier saw Artus coming, he spat something foul on the ground and came to meet him. Artus forced himself to smile. "Oh, thank Hann! It was Reldamar—he almost got me and . . . *ulghh*."

The sentry seized Artus by the throat and threw him against the wall. "I thought I told you not to come back, rat!" He pulled out his dagger. "Now it's time to pay."

Artus dug his fingers into the soldier's arm, trying to loosen his grip. He kicked out with his legs, hitting the soldier in his armored shins. He coughed, scarcely able to speak, *"W-Wait . . . I—"*

The man pressed the knife to Artus's sternum and snarled, "Orders is orders, scum."

Adrenaline surged through Artus's body. He kicked and tried to scream and scraped his fingernails along the man's mailed arm. The man was as immovable as a tree, though, and he leered a yellow-toothed smile at him. "Hope that wheelbarrow fits two."

A shadow fell over both of them, causing the guard to look behind them. Something with huge hands grabbed the man by his tabard and flung him headfirst into the opposite wall so hard, Artus heard something break. The man's body flopped onto the floor and didn't move.

Artus was still gasping for breath when great, furry hands picked him up off the floor and brushed dust and snow off his clothing. Hool's voice was heavy with motherly disapproval. "You are always about to be stabbed by soldiers. What is wrong with you?"

"Did you . . . is he dead?" Artus pointed at the soldier's inert bulk.

Hool's ears swiveled back and forth, as though thinking about it. "Maybe, maybe not. He will not walk again. His spine is broken. Why are you always asking stupid questions?"

"Hool you've got to help me—I've got Myreon and she's . . ."

"Dead," Hool announced. "I can smell her on you. She is dead."

Artus felt the wind rush out of him. "No! No she isn't! She was breathing just a few minutes ago!"

Hool nodded. "And now she has stopped. Dead

things always smell a little different than alive things. I know."

Artus shook his head. "You just said you didn't know if *this* guy was dead—how can you be so sure about Myreon, huh?"

"Because she has been dead for long enough to smell dead. You are wasting time."

Artus looked back in the direction of the wheelbarrow. It couldn't be true! He'd . . . he'd worked so *hard* to save her. He'd come too far to have her die now. It . . . it wasn't *fair.* "She tried to save me." He felt tears beginning to well-up. "She didn't have to do that. It's . . . it's my fault she's dead, Hool."

Hool slapped him in the face. "There is no time for sadness. Come with me."

The gnoll grabbed Artus by the collar and dragged him toward the dark corridor the soldier had been guarding. "Hool! Let go! Where are we going?"

Hool pointed down the corridor. "This way is a lot of blood . . . and magic. It is where Sahand is."

Artus's stomach flipped at the mention of the Mad Prince's name. The terror, though, drove some of his tears away. "Then let's not go that way!"

Hool didn't budge. She took a deep breath and let it out so that the fur on her cheeks rippled. "I have come for Sahand."

Understanding hit Artus all at once. That was why Hool was here, of course—revenge. Not him. Not Myreon. Revenge. "Did you find your pups?"

Hool's ears went back. "Two of them. One of them is alive and hiding outside. The other . . ." She pointed down the dark hallway. "*He* skinned her. Now I will skin him."

The gnoll started down the hall, but Artus grabbed her by the wrist. "Don't go, Hool—he'll kill you, too. He kills everybody—the guy is, like, incredibly dangerous. He killed Myreon, he killed Hendrieux, he . . . he's a monster, Hool. Just take the pup you got and leave."

She looked down at Artus and ran a hand slowly through his hair. "You are a kind human, Artus. But you do not understand."

With that, she took off down the hall, vanishing in the dark before Artus could even say good-bye. He stood there, watching the dark spot where she had vanished, for almost a whole minute. Should he follow? Should he escape? What help would *he* be, anyway?

From behind him, he heard voices shouting. "*Sir, look! It's the mage, sir—he must have ditched her body here!*" and "*Fan out, find him—shoot on sight. Don't give the weasel a chance to talk his way out of it.*"

If the Delloran squad had found Myreon, they had also blocked the only way out Artus knew, and they would find the incapacitated guard momentarily. He drew the guard's broadsword and started down the corridor after Hool. It seemed as though luck was making his decisions for him today.

Tyvian ducked out of a shadowy enclave after the party of Delloran guards had passed and followed them as quietly as he could across the dusty, ice-choked corridors of the inner ruins. The camp and the wide gallery it occupied was just the tip of the iceberg. Corridors and stairwells cut deep into the heart of the mountain, leading to a labyrinthine warren of tunnels, chambers, and dead ends. All around, the eyes of the long-dead kings who once walked these corridors stared out from their endless portraits, bracketed in hieroglyphics that Blue College magi had studied extensively before Freegate had them expelled after the war. Tyvian felt a certain weight of history in this place—heavy, moldering, *dreadful*—that made the way Sahand's goons were casually marching through it all unnerving. They really had no idea how important Daer Trondor had once been, or how much ancient blood stained the flagstones beneath their feet.

The party ahead of him were following a report that said he'd been spotted somewhere down in this part of the ruins, and so Tyvian was following them in the hopes of finding Artus. Since they hadn't run across any mauled or mangled corpses, he guessed Hool was coming in from another direction, which was just as well—he didn't need all these soldiers any more on edge than they already were.

They crossed a grand hall with a fallen-in roof, a great crack of sky visible down the center of the crumbling vaults. The last dying breath of sunlight sent some weak rays spilling across the rubble-strewn floor, but that was all. It was dark, and most of these corridors weren't lit—they had been originally designed to admit as much natural light as possible through the clever use of skylights and, one presumed, some kind of reflecting devices that now were replaced by packs of blue-white ice and drifts of wet snow. Of course, once the sun went down, none of that would matter anymore.

Tyvian had a shard of illumite in his pocket that he had picked up in the armory tent, but he didn't dare bring it out—he might as well ring a bell and shout "Come attack me." He was forced, therefore, to stick close enough to the party of Delloran guards that he could use their light to avoid tripping on anything, but not so close that he himself would be illuminated. It was a tricky business, since the party kept stopping to get their bearings and would occasionally fan out, a shard of illumite apiece, to search large rooms. He supposed in these instances he might have taken them out, one by one, but four fewer Dellorans running around wasn't going to make a lot of difference in the end, and furthermore, the ring seemed to disapprove of stabbing men in the back from the shadows anyway.

Tyvian really couldn't afford to ignore the ring at this stage. He was relying on it too heavily to give him the strength to carry on—its every pulse of goodwill toward his goal of stopping Sahand and, now, rescuing Artus was an essential jolt of energy. He could see how a thing like the ring could become addictive, perhaps even be seen as an asset. Eddereon's behavior was making a bit more sense now, though he still rejected the theory that stated the ring was making him a hero of some kind. Nonsense. It was only natural that he should be exhausted and alone in the dark corridors of some cursed ruin trying to take on the world's most dangerous man and his army of bloodthirsty mercenaries. It was totally in character.

Right.

They were heading down another corridor now, and Tyvian noted a particular smell in the air—metallic, semisweet, sticky. Blood. A huge quantity of blood—it grew in strength with every pace the group of soldiers took in its direction, to the point where Tyvian was having difficulty imagining what terrible event could possibly produce that much of the stuff. There was another scent in the air—an acrid, foul stench, also very familiar. Brymm—definitely brymm, or at least pure Fey energy, and a *lot* of it. So much, again, that it was making Tyvian nervous. What the *hell* was Sahand up to with that power sink? Just how terrible was his plot, after all?

The soldiers in front of Tyvian were getting nervous, too. There was some muttering among themselves that he wasn't close enough to hear, but the body language was clear enough—they knew where they were headed and that they weren't supposed to go there. They came to the top of a broad staircase that dropped about fifteen feet to a wide arch. A pair of soldiers were guarding this arch, and they held up their hands to stop the oncoming group.

"Oi, Farrut—no passing, you know that!" one of sentries yelled.

Farrut—the group's sergeant, evidently—put up his hands. "Yeah, I know—we got word of Reldamar down this way, though. You seen anything?"

The sentries both shook their heads. "Nah—nothing but that stink. Gallo came by, but it was on His Grace's orders, right? Didn't get in the way."

Farrut nodded at the wisdom of this.

Tyvian saw where all this was going long before it got there—they were going to turn around, which meant he needed to beat a hasty retreat. He started back the way they'd come but hadn't gone ten paces before he heard voices ahead of him—more soldiers, coming this way! He looked to his left and right—nowhere to hide, at least not that he could see. Turning back, he saw the group he had been following heading his way, too. He was trapped.

The two groups of Dellorans met at about the center of the corridor, and their lights ilLumenated Tyvian, his saber drawn, at about the same exact time. "Hello, gentlemen—I believe you're looking for me?"

CHAPTER 21

DAMSELS IN DISTRESS

Artus had no idea what had happened to Hool, but he knew wherever he was headed was trouble. Even he could smell the blood in the air now, and it made him uncomfortable. The corridor he was following emptied into a large hall with a partially collapsed roof—a crack in the ceiling was admitting a bit of dying sunlight, and that was it. So it was just about nightfall—Artus realized suddenly it was the first time he'd known what time it was since . . . since whenever he got here. It couldn't have been more than a day, could it?

Focus, Artus.

Though the lighting was poor, Artus could make out several entrances and exits to the hall. Behind him, he could hear the group of Dellorans closing in at a half run, so he didn't have time to consider his route very carefully. He took the closest side-corridor he could and hid in the shadows until the group passed. When they headed down a different way, he breathed a sigh of relief.

"Quiet down!" a man bellowed from somewhere in the dark—Artus thought it came from deeper in the hall he was hiding in. He heard the crack of a whip, and someone screamed; a woman's voice.

Holding the Delloran broadsword tightly in both hands, Artus stalked down the corridor, step after step, eyes straining against the dark to see something that would tell him where the sound was coming from. He hadn't gone very far when he saw the orange glow of an oil lamp flickering from a lopsided arch. Backing up next to it, he hazarded a peek around the corner.

He saw about a half-dozen wretched looking people chained together on a long bench. Over them stood a fat, bald Delloran, a whip in his hand and a heavy wool cape draped across his round shoulders. His arms were bare, too, and covered by a lattice work of scars. Artus had seen scars like that before, in some of the darker corners of Ayventry—you got those from knife fighting, and most people didn't live long enough to get more than a few.

The knife-fighter had his back to Artus, and he was

snarling and cursing at the prisoners in front of him. There were four women and two old men, and all of them looked as Hortense had—starved, terrified, and resigned to their fates.

"No more whining about food!" the knife-fighter barked, "or I'll gut the lot of you freeloading whores!" He waddled then, crablike, to a wooden stool set before a small table and took up a half-eaten loaf of bread. Leering at the women, he took a big bite and chewed, humming to himself as though the hard bread were the finest meal he'd ever eaten.

Saints, Artus thought again, where does Sahand find these ogres?

The next thought came tight on the last one's heels: *Artus, you're going to have to kill this man to save those people.*

His stomach twisted again. He tried to think of another way, but his experience with the kind of soldiers Sahand employed reminded him they couldn't be reasoned with and wouldn't balk at stabbing a kid to death for fun. He couldn't expect Hool to show up *every* time he was about to be murdered either.

And he couldn't just leave them here. He was beginning to identify this as a character flaw.

Artus shifted his grip on the stolen broadsword— his palms were sweaty, despite the cold. He took a deep breath to try and calm his dancing heart. It would be easy—the easiest thing ever. He had the element of surprise. *Just run in, hit him in the head with sword, and bam, that's it.* He tried to imagine how much blood there would be or what kind of sound it would make. He reminded himself that he was doing it to protect innocents, and that Hann would understand. He could be a soldier—it was in his blood. All the men in his family had been soldiers.

Artus counted to three in his head and, with a whooping cry he hoped was terrifying, charged the knife-fighter. The big man's blue eyes seemed to pop out of his head at the sight of Artus, sword held high, running for him. The Delloran stood, put up his hands, and then Artus brought the sword down with all his remaining strength.

The blade sheared off the man's fingers on his right hand, but it missed his head. Instead, it dug itself into the side of the man's neck and moved a full six inches across his torso, only to wedge itself somewhere in his rib cage. Blood spurted in all directions and the man keened pathetically as he contemplated his mangled hand. Then his eyes rolled back in his head and he fell backward with a crash, upsetting the table and stool and knocking the oil lamp to the floor. Artus's face felt wet and warm; he figured he knew why. While he stared at the dead man, he wiped his face absently with his shirt. His whole body seemed to tremble at once. "Saints."

"Who are you?"

Artus blinked and found himself looking at a woman old enough to be his mother. "I . . . I . . . my name is Artus and I'm here to rescue you." He immediately felt himself blush. What a stupid thing to say.

"The keys! Get the keys, boy!" one of the other

women yelled, pointing at the key ring on the dead Delloran's hip.

Artus found himself staring at the body again. "Weird . . ." he said to no one in particular, "he was the first Delloran I've seen who wasn't wearing armor."

As Artus fished the keys off the man's belt, one of the women spat in the direction of the man's face. "He said it made him hot, the pig."

Artus handed the keys to the prisoners and they began to undo their chains. "Did any of you know a man named Hortense?" he asked. "He had a daughter here but the Dellorans took her away. I'm looking for her."

The woman who had asked him who he was shook her head and sighed. "Gone, boy. Sold off, dead, or worse. Poor lamb."

Artus blinked—he didn't know how to react to that. Now what did he do? "But . . . I promised her father . . ."

The other prisoners were heading out the door without even bothering with good-byes. They looked like rats scampering out of a cupboard. One of the old men snorted at Artus before shuffling into the dark. "Forget her, sonny—it's every man for himself now."

The woman patted Artus on the cheek and kissed him on the forehead. "Hann bless you, Artus. Wish I had a son like you. Damned cowards, the lot of them." Then, with a sad smile, she vanished through the doorway.

"Great." He sighed. "Now what?"

The key to successfully fighting multiple armed opponents was to *stop* fighting multiple armed opponents as soon as humanly possible. There were three typical solutions to this: killing them quickly, disarming them quickly, or running someplace where they couldn't all get you at once. Tyvian was currently exercising the third of these options.

He had lost track of the number of turns, twists, chutes, and winding stairs he'd plummeted down or scampered up; he had no idea where he now was. He knew two things, though—he was down to three or four men behind him, which was a great improvement over eight—and the smell of blood and brymm was getting stronger. He hoped very much this was because he was closer to its source and not because of whatever Sahand was doing. He had a sneaking suspicion, though, that it was both.

Tyvian squeezed through a crack in a wall through which a flood of orange light was pouring. He found himself up on a narrow ledge ringing the top of a massive circular chamber. The floor was a complex and asymmetrical pattern of orbs, crystals, and mageglass prisms, all radiating out from a central pool perhaps ten yards in diameter that frothed and bubbled with a thick, hot crimson liquid. Beside it, completely naked and inscribed from head to toe in burning orange runescript, stood Banric Sahand, chanting in a booming voice. Tyvian was dumbfounded by what he saw—a ritual of some kind involving artifacts and magecraft he'd never heard of, let along seen before. "Kroth."

The soldier behind him scuffed his foot along the ledge at the last second, affording Tyvian enough notice to parry a thrust from a broadsword that might have speared his spine. Their blades still engaged, the soldier moved as though to lock them together. In his exhausted state, Tyvian knew better than to put himself corps à corps with a larger opponent, so he disengaged and withdrew two paces, careful to keep both feet planted on the narrow ledge.

The soldier took a wild thrust at his forward leg. Tyvian lifted it clear and slammed it down on top of the man's sword before he could recover. His weapon pinned, Tyvian whipped his saber in a quick cut to the only part of the man's face that wasn't armored—his chin and lips. Blood spurted from the soldier's mouth and he moved a hand to block his bleeding face. Tyvian followed up with a sharp pommel strike to his temple, knocking the man him off the ledge, to crash to the unforgiving stone floor some twenty feet below.

Behind that soldier, though, there was another . . . and another . . . and another . . . and another still, squeezing through the crack. "Kroth," Tyvian swore again. It seemed he hadn't lost as many as he'd hoped.

The next fellow had a short spear and a shield, and he jabbed it at Tyvian's face, backing the smuggler up. This one was more cautious than the last, and Tyvian couldn't find an opening. He beat the spear's shaft away, recalling how *Chance* would have cut straight through the hardened wood like it was a daisy stem. Tyvian wondered if there were any way off this ledge besides falling—one didn't seem to present itself.

"Hyah!" the Delloran yelled, and lunged. The spear nearly took Tyvian in the throat, but he parried it aside at the last second. That let him get inside the man's guard, and grabbing hold of the Delloran's spear-hand, Tyvian turned on the spot and flipped the man over one shoulder with more power than he thought he had in him at the moment. Another Delloran crashed to the floor below.

Another Delloran squeezed through the crack.

"Kroth's bloody Kroth-spawned teeth!" Tyvian's heart was pounding and his situation was not improving. The next man had a battle-axe and a mean, snaggle-toothed grin. "How much is Sahand paying you for this, honestly?"

Below, Sahand completed his chant with a final, guttural syllable. He slapped a hand on the surface of the roiling bloody pool, and for a split second Tyvian thought the world might have just exploded. A cataclysmic roar shook the air itself, so loud it blurred Tyvian's vision and caused his breath to catch in his throat. He and all the Dellorans on the ledge put their hands to their ears as the masonry around them quaked and rumbled, as though being rung like a giant bell. Through his half-open eyes Tyvian could see a fiery red streak of energy sizzling from the pool, through several of the focusing apparatuses, and then in a massive, burning line of power down the primary corridor entering the chamber. The heat and power of the thing blew him back against the wall as though hit with a gust of hurricane wind, and then he fell forward, stumbling on the ledge. Tyvian flailed around to find purchase but found none.

THWUMP!

Tyvian's fall was broken by the corpse of one of the men he had just recently tossed off the ledge. He landed on his ribs and felt at least one of them crack with a white blaze of pain, but was otherwise not seriously harmed. He rolled to his knees, trying to suck air in through his deflated lungs, and cast about for his saber.

He found it, and thanks to the ring as much as anything, pulled himself to his feet. He pointed the blade around him, expecting attack, but found none. All of the Dellorans who had risked stepping out on the ledge had fallen, just like him. They didn't have any of their compatriots to break their fall, though, and lay in broken heaps around him—some injured, some dead.

His ears were still ringing, but he heard Sahand's harsh laugh and turned to see the Mad Prince walking around the edge of the pool toward him. Tyvian moved the opposite direction.

"So, Reldamar, I take it that you have refused my offer, then?"

Tyvian had no idea what he was talking about, but nodded anyway. "Is it that obvious?"

Even naked, Sahand possessed a kind of confidence

that Tyvian felt unnerving. The man probably hadn't been in a room where he wasn't the most dangerous being there in, well, decades. "Surely you don't expect to stop me? What would be in it for you?"

"This is the old power sink, isn't it?" Tyvian asked, trying to stall, eyes casting for a likely escape route. "Gods, Sahand—what have you done to it?"

Sahand stopped walking. Tyvian noted the Mad Prince was now standing in a veta inscribed in the floor and connected by lines of sorcerous script to various other crystals, prisms, and focusing devices. "I have made a weapon, Reldamar. A weapon so potent no one will dare oppose me."

Of course—a weapon. Tyvian knew he was creating a weapon—he had basically told the League as much, but . . . but *this?* "You're using the ley lines, aren't you— the Trell line that runs through Freegate, Galaspin . . ."

" . . . and Saldor, very good. The very lines of energy that network the world together I will use as conduits for my new weapon." He nodded to the pool. "When the Fey energy I have banked in this sink is released, it will send a wave of power down the Trell Valley that will be sufficient to destroy half of Freegate, shatter Galaspin's walls like matchsticks, and set Saldor ablaze."

Tyvian's heart felt still and cold. "You'll kill tens of thousands of people . . . *hundreds* of thousands. Hann's boots, man . . . it's . . ."

Sahand grinned like a tiger. "Spare me, smuggler. I long ago stopped heeding the objections of small-minded men. Today I crush my enemies, tomorrow I make my demands—that is all that really matters. Now," he put his hands over the churning waters of the pool, "I have been distracted long enough. Gallo, if you would . . ."

Tyvian looked over his shoulder to see the hulking, armored bulk of Gallo closing in on him, his vicious falchion in his hand, an expressionless fish-eyed stare fixating on him. Tyvian had seen how much damage Hool inflicted on the life-warded Gallo no more than twenty-four hours ago, and here he was, good as new. Tyvian backed away and then fled from the chamber. Behind him, he heard Sahand's guttural chant begin anew as well as the rhythmic clank and constant wheeze of Gallo in pursuit.

Tyvian couldn't get very far before darkness and the pressure his broken rib put on his lungs was too much, even for the ring, to ignore. He skidded to a halt, propping himself up against a pillar, and turned to face Gallo.

The giant was ten paces away, a shard of illumite around his neck, his weapon at the ready. He walked toward Tyvian as though entering battle was as stimulating as strolling through a public park.

Tyvian's arms shook, his legs shook, the tip of his saber wavered in the pale light. There was no way he could fight a monster like Gallo, but he also couldn't outrun him. He would get one good hit, and that was all. It had to count. A spike through the heart wouldn't slow him, a stab through the leg wouldn't bleed the bastard out, and no amount of slashing or stabbing of his stomach or arms or shoulders would do much good. There was one thing that he could hit, though, that no amount of pain tolerance or sorcerous death-warding would protect.

When Gallo was three paces away, Tyvian lunged for his eyes. The bulky warrior wasn't expecting this—probably didn't think Tyvian had the speed left in him or the skill to pull it off—and his guard was too slow. All it took were two precise thrusts, one to either side of the grotesque wolf's-head helm Gallo wore, and Tyvian was pleased to see the armored juggernaut stumble a pace, groaning with what amounted to the biggest expression of pain Tyvian had ever heard from him.

It was then Tyvian's turn to be surprised—nobody managed to counterattack immediately after being blinded. Nobody, of course, but Gallo. Tyvian was too slow with his own guard to stop Gallo's heavy-bladed falchion from cutting deeply into his side. The aim was fouled a bit by his shirt of borrowed mail, otherwise it would have cleaved the smuggler clean in two. As it stood, Tyvian fell on the ground, blood pumping through his hands as he clutched them over the ragged wound.

Gallo swung again, this time blindly, and Tyvian rolled away. With reserves of energy he never knew he had, he managed to stumble to his feet and run. He didn't go more than ten paces before falling again, and then there was no getting up. It was dark save for the light coming off of Gallo, and Tyvian pushed himself toward the darkness, flopping and rolling as his life's blood spilled from his guts. Each of Gallo's heavy footsteps sounded like a death knell. He got me, Tyvian thought, the faceless son of a bitch got me . . .

Spots danced in his vision and the ring burned and throbbed with a kind of urgent, energetic power that kept his right hand pulling him along the uneven, icy floor. He wasn't dead. Not yet. *Not yet, dammit.*

Tyvian slid down some kind of fissure in the floor and flopped onto his back in another hallway. He could hear Gallo's rasping breath above him and saw the tip of his falchion probing the mouth of the crevice through which Tyvian had slipped. "Too small, you ugly blind bastard," Tyvian hissed, blood bubbling to his lips.

He heard Gallo move away, but knew for certain that Sahand's monstrous henchman wasn't going to give up that easily. He still needed to escape. He needed to find a way to heal his wounds. The pain was almost too much; he found he could scarcely think.

Tyvian kept crawling, though, his ring hand seemingly imbued with an endless strength drawn from reserves far beyond his understanding. Half-baked theories about magecraft and Lumenal energy flitted in and out of his head, but didn't stay long.

It was then that he found Myreon's body.

The wheelbarrow she had been in was overturned, and she lay on her back, her face pale, almost blue, snowflakes frosting her eyelashes and hair. Moonlight poured in from somewhere, and Tyvian, practically nose-to-nose with the body of his old enemy, could see her clearly.

She was certainly dead. He felt something dreadful building in him—something worse than the pain and the exhaustion, something sick and hollowing, as though his heart had been ripped out. He found himself blinking away tears. "Kroth. What . . . what a time to go soft . . ."

What was wrong with him? Myreon Alafarr was a devoted foe to everything he did or wanted to do. She had hounded him across every country in the West, ruined a half dozen of his most profitable plots, and now here they were, dying and dead, side by side—the victims of the same madman.

Tyvian held up his blood-slick ring hand and curled his lips at the humble little band. "You stupid trinket. Happy? You've killed me. You've killed us both."

Wait . . .

Tyvian's overworked heart leapt with a sudden inspiration. The ring! Of course! The ring could heal! Why didn't he think about that before? Ah, yes—the bleeding to death and all that had distracted him. All he needed to do was press the thing to the injury, probably, and sort of do what he had done with breaking the chains, right?

And then what? A little voice in the back of Tyvian's mind, one that sounded suspiciously like his mother, tsked at him. *Just run away while Sahand blows up three of the greatest cities in the world?*

"Why not?" he mumbled. It wasn't like he could stop Sahand—he was no wizard. For all his knowledge, he didn't have the first idea of how to stop a ritual of that magnitude. The only mage who could have possibly helped was dead anyway. Unless . . .

He turned his head to Myreon, thinking. It was a terrible idea; even if it worked, it would just put him in a penitentiary garden for birds to defecate on for the rest of time. It would take the very last bit of his energy, he had no doubt. Better to cut his losses.

The ring weighed in with a mild pinch of displeasure, but Tyvian ignored it. What occupied his thoughts, instead, were the tens of thousands of people whose lives were about to end. The women, the children, the innocents . . .

He really didn't have a choice after all, did he?

Pulling himself to all fours, Tyvian placed his ring hand on Myreon's chest. "Myreon," he said quietly, "I . . . I am very displeased with you for dying. Very irresponsible of you. I demand you wake up. *Wake up,* dammit." He struck her chest; it was like hitting a block of ice. The ring tingled with something—a glimmer of power—but then it was gone. "Wake up! Myreon, I *need* you! Artus needs you! We *all* bloody need you!" The glimmer was there again, but then faded. Tyvian's voice cracked, his strength leaving him. He collapsed on Myreon's chest.

There needed to be something more. Some deeper connection—Tyvian could feel the ring trying to grab hold of something, but he didn't know what. He looked up at Myreon's face, calm, pale, and serene. Beautiful, really. It was so rare that she wasn't scowling at him, that he hadn't had much opportunity to notice just how beautiful she was.

He took a long, ragged breath. "Oh . . . hell, why not?" He pressed his hand to Myreon's chest and whispered in her ear, "Wake up, Myreon. Duty calls." He closed his eyes, and kissed her on the lips.

A torrent of heat and energy poured through his hand and mouth to the point where Tyvian thought he saw lightning bolts shooting across the space between him and Myreon's body. He felt her quake beneath his touch, back arching with the force of the ring's power. At the same time, he felt everything he had, everything that had been keeping him going this past day, siphon out of him and into her. He couldn't pull back from the kiss—he didn't have the energy.

Then, finally, the power faded away. Myreon's eyes opened and shot wide. She pushed Tyvian off as though she were being attacked and scooted away from him on her back. He lay on the ground, so weak he could scarcely move his head.

"What . . . what the hell? Were you . . . *kissing* me? What is wrong with you?"

Tyvian felt unconsciousness coming for him, and soon. He pointed in the direction of Sahand and whispered. "Sah . . . Sahand . . . weapon . . . you've got to stop it. Please . . ."

Myreon was over him then, kneeling at his side. The last thing he heard before he dropped into darkness was her voice, saying softly, "I suppose I have to carry you, too?"

CHAPTER 22

WHAT GOES AROUND . . .

For Banric Sahand time seemed to flow in all directions at once. This much Fey energy—the stuff of chaos itself—confused the senses and confounded all attempts at solidity and logic. He had been talking to Reldamar a moment ago, that was certain, or perhaps he had yet to speak with him—it was hard to say. In either event, it didn't really matter. The time of his triumph was at hand. He was intoning the final phrases— the last part of the ritual that he had been practicing in secret for years, waiting for this moment. The power within the pool was so intense Sahand could scarcely believe it—all of that anger, hate, rage, strength, wild aggression, every ounce of those creatures' beings that had been poured and trapped within its magical confines had been magnified a thousandfold. He was about to unleash a tidal wave that would change the world. Tomorrow, he would be King in the West, the North after that, and after that, the Kalsaaris, and on and on . . .

A world of his own, a world to remake according to his vision. All of it coming thanks to this moment, right here, right now. Were he not focused on placing the proper inflections on all of the incantatory phrases, he would have laughed.

Hool snarled at the last of the Dellorans in her way, and they ran. The pile of bodies at her feet, the blood caked on her jaws—all of this was more than enough to dissuade anyone else from getting in her way. She could smell Sahand now. His scent was buried beneath so much blood that her heart wept to think of the horrors Sahand had made to get it all. She could not understand why anyone would do something like that, even *humans*. She didn't need to understand, though. All she needed to know was where he was, and she could do the rest. She was stalking down a wide stair that was smoking and burning with heat up its center, as though the hottest of fires had burned there but moments ago—that would have been the explosion, she guessed. She was very close.

At the foot of the stairs she saw the chamber and saw Sahand standing at the edge of the foul bloody pool as it seethed and roared with what she could only describe as anger. This was sorcery beyond Hool's wildest nightmares—in the plumes of red water she could see the faces and hear the cries of a thousand slaughtered creatures. She could smell their anger and their need for blood, and it made every hair on her body stand on end. Her ears stood ramrod straight, and she tried to quell her every instinct, which told her to run.

A little, wizened bald man charged from an alcove, a wicked dagger in his hand and murder in his eyes. Hool saw him long before he struck, and his attack broke her from her reverie. She batted the knife away with a swipe of her arm and tackled him to the ground. His hatred turned to terror in an instant. "No!" he squealed. "No kill!"

She recognized this human—he was a brother to the one that had tried to work magic on Tyvian's hand. In what she conceded was a very humanlike moment, she decided he might be useful. She wrapped her hands around his skinny throat and growled, "How do you stop the magic?"

The man spoke quickly. "The power, once collected, cannot be destroyed—it must be released. There *is* no way to stop it! You are too late!"

Hool frowned. "That was a stupid thing for you to say."

She tore out his throat, and decided to look for

Reldamar—she wanted Sahand dead, but she wanted nothing to do with that magic without an expert present.

Artus really wasn't sure what he was supposed to do now. He was thinking about escape, but he hadn't the presence of mind to follow the prisoners out. By the time he thought of it, he had spent too much time trying to retrieve his sword from the body of the Delloran he'd killed and vomiting over the outcome to possibly find them again. It was all so embarrassing, he had trouble thinking about it without blushing.

Currently, he had stopped to rest and was sitting on an ancient stone bench beside some kind of cistern. He cupped some frigid water into his hands and sipped, then sat back and stared into the darkness, trying to figure out what his next move should be.

A pale light gradually rose up from the depths of a stairwell. Whoever that was probably wasn't good for him, so he tried to stand up. He was immediately jerked back down, however, by the fact that his damp wrist had managed to get itself frozen to the lip of the cistern he had just drunk from. "Damn!" he hissed.

Heavy, mailed steps got closer and closer. Artus tugged at his wrist, trying to peel himself off the cistern, but his sleeve had frozen as well as his skin. He pulled harder and harder, but the shirt wouldn't rip. "Kroth!"

Coming up the stairs, he heard the rasping, gurgling breath he had heard once before in the dungeons of Arble Keep. "Kroth's bloody teeth!"

An eyeless, bloody-faced Gallo came up the stairs and turned in his direction, sword drawn.

"I hear you, boy," Gallo rasped. "Come here."

Artus grabbed his stolen broadsword off the ground and tried to somehow cut loose his sleeve without slicing off his arm. His fingers were numb and the blade was heavy, so he dropped it by accident. In the presence of the blind Gallo, the clang seemed the loudest thing Artus had ever heard.

Gallo was coming closer, tapping his falchion against the ground like a blind-man's cane. "Here, boy. Here here, boy."

Artus snatched up a rock and threw it to the opposite end of the hall. Gallo cocked his head in that direction for a moment, but then kept coming toward him. "No good, boy. Not fooled."

Artus racked his brain for any tricks or plans and came up with nothing—he was completely, totally over his head. There was really only one plan left. He yanked his arm loose with a painful tear, leaving flesh and fabric behind, and ran away as fast as he could.

The sound of his feet slapping against the stone floor was loud enough for Gallo to come roaring after him. Artus saw an orange light ahead and went straight for it, just glad to be able to see well enough not to trip. His legs felt like jellied hams, though, and he couldn't manage more than a wheezing job. Behind him, Gallo plowed along in pursuit, shouldering his way past piles of rubble and shattering packs of ice beneath his feet. Looking back, Artus felt his knees go weak. He felt like he was in the midst of one of those nightmares where the arahk slayer or the troll is chasing you and your feet can't get purchase on the ground. Run and run and run, and still you're going to be caught.

Gallo was practically on top of him, his wheezing, gurgling breath blowing spittle far enough to hit the back of Artus's neck. He sprinted through the door to the orange light—inside was a huge chamber, full of magical crystals and orbs, and a giant lake of blood surging with power. The stench of death was overpowering and the roar of the fountain so intense, Artus didn't watch his step. He tripped over a focusing crystal and went sprawling on his face.

The sound of Artus's fall was apparently masked by the roar of Sahand's ritual, because Gallo tripped over him. The monstrous man went airborne, sailing a full two yards before landing, off-balance, just at the edge of the bloody pool. Snarling and gargling, the warrior tried to regain equilibrium, and he would have, too . . .

. . . if Myreon Alafarr hadn't stepped past Artus just then and pushed Gallo with all her might.

With a guttural moan, Sahand's henchman pitched backward and dumped, headfirst, into the seething depths of the power sink. One hand, crimson with blood and smoking with heat, thrust up through the surface, flailing for something to grab, and then burst into flame. Slowly, it melted back into the boiling chaos of the power sink.

Myreon helped Artus up. "Are you all right?"

"Me?" Artus shouted, a smile breaking across his face. "You were *dead*!"

"I was *what*?"

Sahand's voice, barking its violent syllables over the roar of the pool, pitched itself an octave lower. The chamber shook with power; chunks of masonry falling from the ancient dome, crashing to the ground nearby. Myreon grabbed Artus by the collar and dragged him behind a chunk of rubble. "What the *hell* does that man think he's doing?"

"Bad magic, what else?" Hool was with them. She looked at Myreon with her copper eyes. "Why aren't you dead? What happened to Reldamar?"

Myreon frowned. "There are bound to be guards around. What happened to all the guards?"

Hool snorted. "I killed them or chased them away. They are regrouping at the entrance, but won't come down here. They are scared of the bad magic, too."

Artus peered around the corner. He wasn't sure, but whatever Sahand was doing was getting serious. Streamers of multicolored fire were pouring out of the focusing apparatuses, cracks forming along the floor, and the pool had become more of a pillar of seething bloody liquid, somehow part fire and part demon. In the midst of it, Sahand stood within his protective veta, the magical energies roaring around him as he chanted faster and faster in some kind of non-language that made Artus squirm just to hear it. "We've got to stop him somehow."

Myreon looked at the gnoll and the boy and rolled her eyes. "That's the easy part. The hard part is escaping once we do. Get Tyvian and get ready to run."

"I will get Reldamar," Hool announced, and vanished into the dark corridors at a dead sprint.

Myreon said nothing, but simply retreated up the hall a few dozen yards until she came to a pack of snow and ice that had fallen in through one of the skylights. She knelt down, scooped up a big patch of snow, stuck a chunk of ice in the middle of it, and made a snowball.

Artus cocked an eyebrow. "What the . . ."

She took aim and threw the snowball at Sahand, but it vanished into the power sink with a sizzle. "Damn."

"You're . . . you're going to stop him by throwing *snowballs?*"

Myreon smirked. "Snow is full of the Dweomer, which is the antithesis of the Fey. This is basic sorcery, here."

Artus's mouth fell open. "But . . ."

"Don't just stand there!" Myreon snapped, "Start making iceballs, kid!"

Artus dropped to the ground to obey, even as the whole chamber around them quaked with the fury of Sahand's terrible new weapon. He wondered what kind of world he lived in where hair-pulling and snowball-making were life-saving talents. "You sure this will work?" He asked, slapping his singnature killer-iceball-supreme—scourge of his childhood churchyard—into the mage's hand.

"Miscasts can be rough," Myreon said. She took

a couple steps' head start, cocked her arm back and threw. Artus watched, open-mouthed, as the white, snowy sphere arced gracefully across the chamber, in between the gouts of flame, and hit Sahand square in the mouth.

The Mad Prince, Dread Lord of Dellor and Scourge of the Peoples of the West, coughed and sputtered, totally failing to finish his incantation. The massive energies built up on the power sink were suddenly without direction and without control. A miscast.

The pool exploded.

A wave of crimson energy hit Artus with the force of a charging team of horses. He felt himself fly backward for what seemed like forever before he hit a wall, feet first. It hurt, but the fall to the ground afterward hurt more. His arm twisted behind him and his head cracked against the floor. Spots swam through his vision for a moment, but then Hool was there, picking him up. "Run!" she yelled, Tyvian draped across her shoulders, and then was gone.

Artus shook his head, trying to get his bearings. It seemed like everything around him was on fire or exploding. Pulsing waves of orange and crimson energy shot through the air, incinerating supports and vaporizing walls. Staggering to his feet, he saw Myreon likewise trying to stand, supporting herself against a pillar whose top was melting with volcanic heat. Artus charged up to her and pulled her aside before a great flood of liquid rock would have reduced her to ash.

Myreon grabbed him by both wrists and chanted

some quick, precise words. Around them, the air cooled. "We have to get out of here!" she yelled.

"Not without Hortense!"

"Whoever that is, Artus, is as good as dead!"

Artus shook his head, shouting over the flames, "So was I when I went through the anygate, and you came after me!"

Myreon's mouth thinned into a narrow line. "Fine! Hold on!"

Then they were off, the worst of the flames and the Fey energy deflected by Myreon's wards. Artus was amazed at how vital she was—hadn't she been dead a matter of hours ago? It didn't matter—they were running through the burning labyrinth, hunting for Hortense. Artus, though, couldn't remember the way back to the dungeon, and the fortress was coming apart at the seams. Myreon jerked Artus's arm. "We *have* to leave—my wards can't hold out much longer!"

"But—"

Myreon put a hand on his cheek. "Look at me, Artus: I'm only going to let you run off and do something heroic once, okay?"

He looked into the Mage Defender's blue-gray eyes and back at the conflagration that surrounded them. To their left, half the ceiling fell in, white-hot with magical heat. He thought again of his mother, sending him away forever rather than letting him get chewed up by the same war that killed all his brothers. He saw the tears welling in her eyes as he asked to stay one last time, and remembered how hard she had shaken her head. She'd sent him to be safe from a violent death, and here he was, charging into it. Finally, he nodded. "Yeah. Okay."

Together, arm-in-arm, Artus and Myreon fled through the burning air as the ancient ruins behind them seemed to be consumed by the breath of Kroth himself.

CHAPTER 23

DAWN

Through death and smoke, through hellfire itself, Sahand crawled. The runes that coated his body burned like coals, each a unique pain shaped by the chaotic power of the Fey. He had visions—Tyvian Reldamar laughing in triumph, the howl of that gnoll beneath a summer moon. Beings of pure Fey—fiends and gremlins and fire-sprites—danced around him, reveling in the mayhem he had created. There was no light but the fires of creation and destruction, a primordial magma of heat and flame.

Sahand kept crawling, arm over arm, for what

seemed hours. He had no sense of direction nor of place, only that the heat was fading in the face of the cold—good. Cold wind assailed him on a black night. He tasted snow. The feeling of snowmelt upon his parched tongue was like rain upon the desert. He smelled the clear air and rolled onto his back, content at last to rest. Sleep took him.

His eyes snapped open to see the cold, clear light of a winter's dawn. His body was caked in ice; he shivered. "Kroth."

"Well, well, well—here we are again." A woman's voice. A voice he'd not heard for ages, but that he'd never truly forgotten.

Sahand sat up, stiff and sore. "Reldamar!"

Lyrelle Reldamar—or her wraith, more accurately—sat upon a boulder ten feet away. She wore a gown of deepest violet and white brocade, her hair tucked beneath a hat of bleached mink fur, her hands inside a matching muff. She looked older, but not by much.

Sahand roared and tried to stand, but his legs were too numb and he tumbled back into the snow. He sought to call the Fey to him, to burn Lyrelle or the image of her from existence, but it did not come.

Lyrelle chuckled from her perch, swinging her feet beneath her dress. "Oh, that won't work, Banric. You've done a terribly efficient job of siphoning off all the excess Fey in the area, so you won't be so much as lighting a candle without some doing. If only you had studied more broadly, alas."

Sahand could scarcely form words—how could *she* be here? How was this . . . *why* would she . . .

Lyrelle surveyed the slopes of the mountainside as they gleamed in the rising sun. "I must say, you do seem to select the nicest vistas upon which to hit rock bottom. Very pretty indeed."

"This was your doing." Sahand managed at last.

Lyrelle's blue eyes widened. "*Me?* Oh, no no no, Banric—your defeat was not my doing. Not this time." She smiled. "Well, not really."

"Why?" Sahand snarled, teetering to his feet. "*WHY* do you torment me, witch?" He drew a shuddering breath, his body quaking in the freezing air.

Lyrelle pursed her lips in mock concern. "Oh my— poor Banric Sahand, Mad Prince of Dellor. Why ever would the cruel world cheat him of his psychotic whims? Why should a heartless old sorceress inter- fere with his genocidal plots? It hardly seems fair, does it? Poor man. If you live to escape this mountainside a second time, I really *am* going to have to knit you something to keep warm. A fellow who tends to wind up half-dead on mountainsides could really use a nice scarf."

"BEGONE!" Sahand cast a lode-bolt at her, but the blue-white sphere ceased to exist a foot away from her. He roared at her, barely coherent.

Lyrelle's grin was the cruelest thing Sahand had ever seen. "I'll be on my way shortly—no need to over- stay my welcome. I did, however, feel I owed you a thank you in person."

"For what? For failing to burn you and your whole stinking city into ashes? For being unable to crush the life from your bony old skull?" Sahand lunged at the image of Lyrelle, and succeeded only in hugging the boulder.

Lyrelle's wraith re-formed behind him. "The last time we met here, I gave you a means to membership in the Sorcerous League. You didn't have to take it, you know, but I knew you would. I gave you what you wanted—a way at revenge." Sahand began to growl, but Lyrelle cut him off. "Oh, I know you thought you were playing a trick on me—you think you're very clever, after all—but no, Banric. You have been doing exactly what I've wanted you to for the past twenty-seven years." She gave him a shallow curtsey. "Thank you."

Sahand felt the chill in his bones deepen somehow. "No. No, I don't believe you. I was mere moments away from *destroying* you. *Moments!*"

Lyrelle rolled her eyes. "And I suppose it's entirely by chance that one of my former assistants just *happened* to be there to throw a snowball at you at the precise moment? Come now, Sahand—I thought you knew me better than that."

"No!"

"You have wasted twenty-seven years of your life arguing with miserable, cantankerous sorcerers and hedge wizards instead of rebuilding your armies. You have poured your treasury into a long-shot sorcerous ritual that even the Warlock Kings knew enough not to try. Do you know what the best part of it is, too? You, Banric Sahand, have single-handedly done more damage to the Sorcerous League than I or my agents ever have."

Sahand's fist clenched, but there was nothing to strike, nothing to destroy—only Lyrelle Reldamar's smile, delivered to him from the safety of her home, hundreds of miles away. "NO!"

Lyrelle laughed. "You want to know whose doing this all was? That's the beauty of it: *yours*, Banric. It was, all of it, your own idea. I merely had to push you in the right direction, and you basically did the rest. You have, at long last, thoroughly and completely defeated *yourself*."

"I'll kill you. Even if I die in the process, woman, I will drink your blood, understand? You've tricked me twice, but not again. Never again!"

Lyrelle's image began to fade. "My dear Banric, haven't you been listening? There won't *be* an 'again.' These words of mine are the last nail in your coffin, you miserable, harmless old man." She laughed just before vanishing, and the echoes of the illusory laughter rebounded off the mountain slopes, making it seem as though the whole world was, yet again, mocking his folly.

Tyvian Reldamar woke up in his own bed. He knew it was his own bed because the sheets were slashed in the same places Artus slashed them when he had his little temper tantrum. Even in tatters, the sheets on his bed were divine.

He heard somebody bustling in his kitchen and heard voices—his specters didn't bustle and they certainly didn't talk. He tried to sit up but couldn't move. His body was like dead weight. "Hello?" he said. His voice was like the creaking of an unoiled hinge.

The first face he saw was Artus's, bandaged and haggard, as though the lad had just gone ten rounds with a razorboar. "You're awake!" he said in a half cheer.

"Astute, as always, Artus."

Artus was joined by the tall, imposing figure of Myreon Alafarr in full Defender regalia, staff, mageglass armor, and all. Tyvian grimaced at her, and she stared down at him over her statuesque nose. "Tyvian Reldamar."

"Magus Alafarr. I trust that I am in your custody?"

"I am led to believe that I was recently found dead. Is this true?"

Tyvian looked at Artus. The boy was grinning like an idiot. "Truth be told, Magus, my memory is a little hazy from the events leading up to . . . say, what happened, anyway?"

"The whole place exploded," Artus said, "and then Myreon saved me, and Hool saved you, and . . ."

Myreon glared at him. "Artus, bring Master Reldamar some broth."

Artus frowned. "But you said the broth weren't done yet!"

"*Wasn't* done yet," Myreon corrected, and jerked her head toward the door, "and get out."

When the boy had left, Myreon closed the door. "You *kissed* me."

Tyvian groaned. "It . . . it seemed prudent at the time. It is no reflection upon my opinion of you, I assure you."

"You saved my life when you could have saved your own, and you *kissed* me. Explain yourself."

Tyvian opened his mouth to reply and then slammed it shut. "No. I don't owe you any such thing."

Myreon nodded and took up Tyvian's right hand. There the ring continued to rest, quietly comfortable on his fourth finger. "This is a really very *interesting* piece of magecraft. Saldor would simply *love* to get its hands on it, I'm sure."

"I have no doubt they are preparing you a heroine's welcome as we speak," Tyvian grumbled, trying to tug his hand back but lacking the strength to do so.

"Hmmm . . ." Myreon placed his hand back on his stomach. "It's a real shame you will have escaped long before then."

"I beg your pardon?"

Myreon shrugged. "Your elusiveness is well known, of course. No doubt you are already preparing an elaborate plot to dupe me yet again. I'd hardly be the first and certainly not the last. I doubt it would even hurt my career much, given how I single-handedly stopped Banric Sahand from blowing up tens of thousands of people. Don't you think so?"

"You're . . . letting me go? Why? What's the catch?"

Myreon smiled at him for the first time in . . . well, the first time ever. It seemed to make her entire face glow. "Because, Tyvian Reldamar, that ring on your finger is a better prison guard than any penitentiary garden could ever hope to be."

Tyvian found himself smiling, inexplicably, and he immediately masked it with a scowl. "You're just leaving, then?"

Her eyes flashed. "*Just* leaving? What, you expect me to stay for tea, after you *kidnapped* me, sold me to the bloody Kalsaaris and . . ."

"Fine, fine!" Tyvian sighed. "I surrender. Begone with you, then—no tea for you. I merely thought, after all we've been through, it would have been *polite* to offer tea, you understand."

Myreon snorted. "Polite?"

"Look, Myreon, either you're going to sit down and have some tea or you're going to get the hell out. Whatever you do, stop tarrying in my doorway."

Myreon visibly composed herself before speaking again. Her voice was placid, officious. "I sincerely doubt we will cross paths again, sir." She nodded politely. "Good day."

Tyvian cocked an eyebrow. "What, no good-bye kiss?"

The old familiar scowl settled onto Myreon's face like a comfortable hat. "Good-*bye*, Tyvian."

She left—Artus later said she left on the spirit engine for Galaspin that same hour. Part of him cheered at her departure—a weight off his chest, to be sure. Another part, well . . . he kept that part well locked away. It wasn't sensible.

Artus was staying. Like it or not, the boy insisted they were now partners, and Tyvian, seeing how he could scarcely move, was in no position to object. He set the boy about securing them passage on the next spirit engine—unlisted, of course. He had no doubt Theliara's spies were still out there, ready to get vengeance. Then there was the League, and it was possible Sahand survived the explosion . . . gods, a lot of enemies

That night, Hool came in the dark, sneaking in through the still-broken window, Brana at her side. Tyvian woke up with a start, seeing her eyes glowing in the dark above him. "Kroth! Hool, can't you knock?"

"The mountain is still on fire," she stated simply. Brana growled in support. "Sahand is still alive."

Tyvian sighed. "I'm sorry, Hool, but he's beyond my reach now—probably back in Dellor, cooking up some new atrocity to inflict on the world. You could chase him there, but I doubt—"

"We are going with you now."

"Hool, I've got problems of my own, all right? I can't take responsibility for yours."

Hool crouched down and eyed his ring hand, sitting on top of the sheets. Tyvian pulled it out of sight. She sat herself on the bed across from him, her copper eyes flitting from his face to his hand. "That's the ring that Artus talks about. The one that makes you good."

"It does nothing of the kind," Tyvian said, his teeth clenching. "It . . . it just controls me."

"That's stupid," Hool said firmly. "Rings don't control people, not even magic ones. Everybody knows that."

A squeaky howl issued mournfully from Brana, and Hool answered it with a shorter howl of her own. "Brana wants to know if you are okay."

"What does Brana care?"

Hool blinked. "I told him that you saved him. He loves you." She said those last three words as though they were common as the grass.

Tyvian glared at her. "You're learning how to mock, Hool. Good for you."

One of Hool's arms shot out and pressed Tyvian against the headboard as easily as one might topple an empty chair. She loomed over the smuggler, the faint moonlight illuminating only her vast, furry silhouette. "I don't lie to my pups, and I don't lie to you. You think you're a bad person, but you aren't. Bad people break their promises, but you have kept yours to me and Brana. Bad people let other bad people get away with things because they are afraid, but you don't, because you are not afraid. I would tell you stories sung in the Taqar by my people about the heroes of old and the things that they did, but you would laugh at me. I will tell you, though, that if you cut off your paw because you hate this ring, you will be a coward and a bad person, and Brana will not love you anymore."

Hool let him go, and added, "Neither will I."

Tyvian looked up at Hool for a long, cold moment. He began half a dozen clever rejoinders but stopped before he got halfway. "You really will stick by me, won't you?"

Hool grabbed him by the shirt and pulled him to a sitting position. "As long as you are a good person, I will be your friend. Both of us will. Artus, too."

She let him go and he dropped back onto his sheets like a rag doll. She and Brana left, but not before Brana licked his fingers lightly. He recoiled but didn't say anything. He stared at the ceiling a bit and then called, "Artus, are you awake?"

Artus's head popped in the door a few minutes later. "Yeah? You okay?"

"I'm fine, Artus. Say, do you still have that letter Eddereon gave you?"

Artus straightened. "Yeah . . . why?"

Tyvian sighed. He couldn't believe he was doing this, but he had to admit it—he needed these people. He was never going to find the Yldd without them, was he?

"Bring it here," he said. "Let's teach you to read."

ACKNOWLEDGMENTS

Living in a fantasy world is hard to do with bills to pay, so thanks are in order. Thank you to Josh, Will, DJ, Perich, Christine, Serpico, and Deirdre, whose creativity and sense of fun made my world breathe for a time and without whom this project would have been a much duller affair. Heartfelt thanks, also, to my parents, who have always encouraged me; to my wife, who has always stood by me; to my first readers—Katie and Will—and to my editor, Kelly, for making this fantasy real.

My thanks, also, are to you, the reader, for having followed Tyvian this far. I thank you, honestly and sincerely. You people are the greatest.

Hopefully I'll see you all in Book 2, and we can do it all again.

ABOUT THE AUTHOR

On the day **Auston Habershaw** was born, Skylab fell from space. This was a portent of two possible fates: Scifi/Fantasy author or Evil Mastermind. Fortunately he chose the former, and spends his time imagining the could-be and the never-was rather than disintegrating the moon with his volcano laser. He is a winner of the Writers of the Future Award, and his work has appeared in places such as *Analog*, *Stupefying Stories*, and *The Sword and Laser Anthology*. He lives and works in Boston.

Find him online at www.aahabershaw.wordpress.com, on Facebook at www.facebook.com/aahabershaw, or follow him on Twitter @AustonHab.

Discover great authors, exclusive offers, and more at hc.com.